FATAL ODDS

Also by John F. Dobbyn

Neon Dragon

Frame-Up

Black Diamond

Deadly Diamonds

High Stakes

FATAL ODDS

A NOVEL

JOHN F. DOBBYN

OCEANVIEW PUBLISHING

SARASOTA, FLORIDA

ISBN 978-1-60809-372-4

Published in the United States of America by Oceanview Publishing
Sarasota, Florida
www.oceanviewpub.com

10 9 8 7 6 5 4 3 2

PRINTED IN THE UNITED STATES OF AMERICA

There are no words in any language to express how much love and joy I find in my best pal, my total inspiration, my partner in every adventure, my first editor and title writer, and the finest person I believe God ever created—my beautiful bride, Lois.

I also thank God for the one who fills our lives with an abundance of love, laughter, and pride —our third musketeer, our son, John.

FATAL ODDS

PART ONE

ONE

THE MANTRA THAT has soothed the furrowed brows of criminal defense attorneys from the early days of the Old Bailey to current times in Boston's Suffolk County Superior Court is simply this: The Lawyer Always Goes Home.

On the other hand, it provides little solace to one facing that most humbling challenge a lawyer can face: defending a client the lawyer truly believes to be innocent. Doing one's best and "going home" falls painfully short of the mark. The only bearable outcome is winning. And that's a curse.

That curse crowned a particular morning that began with a phone call at 5:45, shattering the first moments of actual sleep I had managed all night. I'd spent the prior six hours playing and replaying an event of the previous day that I could not drive out of my consciousness.

The horses were approaching the gate for the fourth race at Suffolk Downs. I was at the track to watch two jockeys I had known nearly as brothers since their early teens. Roberto and Victor Mendosa were born to my mother's sister on the sunny isle of Puerto Rico. In something of a rescue mission, my mother and I had brought them over in their teens to live with her in what was then the Hispanic bastion of Jamaica Plain—frequently referred to by other Bostonians as "Jamaica Spain".

Both boys had worked with horses in Puerto Rico since the time they were big enough to wield a mucking rake. Again in the form of a rescue a few years later, I got them off the gang-dominated streets of Jamaica Plain and onto the backstretch crew of a horse racing trainer of enormous talent and even greater heart, Rick McDonough. He had an eye for talent. He had them both in the saddle as exercise boys before their sixteenth birthday.

The jump from there to the calling of a jockey required three things: horsemanship, courage, and size. No teacher on earth could instill the subtle arts of horsemanship better than Rick. Courage, on the other hand, is, or is not, inborn, and no man or woman can engage in that most dangerous of all sports without a generous God-given abundance of it. Diminutive size—the ability to weigh in within ounces of one hundred and ten pounds—as Rick often said, also cannot be taught. As fate had it, Roberto and Victor were blessed with all three. By their nineteenth birthday, they were both among the ten leading riders at Suffolk Downs.

The horses were at the post. Roberto, the older brother by a year, was on Dante's Pride in post position three. Victor's horse, Summer Breeze, was beside him in post position four. I remember glancing at the tote board and noticing that Roberto's horse was the odds-on favorite at even money. Victor's horse was the second favorite at 3 to 2. All the other horses in the race were there hoping for a miracle of third money.

I was at the rail as the horses approached the gate. I gave both boys the thumbs up and got a smile and nod from each of them.

Victor's horse walked smoothly into the box like a pro. I noticed that Roberto's horse balked and pranced in front of the gate until two assistant starters locked hands under his tail and urged him into the gate. Nothing particularly unusual there. Thoroughbreds are frequently born high-strung.

I was glued to the three and four post positions during that time-stopping pause while the starter waits for every horse to have all four feet planted and head straight. I could almost feel the adrenaline rush that courses through every jockey in the gate.

Then the break. That ear-splitting bell and the clang of metal gates flying open. In a split second, the guttural breaths of horses driving powerful hips and legs in a burst of acceleration, spraying showers of dirt, were punctuated by the yips and yells of the jockeys.

I half-walked, half-ran down the rail. My eyes were glued to the brothers. Victor's four horse broke fast. He was even for the lead with the five horse to his right. I saw Roberto's three horse stumble leaving the gate. He struggled to gain footing through the first five strides. By twenty feet out, he was still not at full balance, but only half a length short of Victor's horse to his right.

Then it happened—what I kept seeing over and over that night for six hours of abortive sleep. For some reason, Victor's horse shied. He veered to the left. He cut into the path of Roberto's horse.

I heard the sickening click of metal shoe on bone. In an instant, the front legs of Roberto's horse crumpled beneath him. The horse tumbled forward, head into the dirt and body somersaulting forward on top of the flailing body of Roberto.

The other horses continued to race, while the double sirens of the ambulance for Roberto and the med-van for the horse screamed down the track from behind. I wanted to vault the rail and run to him, but the medics were on him before I could make a move. They encased his motionless body in an inflatable brace and got him into the ambulance within thirty seconds. The others were able to lead his horse into the van. Both wagons cleared the track before the other racers came around the second turn.

My strongest urge was to run to my car and drive to the Mass General Hospital where they take seriously injured jockeys more frequently than we want to think. Instead, I ran to the finish line to wait for Victor.

Victor's horse crossed the wire in first place, three lengths ahead of the second horse. When he was able to look around after the finish, he realized that his brother was missing. He was the first one back to the unsaddling area after a sharply foreshortened run-out. He stopped, unsaddled, and weighed in within minutes. I yelled to him. He jumped the rail to come over to me. I told him what I'd seen as we ran to my car.

We arrived at the Mass General emergency room in time for a doctor to call to us over his shoulder. He was following at a run the motionless form of Roberto on a cart headed, we assumed, into surgery.

"Stay in the waiting room. I'll let you know as soon as I can."

"Doc, is he breathing?"

"So far."

TWO

VICTOR AND I waited together at the hospital for the six hours of surgery on Roberto. All through it, I was on the verge of asking Victor why his horse had veered into Roberto's path. Then I'd see the lines of pain, worry, and possibly guilt that creased his face, and the time was never right.

When the doctor finally came out, he looked like he had run a marathon. He wore that "best we could do" look as he explained that bracing and setting bones had been the minor part. Internal bleeding had been severe.

We could see people in uniform wheeling the bed down the corridor with what looked like a collage of plaster, bandages, tubes, and strings. We thanked God that somehow, inside that mélange, there was a breathing Roberto.

The doctor sat down in a chair beside us. "He's a tough kid." That much we knew. "We've got him stabilized for the moment. The X-rays show more fractures than that body can sustain."

Victor and I leaned heavily on each other for what we sensed was coming next. The doctor's eyes spoke the emotional investment he had in his patient. His words were directly to Victor whose family tie was written on his face.

"I wish I could say it's over. We'll know better in the next day. I know what you jockeys can take, but that boy had a trauma most of us wouldn't live through. At this point, we can only pray to God he will."

Victor was first. "Can I see him?"

"Sure." He nodded down the corridor. "Go with your brother."

I started to walk with Victor. The doctor caught my arm.

"Just one. Leave your cell phone number. I'll be here checking on him all night. I'll call you if anything . . . either way."

*　*　*

At 5:45 the next morning, the buzz of the cell phone snapped me out of the restless half sleep I'd dropped into after replaying the first thirty feet of that race for the millionth time. The tug between fear and prayer made me fumble the phone on the first try. I wanted, and didn't want, to hear that doctor's voice. It was a second jolt to hear the raspy voice of the trainer of Roberto's mount, Rick McDonough.

"Hey, Mike, can you get out here?"

"Yeah, Rick. What?"

"Just get out here."

*　*　*

I made Formula One time through the Boston streets from my apartment on Beacon Street, through the tunnel, and down side streets of East Boston that even cabbies don't know. At that hour, I had few other Boston drivers to challenge at intersections and beat on the straightaways.

They knew me at the gate to the backstretch of Suffolk Downs. At least two mornings a week, I take my wake-up shot, black, strong, and jolting, from the coffee shack at the backstretch by the racing stables in the company of trainers, jockeys, and exercise boys. It usually settles my mind, deep in that misty dawn atmosphere, to be among the genuine people of the sport I love. It braces me for the real slings and figurative arrows of the outrageous prosecuting attorneys I do combat with beside my law partner of three years, the redoubtable old lion of the criminal defense bar, Lex Devlin.

This morning there was no comfort and no peace. As I walked the length of the twenty stalls of Rick's barn which housed the horses entrusted to his training, I was picking up a sense of profound eeriness. It's always a beehive of action at that time of the morning. Today it was like a tomb. There was no one home.

I reached the rail of the track and saw all of Rick's hot-walkers, muckers, grooms, feeders, and tackers hanging around inside the outer track rail. They looked like they were on strike.

I found Rick down the track, sitting astride his favorite retired racing thoroughbred, clocking a young roan that was breezing full-out in the straightaway. I walked down and leaned against the rail beside him.

"What's up, Rick?"

He kept his focus on the roan. "Hell if I know, Mike. Any word about Roberto?"

"Nothing yet. Maybe no news is good news."

"You're a hell of an optimist. There's no good news in this thing. You know those two over there by the coffee shack?"

I noticed he never looked over at them. I recognized the over-stuffed middle-agers in suits that might once have fit two slimmer versions. If I was looking for the first good news of the day, this was not it.

"They're Boston cops, Rick. The one with a face like a grapefruit is Malloy. He's in homicide division."

Rick nodded. "You know him?"

"We've gone a few rounds in court."

"You trust him?"

"Yeah. About as far as I could throw that horse you're riding. What do they want?"

"They asked if I'd seen Victor Mendosa. I told them no. They wanted my permission to look through the stalls. I told them to knock themselves out."

"So why aren't they?"

"I might have added that the last one who walked into one of those stalls without one of my people to control the horse is still walking sideways."

"Rick, you're a classic."

For the first time he looked over at me. "They told me to give them a man to go with them. You know how I like taking orders. I told them all of my men are out on the track waiting for horses. They'll be back in a while."

Rick just tapped the walkie-talkie at his side that he used to give orders to the men back in the stables. I got the picture. Apparently all of his men in the stables heard his words to the two police on their receivers and took the hint. Hence the abandoned stables.

The two officers at the coffee shack saw us talking and ambled over, coffee in one hand and a *sopapilla*, the closest thing to a Mexican donut, in the other.

"What the hell are you doing here, Knight?"

"Detective Malloy. What a pleasure. I'm taking in the morning air. And you?"

"Always a smart-ass, Knight."

"Actually, it's true. I do it often. What brings you here?"

Malloy was true to his personal code of giving no information about anything to any defense counsel. "Police business. You seen that jockey, Victor Mendosa?"

Now he had me on the defensive and stifling an outbreak of sweat. "Not in a while. Why?"

"You see him, you put him in touch with me."

He started wandering slowly back to the coffee shack, still waiting for an escort to the stables. I could sense that his ears were still tuned in to me like a wiretap.

I looked back at Rick with the slightest trace of a wink. I knew nothing escaped that old cowboy. "So tell me, Rick. How are things?"

"Okay. Except for that damned Fly Right. She's gone lame again. Nothing but trouble, that filly."

I knew Fly Right. She was made of steel. She hadn't been lame since she was foaled. I picked up Rick's message.

"You got a carrot, Rick. Maybe she needs some sympathy."

He pulled a carrot out of his saddlebag and threw it to me. "Careful, Mike. She'll take your hand off if she can."

He said it loud enough to reach the listening ears. I walked down to stall seven. Fly Right saw me coming and, as always, put her head over the half door to nuzzle my shoulder and get a rub on her neck. She didn't refuse the carrot either.

I said it low, barely above a whisper. "*Qué pasa,* Victor?"

"*Es malo,* Miguel."

We kept it low, although I'd have bet the only Spanish word Malloy knew was "taco." The gist of our conversation was this.

"What's going on here, Victor?"

"I stayed at the hospital with Roberto. He never woke up through the night. Those two at the coffee shack came down the hospital corridor about four this morning. I heard them tell the nurse at the station they were there to arrest me."

"For what?"

"I don't know. I got out of there before they saw me. I can't go to jail, Mike. I mean it. Not here. Sometime I'll tell you why."

The questions running through my mind were piling up faster

than I could ask them. I looked back and saw Malloy and his side-kick walking my way. I grabbed the halter and lead line hanging on an outside hook and slipped it on Fly Right.

"I'll get their attention, Victor. Get out of here."

I led Fly Right out of the stall in the direction of Malloy and his buddy without looking up at them. She was a big filly, around six-teen hands, and she always pranced like she was about to spring. I got to within four feet of them and gave a sharp little tug on the lead line. She was spooky enough to bolt straight up.

Malloy nearly jumped out of his suit. He leaped backwards and came down with one leg in a bucket of wash water. The chill of the water gave him a second leap into a pile of straw and horse drop-pings that had been mucked out of a stall.

He rolled over his protuberant rear end until his flailing feet caught ground and took him as far from the fearsome beast as he needed to go to recover his sense of dignity, if not his temper.

He fired some ripe uncensored words at his junior partner, who almost dropped his sopapilla trying to control an ill-advised explo-sion of laughter. Meanwhile, I led Fly Right back to his stall, which Victor had vacated unnoticed. I slipped out myself before drawing more attention.

* * *

I drove back through the awakening city traffic to the offices of Devlin & Knight on the seventh floor of 77 Franklin Street in the heart of Boston. For the previous three years, I had had the unques-tionable honor of junior partnering with the man who gave birth to more ulcers in opposing prosecuting attorneys than all the rest of the criminal defense trial bar combined. The memory of the trepidation I had experienced when I was first paired with the then irascible icon, Alexis Devlin, had long since morphed into what could be called sincere respect and admiration—but what, closer to the fact, was the deepest love for the man who slipped into that spot reserved for the father I had lost at an early age.

Mr. D. was close to one side or the other of seventy years; and yet, by eight a.m., I could always find him and a pot of hot coffee in his corner office. I knew he was preparing for the third day of an edgy white-collar criminal trial. He was due in court by nine thirty. I also knew that he'd make the time under almost any circumstance for my morning and late afternoon drop-ins. This one was more than social.

I filled him in on what had happened at the track and the hospital and then that morning at the backstretch. He knew Detective Malloy better than I did. He could hardly control his amusement at the detective's morning flummoxing.

He knew without my asking that I needed his clout with the district attorney's office to get answers that were beyond me. He hit a speed-dial number on his desk phone, put it on speaker, and tilted his solid, block-built form back in the groaning chair. The young voice of Mary Cornelius, the receptionist at the Suffolk County District Attorney's office, gave him a greeting warmer than he was likely to get from anyone else in that office, with one exception.

"Mary, would you do me the kindness to ring the only other one in that office of yours with more brains than ambition?"

She was obviously alone at the moment. I could hear the unabashed grin in her voice.

"Mr. Devlin, for you, anything."

"Oh-ho, don't let the Dragon Lady hear that. She'll have your head on a stake."

We could almost hear the grin broaden. "I'll ring Mr. Coyne for you."

From the day I'd met Mr. Devlin, he'd told me with assurance that Billy Coyne, deputy district attorney, was the only career professional in the office with no eye on political or other advancement. He stood head, shoulders, and hips above the rest of the clan in legal acumen and, more to the point, pure old-school professionalism—meaning that if he gave his word, no power in Heaven or Hell could shake him on it. Perhaps because they were cut from the same cloth, their hundreds of one-on-one courtroom jousts had forged a respect that spilled heavily over into an unexpressed affection.

"Lex. How pleasant to start the day with a call from a worthy opponent."

"Opponent to hell, Billy. Can't a man make a call for a friendly chat with a brother at the bar?"

"Lex, don't ever retire. I'd starve without your steady diet of Irish horse manure. What bit of unentitled information do you want to do me out of this morning?"

"Need I remind you of your own Gaelic heritage, Mr. Coyne? If I had a nickel for every snookering you've—"

"Lex, enough. We'll have this out later. I'm due in court. What are you looking for?"

"A simple answer to a simple question. There was an accident at the track yesterday. A jockey was injured. It happens he was family to my partner, Michael. This morning we hear there's an arrest warrant out for his brother. What's that sinister spiderette you work for up to this time?"

There was a pause. "Is Knight there with you?"

I chipped in. "Good morning, Mr. Coyne."

Another pause. "I'm sorry, kid. I'd heard you were close. Roberto Mendosa died early this morning."

It was like a brick wall you see coming, but you won't admit it's there until you slam into it full force. The breath went out of me.

I couldn't have responded even if I could have focused on the conversation. I'd been more a part of Roberto's life, and vice versa, than any member of his family except Victor. And now, in an instant—no more.

The thought of Victor brought me back to the planet.

"Mr. Coyne, what's the charge against Victor?"

"I'm sorry, kid. This is a double belt for you. The district attorney wants him charged with murder."

Mr. D. was up and pacing. "Billy, what the hell is going on over there? I know you can't control her, but this is insanity. It was a racing accident. Michael was there. He described the whole thing. It would hardly call for a steward's inquiry, let alone an indictment."

"You don't have the whole picture, Lex."

"Well, I'm listening."

"I can't."

"Billy, you're the brains and morality of that outfit. Do you go along with this?"

"I've said all I can. I'm due in court. I have a full day. Trial, lunch at the Marliave, trial all this afternoon. I have to go."

There was a catch before Mr. D. said what he was going to say in strong terms. Instead, he said it quietly. "Billy, who else?"

"No one."

Mr. D. hung up the phone. I could see the concern in every line on the old warrior's face. "Michael, I'm sorry."

"I know, Mr. Devlin."

"What about Victor?"

"I've got to find him before Malloy does. I assume we'll be representing him." I looked up for confirmation.

"With everything we've got. Do you know where to start looking for him?"

"I think so. I'll be in touch."

"Billy wants to meet us for lunch at the Marliave. That was his message. He couldn't talk there. I want you with us to hear it firsthand."

THREE

I COULD FEEL the past smothering me when I walked into Pepe's Bar off Hyde Square in Jamaica Plain. I hadn't set foot in the place since my early teens, but I could still walk blindfolded through the layout of tables and chairs to the long bar. The bartender didn't recognize me, but in spite of the aging, I knew him.

He wiped the bar and listened for an order without making eye contact.

"*Hola,* Manuel."

He looked up, but nothing registered. I said nothing. He squinted until a dawn of faint recognition brought back more hostility than I expected. I can't capture the venom in the tone, but what he said in Spanish was this.

"You dare to come back here. You think you walk in here and it's the old days? You're dead in this town." He said it, turned his back, and started to walk away.

"I need to see Paco. Where is he?"

The words stopped him. He turned around and looked in my eyes with the heat of hatred I'd never seen before. "Like it's all over and forgotten, what you left here. You're lucky to be able to walk out that door."

He turned away again.

"It's not your call, Manuel. I'll leave when I hear it from Paco. This is for Victor Mendosa. It's for his life. You call Paco now."

I walked to a table in the corner. I could feel his eyes burning into my back, but I felt sure the old man wouldn't make a move on me without someone's permission. I didn't look back, but I could hear the click of numbers punched into the bar phone. Whatever he said was too low to make out, but I heard Paco's name. I sat down and let the memories burn hot in my mind.

I saw a fourteen-year-old boy who had just lost his father to a heart attack. His mother had moved the two of them from the snow-white North Shore of Boston to the mostly Puerto Rican barrio of Jamaica Plain to be among people of her familiarity and language. She didn't know it, but she was placing her son smack on the violent border between two warring street gangs. To avoid being victimized by both, the boy had to choose between the Diablos and the Coyotes. Either one was a bad choice, but the alternative was to surrender everything from his lunch to his life to the predations of both gangs. For reasons that seem hardly adequate now, he went with the Coyotes.

Coyote headquarters in those days, as apparently in the present, was Pepe's Bar. A younger Manuel was the bartender, and the dominant ruler of the Coyotes was a warrior called Paco. There weren't many to emulate in that strutting, macho collection of outcast juveniles who fell back on violence to mask the constant fear and lack of self-worth.

But there was Paco. He was like a rough diamond in a case of costume jewelry. At somewhere in his thirties, he had come up through the same banishment to an ethnic area outside of the mainstream of "normal" society. But something about him said to that fourteen-year-old boy that there was a higher human quality, an internal strength in this man that would never surrender to self-inflating machismo. This was a *real* man, pure and simple.

The odd thing was that from the day that boy first walked into that bar, there was some invisible, unlikely bond growing between him and Paco. No one else knew it, but to the boy it was almost tangible.

After a trial time with the gang, I could hear the words of one of Paco's lieutenants sending the boy out to pass the first stage of initiation to become a full member of the Coyotes. The boy was ordered to hot-wire a classic Cadillac parked outside of a funeral home during a wake. In those days, that was not beyond the talents of most fourteen-year-olds in that neighborhood. The part the boy couldn't quite carry off was impressing the police in a patrol car within six blocks of the funeral home that he was your average owner of a classic Cadillac.

The trial was brief. The prosecutor wanted the boy tried as an adult to "send a message to the community." Short of that, he was pressing the judge for the maximum number of years in some graduate school of criminality called a "juvenile detention home." Either way, the boy saw it as the end of his life.

Then a miracle happened. The owner of the Cadillac appeared in that pitiful courtroom that was, for most defendants who passed through it, the last station on the road to hell on earth. Miles O'Conner was defense attorney to names on the letterheads of Fortune 500 institutions who found themselves charged with what are appropriately called "white-collar crimes." He conferred with the judge and prosecutor for an interminable twenty minutes before reaching a result that sent the prosecutor off in a huff, and sent the boy off on the coattail of the man who became the boy's guardian, savior, and substitute father.

The boy's life became a different kind of hell, working at the lowliest chores in the North Shore stables of Miles O'Connor every waking moment that he was not in school or studying. But without realizing it, the boy grew into the O'Connor mindset that whatever exertion it took, no standard but perfection would be tolerated. That mindset eventually drove him to the top of his class at Harvard and Harvard Law School. The usual social life and college frivolity of his classmates was never an issue. There was never time for it if he was to insure the man who made everything possible that he'd hear the boy's name among the top prizewinners at every level. When Miles O'Connor died, the boy realized that there was no human being on earth for whom he would more gladly walk off a cliff.

* * *

I was jolted out of the memories of those years when the door of the bar opened. I saw an older man come through the door with hard years written across his face. I didn't recognize him until he turned to look at me. Between the deep, ancient scars on his face, I could read the features of the man I had so admired as a boy.

When he walked toward my table, he limped on legs that were bent and misshapen. I thought I could see a misting in his eyes, but perhaps the moisture was in my own eyes.

I stood up, and we looked at each other. I started to say, "Paco", but the word stuck in my throat. His eyes lowered and he dropped, more than sat, in the opposite chair. As before, he was still more comfortable speaking Spanish.

"*Por qué regresastes,* Miguel?"

He said it with both pain and a softer emotion. "Why did you come back, Michael?"

I sat down with him. "What happened to you, Paco? You were the strongest one of the gang."

He just slowly shook his head. When he looked up, he held up two fingers to the bartender. I could see Manuel open one Dos Equis beer. Paco saw it. He hit the table with his fist. "*Dos,* Manuel. *Dos!*"

Manuel opened another bottle and brought them both to the table. He set one before Paco, and put the other in the center of the table before walking away. I took the bottle and held it. Paco raised his, and we drank that first sip together.

Paco sat back. "You've done well, Miguel. You took the opportunity. You made something good of yourself. I'm proud of you."

"I've been very fortunate."

"Fortunate . . . Yes, you could call it that."

I heard the bartender, Manuel, smash an empty bottle into the trash. He grabbed the lip of the bar and yelled across the room. "Fortunate, you call it, do you? And to hell with you."

Paco shook his head and waved Manuel to break it off. Manuel ignored him. He yelled from across the room, "Sometimes good fortune has to be bought at a great price! A great price!"

Paco looked at me with eyes that seemed to have aged since he came into the room. "Why did you come back, Miguel? It was better to leave it all in the past."

Manuel came out from behind the bar wringing a bar towel between his clenched fists. "You. You think you just walked away from the Coyotes? You ever heard of anyone walking away from the gang and living?"

He walked over close and put his fists on the table. "This man paid your price. You were off somewhere with the big lawyer in the safe, easy life. We didn't even know where. And a good thing for you. The gang found out what this man did for you, and he paid your price. Look at him. I didn't think he'd live at the time."

I looked back at Paco. "I don't understand, Paco. What did you do?"

Manuel leaned down in my face. "He won't tell you. That day your Miles O'Connor came to that court and took you away from a term in prison. You think a man like that just wanders into that pit of a courtroom?"

I had never thought much about why Miles O'Connor came that day. "It was his car that I stole."

"What that car cost him he could make in half of one fee. He could buy a hundred more cars and never miss a meal. It wasn't the car."

"Then what?"

"I was there when this man made a call. He set up an appointment with your Miles O'Connor. He had to plead with his secretary to fit him into his schedule."

Manuel looked down at the bent figure of Paco. He had to force the words. "Paco went to see him. He told your Miles O'Connor there was this kid he thought was worth saving. That's why he went to that courtroom."

I had trouble catching my breath to get the words out. "I never knew. Paco, I swear, I never knew."

Paco just waved his hand as if to wave it all away.

Manuel stood upright. "Then it's good you know now. Because the gang found out. What they did to him was intended for you. Look at him. Even after all that, he's more of a man than you'll ever be."

Paco took him by the elbow and turned him toward the bar. "Leave us, Manuel. Enough. I still have some pride."

Manuel grabbed the bar towel and left with one last meaningful look at me.

I turned back to Paco. "I'm so sorry. I truly never knew. All these years . . ."

Paco held up a hand. "Stop, Miguel. I see what you've done with your life. Do you think I wouldn't do the same thing again? Let's leave it there."

Paco leaned forward across the table. "Something brought you down here today. What is it?"

I leaned closer across the table. This was not for Manuel's ears.

"Maybe I can pay the debt for another one of our brothers. You heard about the death of Roberto Mendosa at Suffolk Downs yesterday?"

"I heard. You know how word travels among the brothers."

"The district attorney is going after his brother, Victor. She's charging him with causing his death."

Paco blew a low whistle through crusty lips.

"I'm going to represent Victor. I'll do everything I can for him. He's not just a client. He's my cousin. And he's one of us."

Paco nodded. "So why does that bring you here?"

"Victor's on the run. I need to bring him in. There's a cop, Detective Malloy. If he catches up with him first, it could be not so good for Victor."

"I hear what you say, Miguel. Still, why does that bring you here?"

I sat back in the chair. "I owe you everything in my life, Paco. I'll never go back on that. Anything you want from me, it's yours. I want you to know that."

I could see those tired eyes come alive with a fire that wasn't there before. "I think you're about to ask something I can't give you, Miguel."

"I need to find him, Paco. Malloy may be the least of his worries."

He shrugged. "I'm an old man. I don't fight those wars anymore."

I leaned forward to whisper, "You'll never be that old. I saw the tattoo yesterday. On Victor. 'NDC.'"

His eyes took on something that looked like a defensive wall. He shrugged. "Lot of our boys have tats."

"Not that one. They wouldn't dare."

Those eyes were ablaze now. The rest of his body just slouched as if in ignorance. "You been listening to fairy tales."

"Listen, Paco. I may be a half blood, but I keep in touch. Those letters mean '*Nyeta de Corazón*'—'*Nyeta* from the heart.'"

Paco just closed his eyes.

I had to crack the shell. I was so close now we could practically touch foreheads across the table. "Don't shut down on this, Paco. Listen to me. I had a cousin in Oso Blanco Prison in Rio Piedras in Puerto Rico. Two guards thought he had a stash of drug money on the outside. They were wrong, but they tried to muscle him into giving it up. He took a beating, but he had nothing to give them. They said they'd come back the next day. They would have killed him."

His eyes were open now. He said nothing, but I could sense every muscle tightening.

"They found those guards that night with their throats cut. Here's a puzzle. Who do you think did it?"

His jaws just shut tighter.

"Talk to me, Paco. Every drop of that Puerto Rican blood in your veins is saying it. The *Nyetas*. They made my cousin in Puerto Rico a *Hermano,* a Brother. He told me about them later when he needed me to defend his son in this country on a drug charge. You and I both know the *Nyetas* started in prison, but they're the strongest organized gang in Puerto Rico. They're strong here too. In the jails, in the city. Are you going to lie to me now, Paco? You going to take the safe road and tell me you never heard of them?"

I put both my hands in a fist on the table in front of him with the forefingers and the middle fingers crossed. I know he saw the *Nyeta* sign, and he knew what it meant. He just looked away.

"You don't know what you're playing with."

"I know they have thousands of members here. They make alliances with local Puerto Rican gangs here to peddle their drugs, and other things we don't need to mention. I think that's what happened years ago with the Coyotes?"

"I never had anything to do with drugs."

"I know, Paco. But you're not the boss now. Just tell me if I'm off base."

"And if I say you're off base, will you just drop it? You're walking a dangerous path."

"I can't. I have to bring Victor in. Right now. I figure he went to the *Nyetas* to go underground. It's the worst thing he could do. I think you could put me in touch with someone who knows."

The fire in Paco's eyes had gone out. He stood up. He took a couple of bills out of his pocket. His voice was strong now. "Nice to see you, *Miguelito*." He threw the bills on the table. "But our worlds are too far apart. There's nothing for you here. I wouldn't come back." The bottom fell out of my heart when he turned and limped his way out the door.

I noticed the self-satisfied grin on Manuel as he focused on washing glasses. I left with a stone in my heart and not an idea in the world of where to go from there.

I walked the two blocks to where I had parked my Corvette. The young boy I paid to watch it was sitting faithfully on the curbstone. He popped up when I held out a five-dollar bill. When he took the bill, he mumbled something in Spanish. He brushed my jacket as he ran past me.

I reached in my pocket for my keys and felt a piece of paper that hadn't been there a moment ago. I was careful to drive out of the neighborhood before opening the paper. It had words in Spanish scrawled in broken letters. They said roughly "Nine o'clock tonight. Bench on west side of Jamaica Pond." In heavier letters, "*Cuidado!*" "Be careful!"

FOUR

I PARKED CLOSE to the office and walked to the Marliave Restaurant off Bromfield Street. Once more it was like walking out of one world and into a radically different one.

The meeting with Mr. Devlin and Billy Coyne, the deputy district attorney, was set for noon—which in Mr. D's world did not mean 12:01. I saw my two lunch companions climbing the narrow steps as I was approaching, and I could reset my watch to 12:00 precisely.

I caught up, as John Ricciutti, the son of the owner and a master chef, was leading the now three-man procession up the stairs to a private dining room. In all of my dinners there with Mr. D., my fingers have never touched a menu. John seated us graciously and spoke with affection directly to the man he put at the head of the table.

"Your Honor, this would be my pleasure. Something with veal. Perhaps prosciutto. I think artichokes. Not too much. Just . . . will you leave it in my hands?"

"John, there are no better hands in the city of Boston."

I could see John's face light up as he summoned the waiter to bring ice water, bread, and his personal stock of olive oil. I was smiling inside to see once again the small annoyance on Mr. Coyne's face at the title of "Your Honor," as John always referred to Mr. D.

"Lex, what the hell is he going to call you if you ever become a judge?"

"I don't know, Billy. 'Your Lordship' would be nice."

He said it with a grin, but I could see it still rankled Mr. Coyne at this slight one-upmanship of his fellow Irishman and almost constant courtroom combatant. Mr. Coyne was, as Mr. D. consistently reminded D.A. Angela Lamb, "beyond purview, the brains and conscience of that office." She had the self-advancing wisdom to leave difficult prosecutions in Mr. Coyne's hands. More often than not, that brought him into a battle of wits and legalisms with my partner, Mr. Devlin.

The preliminaries concluded, and a bowl of the finest pasta e fagioli between Boston and Rome set before each of us, we were left alone with the door discreetly closed.

"You suggested this little gathering, Billy. I take it something's going on over at your little shop of horrors."

"I don't have much, Lex. I just don't want you and the kid here walking into something you don't see coming."

If I should become managing senior partner of Ropes & Gray as a stepping stone to a seat on the United States Supreme Court, I believe I shall always be the kid here I'm resigned.

Alone though we were, Mr. Coyne leaned in close. "What you asked was not for telephone conversation. That jockey that was killed in the race at Suffolk yesterday. You wanted to know why we got involved."

"And, involved with a vengeance. I mean, *felony murder*, Billy? How many times in a year do horses collide? Jockeys taken to the hospital? Even deaths? It's a hell of a profession. Not for the faint of heart."

"Let me remind you, Lex, that more Saturdays of our youth were spent—I didn't say wasted—shoulder to shoulder by the rail at Suffolk Downs than either of us can remember. I don't need the lecture."

"Then what, Billy?"

He leaned back and paused. His timing was impeccable. A knock on the door was followed by the entrance of John and a waiter setting before us a veal dish, the aroma of which alone would send world-renowned chefs into a frenzy of mass suicide.

We all knew that John would not leave the room before gleaning from the look on Mr. D's face at the first taste an expression of sheer rapture. As always, he got it. He left with the waiter in tow and a smile that he'd carry back to the kitchen staff for sheer inspiration.

When the door closed, we all three let the troubles of the world hang in silent abeyance while we devoured something we'd not soon forget. Still, I could see that Mr. Coyne's pleasure was clouded by his thoughts. When the last fork came to rest, Mr. Coyne broke the silence.

"This doesn't leave this room."

I noted that he looked only at me when he said it. The bond of confidence between the two old warriors assumed it without words. I nodded in agreement.

"There's something happening in this city. There's a . . . rumbling below the surface. It's like an invisible tinderbox. If it breaks out in the open, this city of ours could become the murder capital of the country."

"Billy, my lad. This couldn't be your Irish affection for the dramatic?"

He leaned closer. "Listen to me, Lex. I'll admit in this room that our esteemed district attorney will press any flight of fancy that could get her to the governor's chair. You also know damn well that that's not me. I'm telling you, I'm deeply concerned."

"I'm sorry, Billy. You've got our attention."

"Things are happening that don't go together. That race. Take it from me, it was fixed."

"How do you . . . ?"

Billy held up his hand. "It was fixed. Leave it at that. The question is, by whom? Did you ever hear of a gang that started in Puerto Rico? They're called the *Nyetas*."

Mr. D.'s questioning look said "No." Mr. Coyne looked at me and knew that I was in familiar territory. He spoke directly to Mr. D.

"They started in Puerto Rico as a prison gang. The word is they came together in the 70s in the Oso Blanco maximum security prison in Rio Piedras. The idea was originally to protect the more vulnerable inmates, especially political prisoners who were pro-independence, against the more vicious gangs of prisoners—and also corrupt guards. The organizer of the *Nyetas* was Carlos Torres Irriate. He was called *La Sombra,* The Shadow. He built them into the dominant gang in the prison. He tried his best to keep the gang out of using or dealing drugs. That could have been his downfall.

"Their primary enemy was a gang of the most vicious prisoners. Many of them had been expelled from the *Nyetas* for their hair-trigger violence. The *Nyetas* called them '*insectos*'. They call themselves G-27 from an apartment number in a notorious project in Puerto Rico."

I could see he had Mr. D.'s interest. I was a bit stunned to hear this Irish-American prosecutor saying things that are only spoken in whispers among Puerto Ricans. Mr. Coyne leaned in closer.

"Time came when Irriate was killed in prison. Some say the leader of the G-27s, El Monota, put out the contract. They also say some of Irriate's own lieutenants were in on it. They wanted to get the gang into drugs, and other things. When Irriate was away from his followers on a walk with a corrupt guard back from the prison chapel, he was shot and stabbed to death.

"They say the *Nyetas* retaliated against the G-27s. Word is that the *Nyetas* chiseled with spoons, bare hands, anything they could use to break into the cell of El Monota. They stabbed him 150 times, then cut him into 84 pieces. They sent his pieces to specific people, his mother included. His eyes went to the second in command of the *insectos*."

"A sweet bunch."

"Indeed. That's what I'm trying to tell you. Needless to say, I didn't get this off of CNN. And it goes no further than this."

"You know it won't, Billy. And this is all relevant to the jockey's case how?"

"I'm getting to that. Those two gangs are still mortal, violent enemies. They even go to war with the powerful Latin Kings. The *Nyetas* and *insectos* have both established a major presence over here in Puerto Rican communities, mostly in Connecticut, Massachusetts, New York, and New Jersey. They each recruit the local neighborhood gangs to become associates."

He dropped his voice to just above a whisper. "We have serious reason to believe they're on the verge of an all-out war. That would not be pretty."

"Agreed, Billy, but again, why is this relevant to that absurd charge against Victor Mendosa?"

"Because I'm telling you . . . " He looked over at me. ". . . somewhat against my better judgment, we got a tip that that race was fixed by the *Nyetas*."

That chilled my blood. I could remember seeing the *Nyeta* tattoo on Victor. As a boy, I'd heard tales of the *Nyetas* and the *insectos* told in the dark of night by older children to scare the younger ones. They were like Grimm's Fairy Tales. Now they were coming true. I had to ask it.

"The tip you got about the race, Mr. Coyne. Can you tell us from whom?"

"I'll say this and no more. And there'll be no follow-up questions.

The tip was anonymous, but it was detailed enough to carry some weight. The edgy part is that, as far as we know, the *Nyetas* have never been involved in race fixing. Neither have the *insectos*. It's not their thing."

"But you think they are now. And you tie Victor Mendosa to this?"

Mr. Coyne stood. "I said no questions. Whatever puzzles you, puzzles me too. The lady who signs my checks got the tip I mentioned. Typically, she went off half-cocked crusading after Victor to capture some gang-bang headlines. She tossed the file on my desk while she waits for the reporters. No tales out of school there."

"Where are you really going with this, Billy?"

Mr. Coyne picked up his coat and walked to the door. "Wherever it leads me. I just don't want you boys to be blindsided when the fireworks go off. This is not just another case. You know the old saying, 'The lawyer always goes home'. Let's keep it that way."

* * *

The note that had been slipped into my pocket, probably by the boy who had been watching my car outside of Pepe's Bar, was a constant reminder through the afternoon of a date I'd have preferred to break. And couldn't.

At precisely 9:00 p.m., I was walking the now deserted runners' track that circles Jamaica Pond on the border of Jamaica Plain. The pitch darkness was penetrated only by a sliver of moon and the faint glow of too-widely spaced lampposts. The anonymity of the note only multiplied the creepiness.

Halfway around, a faint outline caught my eye. Heaven knows what I expected as I approached the solitary dim figure sitting on a bench, staring at the still water of the pond.

The figure made no move to look up as I edged, more than walked, to within five feet. The eeriness caused me to speak in a whisper. Based mostly on guess and instinct, I said, "Paco, is that you?"

There was minor relief in hearing his familiar muffled Latino voice. "Sit here, Miguel. Do it quickly. There's no time."

I sat. "Time for what?"

"Just listen . . . And remember . . . This is for Victor Mendosa . . . Hear me . . . El Rey de Lechón . . . you hear?"

I kept listening for more. "Do you hear, Miguel? Answer me."

"I do. What is it?"

His breathing was becoming shallow. "No time."

"Paco, I can hardly hear you."

He took a deep breath. It came out in one burst of pent up energy. "Speak only to Benito. Only Benito. You hear me? On your life."

"Should I use your name?"

Only silence. I could feel him tap me gently on the leg with his hand, although he didn't raise it. I looked down. I could just make out the closed fist with the forefinger and middle finger crossed. It was the sign of the *Nyetas*.

I started to stand to face him directly. I felt my foot slip on something wet and slick. The moon was higher, and I could just make out a spreading pool of dark liquid. I followed it to the source, a steady dripping from Paco's wrist. He was steadily slumping forward until he just hung motionless against a cord that bound his chest to the back of the bench.

I don't know which came first, the shock of fear that nearly propelled me off the bench or the numbing weight of loss of one who had been in my corner to the point of death. The result was frozen inaction, broken only when I heard a low voice in Spanish from the direction of the trees just behind the bench.

"On your knees, lawyer. Hands on your head. Not a sound till I tell you."

I was in no frame of mind to argue. I got down on my knees with my hands clasped on my neck. My greatest fear, second to imminent death, was that he had heard Paco's message.

"Now say it. What did he tell you?"

That alleviated one fear. On the other hand, Paco's message, whatever it meant, was delivered at the cost of his life. Fear or not, I couldn't just hand it over.

"I don't know. I couldn't understand him."

"Perhaps you'll understand if I put a bullet through your arm. First the left. Then the right if necessary. I'm afraid it's the last time you'll have use of either one."

He moved a few steps forward. I could see a faint glint of light catch the silencer on what looked like a sizeable handgun.

"Interrupt me when you're ready to speak, Lawyer. I'll count to three. One . . . "

I was actually locked in silence. My loyalty to Paco was probably matched by the paralyzing fear. I couldn't have gotten a word out literally to save my life.

"Two . . . You know what number comes next, Lawyer. Last chance."

"Three!"

I dove face down on the ground into the pool of Paco's last drop of life. The deafening crack of a shot was so stunning that I never noticed that the sound was not suppressed by a silencer.

I braced for the pain, the blast, the shock. Whatever would come. It didn't. It took me several seconds to realize that the shot had come from somewhere along the shoreline of the pond. I looked back to where I'd heard the voice behind the bench. The slim outline of a man was clutching the tree ten feet in back of the bench. He was slowly sliding to the ground.

I looked for the source of the shot down the shore. Nothing. Everything was dark stillness.

I checked Paco for any sign of life, but I knew it was hopeless. I moved to the body behind the bench. With my handkerchief around my fingers and as little touching as possible, I inched a wallet out of the rear pants pocket. By the light of my cell phone, I read the name and address on the driver's license and slipped it back in.

I put some serious thought into what to do next. I called Billy Coyne's private number for two reasons. I had an obligation to report the two bodies to someone in authority. Given the guarded nature of the conversation we'd had at lunch, I thought Billy might want his investigators to be the first on the scene. It would give him a chance to keep any incendiary details out of the press for the time being. If he'd been right about the two gangs, this could be the match to ignite the tinderbox.

FIVE

IT WAS ANOTHER tossing night's sleep—if sleep it could be called. It was like cruising in my restless mind between Scylla and Charybdis with neither actually visible. I had no idea of whether it was the *Nyetas* or the *insectos* or both that had me in their sights the night before, and even less notion of what to do about it.

I figured the best I could do was to keep to public places. It seemed the better part of discretion to finesse telling my senior partner about my personal quandary. I knew from experience that his heartfelt concern for my safety would lead to more restrictive orders than I needed at the moment.

By six a.m., I was at the backstretch at Suffolk Downs. I walked down the rail to the starting gate used for training horses that were new to the track or that had given problems in loading into position for a race. Rick was on horseback as usual. He was watching the assistant starter work with a bay that looked like Dante's Pride, the horse Roberto had been riding in that disastrous race.

"What's up, Rick?"

He glanced back. "Damnedest thing. Watch this."

"Isn't that the horse Roberto was riding in the accident?"

"Yeah. The vet checked her out. She was just shaken up. Had the breath knocked out of her. No lasting injuries."

"So what're you doing here?"

"Watch this."

We both focused on Dante's Pride following the lead line of the assistant starter straight into the open chute in the starting gate as smoothly as if she were walking into her stall. I remembered that she had balked at the gate before the race two days earlier.

Rick kept his voice low. "Now watch."

The starter closed the swinging doors behind her. Dante's Pride stood quietly, four feet on the ground, with the exercise rider just sitting on her back. We counted off a full fifteen seconds before Rick gave the assistant starter a wave.

I knew they wouldn't spring open the front doors unless they wanted to reinforce the instinct to break out at full speed, and it was too soon after her last race to make that demand on her. I watched the starter just open the rear doors and gently back her out.

"So what are we looking at, Rick?"

"A damned question mark. You were there at that race. You notice anything different?"

"She looks like a pro. She doesn't seem to need gate training."

"When she was in the gate for that race, she was like a jitterbug. She never had all four feet on the ground. When the starter sprung 'em, she was off balance. That's why she was stumbling those first few jumps. When Victor's horse bore in on her, it was enough to make her tumble."

I replayed that scene in my mind. He was right.

Rick dismounted and led his horse as we walked back toward the stables.

"Did you hear, Rick? They're charging Victor with causing Roberto's death. They're calling it felony murder."

He stopped short. "The hell you say. They think Victor murdered his brother?"

"Not exactly. They say Roberto died in the course of Victor's involvement in a felony."

"What felony?"

I knew this would not sit well. "They say the race was fixed."

I fully expected the resulting explosion of blistering curses that Rick probably picked up as a boy around the rodeo bucking chutes in Montana. I knew better than to interrupt the flow until he got it all out. He was looking me in the eye when he finished with a steamy, "That boy never rode a crooked race in his life. You can take that to the damned bank."

I've left out a few words, but that was the gist.

"And that's what I've got to get across to a jury."

He was still overheated and ten decibels higher than I wanted since we were approaching other people. "Hell, don't we have something like innocent till they prove him guilty?"

I said it in a low tone, hoping to establish a mood. "Yeah, I know. But sometimes it doesn't work out that way, especially if the prosecutor has good circumstantial evidence."

"I don't know what the hell all that means."

"Anyway, that's my problem. And not the most pressing one at the moment. Victor's disappeared. Very bad timing. Any ideas?"

I could see him thinking as he just shook his head. "You talk to any of the other jockeys? You speak Spanish. I don't. That could give you an edge."

I was thinking of the direction I was heading next and wondering if that edge could get me fitted for a box. I didn't dwell on it.

"Think back to that race, Rick. Other than the starting gate, anything different about it? Roberto was riding Dante's Pride for you. Victor was riding Summer Breeze for another stable. I know that Victor kept on riding after Roberto's spill. His horse actually came in first."

"There's no blame there. Victor didn't see what had happened to his brother. That was behind him. Victor was on the second fastest horse in the race after Dante's Pride. No surprise that he beat the rest of them."

"I suppose."

"Hell, it doesn't even make sense. If it was fixed for Victor's horse, it didn't do 'em any good. The stewards disqualified Victor's horse for interference with Dante's Pride. The win went to the second finisher, Cat's Tale."

"What stable was Victor riding for?"

"Circle A. Tony Lucas is the trainer. His barn's just around the bend there. I'll put my money on Tony, too. He's straight as they come."

As long as I was there, I walked around the bend to Tony Lucas' barn. I'd known Tony from the time some years ago when he'd asked me to sit in with him on his subpoenaed testimony before a state senate committee investigating organized crime involvement in race fixing. My impression at the time, contrary to Mr. Devlin's constant reminder never to trust a client's protestation of innocence, was that Rick was right. Tony was, as they say, clean as a hound's tooth. The investigation had been just a political showpiece anyway. The boys on the senate committee, and they were all boys of the club at the time, were running every horseman with an Italian last name through the committee's witness stand for the main, if not sole, purpose of nightly publicity in the *Record American*. They got their publicity, but there were no irregularities to be found in Tony's barn.

"Hey, Tony, what's up?"

He turned back from the group of exercise riders he was debriefing. When our eyes met, I noticed a degree more surprise, bordering on shock, than I expected.

"Hi, Mike."

That was it. He broke off with his group and walked into one of the stalls. He seemed to busy himself with the ankle of the resident mare. I walked to the door of the stall.

"That was too bad about the disqualification of your horse the other day."

"Those things happen. I'm kind of busy, Mike."

"So I see. You got time for one question?"

That brought what I could only read as a distressed look. "I don't know. What?"

I was getting jumpier by the minute. It seemed a good time to fly direct. "I saw in the program you had a change of equipment on Summer Breeze. You took blinkers off for the first time since her first race. Mind telling me why?"

It was a simple question. For a track horseman, it was like asking if it was Tuesday. He seemed to me to take it like a question about his marital fidelity. There was a noticeable pause, followed by more attitude than the question called for.

"What difference does it make to you?"

"Curiosity. It's not like the formula for Coca-Cola. Any reason not to tell me?"

"Yeah. You questioning my judgment?"

"Tony. I said it's a curiosity. The usual change is 'blinkers on.' Once on, they usually stay on. Why the huff?"

He noticeably relaxed, but I had the nagging feeling it was forced.

"Sorry, Mike. That whole thing with Roberto has me off."

I was thinking, *Maybe, but Roberto never rode for you. You didn't know him that well.*

"So, what about the blinkers?"

"I didn't think she needed them anymore. No need carrying extra baggage."

Since he seemed more settled, I thought I'd go for the big one. I moved into the stall beside him. "Has Victor been in touch with you since the race?"

"No. I really am busy, Mike. Let's get together some other time."

It may have been my super sensitivity, but now I was wondering why he wasn't curious about why I was asking about Victor. Nevertheless, for whatever reason, that well had apparently run dry.

There were at least two propelling motives for my next move. The first was to find Victor. But the second, right up there with it, was to find out who was behind the killing of Paco and the ambush of me, personally. That last part could well recur with more successful results.

My only lead was what Paco had said with his last breath. "El Rey de Lechón." At first, it made no sense. "The king of suckling pig." On a hunch, I fed it into the computer and came up with a restaurant off Roslindale Square in the western part of Boston. An iffy lead at best, but when a straw is all you have, you grasp at it.

* * *

El Rey de Lechón was a stand-alone café on a busy street. It was not Beacon Hill, but I had no qualms about parking the Corvette in the attached lot. The décor inside was my idea of a country restaurant in a village in Puerto Rico. The sign boasted the best Puerto Rican cooking outside of San Juan.

My first effort was to blend. At eleven forty-five a.m., there were half a dozen men scattered in groups at the tables. The tone of the voices was exclusively casual Spanish. The next thing I noticed caught me by surprise. I had not quaffed that *aroma de cocina casera*—aroma of home cooking—since my last dinner at my mother's about a week previous, and it practically reduced my taste buds to groveling supplicants.

I slid into one of the booths. The waitress set the tone with a warm, *"Buenos días, Señor. Agua frío?"*

My acceptance of the offer of ice water was as gracious as the offer, and in Spanish. There was business to do, but I was beginning to believe the boast of the sign outside. If I hadn't come with an appetite, I had one now. I ordered the *lechón*—suckling pig, *arroz con gandules*—yellow rice with peas, and to put the chef to the real test, the *chicharrón*—fried pig skin.

An hour later, I made a vow that if I had, by chance, walked into the national headquarters of both the *Nyetas* and the *insectos*, and they had united for the sole purpose of terminating my life, I would nevertheless return for the *lechón*. The *chicharrón* were so worth every artery-clogging drop of cholesterol that, if I were to tell the truth, this Puerto Rican chef had moved my mother's *cocina* to a close second place. May she never hear it.

I was wading into the *budin de pan*—bread pudding, when the waitress, Maria, according to her name tag, dropped by to check on my needs. It reminded me of the "need" that brought me there. Since we had become easy with each other in Spanish, I kept it that way. I remembered the warning in Paco's last words.

"Is Benito here?"

She smiled. "You should know. You've been enjoying his cooking."

"Any chance I could talk to him. He deserves my compliments in person."

She left me with a mug of rich Spanish coffee. In about thirty seconds, there was a chef's apron on a tall, well-proportioned, red-haired man somewhere in his late twenties standing beside me. I held out a hand. He took it and slid into the opposite bench.

"First time?" He said it in English with no trace of an accent.

He caught my hesitation and filled the gap. "I don't speak Spanish. How's your English?"

"I can get by. I was asking for Benito. Are you . . ."

"Yes and no. I'm Benjamin. Ben Capone. It's Italian. They like to call me Benito around here. Good for business."

"I don't believe it. You cooked this?"

He had a pleasant, genuine laugh. "My grandmother, my mother's side. She was direct from Puerto Rico. She lived with us in the North End when I was a kid. She taught me everything she could about cooking her style."

"Unbelievable."

He laughed again. "Actually, you could take every drop of Puerto Rican blood in my body and put it in a shot glass. But I love doing the food. What brings you in?"

After what I had just heard about this Benito's ancestry, I was thinking, *a dead end.* I had one last hope. I said it softly. "Is there another Benito who's a regular around here?"

"Yeah. About four of them. It's a common name."

Now I was at a dead end, until he looked around and leaned closer. "I get the notion you didn't drop in just for the *lechón.* You look like you want to do some business. Yes?"

"And if that were true, could you sort out the Benitos for me?"

He had that same easy grin. "Understand, my only interest in this place, these people, whatever else goes on here, is the cooking. I mean, where else can you get paid to cook Puerto Rican? But I notice things. I think maybe you want to tap into a more serious group that hangs around here."

I knew I was on something between thin and no ice. But I had nowhere else to go.

"I need some information. I'm a lawyer. I represent a client, Victor Mendosa. I need to locate him. Have you heard the name around here?"

"I told you. I don't speak Spanish. And those . . ." He nodded to the customers across the room. "They don't speak English. So there's not much communication."

I opened my billfold and took out the hundred-dollar bill I keep folded for moments like this. I put it under the bread plate and slid it halfway across the table. I could see his grin broaden. He reached over and plucked the bill from the plate. He just looked at me for about five seconds before he gave that warm Italian laugh. He reached over and tucked the hundred-dollar bill into my suit coat pocket.

"Like I said. I'm only here for the cooking."

He must have seen my spirits drop. He laughed again. "But I'll give you this. One of those four Benitos. He comes in here every afternoon about three. They all just about kiss his ring. I don't know what he's into. I don't want to, as long as it doesn't get this place closed. Let me have your card. I'll tell him you want to do business." He held up his hand. "And don't tell me what business."

* * *

I was in my office on Franklin Street that afternoon. Julie, my secretary through every phase of my life since law school, buzzed my line.

"Michael, you better take this one."

"Who is it?"

"I think it's Mr. Universe. Could this man possibly be as charming as he sounds?"

"Give me a hint, Julie."

"He says it's Ben Capone. He could be Leonardo DiCapro."

My taste buds instantly recalled the *lechón*. "He has his ways. Put him on."

I waited for Julie to click off. "What have you got, Ben?"

"A message. And then I'm out of it. Be in front of your office at nine tonight."

"For what? Did he say?"

"End of message."

"I understand. Many thanks, Ben."

There was an uncomfortable pause. "Don't thank me yet. This may not be a favor. I could be reading your name in tomorrow's *Globe*. And I don't mean the society page. I've seen this dude."

"And?"

There was no smile in the voice this time. "Better you than me."

SIX

THE AFTERNOON GAVE me some much needed time for an inventory of goals. Top of the list was finding and bringing in our client, Victor Mendosa. The longer he stayed out, the deeper the hole he was digging. The second goal was keeping intact and functioning the concept that "The lawyer always goes home."

At exactly 9:00 p.m., I was standing in front of our office building on the corner of Franklin and Arch Streets. At 9:01, a black Lincoln with clouded windows glided to the curb. The back door swung open. A low voice from the driver's seat said "*Sube al caro, Señor*"—"Get in the car." My inner voice was screaming in two languages, "*NO sube al caro!*" When you have no choice, you have no choice.

As the sole passenger, I watched familiar safe environs flash by the window. We headed south on Tremont Street, deeper and deeper into the bowels of the South End of Boston. When we passed Dartmouth Street, I'd have bet what little value my life had at that moment that I could guess the destination. If the rumors of gang violence at the predominantly Puerto Rican housing project I had in mind were factual by half, it would be an interesting evening. I could see flashes of recent newspaper articles condemning the lethal clashes between the resident gang there and the one at Mission Hill.

We finally pulled to the curb outside of the very place I had in mind. The car door opened. There were two escorts the size of Patriots linebackers on either side. Between them stood one tall, slender dude with facial scars that bespoke a violent rise through the ranks of whatever gang was playing host. He made a finger motion that said in any language, "Out of the car—follow me." The word, "please," was not implied.

An ominous silence reigned as we marched to a door at the side of the old stone-and-stucco building. Slim took the lead, I occupied the middle, and the two linebackers kept the ranks closed from behind.

We passed through small clusters of onlookers. Each one hit the mute button as we approached. It was like the palace guard conducting a foreign visitor to the presence of Caesar. I read the stony stares we passed as either honoring Caesar's guest or praying thankfully, "There but for the grace of God go I."

We entered the building by a side door that was flanked by two males with bulges where chest muscles don't grow. It reemphasized the idea that if this lawyer were to go home, it would be with the permission of Caesar.

We passed down a long corridor as dark and foreboding as my thoughts. When we reached the door at the end, my guide, Slim, knocked softly. The order to enter came in Spanish.

Before touching the door, Slim turned and patted down every area of my rigid body that could conceal a weapon or microphone. I've been through less thorough medical examinations. Needless to say, I raised no objections.

Slim knocked softly again. The door opened from the inside. A solid nudge from one of the linebackers ended any hesitation I might have entertained about entering.

I found myself standing in a bare-walled room behind a plain wooden chair in front of an ancient, oversized desk. The man sitting behind the desk was heavy in build, dark-complected, and probably within ten years of the age of Mr. Devlin. The other thing they had in common was an unmistakable aura that said that you were in the presence of one who could command your respect by sheer weight of character. I was taken by surprise, because only two men I had met in a lifetime had so affected me on first meeting—Mr. Devlin, and my surrogate father, Miles O'Connor.

He rose and extended a hand toward the chair. It seemed more an invitation to sit than a command. His voice was deep and low, and seemed to lack the need to instill fear.

"Mr. Knight, please."

I sat, and when I had done so, he also sat. He gave one nod in the direction of Slim, the linebackers, and one resembling Slim who had apparently opened the door. They took the signal and left us alone.

I was further surprised that he spoke to me in English.

"I understand that your Spanish is excellent, Mr. Knight. Nevertheless, I think it would be easier for you if we converse in English. It's important that we clearly understand each other. Yes?"

"If you say so."

My tone may still have been tense, but it was not hostile. He smiled, perhaps pleased.

"Good. My name is Ramon Garcia. I assure you, that's my real name. Some choose to call me Benito. It was a childhood nickname. Long story. I say this because, regardless of what you might have heard or anticipated, I want your trust. Not your fear."

The smile that appeared on his face seemed completely genuine. I continued to be surprised at the impression he was making on me with every word. He had not asked a question, so I just nodded.

"I hope my people who conducted you here have done nothing to discourage that trust. Certain precautions are . . . perhaps you understand."

"I do."

I didn't, but it seemed the thing to say.

"Good. Then we start fresh. I'm sure you'll have questions."

I managed a small smile. "The first would be what in the world I'm doing here."

He laughed a gentle laugh. "Yes. That would be first. Actually, that would be second. The first concern is that I want to assure you that after what I hope will be a pleasant and productive conversation, you will be escorted to your home. In spite of what you may have heard of our little community here, you're in no danger. Do you understand that I can and do give that assurance?"

I sat back in the chair as an intended sign of trust. "I do. Perhaps you understand that you've just restored ten years to my life."

The laugh this time was open and hearty. "I've been told that you have a certain steel in your bones when in, shall we say, difficult situations, Mr. Knight. The mere fact that you chose to come here tonight, well . . . we both have much to learn of each other. So, to business."

He leaned forward with his elbows on the desk. "Mr. Knight, we have a mutual acquaintance. Victor Mendosa. I believe you have a close relationship."

I figured I was giving him nothing he didn't already know by saying, "He's the son of my mother's sister. My cousin."

"Yes. And I believe the relationship is even closer than that."

"If you mean we've been close friends since he and his brother, Roberto, came to live with us when he was fourteen, yes. You're right."

"That's good. Let's get directly to the point. Cards on the table, as they say. Victor's in legal trouble. Our Suffolk County district attorney wants to try him for involvement in his brother's death."

"As far as I know, there's been no public announcement." I was getting edgy about breaching the confidence I promised to Billy Coyne. He smiled and leaned back in the creaking desk chair.

"We could play games with each other and waste the evening without ever reaching the point, Mr. Knight. That would be unfortunate for the three of us, Victor included. Why don't we assume for discussion, merely hypothetically, that I have information about an impending indictment of Victor for felony murder based on the D.A.'s suspicion that the race was fixed? No actual admission or commitment on your part required. Is that fair?"

I was still uncomfortable. "I'm willing to listen."

"Very good. Then we can assume, hypothetically of course, that Victor is left with two choices. We both know that Victor is . . . missing. He could stay that way indefinitely and avoid trial. That's not a good choice. He has a promising career. The alternative is to turn himself in and stand trial."

"When you say 'missing,' Mr. Garcia, can we also assume—hypothetically—that you know where Victor could be located. That assumption could, as you say, advance the conversation."

There was a pause. His smile was frozen for a few seconds before thawing. My guess was that he seldom heard more than the word "yes" or "no"—mostly "yes"—from someone sitting in that chair.

"I'm acquainted with your senior partner, Mr. Devlin. You've picked up his direct ways. I see you also have the backbone to carry it off. I hope we'll get to know each other better. Until then, let's hold that assumption about Victor's whereabouts in abeyance."

"I'm still listening."

He nodded. "I have an interest in seeing Victor cleared of that charge. He's a fine young man. But you know that."

"Would you mind if I ask what that interest is?"

He raised his hands in an ambiguous gesture as he noticed that the questions were flowing in his direction.

"I'll give you the simple answer. Too many of our young men have their futures, their lives, stifled . . . stamped out in their teens. Violence seems endemic to our community. Your path was different, thank God. But you understand how things are here."

He looked over. I said it all with a nod.

"I don't want Victor's life to end here. I want him to have the best defense counsel possible. I'm told that would be the firm of Devlin & Knight. I'm also told that the fee would be at an appropriately high level. I'm prepared to write whatever check is necessary to ensure your services."

"That's very generous, Mr. Garcia. But it doesn't answer the question."

His eyebrows rose significantly, as did my blood pressure. But I needed an answer to the question before I could make a commitment. This could be rough sailing. Mr. Devlin and I agreed when we first came together as partners that while we'd be representing criminals—many of them guilty—we'd never take on representation of anyone whose occupation involved cold-blooded murder. That eliminated organized crime personnel, whether Italian, Irish, or Puerto Rican. I owed it to my partner to honor that commitment, regardless of circumstances. He would have done the same.

He held up his hands in a silent question.

"Your real interest, Mr. Garcia. It matters. I'll tell you why if you'd like. As you say, Victor's a nice young man and a good jockey. Neither of those facts would cause most people to open their checkbooks."

There was a slowly kindling fire in his dark eyes now that was setting off alarms in every corner of my mind. It was only deep-rooted loyalty to Mr. Devlin that recalled the phrase, "Damn the torpedoes, full speed ahead."

"Perhaps, as you say, Mr. Garcia, it's my turn to put all the cards on the table."

He was piercing me with those deep eyes at this point, but there was still no hostility in his voice. "By all means, Michael. May I call you Michael?"

"I'd actually prefer to keep the formality, if you don't mind. You'll understand when I tell you why I need to know more before I commit. Mr. Devlin and I made a solemn promise that neither of us would represent anyone whose occupation involved murder."

"Victor's a jockey, Mr. Knight."

"I was with Victor in the hospital. He had come right from the track. He took off his jockey silks in the waiting room. I saw the tattoo. 'NDC.' That's the symbol of an organized crime gang called the *Nyetas*. I may not live in Jamaica Plain now, but I'm not totally out of touch either. The gang that rules in this housing project is rumored to have connections with the *Nyetas*."

I looked for something in his eyes—agreement, disagreement, anger. I could at least read nothing that said I'd walked off a cliff so far.

"I think you brought me here for this meeting because I've been asking questions about Victor. Clearly you're not the building superintendent here. You're a man of power. I think you see where this is going."

He sat back in his chair. There was a studied calm in his features that I'd seen in Mr. D.'s when the game was on and the stakes were high.

"Ask your question, Mr. Knight. And make it direct. Leave no room for later doubts."

The gauntlet was down, and I had one chance. "If we take on the representation of Victor, will we be representing solely the interests of a jockey with a promising career, or will we be furthering the interests of an organization that deals in drugs and death?"

I held my breath. He stood. I don't know why, but I did, too. He had my eyes locked with his.

"This boy with the tattoo. You didn't know him when he and his brother were young boys in Puerto Rico. You were not living in your mother's house when they came here. It was your mother who answered the pleas of her sister in Puerto Rico to bring the boys to this city before their lives were compromised by the gang. But your mother never knew the full story, either. And just as well."

He walked over to my side of the desk. "I'm in a position to know more about you than you think. May I just say that your own past was not unlike that of Victor. You may not have been left with a tattoo to carry for the rest of your life, but I'm sure you have other scars, up here." He pointed to his forehead. "You made a new life. So has Victor. What Paco did for you—yes, I know about that—I also did for Victor. The difference is that I had the power to grant his release without suffering the price Paco paid for you."

He turned his head, I think possibly to hide any trace of an emotion that could seem to some like weakness. "Victor has been like my son."

He walked back and sat down. I sat as well. Our eyes were locked again. "No, Mr. Knight. You have no worry on that score. I make no apology for my life, but you won't be representing me or any organization. You'll be defending a boy against an ambitious and powerful prosecutor. I believe you and your partner can live with that."

There was that same tiredness around his eyes that I see in Mr. Devlin's all too often. But I could find no resentment there for my asking the question.

There was one more devil that had to be exorcised. "Mr. Garcia, are you aware that Paco is dead?"

"So I've heard. That is regrettable."

"Are you also aware that I came within a count of three of being shot by the man who killed him?"

This time I saw his eyes come to full alert. I recalled the name on the identification I found in the wallet of the man with the gun, the man who also died that night from a gunshot out of the shadows.

"Mr. Garcia, who is, or rather was, Hector Martinez?"

I could have read his expression as either shock or anger. Either way, it was momentary. A look of calm resolution took its place almost before I could read it.

"Mr. Knight, this is a dangerous world you and I have chosen to inhabit. You represent people who are involved in matters that must occasionally touch your life with certain risks. It would be naïve to believe these risks could be totally avoided by saying you're just the lawyer. Am I correct?"

I thought back over the past three years and counted the number of times I'd sworn never to take another case more dangerous than drafting a deed.

"Granted. But ..."

"Allow me, Mr. Knight. And then you choose, once and for all. You recognize that I'm a man of a certain power in this community. May I say modestly, that you have no conception of the extent of that power. That said, I'll swear to you now that I'll use every resource at my command to shield you and your partner from any threat that might result from your representation of Victor. More than that, I cannot offer."

I sensed that that was all he had to say on the matter. It was in or out on that basis. I sat silently for a few moments. I wanted him to know that what I was about to say was fully thought out.

When I looked up, I could see that he was giving me the time for thought, but that he expected an answer.

"Mr. Garcia, Victor is my cousin. But we're more like brothers. Before you brought me here, Mr. Devlin and I committed to his defense. I could have said that at the beginning, but I had to know what part you play in this. As long as the business of the *Nyetas* is out of this equation entirely, our commitment to Victor stands."

His smile was genuine. He took a checkbook out of his coat pocket. I held up a hand. "That's not what I want. I need something more important."

His eyes asked the question.

"I need information. Where do I start? You didn't say you knew where Victor is. But you didn't deny it either. There's no time for games now. We trust each other, or we don't. It can't be halfway. I could be walking into a lion's den."

He nodded as if a decision had been made. "You're an interesting young man. You and Lex Devlin are well matched. I'll say this just once. When I give my trust, like your partner, it's not halfway. I fully expect the same. I don't think I need to be more explicit."

We both stood, and when our eyes met this time, a compact was made. Words were unnecessary. The handshake merely solidified it.

He walked me to the door. "Now may I call you 'Michael'?"

"Now, and from now on, Mr. Garcia."

"I'll be in touch by tomorrow with the information you need. If you have to contact me, do it through the chef at El Rey de Lechón. He's not of our blood. But you can trust him. And there are not many. As we say, *cuidado,* Miguel."

SEVEN

I KNEW THAT certain questions needed solid answers before I could make a pitch to Victor to turn himself in voluntarily. First, was that race, in fact, a boat race as the old touts used to say—fixed? Secondly, if so, was Victor in on the fix? Two affirmatives to those questions would dictate a radically different approach to the defense from the one I had planned on the assumption of Victor's innocence.

My only lead as to his whereabouts was the promise of a message from Ramon Garcia. That involved waiting—a skill I never fully mastered. I decided to make the best use of the time.

There had been a bug in the back of my head ever since the previous morning when I'd watched Dante's Pride, Roberto's horse in that disastrous race, walk calmly into the training starting gate on the backstretch. He even stood still in the box as if he were posing for photos. Rick had called to mind the contrasting image of the Pride in the starting gate the afternoon of the race. He was jumpy as a cat on a griddle. He never had all four feet planted on the ground before the gate sprung open. The result was predictably a stumbling start over the first eight strides.

When facts don't readily rear their little heads, the next best thing is a hunch. As Sherlock Holmes was wont to say, eliminate the improbable and what's left is high on the probability chart. I remembered hearing a story from Rick years before about an old

Montana horse trader's trick to make a horse look lame in order to reduce the asking price.

That thought had me at the Suffolk Downs backstretch the next morning before the sun cleared the horizon. I walked down the track to the starting gate where the crew of assistant starters were standing around in a cluster, waiting for the day's crop of horses for training.

I caught the eye of Fred Rothman, the only one I knew. Rick McDonough had referred him to our law firm years before when he was charged for an incident of high-speed driving. I had lucked out in discovering an out-of-date calibration of the radar equipment used at that time by the local police. The judge dismissed the charge. That put Fred and me on friendly footing when he walked over to the rail.

"How's it going, Counselor?"

"We'll see how the day shapes up. I need a favor, Fred. Just a curiosity. You were working the starting gate the day Roberto Mendosa's horse fell, weren't you?"

Fred just shook his head. "That was the worst, and I've seen all the bad ones. Roberto was a good kid. What's this got to do with you?"

"Curiosity. Do you remember which starter loaded Dante's Pride for that race?"

"Yeah. Dante was number three post. That was . . ."

He started to turn around toward the group of starters, some of whom were looking in our direction. I caught him in mid-turn.

"Fred. Look at me. This is confidential."

"This is more than curiosity, isn't it, Mike?"

"That's the favor I mentioned. You and I are just chatting about the weather, right?"

"Looks sunny to me. I was about to say it was Ronny Stone. I remember he loaded Dante's Pride."

"How do you remember that?"

"Because I had to help him. It was unusual. Pride's usually the coolest horse in the race."

"Without turning around, which one is Stone?"

"He's the guy with the blue cap."

That did it. I spotted him in the group and thanked Fred.

"Whoa, Mike. What's up?"

I smiled. "Nothing, Fred. When do you fellas take a break?"

"At eight thirty. We've got a list of horses to gate-train coming down now. Then they drag the track. Everything shuts down for fifteen minutes. You know the routine."

"Then here's the second part of the favor. Would you tell Mr. Stone I have a message for him? Confidentially. I'll be at the coffee shack during the break. He doesn't know me. No names. Just tell him quietly the guy at the rail said he's from a man he knows in the city. You don't know anything more than that."

"Now you've really got me curious."

"How about if I satisfy your curiosity over dinner at Durgin-Park in about a week. Until then, you don't know anything."

"My mind is a blank."

"Then put a smile on your face, deliver the message, and dream about that prime rib."

* * *

I was at the coffee shack, when the breezing and galloping horses all came off the track to allow the tractor brigade to drag heavy planks with three-inch studs on the bottom around the track to break up clods and smooth out the surface. I had two steaming cups of the heavy dark brew in front of me when I saw a blue cap ease up to the counter a few feet away. He had the rugged build of a man who pushed and pulled ton-and-a-half horses into confined metal enclosures for ten races every day.

He never looked in my direction, but I could sense the tension in every muscle. The counter man looked for an order, but he just waved him off. I slid one of the coffee cups down in front of him. He just looked at it. I smiled and hoped he could hear the smile in my voice. One of us had to set the tone for some conversation.

Most of the chatter of the jockeys and exercise riders down the counter was fortunately in Spanish. I kept my voice below the chatter level in English.

"Good morning, Ron. That coffee's for you."

He picked it up and blew the steam off the top. Still nothing but tension. That actually brought a bit of joy to my heart. I turned and gave him the most beaming, comforting smile I could muster at that hour.

"Smile, Ron. Relax. I'm like an insurance salesman. You know what insurance is, don't you? Some people say they can't live without it. Let's take a walk."

I left it at that vaguely ominous suggestion and moved away from the counter in the direction of a vacant section of the track rail. If there were anyone within earshot—which there wasn't—the rumble of the tractors would have provided privacy.

I looked back and watched him ease away from the counter. He gave it his best casual saunter in my general direction. He looked about as casual as a Marblehead sloop tacking into a headwind. And every reluctant step he took confirmed in my high-fiving mind that on a hunch, I had cast my net over a major catch.

He settled at the rail about four feet away looking toward the grandstand across the track. I moved a foot or two closer.

"So, Ronny, we meet. I've been hearing about you from . . . you know. I don't think we need to speak names here."

He just looked at me with the blank look of a dog that doesn't know if it's going to get a pat or a kick. That was my security blanket. He stood a good six foot five. With those enlarged horseman's hands, he could have tossed me the width of the track on a whim. That meant that the anxiety that was tightening his grip on the rail was generated by his assumption that I was connected with someone with serious threatening power. As I hoped. Game on.

"Ronny, you look pale. You should get out in the air more often."

He looked befuddled.

"It's a joke. Relax. I have good news for you. He's happy. He wanted me to tell you that you pulled it off perfectly. Couldn't be better. He used the word great. You hear that?"

He looked at me in disbelief. Not what I was looking for, but at least it jarred him off dead center.

"Great? Did you say 'great'?" He was spitting out the words in a forced whisper. "That kid died. You call that great? What the hell is it with you people?"

The only thing I heard was "you people." That meant the hook was set. Now the trick was to ward off an explosion that could release my catch.

"Relax, Ronny. You're right. That was a hell of a thing. I'll tell you this. His family'll be taken care of."

He gave me a disgusted look as if I'd missed the point entirely. That, too, was more or less welcome. He had so completely bought into who he thought I was connected with that I was even beginning to dislike myself. It was time to reel in the fish.

"The point here is twofold. He wants to see you. Same place. This morning. Eleven o'clock. You'll be back in time to work the races this afternoon. I would imagine."

He backed off the rail and turned face to face.

"Like hell! He said this was just one time. Why the hell does he want to see me?"

"I told you there were two things. First, he wants you to do it again next week."

His face flushed, and a string of expletives poured out like a volcanic eruption. I let it run its course.

When it stopped, I just shook my head and smiled. "Whoa, Ronny. I don't think I'll deliver that message. You know the old saying about shooting the messenger."

That seemed to remind him of whom he thought he was talking to. He settled into a grouchy funk.

"I said two things. He wants to give you a bonus for the last time. Don't say I told you, but he also mentioned a figure that's about twice the price for the next time."

To his credit, that seemed to make no difference whatsoever. I was beginning to regret the wringer I was putting him through, but then I remembered the last time I saw Roberto. I decided to push it one last yard for confirmation.

"Incidentally, Ronny, what did you use? He may ask out of curiosity. I like to have answers for him. You know how he is."

He answered by kicking up some of the half-inch stones on the path underfoot. Bingo. Hunch dead on. The story I remembered Rick telling me was that an old Montana horse trader he knew years ago would walk alone into the stall of a horse he was intending to buy. He'd throw some pebbles into the straw bedding under the horse. It generally caused the horse to keep lifting his feet to find a safe spot to avoid the painful pebbles. The trader could claim the horse was lame and the price would drop. I had a feeling that something like that had caused Dante's Pride to prance around in the starting gate. That way he wouldn't have all four feet on the ground at the start of the race. He'd get off to a slow start and probably get boxed in by other horses well off the lead. So much for his being the speed horse in the race.

The other half of the hunch was that the most likely one to pull it off would be the assistant starter who led the horse into its post position in the gate. He could drop the pebbles or whatever on the ground inside the gate at that position just before leading the horse into the gate. Immediately after the race, the tractors would pull the drags over the track for the next race and bury the evidence.

"Well, that's it. Eleven o'clock this morning. I wouldn't keep him waiting. But I guess you know that."

I started to walk off and leave him with his thoughts. I got a few steps when I heard the question I least wanted to hear.

"Hey, who the hell are you, anyway? What's your name?"

I kept walking, but I spoke back over my shoulder. "What's the difference, Ronny? We won't be dating. I'll tell him to expect you."

*   *   *

On the walk to my car, I speed-dialed the same security service that Mr. Devlin and I had used since our law firm began. Tom Burns' agency provided confidential investigation, protective security, and other services at a level that justified a fee scale that would make any of his competitors blush. I had the number that put me in direct touch with Tom without other ears intervening.

"Tom, I need one of your very best men."

"Mike, you should know by now. There's no such thing."

"Meaning?"

"That with one exception, any man who's not the best in the business doesn't work for me. There's no ranking."

"Who's the exception?"

"The only one who perfectly fits your description."

"And that would be? Wait a minute. Spare me. That would be you."

"You're a clever lad, Mike."

"And you're the soul of modesty."

"If I were the soul of modesty, I couldn't send those bills you never seem to object to. What do you need, Mike?"

"There's an assistant starter at Suffolk Downs. He's working the training gate right now. When they finish for the morning, he'll be keeping an appointment he thinks he has with someone who's used him to fix a race. I need a man on his tail. I need the name of the man he tries to meet with."

"Consider it done. Describe the assistant starter."

I did.

"I'll call you, Mike."

"Let me give you a heads up, Tom. We're probably talking about someone high up in one of the dicier Puerto Rican gangs."

"In race fixing? That would be unusual for them."

"Nevertheless, tread lightly. Those boys do not play nice."

EIGHT

I WAS FEELING the first faint glow of relief since Roberto's fall. The fact that whoever fixed that race had to depend on the pebble trick to neutralize Roberto's chance of winning suggested that Roberto was not in on the fix. The glow faded when I realized that that did not absolve Victor. In fact, it was the swerving of Victor's horse into the path of the stumbling favorite, Dante's Pride, that took him out of the race entirely.

To go one disheartening step further, the fact that Victor clearly veered into Roberto's path practically ensured that Victor's own horse, the second favorite in the race, would be disqualified on a foul by the stewards—as he was. That put the two favorites out of the money, leaving the win to one of the long shots. It was, in fact, Cat's Tale in post position five outside of Victor's horse that ultimately won the race at odds of 15 to 1.

To complete the math, with only seven horses in the race, if you subtract the two favorites, and the winner, Cat's Tale, you have four left. Two of those four had tired, sore legs from over-racing. I'd have had a better chance of beating Cat's Tale on foot. That left just two horses, Mark's Delight and High Justice that had to be eliminated from contention to make Cat's Tale a shoo-in as the winner.

That was depressing. It appeared on circumstantial evidence that Victor played a pivotal role in the fix. On the positive side, I'd known Victor for his entire adolescent and young adult life. My strongest intuition was that he would never deliberately place his brother in jeopardy by a move on the track that reeked of potential disaster. Again, on the negative side, my intuition and five dollars would barely buy a cup of Starbucks' daily brew.

I took the shore route back to the city along Winthrop Parkway. It was fifty degrees in a stiff easterly wind. I had both windows down. Nothing clears the cobwebs like chilled salty air right off the ocean. By the time I reached Pearl Avenue, I was ready to surrender to Mr. Devlin's theory that you can't base a defense strategy on the belief that the client is innocent.

Then it hit me—like a curtain lifting. Damn it! It wasn't Victor's play at all. He was just along for the ride. Why the hell didn't I put those pieces together before?

I whipped the Corvette in a U-turn that covered half the sidewalk and nearly put two cars into the beach wall. It was rush hour, but the rush was in the opposite direction. I could treat the speed limit as a mere suggestion all the way back to the backstretch.

As I passed through the gate, my cell phone came to life. I cut the pleasantries to the core.

"Tom, what have you got?"

"Good news and bad news, Mikey."

"Give me both in one sentence."

"Good news: I've got a name. Your assistant starter flew direct, but not where you thought. You said he'd go to one of the Puerto Rican hotshots—as in the South End. Not so."

"Then where?"

"That's the bad news. He went direct to D'Angelo's Restaurant on Prince Street in the North End. My man parked and went in right behind him. Your boy gave the bartender a message that went direct to the back room. In about ten seconds, one of the goons came out and escorted him in an ungentlemanly manner to the back room.

My man says there was a crap-storm touched off that you could hear at Paul Revere's house."

"Did he come out?"

"Not yet. That's the bad news. Here's worse news. In case you don't know it, that's Paulie Caruso's den. Allegedly, as they say, he's the number two boy in the Italian mob these days. And to hell with the 'allegedly.' You listening, Mike?"

That was a twist that had me reeling. Every time I thought I had this mess contained, it sprung another leak. "I'm here, Tom."

"Yeah, but are you listening? Some of those North End *mafiosi* kill for business. This one's a certified lunatic. Not to spoil your breakfast, but you'd rather have been on Whitey Bulger's hit list on his worst day."

"I'm thinking back. I never gave my name to the starter. He showed no sign of recognizing me. What could he tell Caruso?"

"You've got your head in the sand, or someplace else. He could give your description. You were probably the only one at the back-stretch this morning in a suit. It could take Caruso five minutes to have you identified. It'd take me about one."

"You make a point."

"Thank you. Here's another one. Paulie Caruso now knows that you know he was the fixer in a race that caused a death. He didn't get where he is by leaving witnesses in good health."

"So I've heard."

"Then hear this. The starter didn't come out, but two goons right out of the cast of *The Godfather* did. My man's on their tail. They look like they're heading for Suffolk Downs. Where are you now?"

"Guess."

"Oh, crap. Get out of there now, Mike. These are pros. Have you started carrying a gun like I've been telling you?"

"Guns make me nervous. I'm a lawyer."

"Oh, good. Be sure to mention that when those two start shooting. *Leave now.*"

"No use, Tom. They could find me at the office, at home, anyplace."

"Then you, my friend, have a clear problem."

"Maybe not. Is your man still on their tail?"

"So far."

"I have an idea. What's your man's name?"

"Let's say 'Frankie'. He's always liked that name."

"Good enough. Here's what I need."

*   *   *

I picked up another cup of coffee for grit and walked to the rail down by the training gate. The assistant starters had gone for the day. It was just me in my blue suit and a few pigeons.

It was my turn to feel a world of violence closing in. They say if you want to judge a matador's courage, watch his feet. I planted my feet and got a grip on the rail to keep them there. I had ten minutes to regret everything that brought me to that moment, going back to filing an application to law school.

In exactly ten minutes, I could sense the curtain going up. It was showtime. I sensed two massive presences approaching, one on each side. This was confirmed by the pressure of a dull object just under the ribcage. Then a baritone voice in that distinctive North End accent.

"Mr. Caruso sends you a personal message. You got into his business. And he takes it … personally."

I knew that the worst part of that was the open use of Caruso's name. The chances of my being left alive to repeat it on this earth were nonexistent.

"Suppose I could assure Mr. Caruso that he has nothing to fear from me about his fixing that race two days ago."

"That's not a chance Mr. Caruso chooses to take. Let's take a walk. Over here."

I turned around and saw the gun I'd been feeling gesturing in the direction of an empty row of stalls. I started to move in that direction at the slowest pace I thought I could get away with. A couple of nudges in the back with the same cold steel put a limit to that ploy. I was down to my last move—a prayer that Tom Burns was not all bluff.

We passed several empty shed rows. I got the "Stop" command in front of the next empty stall. My escort said the last thing I could expect to hear in this life. "Inside."

Before obeying that last order, I turned around to face them. I knew my lines, but saying them in anything under a soprano voice was a challenge.

"Just one thing, boys. I have a message for your boss."

That bought me a few seconds. I looked into the two stone-cold faces that could as easily have been ordering a pizza as ending another human's life. I looked beyond them for a glimpse of something to ignite a hope. Nothing.

I fell back on blind faith and said the line I'd rehearsed at full stage volume.

"To hell with it, boys. You'd screw it up, anyway. I'll deliver the message myself."

There were grins on both faces. "Not likely."

I yelled the punch line. "Like hell!"

I dropped to the ground as if my legs had been kicked out from under me and clung to the earth. Two gunshots pierced the air. My body went rigid waiting for the impact. It didn't come. The only sounds that followed the shots were two screams and a mixture of curses, grunts, and groans of pain.

One spin rolled me into the dark of the stall. I looked back and saw two overstuffed bodies writhing on the ground. Each had dropped a gun to grab a leg just above the knee. The location of the blossoming pond of crimson on each said that Tom's marksman had shattered the bone.

I was on my feet with their two dropped guns in hand. It's amazing how a change in circumstances can restore the self-confidence. In spite of their pain, I had their full attention with a gun in each hand, barrels pressing on the center of each of their temples.

"If you ever come within half a mile of me again, my man will aim higher. Is that understood?"

They just stared. A slight rap on the side of the head with the barrel produced a response.

"Yeah."

"Good. Now take one hand, reach in your pocket, and take out your wallets."

I could see the pain in their faces when they moved, but this time they were the ones with no choice. I put down the guns long enough to take out their driver's licenses and dropped the wallets beside them.

"The man who sent you to kill me—that would be Paulie Caruso, right?"

The code of silence kicked back in. I aimed each gun at the same point above the knee of their good legs. I started to squeeze the trigger. None of us, including me, knew how close the guns were to firing. "It's your choice, boys."

One of them cracked. "Wait! Don't do it!"

"Say the name."

"Awright. Mr. Caruso."

"Is that Paulie Caruso?"

Silence. Another half squeeze.

"Yeah. Yeah."

"Say it."

"Paulie Caruso."

"Thank you, boys. *Arrivederci.* Try to stay out of trouble."

* * *

For the first time in my life, I was chomping at the bit to get away from the backstretch. There was just one last matter to attend to before the moment passed. A small curious crowd was moving in the general direction of the gunshots, which I guessed came from somewhere in the infield of the track. It wouldn't be long before the search expanded to the boys on the ground.

I moved double-time toward the barn of Bill McClosky, the trainer of the winner of that race, Cat's Tale. I knew that Bobby Cataldo was the jockey for most of Bill's entries. He was at the backstretch to exercise the horses he'd be riding in races.

I saw Bobby just coming off the track from breezing one of Bill's horses. I caught him as he dismounted and whispered a few quick words. He debriefed Bill on the workout, and hustled to where I was waiting alone.

"There's no time for niceties, Bobby. Just listen. You were part of the fix of that race that killed Roberto."

He pulled back. "What the hell are you talking about, Mike?"

I took him by the arm. Since I had eighty pounds and six inches on him, it was not difficult to walk him in the direction I had in mind.

"Like I said, no time to be nice. I've seen you ride a hundred times. You're right-handed. You come out of the gate with the whip in your right hand. That day you had it in your left."

"So what?"

He tried to pull away, but I had him, and we were moving at a good clip.

"Alone, nothing. But that was the one day that the horse on your left was Victor's horse, Summer Breeze. She had the blinkers off. Tony Lucas always had blinkers on her because she shies at anything she sees beside her. Put those two together and it's clear why Summer Breeze veered into Roberto's path. You just had to flick your whip beside her right eye."

"The hell. That doesn't prove I was in on anything."

"I don't want to prove it, Bobby. You and I both know what you did. That's for you to live with. I just need some information between you and me."

We kept up the pace, but he went silent. "I think I know why you did it. I can imagine the threats from the North End. I've got something to show you."

We walked around the end of the empty stalls. When he saw the two goons on the ground he went snow white. I had all I could do to drag him in front of them. They were still clutching a leg. The curses and grunts were down to moans.

I rapped each of them on the good leg. They looked up. It was clear that they recognized Bobby as he stood over them in my grip.

"One last question, boys. Is this one of the jockeys you threatened to get them to fix that race?"

Their silence meant that I had lost some of the previous momentum. I let go of Bobby and took one of the guns out of my waistband. I was beginning to feel like Wyatt Earp with the unaccustomed leverage of a gun in my hand. I took aim at the good leg of the one who had spoken before. Bobby's eyes were practically coming out of his head. Even without my grip, he was frozen to the spot.

"It's all the same to me, boys, but I'd think you'd want to have one good leg."

Nothing. I pressed the gun into the flesh of the good leg of my previous conversant. I began to squeeze. Again, he had no idea of how close my pressure on the trigger was to firing—and neither did I. We were probably both praying.

The goon broke again before either of us suffered a lifelong wound. "Yeah. That's him."

I pulled back the gun for the sake of both of us. "Good. Then we're ready for the final question. Let's pretend you're both under oath, and you are. Because if I ever find out you lied, we'll be back in this position. Am I clear?"

The speaking man on the ground nodded. I looked at Bobby. "I know why you did it, Bobby. I have no interest in causing you more trouble. I just need a straight answer."

I looked first at the man on the ground. "Was Victor Mendosa in on the fix?"

He'd gone this far. There was no need to lie now. He just looked blank.

"I'll have an answer. *Now*."

He just shook his head. I thought I had finally made first base until he followed it with "I don't know."

I brought the gun into position again. "One more time."

"I swear it. I don't know. Mr. Caruso had other men on it. I swear I don't know. Just not by me."

I looked over at Bobby and almost willed an answer. He looked totally spent, but he seemed to be thinking.

"Tell me one way or the other. I don't care which. I just need the truth."

He was almost in tears. I could feel the weight he was carrying because of Roberto's death.

"Say it, Bobby."

"I can't."

"These two will not hurt you. Or your family."

"I mean I can't. I really don't know. I only know what they made me do. I don't know about Mendosa."

That was a brick wall. I felt like I had run a marathon, only to wind up right back at the starting line—except at the starting line, I didn't have Paulie Caruso at my throat.

NINE

THE EMOTIONAL HEAT rose to a boil as I ran back to my Corvette. I could sense the growing specter of never knowing for the rest of my life when a bullet from one of Paulie Caruso's thugs would close the curtain forever. My more rational sense of fear was screaming *"flight, not fight."*

I took every back road toward Boston that would let me keep the gas pedal close to the max without police interference. I even cruised through the tunnel to the North End at close to the same speed. I only knew that I was trying to outrace the cooling of the impulse to leap into the snake pit. Without that propelling impulse, I'd be certain to wimp into a protective cocoon.

It was nine thirty a.m. when I slant-parked in half a space on Prince Street in the North End and double-timed the walk to D'Angelo's Trattoria. I was still moving at ramming speed when I went through the door. The only human life inside was a bartender cleaning glasses to the right, and two trim but sizable members of the palace guard who bolted into a defensive line position when it appeared that I was on a direct course to what looked like the office door in the back of the restaurant.

One grabbed me by the arms and spun me around while the other did a rapid frisking that came to an abrupt halt when he reached the two guns still tucked into my belt. At that point the frisker made a battlefield decision and turned one of the guns on me. I froze the situation with just two words.

"Paulie Caruso."

Only I didn't say them. I bellowed them at a volume that made both of them jump. I was still hearing echoes when the office door flew open.

"What the hell's goin' on out here?"

The words came out of the five foot two, balding image of a cannonball with limbs in the doorway. The gun in the hand of the frisker was touching the side of my neck.

"I'll take care of him, Mr. Caruso."

"Wait a minute. Frisk him."

"I did, boss." He held up the two guns as evidence.

"Do it again."

He did. No new discoveries.

The cannonball walked slowly to within a few feet while the frisker kept the gun at my neck.

"You got a death wish or something? Who the hell are you?"

Under any other circumstances, I'd probably be fluctuating between praying and pleading. But not today.

"I'm someone with a message that could do us both a hell of a lot of good."

He looked at me like some unknown species. "I don't hear nothin' from some guy I don't know his name. Like I said. Who the hell are you?"

I knew the next two words could buy me time or a bullet in the neck. Either way, the chips were irretrievably down. "Michael Knight. I've got a proposition for you, Mr. Caruso."

A grin started on the jowled face and just grew as he took a slow reconnaissance lap around me. When he completed the circle, he just looked up at me eye to eye.

"Would ya look at this, boys? This guy in his nifty dark-blue suit. He walks into my place. He's got two popguns. He's gonna make me a proposition."

That brought grins from the two-man peanut gallery. I remembered Tom Burns' description of Caruso as a homicidal lunatic. On the other hand, I was still breathing. Rapidly, but breathing.

"Bring this guy in the office. Put him in a chair."

They did. Caruso stood in front of me, which gave him the advantage of looking down. He crossed his arms with all the swagger of someone with two goons to keep the dark-blue suit in submission.

"So what've you got to say? This better be good."

I went to put my right hand in my pocket. Caruso jumped two feet back. The goon on my right brought the gun down in a chop to the soft part of my shoulder. The pain generated stars in my vision, but it was no time to wimp out. I held my right hand open and moved slowly again toward my pocket. This time I managed to pull something out of my pocket. I held it out to Caruso.

He squinted down at the driver's licenses I'd taken from the two he'd sent to the track to terminate my existence. The grin was gone in an instant of recognition.

"What the hell is this?"

The goon who had frisked me looked at the licenses over my shoulder. "Hey, boss, this is Gino's gun he had. I know the crack in the handle."

One look from Caruso silenced the goon, and his eyes were back on me. It was showtime in spades.

"I'm afraid the boys you sent won't be coming to work tomorrow, Mr. Caruso. They'll be in need of some sick time."

He just looked at me for five seconds as if he'd discovered a new life form. "You walk in here and tell me this? Why do I let you breathe for one more second?"

I held out my open left hand like a magician making a show to the audience. I slowly moved it into my left suit coat pocket and pulled out a tiny device without which I would not dream of leaving home. I put it on the wooden arm of the chair and touched one of the micro switches. A voice came out of the recording device that was louder than its size would suggest. I replayed my conversation at the stable that morning with the talkative thug who had named Caruso as the one behind the fixed race in which Roberto died.

I could see tiny beads of perspiration on the bald pate in front of me. It boosted my draining confidence for an instant. In a flash of the temper I'd expected, Caruso's short arm shot out. He brought a chubby fist down like a hammer on the device. The playback was instantly squashed. The fat face resumed the grin and came within a foot of mine.

"You got any other cards you want to play before I . . ."

I was my turn to grin—more of a smile—while I controlled my breathing. "Can you imagine on your luckiest day, Mr. Caruso, that I wouldn't have made copies? And had witnesses to authenticate it? And made arrangements to get it to the federal and state prosecutors if I leave here with even a crease in this blue suit you seem to admire."

I let it sink in during the almost tangible silence that followed. I gave it five seconds, while I tried to forget that no such copies actually existed.

"I told you I had a proposition that could help us both, Mr. Caruso. Shall we go on playing King of the Hill? Or do we talk business?"

He turned and walked back to sit behind the desk. I knew his little mind was racing at warp speed to adjust to a situation he'd probably never experienced. He had an unarmed man in his den, with two goons and two guns that could end the conversation as easily as squashing a mosquito. And still he sensed that he was not in control. It threw him, and he could not show it in front of his goons.

"So what's this proposition? I'm just listenin' here."

I sat back in the chair like one of two businessmen dealing on equal terms. "Here's the deal. On my side, I have a recorded statement by your employee that could bring a charge of felony murder against you if it reached one of our eager prosecutors. And I can assure you that it will if you choose to act in an ungentlemanly manner."

A good place for a dramatic pause. I saw no need to add that the recording would be inadmissible in any prosecution under the hearsay rule, best evidence rule, right to confront witnesses rule, and probably a dozen more. His silence suggested that that legal nicety had escaped his upbringing. The ground was prepared for point two.

"That said, here's the good news. Please take this to heart. I haven't the faintest interest in your business, your organization, your hobbies, or anything else that seems to keep you on the front page of the *Globe*. Absolutely none. When I walk out of this room—and that will happen—you have absolutely nothing to fear from me. Do you understand what I'm saying here?"

He had beady little eyes, and they were in full squint. For a man whose idea of bargaining was "My way or a bullet in a vital organ," I was truly a horse of a different hue. On the other hand, I was well aware that the toothless bluff of the recording was all that had him off-balance enough to listen, and its shelf life was uncertain at best.

"Get to it. What do ya want? I'm just askin'."

"I want nothing. I want you to know that I am no threat to you. I want you out of my life. No more goons with guns. No threats. Nothing. And the price I pay is that I never use that recording against you in any way. I walk through that door, and we're out of each other's lives. Permanently. That's it."

"That's why you came? That's why you march in here? I give you my word and you give me all the copies of that thing?"

"I intend to trust your word as coming from a man of honor. We do this like gentlemen. We shake hands on the promise to do each other no harm. Ask around. You'll never get a better deal than my word. I'll put the same trust in yours."

I stood. I held out my hand while he grasped for a decision. I was drowning in the realization that I was playing a death scene in the theatre of the absurd. I was exchanging words of honor with a lifetime thug who never made a decision that didn't flow from the power of a pointed gun. The word "honor" was as alien to his entire life as a unicorn.

The seconds ticked . . . five . . . ten. What the hell was he waiting for?

Then it crept into my skull. That was it. No one in his entire life had ever dealt with him as a man of honor. The words "holy crap" were clearly forming in my mind. I looked at him standing there, actually looking maybe an inch or two taller than when we came into the room. He seemed to be growing into the idea, particularly in front of his goons.

"And you turn over all copies of this thing."

"First I want your word. Then I give you all I've got. And the promise to stay out of your life. That's it."

I could see him take in the expressions, such as they were, on the faces of his two goons. I think he was reading, at least in his mind, a sort of respect that didn't come out of the barrel of a gun. It was undoubtedly the first time, and it was a kind of baptism.

He reached out and took my hand, and the pact was made. I still can't explain why I felt a ton and a half lift from my shoulders. But I did.

"Now what about them copies?"

I was back in the soup. This could unravel the whole deal, but you can't give what you don't have.

"There are no copies, Mr. Caruso. I never had time to make any. I came here right from the track."

He looked me in the eye with an expression I couldn't read at that moment. Then a grin. He looked at the goons when he spoke.

"Look at this here. This is a piece of work, this guy." He turned to me. "You know what, Knight? I believe you. Boys, escort Mr. Knight to the door, like a gentleman."

It was on shaky legs that I counted every step to the door of the office. Just before I left the room, I heard from behind, "Needless to say, if I ever hear . . ."

"You never will, Mr. Caruso. You have my word on it. And I have yours."

"Yeah."

* * *

I was driving through the city streets of Boston to my office on Franklin Street. For the first time in recent memory, I had no need to check for patrol cars. I was actually within the speed limit. I never even challenged other cars entering intersections, which tended to confuse the other Boston drivers.

I had just parked when my cell phone came to life. It was the call I'd have been expecting if the morning had not held other diversions.

"Michael, this is Ramon Garcia."

The name called to mind the other harrowing interview I'd experienced lately, this one the previous evening in the housing project center of the Puerto Rican version of organized crime.

"Mr. Garcia, thank you for getting back to me. You were checking on where I could locate Victor Mendosa. Any word?"

"I think what we have to say to each other should be done in person. Do you suppose you could meet me at a restaurant in Roslindale? I believe you know El Rey de Lechón."

The mere utterance of those words flooded my salivating mouth with the taste of the *lechón*—the suckling pig. I forced my mind back on the business at hand.

"I do."

"Shall we say around midnight this evening?"

"Fine."

"And, Mr. Knight, just a precaution. Could you park up the block on Cummins Highway and walk? You might come in by the kitchen entrance in the rear. The chef, Benito, will bid you welcome."

Why not? It seemed that every entrance through every door I'd made in recent memory had been written by Lee Child for Jack Reacher. I swore an oath to myself that when this case was finally put to rest, I would head up a new "wills and trusts" division of our firm. And I'd enter every building for the rest of my life by the front door, unescorted.

TEN

THE LIST OF things to do before *sneaking* in the back door of the El Rey de Lechón Restaurant at midnight to meet with Ramon Garcia was beginning to multiply. The purpose of most of them hinged on my eventually finding our elusive client. Part of the tenuousness of every possible move lay in the fact that I seemed to be playing three separate chess matches with three apparently unconnected opponents—the Italian mafia, the Puerto Rican *Nyetas*, and possibly their deadly enemies, the *insectos*.

For the moment, I let myself revel in the hope that I was at least off of Caruso's hit list. During the meeting with Caruso, the thought had occurred of asking him the burning question—was Victor in on the fixed race? Thirty seconds into the conversation, I concluded that it would not be worth confusing the issue. Caruso would likely not have the foggiest idea. The fixing of that race was a complex masterpiece. He probably ordered it. But the complexity of planning and pulling it off was as far above his mentality as isolating a genome. That plan required a master of the fine art of race fixing. I had one in mind, but that was for another day.

I was back at the office at 77 Franklin Street a bit before noon. My secretary and right hand, Julie, rose from her chair with arms raised.

"Can this be? A personal appearance in his very own office by Michael Knight. Heaven is truly smiling on us."

I must mention that I suffer Julie's dramatics with unflustered aplomb. Her only serious flaw is that she is bright, young, and beautiful. I live in constant dread that some knight-errant is going to wise up and sweep her into the arms of matrimony—and out of my professional life. On that day, I'll probably take up plumbing or landscaping. When one of these all-consuming cases bleeds every speck of attention and energy out of my day, Julie holds the rest of my practice together like a mother hen.

"Good to see you too, Julie. Any important messages? And by that I mean earthshaking, titanic. Nothing less."

"Oh, I don't know, Michael. If you can find the phone on your desk under the message slips, you might just answer several hundred at random. And keep this in mind. Every one you answer is one less client or lawyer who will not be saying the most distressing things to your sensitive assistant."

"Julie, if I could, I'd run the whole list. Not possible. Tell you what. Pick the ten that are giving you the most aggravation. I promise. I'll get to them. Is Mr. Devlin in?"

"And if I say 'yes, he is', does that mean you finesse answering messages?"

"Julie. A promise is a promise. But I'll take that as an affirmative."

* * *

Mr. D. cut a phone call short when he saw me walk into his office.

"Michael, I've been worried about you. I heard you've been leaving a trail of bodies. First Jamaica Pond, then two at the track. Tom Burns told me about your morning. What the hell are you up to?"

I settled into my usual chair. "I wish I knew. It's like whack-a-mole. Every time I knock down one problem, another one pops up. Have you heard from the D.A.'s office?"

"Billy called this morning. The Dragon Lady's flustered about not being able to find our client. Are you any closer than she is?"

"Maybe yes. I have a meeting tonight with Ramon Garcia. I think he's the head of the *Nyetas* around here. He called the meeting. It's about Victor. I'd rather not tip it to the D.A.'s office until I hear what he says."

"What's the danger level, Michael? That was a hell of a risk you took this morning. I want no more of that."

I told him about my deal with Paulie Caruso. His expression showed no great relief. "This is your life we're talking about. You know who he is. How much faith can you put in his word?"

"I don't know. For some reason, our so-called deal's given me some peace on that front."

The furrows remained on his forehead. "I don't like it. I'm going to have Tom Burns put a man on you for protection."

I shook my head. "Not necessary. It could even kill any chance of getting information from Garcia tonight. I do think we need to touch base with Billy Coyne. Very privately."

Mr. D. dialed Billy's private line and put us on speakerphone.

"Billy, I have Michael here. Can we talk?"

"Hold on, Lex."

There were some muffled voices, a door closing, and Billy back on the line.

"We're okay now. What the hell have you been up to, kid? People seem to be showing up shot wherever you've been."

"Mr. Coyne, I'm going to level with you. As I promised. I just need to know for sure that it stays between the three of us. If your boss starts mucking around in this, there could be a lot more bodies, starting with mine."

That brought Mr. D's eyebrows up to full alert.

"Go ahead, kid. Lex knows it'll stay between us."

I filled him in on my escapades of the past few days, including the fact that I had a meeting scheduled for midnight that night.

"Who are you meeting with tonight?"

"That one I can't give you. I gave my word. I can say this. I'll let you know whatever I can after the meeting without breaking that confidence."

There was a pause. "All right, kid. Hey, Lex, I hope you've got a leash on your junior partner."

Mr. D. looked at me. "It's my every wish, Billy. The trouble is he's too much like me."

That thought brought enough joy to my heart to re-fire my engine for the night ahead. I jumped in. "Mr. Coyne, I have to ask. Last time we talked, you mentioned a tinderbox about to erupt. Can you be more specific? I need to know which way to duck. Our only interest is Victor Mendosa. But I'm sensing threads from the *Nyetas,* maybe the *insectos*, and now, for the love of Pete, the North End mafia. Do you know of any connections?"

Billy's voice dropped to just above a whisper. "Nothing specific. I've been getting the same vibes you are. The Puerto Ricans have never gone in for race fixing. Everything else, but not that. And yet I get the feeling they're all over that race with the Mendosas. That business at Jamaica Pond. That smacks of the *insectos.* They've been at war with the *Nyetas* for decades. Does your Puerto Rican side agree with that?"

"Completely, but—"

"Hold on. Then we have the Italian mafia boys. That fixed race has their fingerprints all over it. Which leaves the question, what's the connection? The P.R.s and the Italians have never been bed buddies. And if they are now, this thing jumps to a completely different level. And that scares the hell out of me."

"On the Italian side, are you thinking of the same name I am?"

"You're learning fast, kid. There's only one I know who could handle that fix."

"Fat Tony Cannucci."

"The same. I heard he was operating in Florida. Last week he was spotted in the North End."

"Anywhere near D'Angelo's Restaurant on Prince Street?"

"No. He's too smart for that. But your new friend, Paulie Caruso, was seen coming out the back door of Julio's Pizza Shop on Hanover Street just after Fat Tony had dinner there. Two plus two, right?"

Mr. D. and I exchanged agreeing looks that said the dimensions of this thing had grown exponentially since we took on a relatively simple case of race fixing.

*　*　*

I left the office later that afternoon with a deep sense of the futility of doing anything until I heard whatever Ramon Garcia could tell me. With everything on hold, I took the luxury of admitting to myself that there was a complete other side of my existence that had been ignored far too long.

At six o'clock, I was weaving the fenders of my Corvette through a gaggle of Boston's most aggressive motorists—which is saying a mouthful—in competition for entrance to the tunnel leading to Winthrop's oceanside peninsula across from Boston Harbor. There was not a single Puerto Rican or Italian mobster on the radar screen of my mind. Every sensory cell was filled with the vision of the one who could turn my occasionally helter-skelter existence into a world I wouldn't trade for Shangri-La.

By six thirty, I was on the doorstep of 2 Andrew Street, roses in hand, knowing what would happen when that door opened. And it did. It always did. Terry O'Brien opened the door, and I was almost struck dumb with disbelief that this smile, this radiance, this brilliance and beauty had agreed to marry this lawyer who seemed all too frequently to defy the rule that the lawyer always goes home.

By seven thirty, we were into cocktails before dinner at our favorite table in the majestic dining room of the stately and historic Parker House on School Street in the heart of Boston. That table had taken on special significance since our engagement. It was never out of my mind that it was next to the table at which Jack Kennedy proposed to his Jacqueline.

I was into the first of three fingers of Famous Grouse Scotch over four ice cubes, and Terry had begun to make inroads on a wine spritzer—lime, not lemon—when, like a gust of wind, our expected guest for dinner breezed in. Janet Reading was Terry's wedding planner of choice, and once I had met her, mine too.

From that point on, dinner conversation covered everything from colors of bridesmaids' dresses, to choice of flowers, to seating of guests at the head table, which would, of course, be at the Parker House. Ordinarily, discussions of these details would send my mind drifting into recollections of past Bruins games or concern over an injury to quarterback Tom Brady of the Patriots. I have to admit, after the previous three days, the serenity and nonthreatening calm of the subject matter actually caused me to pay attention.

After a dessert that only Chef Alexander could concoct, Janet left us in a similar whirlwind with a kiss for each of us. Within twenty minutes, Terry and I were cruising up the north shore coast to a spot that will always mark a major turning point in our lives, the Molly Waldo restaurant in Marblehead.

We took a table in the corner. John Kiley, the organist who played regularly for Bruins, Celtics, and Red Sox games, and on weekends, for dancing at the Molly Waldo, was on break. We ordered two Black Russians. Within ten minutes, John was back behind the Hammond organ.

He spotted us and gave a courtly bow before beginning his own rendition of the exquisite "There Will Never Be Another You." Again it cast a spell. We had been on that floor dancing a month previously when John worked his magic with that very song to produce the perfect moment to propose to my future bride. As always when I was with Terry, I could feel every eye in the house on her, and I had no idea how to thank God for putting her in my arms.

By the last touching phrase of the song, we had danced our way to a spot beside John.

"Michael, I see she hasn't given up on you yet. In spite of the ridiculously dangerous situations you get yourself into, at least according to the *Globe*. Terry, dear, there's still time to come to your senses."

"How can I when you play that romantic music, John? I think it was your music that made Michael propose in the first place."

"Ah, that's a burden I'll carry through life. Michael, I hope you've assumed a more placid life to share with this charming young lady?"

I flashed through the previous two days and changed the subject.

"We have a question, John. To ensure the right answer, I'll let Terry ask it."

Terry flashed him a smile that could melt the faces on Mount Rushmore. "Like it or not, John, you're a part of our life. We've set the date. It will be June 28. Eight months from today. We want you there as our guest. But we'd be so happy if you'd play the song for our first dance at the wedding."

I've known John for some years. He shows a suave, cultured, sophisticated persona to the world. But when Terry asked the question, there was a flush to his face, and something in his throat that he had to clear to answer. He took her hand and kissed it gently. He spoke directly to Terry.

"My dear, I believe I have just the selection."

Now Terry began misting. "I'm sure you do, John."

He turned to me. "And you, Michael. You keep this young lady out of danger or you'll have me to deal with."

"I understand, John. I will."

I said, "I will," but John's words brought back the thought of the meeting I had at midnight to intrude on the spell of the evening. It was ten thirty, and time for just one more dance before taking Terry home and driving to the El Rey in Roslindale.

When we had arrived at the Molly Waldo, I had refused the valet parking service in order to park the Corvette myself in the rear of the lot. I admit to being somewhat compulsive about protecting her from the dings of car doors. In leaving, however, I handed the key and a ten dollar bill to induce caution to the young parking valet while I waited with Terry.

I was making the mental transition from the dream world we left to the reality of the meeting ahead. I had a foot in both worlds, while my eyes instinctively followed every move the valet made in approaching and entering the Corvette.

I can't really explain this, but something moving in the trees at the back of the lot caught my notice, and every sensory nerve went into full-scale red alert. It was partly what I saw, and partly an intuitive leap. Whichever predominated, it propelled me into a sudden burst of the top speed I could reach across the parking lot.

I was screaming to the valet at the top of my lungs. The young man was just seated. He had the key in the starter and had just brought the engine into its full-throated rumble. He couldn't make out what this lunatic was yelling. I could see him about to put it in gear, when I reached the driver's side.

I jerked open the door, grabbed him by the shirt collar, and yanked him out of the car. I pulled him stumbling across the lot too fast for him to gain his footing.

I was still running on intuition. When we made it forty feet from the car, I forced him to the ground and draped my body over him. Fortunately, he froze under the weight of his insane attacker.

If nothing had happened at that point, I'd have forgiven him for having me committed. But in three seconds, in a burst of deafening sound and blazing light, what had been the second love of my life turned from a pristine blue gem into a ball of red, yellow, and orange flame, exploding out the open door and bursting vertically through the disintegrating convertible top.

When I managed to get my stunned senses out of complete lockdown, I could hear the boy gasping for breath beneath me. I rolled off him, but he seemed frozen to the ground. I pulled him to his feet and jerked his head around to look at me. I yelled, "Call 911!" and pushed him off in the direction of the restaurant.

Terry was still standing where I left her in a state of wide-eyed shock. I ran back and took her in my arms. People began pouring out of the restaurant. John Kiley was among them. He took in the scene in a glance and gave me a look of total concern and frustration. "Michael, what—"

"John, please call a cab. Right now."

With cold rationality fighting for control, my first concern was getting Terry out of there. The figures I'd seen in the woods probably saw me park the Corvette myself and assumed I'd be picking it up myself. They had built just enough delay into the car bomb to let me buckle my seat belt and settle in before being incinerated.

I figured they could be some distance away, enjoying the apparent success of the explosion. On the other hand, they could have stayed close by. If they saw my escape, they might make a second attempt.

Within a couple of minutes, a taxi pulled in ahead of any police response. I could handle police questioning later. My first priority was to get Terry and me in the cab, heading south at full speed toward Winthrop. A twenty dollar bill over the shoulder of the driver accomplished that.

On the ride, I did what I could to calm Terry's fears, but it was impossible. I could scarcely get control of my own. I kept a close check on the road behind us to be sure there was no immediate follow up.

When we pulled up at 2 Andrew Street, I told the cabbie to wait. I walked Terry to the door. She had regained most of her composure and was left primarily with an intense concern for me. I stayed a few minutes to give her what assurance I could that I'd set up protection for both of us. I left her with the promise, which unfortunately even I couldn't believe, that our lives would soon return to peace and serenity. I knew that words couldn't accomplish it, only actions.

On my double-time walk back to the cab, I speed-dialed Tom Burns. I gave him a flash update and asked him to put a protective detail around Terry. He asked about me, but I was still concerned about shutting down any flow of information from Ramon Garcia if he spotted a tail. The time of that meeting was approaching fast. But first, I had one essential errand.

I gave the cab driver the address of D'Angelo's Restaurant in the North End. By now, his adrenaline was flowing almost as fast as my own. Another twenty over the shoulder spurred him into a speed that I'd bet he'd never reached before. By the time we were flying through the tunnel, I had morphed my initial panic into a blazing anger at what could have happened to Terry.

We pulled up directly in front of D'Angelo's Restaurant in the North End. Again I had the cabbie wait. This could go either way in terms of survival, but there was only one way to get an answer to my most burning question.

I got a firm grip on every violent impulse that was raging for control and walked calmly through the door. It was well past eleven.

There was practically no one there. I saw Paulie Caruso at a table in the back at a late dinner with his palace guard.

I stayed out of his vision as I approached the table. I needed a close-up look at his face when he first saw me. His head was down a few inches above a bowl of linguini as I moved closer. The two thugs beside him had been in the office that morning. They saw me first, but recognized me as being allowable at close range.

I was four feet from Caruso when he looked up. "Hey, Knight. What's up? You want some dinner?"

I looked for any indication that he was in the slightest shocked to see me still alive. Not a trace. It said more clearly than any words that he was not the one who had sent the car bombers. It also left me floundering for some excuse for being there.

"Hi, Mr. Caruso. I was just in the neighborhood. I hear they make the best pizza in town here."

"You heard that, did ya? Well, they're right. Grab a chair. Hey, Mario, go tell the cook I want the best pizza he can make."

I was out of one spot and into another. I had to be in Roslindale on the other side of the city in twenty minutes. I talked Caruso into just one slice of already made pizza for a take-out.

I was out the door and back in the cab in five minutes. I gave the cabbie the address of the El Rey in Roslindale and was holding another twenty over his shoulder. He pushed my hand away.

"Forget it, buddy, this one's on me. I ain't had a night like this in my whole life. Can't wait to tell the wife. You better buckle up for this one."

ELEVEN

THE CAB RIDE to El Rey de Lechón in Roslindale was almost as hair-raising as the bombing incident. Carlos—the name on his cab license—made good on his promise to get me there in the twenty minutes I had to the midnight meeting with Ramon Garcia.

I asked Carlos to wait for me. Even among cabbies, who engage in automotive combat with Boston drivers for a living, I doubted that I'd ever find his equal.

As requested, we parked two blocks from the restaurant. I took the alleyway to the back kitchen door. It was open to release the heat of the evening's cooking—and with it, aromas of viands that could convert a committed vegan.

Through the screen, I caught the attention of the chef, Ben Capone. He dried his hands and swung open the door.

"You're back, Michael. I knew you couldn't stay away. Unfortunately, the hour . . ."

"Not a problem, Ben. Your *lechón*'ll have to wait. I have an appointment."

"I know. Come on in. He's inside."

He led me through the kitchen into the small dining area. I noticed that the window shades were all drawn. It was empty, except for Ramon Garcia. He was seated at a table alone in the far corner. I hesitated to approach until I caught his attention.

Mr. Garcia saw me and stood. He had a warm smile, and more to the point, no trace of shock that I was still among the living. That was the second one passing the litmus test.

He waved me to the table and offered the chair beside him. There was a brandy snifter before each of us. Mr. Garcia gave Ben a nod and turned to me. "Please allow me to offer a toast to a friendship built on trust."

Ben returned with a bottle I had never seen before. Another nod from Mr. Garcia and he poured a generous amount into each glass.

"Michael, have you ever tried Apidoro?"

I was sure I had not.

"Before we drink, may I just say I selected it carefully. It's made in Ponce, Puerto Rico. You won't find it here. It's only available in Puerto Rico."

"Then how did you find it?"

He shrugged with a smile. "With the right connections. You know how it is."

"I'm impressed."

A deeper smile. "I'd hoped so. May I impose? It's the teacher in me. Apidoro's a wine made from fermented honey. The name means golden bee. Perhaps you know honey wine as mead."

"That's familiar."

"Honey mead goes back over 9000 years among the Chinese. The first grape wine wasn't made until 2000 years later among the Persians. Before Dionysus, the Greek mythical god, drank grape wine, he drank honey mead. As they say, 'nectar of the gods.'"

He raised his glass, as did I. "May I toast a lasting friendship built on the most ancient foundation—trust? Were he not a myth, Dionysus would join us to solemnize our toast."

Our glasses came together. It was the sound that ushered in a course of events that, had I known at the time, would have sent me bolting for the door.

We sat. I waited for him to initiate the conversation. We both knew the subject. Mr. Garcia's optimistic smile gave way to a forehead furrowed with obvious concern. His voice dropped as well.

"But you didn't come to hear about wine. I wish I had something better for you. When Victor Mendosa heard that on top of the loss of his brother, he was to be charged with Roberto's murder, his first thought was to run."

"How did he hear about the indictment, Mr. Garcia?"

"From me."

"And how did you . . ."

"That's another matter. Perhaps someday. In any event, I persuaded him to stay until I could arrange counsel to set this thing right. He moved into the housing project where you and I first met. My people could take care of him. Provide protection."

"Was he there when we were there?"

He held up a hand. "I'm getting to that. No, he wasn't. Sometime during the night before we met he was gone."

"Did he leave any word?"

"No. But it's worse than that. The two men I had staying with him for his protection were found behind the building. They were both dead."

I was in total disbelief. "Was it Victor?"

"I'm sure not. The manner of the killing. You're one of us by blood. But how much do you know about the ones called '*insectos*'?"

"I know . . . not much. They began in the Puerto Rican prisons like the *Nyetas*. They're a rival . . ."

"They're blood enemies. The manner of death of my two men, it's their signature. I needn't be descriptive."

I needed a few seconds to absorb what I'd heard. "To be clear, Mr. Garcia. You're not saying that Victor is a member of the *insectos*?"

"I'd bet my life that he's not. From the time Victor left the *Nyetas*, he was free of it all."

"You seem sure of it."

"It was with my help alone that he could leave the *Nyetas*. And still live. I haven't seen him as much in the last few years, but he's still like my son. I know my son."

I nodded. I wanted to believe.

He leaned even closer. "Victor had time—I assume while they were doing what they did to my men—to scratch something with a knife into a table in the room before they took him. It's all I can give you."

He took a pen out of his shirt pocket and wrote something on a paper napkin, folded it, and slid it over to me. I glanced at it and slipped it into my pocket.

"But do you know where more specifically?"

"There's a farm outside of the city of Mayagüez in Puerto Rico. It's an *insecto* stronghold. If they took him anywhere, that would be my guess. I have a man watching it now. If anyone comes in or out, he'll know it."

We both sat back in the chairs, but our eyes were locked in some kind of silent bargaining. I knew what I had to say next, but I couldn't get the words out for several seconds.

"Mr. Garcia, I think you're asking me to go there to find Victor."

I could see deep concern in his eyes. "All of our men are known to the *insectos*, both here and there. There'd be no chance of bargaining. Besides, I think you know yourself that as his lawyer, you're the only one who could convince Victor to come back to stand trial." He leaned closer to me. "If there were any other way, Michael, we wouldn't be sitting here."

My mind was under attack from every side with arguments for

and against what he was suggesting. I knew he wasn't asking this for himself. I believed that his concern was for Victor. I also knew that I had my own obligation to Victor as a client, if not as a blood relative.

On the other hand, I had an obligation to Terry and our future, if there was to be one. And most certainly an obligation to Mr. Devlin, who would veto the idea in an instant.

The argument raged in my mind while I sipped the sweet honey mead that I now can't even remember tasting. I finally stood. Mr. Garcia stood opposite.

"Michael, as much as my heart is in this request, if you say no, I'll know you have reasons that have nothing to do with character. You'll stand tall in my eyes whatever your decision. For what that's worth."

I held out my hand, and he took it. "It's come to mean more than I thought it would, Mr. Garcia. Sometimes we think we have a choice, but we don't. What's inside of us always determines the decision, doesn't it? The rest is just mental ping-pong. I'll leave as soon as I can. Tomorrow."

He held my hand, but his head was bowed. He shook his head for lack of words. He simply whispered, "Thank you, my friend."

He took back the paper napkin on which he had written Victor's message. He turned it over and wrote a name on it followed by an address in Mayagüez, Puerto Rico.

"Start here, Michael. It's a bar, a club of sorts in the city. Ask for that name. I'll get word to him. He'll take you where you need to go. I would trust him with the lives of my grandchildren. His loyalty is beyond question. But . . . be careful. *Cuidado,* Miguel. In spite of appearances, trust no one else."

That sent chills through my spine that could have called off all bets, but I'd just given my word.

"Please keep me advised, Michael. I may be able to help when you need it. You can always reach me through Ben." He nodded toward the kitchen.

"*Vaya con Dios,* Miguel."

* * *

I sat in the back of Carlos' cab while he drove through the city to my apartment, this time at a legal speed. The list of things I had to accomplish within the next day was spinning through my mind like a roulette wheel. At the top of the list, I owed it to Terry to explain where I'd be for the next . . . who knew how many days. Although half of my ancestral roots were in Puerto Rico, I'd never set foot on the island. Based on a brief message Victor had carved into a table, that was about to change.

* * *

After a fitful attempt to score five hours of rest, if not sleep, I was back in a cab on the way to Winthrop shortly after sunrise. Much as I loved having time to think while someone else drove, I was beginning to miss sorely the cockpit of my Corvette. I made one call to the personal home number of the dealer who shared my passion for those obsessions on wheels. I set Bob Herman to scanning his computer for an identical replacement—ASAP.

A second call woke Julie, my secretary, out of a sound sleep. I asked her to book me on a flight that evening to Mayagüez on the west coast of Puerto Rico. She jumped to the conclusion that it was the weekend vacation she had been badgering me to take for months. I took the easy path and left that happy assumption intact. On the other hand, that quick, intuitive mind of hers was ringing with alarms when I asked her to leave the return open-ended.

"Michael, what are you up to? If this is more than the weekend, you've got me worried."

"And when I return with a golden tan, you'll be jealous instead of worried. I just don't want to be pressured by a return date. I may take a day to see relatives."

That seemed to get us over that bump in the road without actually lying. As far as Mr. Devlin was concerned, I knew I'd do better to inform him of my plans, such as they were, once I'd landed in Puerto Rico. Unlike Julie, Mr. D. had the power to veto the whole excursion.

Then I turned my full attention to the one for whom there could be no slick avoidance of the facts. I was at Terry's door in Winthrop before she left for work in Boston.

Given the events of the previous evening—and not for the first time—if she handed back the ring at the door and opted out of a life that no sane person would voluntarily walk into, I'd have no reasonable argument.

I heard bare feet running to the door. Those same groundhogs that gnawed at my stomach lining the evening I proposed were back with puppies.

I stood there frozen. The door opened, and she was in my arms. I could feel her tears on my cheek. When she could, she said, "Michael, that was too close. What are you going to do?"

The only thing driving my next words was the absolute necessity to tell the truth, and all of it. I had a minute to think, while we came into the kitchen and she poured us each a cup of strong coffee.

I started at the beginning and let it all pour out—everything from the moment I saw Roberto fall under the weight of his horse to my meeting with Ramon Garcia just hours before. I told her about the promise I had made to Mr. Garcia and what might lay ahead in that city in Puerto Rico. I had perhaps never been so thoroughly honest in my life.

I knew she was shaken. I could only add two thoughts. First, whatever lay ahead of me in Puerto Rico, I had to face up to it because I'd made a promise. My training at the hands of both Miles O'Connor and Lex Devlin made that binding. I could only add that when I would pledge the oath of faithfulness in marriage to Terry, it would be equally unbreakable.

When I finished, we sat in silence. Now it could go either way, and everything that made life worth living from that point on was in her hands.

When she looked up at me, there was a calmness in her expression that gave me no clue. I took her hands and forced myself to meet her eyes for a decision.

"Where do we go from here, Terry?"

She spoke in a calmer tone than I expected. "You do what you feel you have to do, Michael."

"And you, Terry?"

"I wait for you to come home to me. And then I marry the man I love."

The relief must have shown in my face.

"Michael, I know what a promise means to you. It's part of the man I love. And respect. But do you think you're the only one? I knew about your life that night that I promised to marry you."

"Terry, I promise that after this case ends, I'll never—"

She put her hand on my mouth. "Wait, Michael. Don't make a promise that you may not be able to keep. I trust you to do what's right for us both. Always. Let's leave it at that. And come home to me as soon as you can."

PART TWO

TWELVE

*A village deep in the Amazon rainforest
on a remote tributary of the Amazon River, Brazil*

THE MOST DEADLY poison known to man is found in a tiny frog called the golden poison dart frog. It is smaller than 1.5 centimeters, but it has the power to kill twenty men, or 10,000 mice, or two African bull elephants. Yet in the hands of an enlightened man, that same poison can be used to relieve pain and cure many diseases. I learned that, and almost everything I know, from my grandfather as a young boy.

His name is Ancuro and he was the shaman of our small tribe. I have always treasured my name, Ancarit, because it says I am his grandson. He was the only one in our village who ever traveled by raft down the river the outsiders call the Jaraucu, and into the great river that he said was beyond all of our imagining, called the Amazon.

He spent most of the years while I was growing to the age of fourteen beyond the river's bend. When he returned, the older members of my tribe said that he was changed. I asked how, but none could explain it.

I remember countless evenings after his return, fighting for a place on the ground close enough to him to hear every story, every

word of knowledge and wisdom he would speak to us. What worlds
he opened. For us, the bend in the river marked the boundary of
our venturing in safety because of teeming death from black caiman
in the river to jaguars, killer bees, anacondas, and more under the
dense canopy of trees. He said that this forest we knew, where it
nearly always rained, was like a speck in the eye of the great God
who made lands we could not fathom.

He told us what a city was and what it did to the people steeped
in fear and ambition who lived there. He said they were not like us.
He warned that someday they would come to our village in great
boats, and our lives would be changed.

I asked my grandfather how they were different. I saw something
pass over his face that I could not understand then. He just shook
his head, and I didn't ask any more.

At fourteen, I was of an age to absorb everything he could teach
me. Our tribe lived mainly on the abundance of fruits, berries, and
plants there for the picking, but when we could, we also feasted on
the meat of the monkeys that darted through the branches of the
thick canopy of trees above us. That was rare until the return of my
grandfather. Our simple blow-darts would seldom do more than
annoy them with pricks of the skin.

When my grandfather returned, he took me deep into our forest. He told me to watch every move he made and learn. He first
covered his hands in the broad, leathery leaves of a plant that clung
to the great Kapok trees. Then he moved silently deep into the forest, making small marks on the trees as he went. I followed closely,
heeding his caution to keep silent.

He scoured the ground close to the trees until he saw what we
had always been taught to avoid—the swarming activity of a colony
of venomous ants. He sat quietly on the backs of his legs within a

few feet of their circle. He gestured to me to do the same. Within minutes I saw his eyes riveted on the approach of a tiny frog the size of my thumbnail. It was the color of pure gold all over its body.

We watched as the frog moved in small hops to within inches of the ant colony. It sat quietly for a few moments until, rapid as a flash of lightning, its long tongue shot from its mouth. A dozen tiny ants were stuck to the moist tongue when it snapped back into the frog's mouth. While this happened again and again, my grandfather crawled behind the frog. Finally, at one flick of the frog's tongue, my grandfather pounced and held the frog tightly between the leaves on his hands.

He told me to make a fire while he secured his grip on the back legs of the tiny frog. When I came close to see it, he waved me back. But he said to watch closely.

He turned the frog and held its back closer and closer to the fire until a frothy white foam oozed out of the pores of its back. My grandfather took out of his quiver three of the darts I had seen him fashion out of bamboo wood the previous day. He rubbed the tips of the darts in the foaming ooze and stuck the dry end of each dart into the ground to let the foam dry. He released the frog unharmed and let it hop back to the ant colony to finish its meal.

When the dart tips were dry, he led me deeper into the forest toward the chattering of a cluster of spider monkeys lazing in the afternoon sun toward the top of the tree canopy. My grandfather waved me to sit quietly on the ground. He took one of the coated darts from his quiver and loaded it into his long blowpipe. He took careful aim at a large male that had draped himself over one of the lower branches. With one rapid burst of air from his lungs, he sent the dart on a true course to the belly of the monkey.

He whispered one word. "Watch."

I had sent many blow darts on courses just as true. The monkeys they struck cursed us for the annoyance of the pinprick and moved to a higher branch.

This was different. The monkey began to climb higher, but within a few seconds, its arms and legs stopped moving. It was dead weight when it came crashing through the tree branches to the ground beside us.

That evening, there was fresh meat over the fire in the center of our village. It was roasted and shared by all. There was great celebration, because what happened that day could happen again the next day. Our village would be blessed with fresh meat from then on.

The praise spread to me since I had also returned with the miraculous catch. When I cast the glory onto my grandfather, he said to me, "Tomorrow, the catch will be yours."

And so it went. What I learned from my grandfather over the next few years could fill many books. I learned that the yellow dart frog poison that killed the monkeys was harmless to us once the meat was well cooked.

With this wonderful knowledge, my grandfather and I brought to the daily feasts of our village the succulent meat of the hundred-pound capybara that could previously dive and swim great distances underwater lest we catch it.

My grandfather also taught me to use bits of the frog poison in combination with the excretion of particular plants to cure many of the illnesses of our people and to relieve pain. It became clear that he was preparing me to replace him as shaman when his time came.

And he taught me something else. He taught me the language of the large tribe he called the Portuguese who lived in the cities far beyond the bend in the river. He also taught me some of the language of the people he called the English. He told me I had to be prepared for the day the great boats would come to the shore of our village.

I took his lessons to heart, though I'll admit now that I had no real sense of what it was that drove him to teach me as if time were running out.

* * *

On the day that a boat nearly a quarter of the width of our river came around the bend and approached our shore, there was no fear, only excitement among our tribe. Our people flocked to the shore to see what this ark brought to us.

Men whose bodies were covered with much more clothing than we wore came onto our shore. They clutched things in their hands that looked to us like a different kind of blowpipe. I have since come to call them by a name that I wish I had never heard—guns.

They walked cautiously and kept close together until it became obvious that our people wanted only to greet them with smiles and warm words. They could not understand the words, but they could sense there was no danger. It was not long before they lowered the guns and returned the smiles.

My grandfather and I had been in the forest hunting. I returned ahead of him with part of the day's catch. I remember my first sensation when I saw the boat and our people swarming to greet the strangers. Our people were innocent of all doubt of their goodwill since no outsider had ever come beyond the bend in our river. I'll admit that I would have shared completely in that innocence, but for my grandfather's forecasting of an ominous change.

I moved through the cluster of our people around the man who seemed to be their leader. When I said words of welcome in the language of the Portuguese my grandfather had taught me, I was almost stunned to hear words in their language that I could understand.

We exchanged greetings that assured peaceful intentions on both sides, and my initial fears began to subside. While some of their number remained on the boat, I welcomed their leader and the group with him to the center of our village.

The excitement of that first meeting was raised to fever pitch by their generous offering of gifts of food we had never seen. Before long, those on the boat brought shiny pieces of stone on strings that they placed around the necks of our women.

Although our tribe had never experienced guests, it seemed natural to prepare a feast. A cooking fire was built, and large samples of every species of meat that we had come to include in our meals were brought to the flame to prepare for our guests.

We were well into the preparations when my grandfather came back from the hunt. I watched his face as he took in the presence of the boat and the men it brought. For the first time, I saw a look of fear and, I don't know, perhaps something deeper.

I ran to meet him. I wanted to share my pride in using the language he had taught me to pave a path of peace and friendship with our guests. He listened in silence. My words seemed to have no effect on the bitterness I saw in his eyes.

"It's all right, Grandfather. They mean us no harm. They bring gifts."

"It's not all right."

He said it with such conviction that I was stunned. I finally asked, "What should we do?"

He had a grim look on his face as he seemed to be counting the number of strangers. He looked carefully at the sticks called guns that the strangers had let drop to their sides, but which they still held.

"Nothing." There was a strange resignation in the voice of this man I thought to be in command of everything in life.

Together we walked to the center of the village. When he

approached their leader there seemed to pass between them looks that left me stunned. There was a look of domination in the eyes of the stranger, and, with a sadness I'd never known, I saw a look of surrender in the eyes of my grandfather.

The powerless feeling I had at that moment eased as the afternoon passed in the sharing of the greatest feast I had ever experienced. We favored our guests with every delicacy we had from the tenderest young monkey meat to slices of the rich meat of a manatee fresh from our river. We only refrained from the harvest of the pink river dolphin because of myths and legends our people held sacred.

There was no less an outpouring of generous provisions on the part of our guests. From their boat, they brought us delicacies they called breads and meats of animals we have never known. It was a feast of food and friendship that left me for the first time in my life doubting the thoughts of my grandfather.

When the eating was done and the feast settled into a restful slumber for our guests and most of our own people, their leader found me and my grandfather. He asked in his language that we walk with him a ways into the deep forest.

My grandfather seemed reluctant but resigned. The three of us took a path that my grandfather favored when we went hunting.

We walked in silence, while I noticed the leader scanning every movement in the great canopy of trees above us. We passed under colonies of spider monkeys that were equally interested in us. As we passed below capuchin monkeys, wooleys, red howlers, and pygmy marmosets, I answered every question about what we were seeing while my grandfather kept his silence.

The eyes of our guest almost blazed with interest when we passed beneath the rare golden lion tamarin. He took an even greater interest in the screams and caws we heard at a distance. He asked to be taken to see the great birds that made a noise he seemed to recognize.

In my innocence, I began to lead the way to where the hyacinth and scarlet macaws nested. I knew the place well. Our people believed that these enormous birds, colored in the most brilliant reds, greens, and deep purples like no other creature in our world, were the sacred gifts of God to keep us aware of the joy of life. In homage to God, we brought to their nesting area every day the best fruits and nuts as a thanksgiving for the sacred message these creatures brought from God.

Before I could move far, my grandfather caught my arm. He spoke to our guest, but he was looking at me.

"It's too late in the day. We have to be out of the forest by sundown. The anaconda wait in the trees and the jaguar hunt in the darkness."

I had never heard of the giant boas or the jaguars being night hunters, but I would never contradict my grandfather. I noticed a reluctance in our guest to turn back, but my grandfather's words prevailed.

When we reached the outskirts of our village, our guest asked us to stop. He motioned us to sit under a kapok tree and talk. I could sense a foreboding in my grandfather, but I had no reason to fear the words of the stranger.

Our guest spoke slowly, perhaps so that there would be no misunderstanding. "We've just feasted on the meat of these animals of the forest." He gestured upward. "I have a different interest. I want to take some of them back with me. There are people of great wealth who'll give them fine homes as pets. They'll be well fed and live in comfort."

My grandfather was stone silent. Someone had to speak. I said, "They're well fed now. Look at them. They're comfortable with their families."

Our guest laughed. "So they appear. But remember, there is

death waiting for them on every side. Day and night. The jaguars can climb trees. Boas are waiting to strangle them and swallow their young. Every animal here has predators. In these homes there will be no predators."

"Perhaps. But even so, what does all this have to do with us?"

He leaned toward me. "We need you to catch the birds and animals for us."

I just smiled. "We can't. It's impossible."

"But you did. We feasted on them this afternoon."

I shook my head. "No. We can kill them with blow darts up there at a distance when we need food. We can't catch them."

Our guest sat back with an enigmatic smile. "But suppose for a minute that it were possible. It would be good for the animals. It would be good for you and your people too. You enjoyed the food we shared with you today. There could be more. There could also be knives called machetes made of this." He held up the hard pole called a gun. "Sharp enough to carve darts, blowpipes, even hollow boats to fish the river. You'd be well paid. Life could be better for you."

I smiled and pointed at the gun in his hand. "Perhaps even these poles you call guns."

My grandfather suddenly went from sadness to bitter anger. "Enough! No more of this!"

He stood and began to walk back to the village. Our guest caught him in the crook of his arm with the gun-pole. He kept the smile while he said, "Give me a moment with your grandfather, Ancarit. I think we can reason together."

I walked out of earshot. I turned to watch them. The stranger kept his hold on my grandfather's arm. He did the talking. At times he lifted the gun-pole into my grandfather's vision. At one point, the stranger looked at me and smiled and waved. I saw my grandfather's anger fade. He simply sank into a look of deflation, defeat.

Whatever else was said between them caused my grandfather to look back at me and simply nod. Somehow I sensed for the first time in my life that there is a power of evil in the world, and that a deal had been struck that would, as my grandfather predicted years earlier, change us all, perhaps not for the better.

THIRTEEN

TO THIS DAY, I remember the hunt with my grandfather on that previous morning before the boat arrived like no other. It was the last time I saw him smile.

The following morning, I felt a nudge at my back calling me from sleep. What little sun filtered through the dense canopy of trees was barely announcing dawn.

"Come, Ancarit. I need you. It's beginning."

I followed my grandfather into the narrow path we always took hunting. By the time we reached the point where our village was shielded from sight by hanging vines, he would always be well into a story about what happened in a city called São Paulo or Rio de Janeiro. This morning there was only silence.

We came to a small clearing under a chattering family of squirrel monkeys. He took a blow dart out of his quiver. I kept silence, but touched his shoulder and looked in his eyes. He could read my question. Squirrel monkeys are not good for eating. Why would we kill one?

I could see the frustration in his tired eyes. I knew he hadn't slept. He motioned me to sit, and he sat beside me. He had difficulty beginning, but I sensed that he had to explain.

"Our lives are no longer our own, Obanti."

This was the name he'd chosen for me. It means "One who will lead." I was sure he meant as shaman of our people. I just listened.

"These men with guns are not what you think. You must know two things. First, they are capable of acts of evil beyond your imagining. Their words mean nothing. You must know that from the beginning."

"I believe you, Grandfather. But then why do we—"

"Listen to me. Carefully. There is power in those sticks they carry that gives them control over us. For now, for the sake of our people, we have to obey them. Do you understand?"

I didn't. And I couldn't lie to my grandfather. "If we do what they say, will they leave?"

He would not lie to me either. "I don't know. For the time being..."

He took the dart and rested it on a leaf. We performed the usual ritual to excrete the poison from a frog. This time he gathered it on a leaf. He crushed the juice out of several leaves and twigs of a bush that he pointed out to me with the words, "Remember this. This won't hurt the monkey. He'll just sleep."

He mixed a tiny speck of the poison with the juice from the bushes and coated the dart. When he raised the blowpipe to his lips, I saw moisture forming in his eyes. He wiped them and took aim. He blew the dart straight into the chest of a male squirrel monkey. It jumped in alarm at the slight sting and began climbing. I waited for it to drop through the branches.

This time it simply slowed up and made clumsy motions with its hands. My grandfather stood beneath it. When it finally missed a branch and tumbled down, he caught it gently in an armful of leaves.

"It's not dead, Ancarit. It will wake up about midday. We have to work quickly."

He set the sleeping monkey on a bed of leaves under a tree. Together we did the same thing again. In a short time we had seven sleeping squirrel monkeys.

We moved on to where a family of red howler monkeys was

playing some game in the canopy. My grandfather captured seven of them in the same way. When we finished, he straightened up with great difficulty. I asked him to rest, but he shook his head.

"No rest. Not now. We have to get these to the boat before they wake up."

I carried as many of the sleeping bodies as I could, and my grandfather carried the rest down to the shore. He called to the man in charge. He came out on the deck with what looked like a staggering walk. My grandfather pointed to the sleeping monkeys. The man wiped saliva from his mouth and almost fell against the rail. His voice was raspy and slurred and coarser than anything I'd ever heard.

"What the hell! They're no good to me dead."

The disgust showed in my grandfather's low tone. "They're alive. They'll all be awake and hungry by the time the sun goes down. Where do you want them?"

The man seemed to be slow understanding. He finally called behind him. Two of his men, not much more alert than he was, came out of the cabin. They followed his orders to come down and gather up the monkeys.

Everything inside of me was rebelling. These monkeys were as much a part of this forest as we were. Since I was born, we'd referred to every animal and bird as a brother or sister. Yes, we killed to eat, but we never made one of these brothers suffer.

When the workman from the boat grabbed the first of the monkeys roughly, my reaction was instinctive. I gave a hard shove to his shoulder with both hands. His unsteadiness gave way to the blow. He tumbled backwards away from the sleeping monkey.

The leader on deck shouted down with a crooked grin. "Hey, kid. It's all right. We got a good safe place for the monkeys. They'll have plenty of room. We got food for them. They'll be good. Manuel, go easy with the monkeys."

He was forcing a smile and waving his hands. "It's okay, kid. Ask your grandfather."

I looked beside me. My grandfather's head was down. He wouldn't look at me. He just said, "Come, Ancarit. Come."

"But what's going to happen to the monkeys? We brought them here."

He turned and walked away from the shore with his head down. I was torn to the point of feeling ill. With no better basis for deciding, I followed, as I always had, my grandfather's lead.

The slurred voice from the deck boomed behind us. "More monkeys. And I want the birds. We don't leave till we get the birds."

Neither of us looked back. We just walked. I was so worried about my grandfather that I scarcely heard the slurred words. "And a tamarin. I want a golden lion tamarin. You hear me?"

* * *

The sun was high above when we went deeper into the forest. We found another family of squirrel monkeys. I could see that the strength and even the heart of my grandfather had been drained. I made him sit beneath a kapok tree while I repeated what we had done that morning. Within an hour, I had seven more sleeping spider monkeys.

I helped my grandfather to his feet and started to lift the monkeys to bring them back to the boat. He took my arm gently and looked in my eyes for the first time since we had left the shore.

"Ancarit, this will be hard. We have to bring them the great birds."

Now I could see clear moisture in his eyes. I remembered that their leader was demanding birds. I realized for the first time that he meant the hyacinth and scarlet macaws. How could we do it? We believe that these radiant birds that stand high as a year-old child are the sacred gift of God.

It was too much. "We can't, Grandfather. You know we can't."

"What I know is that we must. On the lives of our people. Let's do it quickly. Then we'll pray for forgiveness."

It took until midafternoon. We walked to where the loud calls and shrieks came from branches that were alive with color. I saw my grandfather's hands tremble as he prepared the darts that would bring into our hands what was intended to light the skies.

When we had four brilliant sleeping macaws, we held them in our arms while we pulled sleds of bamboo branches on which the monkeys slept like children. Every step we took was an assault to our hearts, but we did it.

Their leader was steadier on his feet when we got back. We laid the sleeping monkeys and macaws on the shore to be taken by his men onto the boat. I wanted to plead for the release of at least the birds, but when I looked into the cold eyes of their leader, I knew my grandfather's words were true. We had no control.

As we walked back to the village, I tried to feed our spirits with the words, "He said they'd be better off in the homes of their new owners."

My grandfather put his arm around my shoulder and started to speak, but he couldn't lie to me, and he knew no truth that would give either of us comfort.

The last word I heard from the deck of the boat was wrapped in a curse. It was a repeated demand for a golden lion tamarin.

My grandfather's energy was spent. I brought him back to where my mother had prepared supper for us. I left him there and stole out of the village. The last part would be up to me.

The golden lion tamarin is so rare that whenever we caught a fleeting glimpse of it, we considered the day blessed. It tore at me as never before, but I prayed for success in doing what my heart knew was evil. It was in the last rays of the day's light that I saw high on a branch, a small golden body that could fit in the palm of my hand. It was a mature male, though its large innocent eyes made it look like a child.

I asked for forgiveness from all of nature as I prepared, according to my grandfather's earlier instruction, the weakest solution that would put it to sleep. I sent the dart to its mark, and stood to receive the tiny body in a soft bed of leaves. I sat holding it for several minutes of indecision before beginning the long walk to the boat.

When I arrived at the shore, there was no one in sight. I called, but there was no answer. I walked up the plank that led to the deck and called again. Still no answer.

I walked through the door that led into the house that sat on the deck. A sickening, pungent smell of what I later learned was called rum stung my nose. There was a small flame in a lantern in the house that lit the bodies of sleeping men on the beds and on the floor. I saw the unconscious face of their leader and nudged his shoulder. There was no movement and no way to bring him to wakefulness.

There was an opening in the middle of the floor with a set of six steps leading down to the chamber below. It had to be where they were keeping the animals. I decided to look for a cage below and leave the tamarin behind.

I took the lantern in one hand and cradled the tiny tamarin in the other as I took each of the steps slowly. When my foot left the last step and the light reached into the corners of that small room, my body was frozen.

There was one cage in the center of the room. It held all of the monkeys we had brought that afternoon. Their eyes broadcast a fear that must have been reaching panic. I felt in my heart the deepest violation of every law of nature to see that natural wildness that I had never seen other than in play, caged and rooted to the floor of that small room. The chattering that was their language was stifled into squeals that left me stunned.

When I could think, I turned my head to the side and saw another cage holding the macaws. It seemed the grossest contradiction to see those radiant colors of freedom and joy grounded and boxed into a small cage. I would have welcomed one shriek of protest. But there was nothing but silence.

I finally realized that I was grasping the railing to keep me on my feet. My mind was sinking under the weight of the evil in that dark room—and the burden of knowing my part in it.

At first I was lost. My only conscious thought was to bolt and run and keep on running until I could pass out in total exhaustion.

But I didn't. And the longer I stood there, the clearer my mind became. I was the grandson of my grandfather. Someday I would be the shaman. I'd be the source of strength and wisdom and leadership for our whole village. Like it or not, that day was today.

My thoughts were cool and crystal clear. I began with the caged monkeys. I yanked the spike out of the latch that bolted the door. I didn't open the door—I ripped it off its hinges. The monkeys first tumbled off-balance onto the floor. I waved my hands in big circles to drive them up the stairs and out the door. When they ran through the upper chamber and burst into the fresh air, there was nothing that could silence their squeals and chattering of freedom.

My only fear was that some of the men upstairs might come out of their stupor. Fortunately, the rum had done its best or worst. None stirred.

I was more gentle as I took apart the cage of the parrots. I carried them up to the deck. They needed to be kept from panic while I gently removed the strings that were wrapped around their bodies without harming the wings that would carry them into the highest levels of the tree canopy.

One by one they took flight in a gust of feathered wind that sent my heart to a new height. When the last magnificent macaw was loosed and restored to where it was intended it to be, I was bathed in sweat. My hands were shaking from tension and exertion. But I was less tired and more refreshed than I had been since my grandfather had wakened me that morning.

Only God knew what my action would bring. I only knew one thing with total certainty. What I had done was right.

* * *

I carried the still sleeping tamarin in my arm and passed quietly between the rows of unconscious bodies in the upper deck. At one point, the lantern's beam glinted on a long, slender piece of hardness like the gun-pipes. It had a sharp edge that could slice through a bamboo tree. I picked up what I later heard men call a machete and walked down the board leading to the shore.

If I had one wish at that moment, it was to send that arc of evil as far from our village as it could go. I made one more decision that night, for whatever might be the result. I grasped the machete with both hands. I prayed God to grant my wish, and I swung with every ounce of conviction in my body. The machete sliced through the rope that held the boat to the shore. The strong current of the river did the rest.

I watched that cursed thing float more and more rapidly away from our sleeping village until it was carried around the next bend in the river—and out of our sight. I walked to my hut and dropped into a sleep of peace.

FOURTEEN

IN A DEEP sleep, I dreamed of chattering spider monkeys making flying catches of limbs high in the canopy, playing games with their young that only they understood. In my dream, there were also splashes of brilliant color illuminating the highest limbs of giant kapoks where macaws clustered to preen themselves.

The sun was high overhead when the sounds of my mother preparing food broke into my dream world. Disturbing recollections of the previous day invaded my sense of calm. The worst yesterday of my life played on my mind like a cascade of painful scenes until the last one remained in my consciousness. The conflicted picture of that demon ark being carried away on the river's current was stuck in my mind. It was conflicted because I never fully believed that that sweet victory would pass without payment in pain.

My first conscious thought was to give my grandfather a recounting of the last events of the previous evening. He had to know what it was that could bring retribution to our village.

I ran across the village from my hut to the hut of my grandfather. On my way, I scanned the shore of the river. It was a comfort to see the shoreline unbroken by the demon ark.

I was a bit shaken to find my grandfather's hut empty. Then I realized that, given the height of the sun in the sky, he would naturally be out about the work of the day.

I walked back to our family's cluster of huts. My mother was preparing the fruits and cracking the shells of nuts she'd gathered for the noon meal. She stopped and called me to sit beside her. I knew she had no inkling of what my grandfather and I had been through at the hands of our visitors. We chose not to disturb the tranquility of anyone in the village if we could keep it to ourselves.

"I have a message from your grandfather, Ancarit."

For some reason, those simple words set demons tugging at my nerves. I sat to listen.

"The men from the boat came back early this morning. They came to wake you. Your grandfather stopped them before they got to your hut. They seemed very angry."

"What did they say? Tell me every word."

"They said you owed them something. They said you had to help them with a hunt. Your grandfather asked them—he pleaded with them—to leave you asleep. They said no. You had to come with them. But he insisted. He promised he could give them what they wanted. They argued until they agreed that he could go in your place."

I tried to keep the fear and anger that was boiling inside from my mother.

"Mother, don't be alarmed by this question. I'm just asking. Did they hurt him?"

"Why would they hurt him? No, of course not. After they talked, he led them into the forest where you go to hunt."

I leaped to my feet. Before I could run after them, my mother took my arm.

"They're not there. They were gone most of the morning. When they came out of the forest, some of the men were carrying what looked like dead monkeys. Some of them had some of the large birds in their arms. They carried them to the boat. I didn't see them come out. Ancarit, why would they take the birds? They're sacred."

"Not to them, Mother. Where did my grandfather go?"

"He came back and gave me a message for you. He told me not to wake you until he'd gone."

"Gone where?"

"In the boat with the men. They went down the river, around the bend."

"Did he say anything else?"

"He said that the men wanted him to go with them. They were going far away, to the big river he told us about, to one of the cities."

"Did he say a name?"

She thought for a minute. "He said the word, 'Macapá.'"

I'd heard him speak of that city before. From the moment I heard the word, there was no indecision, no confusion. Every doubt about what I had to do next was resolved.

My mind was racing with thoughts of preparation before leaving the only village I had ever known, and may never see again. I stood and began to run to my hut. My mother stopped me.

"He said one more thing, Ancarit."

I knew what it was, but I listened anyway.

"He said you were not to follow. He wanted to know you'd be here when he returned."

For only the second time in my life, I was about to act contrary to my grandfather's wishes. I was driven by two truths. First, I would follow his path no matter where it led. Second, I was absolutely certain that if I failed, we'd never see him again in this life.

"I have to go, Mother."

She knew the strength of the bond between my grandfather and me. She held back tears, but she simply said, "I know."

I ran to my hut for the only possession I would need—a blowpipe and a quiver of darts treated with the excretion of a yellow dart frog. The forest would feed me, and the river would guide me.

The sun was further along than I'd wished when I took to the riverbank. I ran blindly on the edge between forest and water at a pace I could keep up without rest. I insulated my mind from fear by forcing out every thought that was not of my grandfather.

I ran until the sun dropped out of sight. Since no moon took its place, I could not keep on. I used the last flicker of light to gather enough nuts and berries to calm my hunger. I saved enough to fuel my legs for the run in the morning. I knew I needed to keep up the pace. It was not just that the boat was increasing the distance. There were dangers. If I slowed, a lurking boa could drop from a branch and clench me in its suffocating grip before I knew it was on me. At a good pace, I could even pass a waiting crocodile or caiman in the shallows before it could spring.

By the time I stopped running, it was impossible to build a protective hut in the dark. Instead, I lit a fire in a pit of rocks. I slept close enough to the flame to pull a burning stick out of the pit if I had to defend myself.

Whether I slept at all or just gave in to a fitful rest I have no idea. At the first glint of sunlight, I was back on my feet. I ate the berries and nuts I'd set aside while I ran.

While the sun traced its arc, I kept the same hypnotic pace without rest. By midafternoon, I had underestimated the depth of my exhaustion. I was unaware that my feet were barely skimming the ground until a tree root snagged a dragging foot. I pitched forward on my knees. When I rose and started again, I'd been shaken into alertness, but I was moving at half the previous pace.

Within minutes, I passed below the hanging branch of a castanha tree. I either heard or sensed a slight rustling of leaves above me. It triggered a terror. I didn't even look. I ducked and sprang to my left. In that instant I felt a massive body brush my right side, scarcely missing full impact with my shoulders.

The body rolled and scrambled to its feet. For a fraction of a second, I was looking into the eyes of a male jaguar, fully as heavy as me, crouched and poised for the attack on an easy prey. I knew he'd go for my head. Jaguars kill by crushing the skull of their prey in the vice of their powerful jaws.

I had precious few options. I pulled a dart out of the quiver and braced for the blow. It came swiftly as lightning. Driven by all of the power in the back legs, the gaping fangs came at my face. I bent this time to the right. As the spotted yellow blur passed shoulder high, I rammed the dart into his throat.

He twisted with pain in midair. I held the dart fast. In his moving flesh, the dart must have caught and split an artery. A fountain of the creature's blood spurted out on the bank and dyed the river water crimson.

The pain distracted him. He stood shaking his head and spinning in circles. Within seconds, I could see the poison grabbing hold. He finally lost his balance. He fell thrashing into the tinted water.

I stood frozen where I was, watching the jaguar's flailing legs disappear in a vortex of crimson foam and splashes. Through the turbulence, all I could see was a frenzy of scales and teeth. It took less than a minute for hundreds of snapping piranhas to reduce the jaguar to a skeleton.

I didn't realize how much the attack had taken out of me until I tried to resume my pace. After a few clumsy steps, I fell forward again. I just lay there, knowing I had to rest or I'd be easy prey for a dozen different predators. It was unlikely that another jaguar was in the area since they are solitary hunters. That still left too many threats to ignore.

I resorted to my only defense. I built a large fire in a rock bed. I gathered and ate some of the fruits and berries that the forest provided close at hand, and then fell into a deep sleep beside the fire.

* * *

Again I slept until the first rays of dawn. Much as I regretted the time lost, I knew I had limits. This time, I ate enough of the fruit of the mango tree and nuts from the castanha to last me through the day.

It was midafternoon when I rounded a curve in the river and saw downstream a village several times the size of my own. There were large huts made of sheets of wood instead of just branches. I saw that the villagers wore pants and shirts and moccasins, much like the men on the boat I was following.

By the shore, there was a boat with an engine that could hold ten men. It was tied to a wooden walkway into the river. I could see men on the boat leaning over the side. Something disturbing had their attention.

I wanted to ask about the boat carrying my grandfather, and these river people seemed the best to ask. I walked down to where the boat was tied and listened. It was clear that they were too involved with their own problem to answer my questions, so I asked about their problem.

They looked at me, dressed in the scant amount of native clothing I wore, and turned back to whatever had their attention over the side of the boat. I finally got one of the younger men to explain to me that a thing called the propeller had become tangled in a rope. The boat couldn't move.

I yelled to them and asked why they didn't just take the rope away. Most of them dismissed my question in disgust. The young boy looked at me almost in disbelief, but at least he spoke.

"What's the matter with you? We can't go in the water."

He turned away, but I got his attention again. "Why not?"

His grin seemed to be in disbelief at my stupidity.

"I mean it. Why not?"

He grudgingly answered. "Don't you know what piranhas are?"

"Of course I do."

"Then just look. There are thousands of them. Probably millions of them in this river. You think we're dumb enough to go in there?"

All of a sudden several ideas came together. I leaned over the side of the boat and tapped the shoulder of the man who seemed to be in charge. He turned around in obvious impatience. I smiled.

"I've got a deal for you."

He turned away. I tapped him again. "This will interest you." Perhaps it was hearing a native speak Portuguese, but for whatever reason he turned back. He seemed to be listening.

"If I can get the rope off the thing you call a propeller, will you do something for me?"

He looked doubtful, but he didn't turn away. "And how are you going to do that?"

"Leave that to me. Can we make a deal?"

Now he was looking right at me. "What do you want?"

"I want clothes like those." I pointed to what he was wearing. I knew if I were to find my grandfather in the city called Macapá, I'd need to blend in.

"Yeah?"

"Wait. There's more. I need to ride with you down the river to Macapá. Is that where you're going?"

"Yeah, but so what? That rope's wound tight. No one can get down there alive."

"Just say one word. I'll trust you. Is it a deal?"

He shook his head. "Don't try it, kid. Nothing's worth it."

"That's up to me. Will you make the deal?"

He hesitated, then he held out his hand.

I took it in mine as a sign that we agreed.

"Done," I said and climbed into the boat and crossed the deck to the river side. I handed my blowpipe and quiver of darts to the man at the rail, and I vaulted over the side into the river.

The water was so deep at that point that I couldn't touch bottom. I looked around for signs of crocodiles or caiman and saw none.

I dove deep in the water and swam under the boat. I could see the end of a thick rope dangling from a circular thing with blades. I knew my breath was limited. I began uncoiling the rope as fast as I could. It took five turns before the rope came free. I held the end of it and swam to the side of the boat.

When I held up the rope, I heard cheers mixed with laughs. Three arms and hands reached overboard to pull me back onto the boat. Their leader was the first one beside me when I stood up.

"How the hell did you do that? That damn river's full of those killer fish."

I could have told him that piranha prey on the fish in the river for food. They have no interest in attacking anything alive as big as me as long as there is no blood in the water. My people swim and bathe in the river all the time. It was the blood of the jaguar upstream that caused them to attack and devour it.

But I didn't say that. I just said, "I really need the clothes. And don't forget the ride to Macapá."

"Hell, I'll take you anywhere you want to go. Damn. I never saw anything like it."

He called one of the men over. "Take this kid. Hey, kid, what's your name?"

"Ancarit."

"Take Ancarit to that trading post in the village. Buy him whatever he needs." He looked up at the sun. "And hurry it up. We're going to get this kid to Macapá."

FIFTEEN

IT TOOK TWO and a half days of cruising with the current to come within view of the city of Macapá. At about halfway, where our own river spilled into the majestic Amazon, the size of my entire world burst open at the seams. I had never imagined that such expanse, such rushing power could exist.

The city of Macapá on the bank of the Amazon River was just as my grandfather had described it to me. There were no huts, only solid buildings taller than ten of our huts on top of each other. People filled the streets. They seemed to pass among the buildings, trading in shops for the things we would make or hunt—and much more.

Our boat pulled up alongside one of many piers that ran beside the river. From where the piers ended, the great river flowed into a body of water so massive that there appeared no land on the opposite side.

There were boats and ships from tiny to grand tied to the docks. I could have spent the day staring at things I could never dream, but I had a more pressing priority.

I scanned every vessel for the length of the piers until I saw it. That demon ark was tied to the pier a blow dart's flight from where we docked. I was off the boat as soon as it was made fast. I stayed in the shadows of the buildings until I came to a good watching place.

There was no movement aboard that ark. I settled down to watch. Through that evening and night I saw nothing. In the morning, men with skin like mine and faces that could have belonged to our village walked by my watching place on the pier. Their looks in my direction told me that I needed to be less obvious.

There was a ship that could hold my entire village at the dock next in line to that demon boat. The men who passed by me gathered around a plank that led from the pier to the deck of the ship. When the sun was well up, a man came down the plank from the ship. Everyone gathered around him. He barked some kind of order I didn't understand, and everyone clustered closer.

There was some pushing and jostling among the men. I thought a fight might break out, but before it could happen, the man on the plank threw two fistfuls of small round coins of white metal into the midst of the crowd. The scrambling and diving of the men after the coins made me believe they had great value.

When each of the coins was snatched off the ground, those who had managed to grab one gathered around the man. The others drifted away. As I watched, I realized that the coins were the offer of a day's work loading things on the ship.

I watched while the men listened to the orders barked by the man. They turned and went into a building behind the dock. When they came out, each was carrying a massive branch of bananas or a net filled with coconuts. I saw them struggle under the weight as they carried their burden up the plank and down a hole in the deck of the ship.

I was still getting curious looks from any men who passed me. I was the only one not engaged in some heavy labor. I needed a reason to stay where I could watch for my grandfather on the boat.

I walked to the door of the big building that housed the bananas. When one of the men, sweating and panting from the exertion, passed me on the way to the plank, I walked beside him. When he looked at me, I spoke in the language of my village. He seemed confused. I spoke in Portuguese, and he understood.

"I'll make you a deal. Give me your coin. I'll do all the work for the rest of the day. I'll give you the pay at the end for doing nothing more."

With good reason, he didn't believe me. Before he could walk on, I caught his arm.

"I mean it. I won't leave till I give you what they give me. You can watch me from here."

Either because of the exhaustion he was feeling in the heat or some desperation in my voice, he dropped the heavy burden of bananas at my feet. He handed me the coin with a threat about keeping my word. I hoisted the bananas on my shoulder and mixed in with those climbing the plank.

The higher I climbed, the better view I got of the deck of the demon boat. There was still no movement on the deck and not a person in sight. I knew I had to continue the watch since it was the only place in the city I knew to look for my grandfather.

I lost count of the treks I made in the heat and humidity. I know that neither the weight of bananas and coconuts, nor the perspiration that stung my eyes deflected my attention from the deck of the demon boat.

When the sun was shedding its last rays, I finally saw movement. The leader and four of the men of his crew came out on the deck of the boat. They seemed to be arguing loudly as if the afternoon's rum was taking its grip. The heavy plank groaned and creaked under their stumbling steps to the dock.

They left one man on the deck as a watch. Once they were clear of the boat and the dock, he spread himself flat on a rolled canvas. Within minutes, his deep breathing signaled sleep.

It was my chance. The exhaustion of my fellow banana loaders would keep them from noticing that I fell out of line. I found my blowpipe and quiver of darts where I had hidden them. I used the water of the river to dilute the poison on one dart.

When I had climbed the plank with the last stem of bananas from the pier to be loaded, I slipped away from the group. The other laborers began clustering around a table on the deck to be paid. From the height of the ship's deck, I had a clear shot with the blowpipe at the demon boat's watchman. The sting of the dart barely interrupted his slumber with a flinch.

I came back and fell in line with the men to hand in the coin and collect the day's pay. By the time I delivered it to the man on the pier who gave me the coin, I was sure I could march a herd of armadillos up the plank to the boat without waking the watchman.

My heart was pounding out of my chest when I ran up to the deck of the boat. The watchman never stirred. I pushed through the door of the house on the deck and stopped for an instant at the hatch that led to the room below where they kept the animals. I prayed to God that it was not in vain.

When I pulled open the hatch, my first sensation was the wave of stench that poured out of the confinement and stung my eyes. But enough light poured into chamber to light the image I'll never forget. For a few seconds, my grandfather was standing there below, shielding his eyes. When his blinking eyes could look up, there was a burst of joy that lit his face like the sun itself.

That was his first reaction. His second was a look of pain. "Ancarit, why did you come? Run! Before they come back!"

I ran, but it was down the steps and into the arms of my grandfather. He kept telling me to run to safety, but his arms clung to me as if I were his very life. It was no matter. I would not have left him there if the universe depended on it.

"Come with me, Grandfather. There's no one to keep us."

"I can't. Something big is happening." He nodded to the caged animals and birds. "These all depend on me. I can't leave."

I sat beside him. "Then we stay together."

He started to speak, but I cut in. "Those men up there, do they ever come down here?"

"No. They can't stand the smell."

"Then we wait here together."

* * *

A little after dawn, I heard faint voices above. I crept up the stairs and saw no one on deck. I opened the door a crack to see that the banana ship was no longer there. Another massive ship had taken its place. I saw the leader from the demon boat talking with a heavy man with a beard on the deck of the newly arrived ship. They were grinning about something. Then I saw the heavy man hand what looked like a large wad of paper to the leader.

The heavy man shouted orders, and four men from the ship came to the boat. My grandfather and I crouched behind the cages of animals. Each of the four men came down the stairs and picked up a cage. They carried them up to the deck, across the pier, and up the new ship's plank before they disappeared from sight.

My grandfather whispered, "We have to see where they take them."

When the men came back for a second load, I told my grandfather to wait there. I hoisted a cage and followed the men with my head down. As I hoped, the men from the ship thought I was a helper from the boat. The men from the demon boat were on the dock. When I passed them in the dark, they must have thought I was from the ship, because they never looked at me.

I followed the men carrying cages down a passageway on the ship's deck and downstairs into a chamber below. I waited for them to leave their loads and go back for more. I carried the cage following the faint light down the steps. What I saw below is so burned into my memory that I'm sure I'll carry it into the next world.

Several dull lights lit a room that seemed nearly half the size of my whole village. It was stacked with cages crammed to capacity with nearly every bird and animal I had ever seen in our forest. Every species of monkey was packed so tightly in the cages that they could scarcely move. Anteaters and armadillos were crated together. Giant sea turtles were strapped and boxed tightly one on top of the other.

I was reeling in horror. I looked beyond the boxes of animals and saw cages stuffed with birds from ibises and macaws to delicate flamingoes, and even the rarely seen toucans, all packed so tightly they couldn't move.

The air was stifling. I had all I could do to keep my consciousness. It was clear that most of the animals and birds had been confined there for some time.

When I came back onto the pier, I saw the leader gathered with his men on the deck of the boat. He took out some bills from the wad of paper he got from the bearded man on the ship. He handed some to each of his men. When they each got their share, they came down the plank to the pier and wandered off into the city.

One of the men remained on the boat with the leader. By now

the sun was down. The lights on the pier cast just enough light on the deck of the boat to make out the figures. I heard the leader give an order.

The man went into the shed on the deck. When he came back out, he was holding my grandfather by the neck and pushing him onto the deck. My grandfather's hands were tied behind him.

I heard another order given, though I still couldn't make out the words. The man pushed my grandfather across the deck to the rail of the boat toward the open water. He stood him up against the rail.

The leader gave one more order, and the man left the boat to join the others. When the man was out of sight, I saw the leader raise the gun in his hands. I could see by the glint of light on the barrel that he was pointing it directly at the head of my grandfather.

I had never in my life acted to injure another human being until that moment. But without a single thought or hesitation, I pulled a fully poisoned dart out of my quiver, loaded it in the blowpipe, and sent it straight to the neck of the man who would kill my grandfather. I put such force behind it that it opened a gushing spurt of blood.

The leader dropped the gun. The powerful poison in his bloodstream took effect quickly. He stumbled backwards toward the rail by the open water. His momentum carried him over the rail in a spiral of arms and legs. The outpouring of blood tainted the water just before he hit it. There was no power on earth that could have saved him at that point. I could hear the splashing of hundreds of piranhas. I knew to a certainty that he would cause no more pain to men or animals on this earth.

I ran to my grandfather. I untied the cord that bound his hands behind him. Whether we had the time or not, he grabbed me in his arms and we hung onto each other.

I made use of the next minute to tell him what I had seen in the hold of the large ship. We knew that this thing was too vast for us to stop it. We also knew that we had to do whatever we could—however little that might be.

I could hear the drunken voices of the members of the crew coming back down the pier. We each grabbed one of the empty cages left in the hold. I figured that we could carry the cages to the ship's hold where they kept the animals without attracting attention. It was too dark for anyone to see that they were empty.

At the last instant, I told my grandfather to go down the plank to the pier and wait for me. There was one last bit of evil that needed to be scoured from the face of the earth.

I picked up a heavy hammer used to drive stakes for anchoring. I tied a cloth around it to prevent sparks and ran to the engine room. With every ounce of energy I had left, I smashed a gaping hole in the bottom of the engine's gas tank.

I gave it ten seconds to let the gas flow freely while I uncapped cans of extra gas. I doused the cloth-covered head of the hammer in gasoline and climbed the stairs. I found the matches the leader used to light his cigars and set the cloth ablaze. With one last yell, I threw the flaming hammer into the engine room and ran down the plank to join my grandfather.

We carried the empty cages quickly past the drunk and staggering crewmen. They were far too much into the rum to recognize us.

My grandfather and I were halfway up the big ship's gangplank when an explosion rocked the pier. Splinters of flaming wood from that demon ark showered the water like a meteor storm. What was left of the boat was brilliantly ablaze before it sunk below the black surface of the water.

In the confusion that followed, no one saw me lead my grandfather down to the giant chamber that housed those pitiful animals. When he saw them, I saw the look in my grandfather's eyes. I knew that in the midst of all of that misery, his heart was breaking.

He took me by the shoulders and whispered. "You have to leave right now. This ship could leave port any minute."

"You're right, Grandfather. Let's go."

"You go. I can't."

"Why not?"

"I have work to do here. I've seen this before. They've bought these animals from poachers all along the coast from São Luís to here. They'll take them to sell on the black market."

"But what—"

"Listen to me. I can't leave. These animals can live without food, but not without water. Many of them will be dead by the time they dock."

I looked around at the hundreds of frightened faces. "Why do they do this? They can't sell them if they're dead."

"It's all greed. They figure that if they pack in this many animals, enough will live to make a bigger profit than if they showed compassion for the animals. They learned this numbers game from the old slave traders."

I was sickened and infuriated. My grandfather could see it in my eyes. "If you have work to do, Grandfather, so do I."

He saw my resolve and just nodded.

By two dim lights at either end of the room, we found two long hoses, probably used to flush out the room between shipments. My grandfather turned on the spigots. He tasted the water to be sure it was not salted from the sea.

We turned the spigots down to a trickle of water. I watched him carry one of the hoses to the first cage. He held the dripping nozzle to the mouth of one of the monkeys. The monkey nearly swallowed the nozzle to get to the water. My grandfather let him drink for ten or fifteen seconds before giving water to the next monkey.

"Don't give them too much right away. They may be badly dehydrated. They need to get used to it."

I started on the other side of the room with the other hose. I had never seen such desperate need in an animal.

We had each finished two cages of monkeys when we felt the ship take a sharp lurch. We looked at each other without words. We knew the ship was going to sea. For us, the die was cast.

It took us half the night to finish the first round. After bringing water to the last cage of birds, I fell back on the floor with my eyes closed. I couldn't imagine how tired my grandfather must have been.

He shot a spurt of water out of the hose at me. When I jumped, he said, "No rest for us yet. They're only half-saved."

We started again at the beginning. This time we let them drink their fill. When I dropped down after completing the second round, I thought nothing on earth could rouse me to my feet. My grandfather came and sat beside me. He just patted my arm. No words were necessary.

After a minute of silence, I turned to him. "What now, Grandfather? We need rest or we'll be no good to us or them."

He nodded.

"Should we release them from the cages?"

"No. Under these conditions, this stress, they'd fight. They might hurt each other."

It was the last word I heard before a black, dreamless unconsciousness took away all thought. We slept for what must have been half a day until I felt the nudge of my grandfather's hand. It was time to start the watering again.

When we finished that round, I asked my grandfather what had been on my mind since we entered that chamber of death.

"It's good that we ease their suffering and keep them alive. But what do we do when we reach port and they unload them?"

He looked over the sea of small, terrified faces, for which we'd both taken on a kind of responsibility.

"I don't know, Ancarit. I only know that by my God who made them, I'll do something."

I felt the resolution in his voice. It became mine, too.

PART THREE

SIXTEEN

Julie's cell phone message confirmed a one-way plane ticket to Mayagüez, Puerto Rico. Wheels in the well that evening at nine thirty. That gave me nearly twelve hours. I'd have no trouble filling them. The question was the order of priorities.

Two thoughts coalesced into a decision. Thought one: the purpose of the trip was to convince our evanescent client, Victor, to come out of hiding so I could work on a court verdict that would give him back a life. Thought two: the pitch I'd make to Victor would depend on whether he was guilty or innocent of aiding in the fixing of the race that resulted in the death of his brother, Roberto. And as yet, that for me was a coin flip.

I realized that I'd been nibbling around the edges of that issue in terms of the people I'd talked to about the race. Impossible as the idea sounded, with just hours left before flying out, I decided to take a stab at getting it straight from the horse's mouth, in a manner of speaking.

The one point of total agreement among Mr. Devlin, Deputy D.A. Billy Coyne, and me was that a race fix of that complexity called for a level of expertise in that black art far beyond that of the average mafia hood—Italian or Puerto Rican. There was only one name that jumped out of the box.

Fat Tony Cannucci had the reputation for orchestrating every major fix of a horse race between Miami and Maine over the past twenty years. The newspapers dressed it up in the word alleged because neither federal nor state prosecutors had ever laid a glove on him. But if you asked any twelve-year-old kid within the confines of the North End of Boston who was "the man" in race fixing, there would be no debate.

The problem was that Fat Tony was as elusive as our client. He could be anywhere you find a racetrack on the East Coast. My only hope was that, with the exception of Ramon Garcia, who apparently had an inside source, word of the impending indictment of Victor was still the district attorney's dirty little secret. That left open the possibility that Fat Tony might have stayed in the neighborhood to repeat his performance.

According to my figuring, the only two horses other than those ridden by Roberto and Victor that had to be neutralized in that race to insure a victory for Cat's Tale were the one-horse, Mark's Delight, and the seven-horse, High Justice. The two jockeys involved were Manny Santiago and Juan Colon.

A quick check of the *Boston Globe* told me that they were both riding in the first race at Suffolk—post time: twelve noon. Since neither had mounts in the second, I got to the track in time to wait outside the jockeys' dressing room for the other jockeys to come out for the second race. I figured that would leave Manny and Juan resting or exercising on the mechanical horse in the jockey's room.

I knew that not even the Secretary-General of the United Nations is permitted in the jockeys' room during a racing afternoon. I caught Ed Goodavage, the valet for several jockeys including Manny, coming back from delivering the saddle and numbered cloth to the paddock for another jockey for the second race. I knew him casually from a bar that people from the track favor after the races.

Since the valets have access to the jockeys' room, I asked Ed to deliver a message to both Manny and Juan. The message was that their agent had word about adding a mount for each of them that afternoon, and that he needed to see them outside. Whatever might have seemed unlikely to Ed about my delivering the message was smoothed over by my most ingratiating smile and a twenty dollar bill. The smile was probably superfluous.

As I figured, once the "jockeys up" call was given and the horses left the paddock for the second race, the crowd of spectators went with them, either to the stands or the betting windows. I was standing alone when Manny and Juan, both in their silks for the third race, came to the side of the building looking for their agent.

"Hello, gentlemen. I'm the messenger."

The lure of getting another mount that afternoon brought them both over with smiles and a handshake. I hated to have to disappoint them.

"Actually, I'm not from your agent. I'm sorry. I need a word with both of you. I take it you're both familiar with the name Fat Tony Cannucci?"

The facial changes could not have been more abrupt or stark. Manny came about up to my collarbone, but he grabbed me by a fistful of my suit coat in the vise-grip of his powerful jockey's hand. He erupted in a torrent of Spanish curses. It began, roughly, "Listen you—You can tell that . . . slimeball for me and every other jockey—"

He punctuated the last words by storming back into the jockeys' room. That left me standing with Juan, who had a look somewhere between fear and panic.

"Manny's very brave, Mister. I wish I could say the same things he did. If I didn't have a family . . ."

"Whoa! Juan! Listen to me. I'm not from Fat Tony. I have nothing to do with him. I just need information. Can you settle down just for one question?"

The look softened, but not by a lot.

"Thank you, Juan. This'll just take a minute. And I promise you, no one will know."

Another slight degree of softening.

"I take it Mr. Cannucci's not high on your list."

Juan looked at the ground. He took a few seconds, I think to decide whether to speak or take the safe ground. When he looked up, he had a look that took my complete attention.

"Listen, Mister . . . What do I call you anyway?"

"My name's Michael Knight."

"All right, Michael Knight. Think about this. I got a deal for you. You want to take my ride in the third race? You want to ride that race? The horse is Sweet Charlie. He's a two year old. He's put two exercise riders in the hospital. He don't give no warning. He just explodes and you can't see it coming."

"I don't think—"

"Just listen. That's only part of it. I have the one post position. I got two speed horses outside of me. If I don't break on top, they'll be driving me into the rail. That's okay. I'd do the same. But if we come too close and click hooves . . . last year that put me in the hospital with three broken bones."

"Juan, I know—"

"Like hell you know. Nobody knows who hasn't hit forty miles an hour on the neck of an animal that could break a leg at every step. And there's not a jockey out there that hasn't taken that flying ambulance ride to the hospital."

"I know what you're saying, Juan."

"I'm not through. So why do we do it? What do you think, Mr. Michael Knight?"

"I guess . . ."

"We do it five, six times every day because we love it. Because we love the competition, the sport. We love the horses. It's a gift from God that we can be on the back of a horse that flies like the wind to beat every other horse. In spite of everything I said, we'd never give up this thing we love. Never. You hear that?"

"I do."

"Then hear this. Along comes this piece of crap. This Cannucci. He tells us that if we don't make this thing we love meaningless, a joke, he'll do things to our family, our children. If we don't do things so no matter how many chances we take, no matter how much heart our horse gives us, he can't win the race. This beautiful thing we love becomes dirty, it's an obscenity, so that gangster piece of garbage can pad his pockets."

I let him run his course. For as little as I could do about it, it might have released some pressure for him just to get it out.

"Juan, I agree with everything you said. I need to talk with that particular piece of garbage. I'm a lawyer. I represent Victor Mendosa. He lost more than a race the other day. He lost his brother. He could lose even more if I don't find the fat man fast. I need information. He may have it. Have you heard from him again?"

Juan was grinding the dirt on the ground with his shoe. "Maybe. What do you want to know?"

"Is he still in this area? Is he setting up another fix?"

"He came to see a few of us last night. Him and a couple of his goons. I think this is a big one."

"When?"

He looked around. "How do I know you're not from him?"

I showed him my bar membership card. "We've never met, but you must have seen me at the backstretch a few mornings every week. More importantly, Juan, I'm cousin to Roberto and Victor Mendosa. I can only swear to God I'm on your side."

He shook his head. "What the hell. I gotta trust someone. I can't live in the back pocket of that slimeball. What do you want?"

"When is the next fix?"

"It's not set yet. They just said it's coming. Sometime next week maybe. He'll tell us which race and who wins when the time comes."

"Thank you, Juan. Manny's not the only brave one. That took courage. I need to find Cannucci this afternoon. Is there anything he said that can give me a clue?"

He was silent for a few seconds. "Not this time, but last time. He was bragging about playing in a big twenty-four-hour poker game. He goes there in the afternoons when he's in town."

"Where?"

"It's in East Boston. That's all I know."

"That may be enough. Be careful, Juan. Maybe someday I can return the favor big-time."

* * *

While I drove my rental car in the direction of East Boston, I called Tom Burns, our personal source of information, licit and illicit.

"Tommy, I need some information. And you are like the Library of Congress in certain areas."

"What do you mean, 'in certain areas'?"

"Let me rephrase. You are the Encyclopedia Britannica. Period."

"That's a fair representation. What do you need, Mike?"

"There's a high-stakes twenty-four-hour poker game somewhere in East Boston. Do you know it?"

"Of course."

"Who do I have to know to get in?"

"Benjamin Franklin, ten times over."

"In English."

"You need ten hundred-dollar bills. A thousand dollars. Cash, no checks, money orders, or stamps. And definitely no credit cards with names on them."

"You mean I just knock on the door, hand over a thousand dollars, and I'm in?"

"A customer in good standing."

"If it's that easy, aren't they afraid of being raided? Closed down?"

"By whom? The mayors and police chiefs of most of the cities around there are customers. Throw in half the big-shot politicians in the State House. Who's going to close them down?"

"How about Boston's crusading District Attorney Lamb?"

"Are you kidding? She needs all the political clout she can get to hoist her ambitious, if incompetent, hind-quarters into the governor's seat. She's not going to rattle that hornets' nest."

"How about the feds?"

"It's a tight operation, Mike. No organized crime involvement. At all. The big wise guys come to play, but they have no ownership. That means the feds have no interest."

"Dare I ask if you're a member, Tom?"

"Dare on. No. Of course I'm not. It's a sucker's game."

"You mean it's rigged?"

"Not a bit. One slight whiff of a crooked table and they'd be out of business. No, look around if you go there. It's more plush than anything Donald Trump ever put together. Who do you suppose pays for all that fru-fru?"

"The suckers."

"You're a quick lad. The games are straight. The customers play against each other. The house takes 10 percent of every pot. And the pots can be astronomical. What do you suppose that cut for the house does to the suckers' chances of winning in the long run?"

"I hear you."

"So why do you want into a poker game there? It's a shark tank. The players in those games would eat you alive. You might as well just drop off your losings in an envelope and save the time."

"I need to connect with Fat Tony Cannucci. I hear he's there in the afternoon."

"Holy crap, Mike. You do lead an interesting life. Would it do any good to tell you to stay as far away from that round mound of feces as possible?"

"It'd do me more good if you tell me how to find this place."

"I doubt that. But it's your show. Just walk softly. There's more power in that room than in the whole State House."

When Tom hung up, I had a call waiting. It was the golden voice of Bob Herman. He said the words that gladdened my heart—"I have a brand new, identical replacement for your Corvette on the way to the showroom. It'll be waiting when you get here."

In terms of priorities, that trumped almost everything. I was there within twenty minutes. I dropped off my rental for pickup, and slipped behind the wheel of an absolute clone of the car that had been bombed out of my life. It was like slipping into a perfectly fitting velvet glove. In the words of an old singing cowboy, Gene Autry, I was back in the saddle again—and on my way to East Boston.

SEVENTEEN

ARMED WITH AN address and five thousand dollars in hundreds that I drew out of my checking account, I found the building in East Boston. I had always assumed it was a warehouse for one of the Boston department stores. It was totally unprepossessing on the outside. On Tom's word, I parked in the lot behind the building and rang the bell.

I couldn't believe that it was that simple, but when I knocked, a neatly turned-out tuxedo opened the door. I handed over ten crisp new hundred-dollar bills. He seemed to know just by the heft that it was all there. The door opened wide, and I stepped into Wonderland, Oz, and Disneyland for the well-heeled.

Every inch of what surrounded me spoke of plush luxuriance in the extreme, from the carpeting and wallpaper that had to run in the hundreds by the foot, to the movie-star quality of the staff in formal wear and gowns that were, even to my untrained eyes, not knock-offs from Marshalls. The comforting soft music came not through a wire in the wall, but from a live string ensemble. Each of the discreetly small rooms housed a velvet clad poker table and well-padded chairs. Each had a bar that, at a glance, showed no whiskey less than twelve years old.

I felt as underdressed in my conservative blue suit and understated striped tie as a well-digger at a coming-out ball. And yet, when I converted the other four thousand dollars into forty chips,

I was made to feel as welcome as the flowers in May by the liveried escort who asked if he might see to my needs.

Contrary to my expectations, there was not a hint of expensive prostitution, drugs, or any vice other than inoffensive gambling. These entrepreneurs were truly the soul of restraint. I began to understand how they survived the occasional wave of anti-corruption politicians.

At my request, he escorted me to an unoccupied room with a table and five chairs that undoubtedly went for more than all of the furniture in my four-room apartment.

I asked my escort if he would do me the kindness to deliver a note to Mr. Anthony Cannucci. He took the note while I took a seat. Within a few minutes, Mr. Cannucci walked through the door. I found myself sitting in front of the most massive block of corpulence I had experienced since my tour of the Patriots' dressing room. The term, "Fat Tony," applied to every inch of his six-foot, five-inch frame. I doubt that the set of scales has been created that could measure his bulk in poundage.

He had the confident smile of one who towers over most of the world's inhabitants. I introduced myself, and we shook hands. He waved my note in front of me.

"Intriguing. And how do you happen to favor me with this invitation?"

In the note, I had invited him to a single hand of showdown five-card poker, no draw, for a thousand dollars.

"I've heard you're a sporting man, Mr. Cannucci."

"Yes. I bet you have. And yet?"

I invited him to take one of the seats.

Before sitting, he repeated the question. "As I say, Mr. Knight, and yet?"

"Let me explain the terms of the bet more fully. I thought you might be interested in one hand of thousand-dollar showdown poker. If I win, you pay me the thousand. If you win, I pay you the thousand . . . on condition that you accommodate me with certain information."

The smile was turning into an amused grin. "And what would that information be?"

"Nothing that will ever compromise you. I'll assure you of that. You'll understand more fully if you accept the wager. You're a sporting man. Think of it as part of the gamble."

"Ah, but the odds seem unequal, Mr. Knight. What do you add to the pot to balance the addition of information on my part?"

"Quite simply this. We use your deck of cards."

The grin held, but I noticed his eyes narrowing a bit. "Are you suggesting something?"

"Nothing untoward, Mr. Cannucci. Merely setting the rules of our game. Shall we play?"

He never took his eyes off of me while he slowly sat in the chair opposite me.

"I assume you have a deck with you."

He reached into a vest pocket and took out what appeared to be a fresh unopened deck of Bicycle cards. His eyes still remained on me as he shuffled the cards with hands far more nimble than their size would suggest.

He handed the deck across to me. "Shuffle if you wish, Mr. Knight."

I merely tapped the top of the deck.

"Then cut the cards?"

Again I merely tapped the deck. He had the hesitation of one who is invited to fire competitively at a quarry that is staked to a post. It seemed far too easy. And yet I could read it in his eyes. When a sucker places himself so willingly on one's plate, it would be almost immoral not to feast.

He dealt each of us five cards in turn. He picked up his cards and examined them close to his chest. True to the code, his facial expression remained frozen as he looked at me to do the same.

I nodded to him without moving toward my cards. Since it was showdown poker, he simply spread his hand on the table face up. He had three queens.

My eyes were locked on his as I gathered my cards. I stacked them together without looking at them and tossed them to the center of the table.

"You win, Mr. Cannucci."

"How do you know? You haven't seen your cards."

"Do I need to?"

His expression stiffened. Again with my eyes on his, I reached for my cards and spread them in front of him, face up. I had two pair. I merely shrugged. I took ten hundred-dollar chips out of my pocket and set them in front of him. He merely looked at them.

"And now, Mr. Cannucci, the information."

That brought his eyes up.

"Let's assume for the moment that there was a fixed race at Suffolk Downs last week."

"Astonishing, Mr. Knight. A fixed race at Suffolk Downs?"

"I know. Unimaginable, isn't it? And yet, let's just suppose the fix happened to result in the death of a jockey. I'm a lawyer, Mr. Cannucci. Michael Knight of Devlin & Knight."

"And that would be Alexis Devlin?"

"It would. We represent one of the jockeys in that race who may be facing a charge of felony murder."

I could see in his eyes that he was making the leap to a possible spillover of the charge to include himself.

"There's one piece of critical information we need for his defense. Was Victor Mendosa a knowing party to the fix?"

"And why in your wildest dreams would you imagine that I'd give you that information, if in fact, I had it?"

"Because you're a clever man. It would be to your distinct advantage for us to get a court ruling that the entire incident was something that should be out of the criminal courts and handled by the track stewards. The stewards have jurisdiction to suspend the jockey, but they can't touch you. That would make it worth your while to give me the benefit of an answer."

I could see him playing with the ten chips in front of him while his mental machinery spun at full speed. The legal advice I had just given him was worth exactly what he was paying for it—zippo. But then he wasn't my client. He could take it or leave it.

When he looked up at me, he took one of the hundred-dollar chips and flipped it over to me.

"Suppose I buy a bit of insurance. That hundred dollars retains your services as my counsel. Agreed? That way, anything I might say is covered by attorney-client privilege."

I flipped the chip back to him.

"Doesn't work that way, Mr. Cannucci. Neither Mr. Devlin nor I would represent a slimy piece of parasitic crap like you if our lives depended on it."

Actually, I valued my kneecaps far too much to have said those heartfelt words. What did pass my lips was, "We can't accept your offer. It would raise a conflict of interest with our client. On the other hand, Mr. Cannucci, you have a far more effective form of insurance."

"And that would be?"

"Mr. Devlin and I walk past the duck pond in public garden almost every day. If we violate your interests in any way, the birds in that pond wouldn't be the only sitting ducks. That's better insurance than any code of legal ethics. Yes?"

He looked down at the chips he was fingering. "You're a clever lad. But in the end, I really don't know you, do I?"

It was my turn to smile. "Really? I'll make you another bet. The note I sent you was on Devlin & Knight notepaper. It was intended to give you a chance to check us out on your cell phone. I'll bet you another thousand that you did just that before you came into this room."

He looked me in the eye and smiled. "You are definitely a clever lad, Mr. Knight. Perhaps too clever."

"One last thought, Mr. Cannucci. Obviously, I already have enough information to connect you with the fixing of that race. Otherwise, I wouldn't be bringing the question to you, would I? And as we see, you're still at liberty. Does that tell you something about my discretion?"

He leaned back in the chair. This time his expression said it was time to do business. "Ask your question, Mr. Knight. And then I have one of my own."

"I did ask it. Was Victor Mendosa aware of and party to the fixing of that race?"

He looked away when he spoke. "I admit nothing. But one hears rumors. One hears that the payoff for the fix was sent to each of the Mendosa brothers. Roberto rejected the offer. He sent the money back."

"And Victor?"

He took a deep breath. "Victor seemed non-committal at first. He didn't take the money. A day later he sent word that he wanted in. The payoff money was sent back to him. But his ambivalence left room for doubt. Other arrangements were needed to insure compliance with the fix. Other arrangements were made. As you apparently know, when all was said and done, the right horse won the race." He smiled. "At least that's the rumor."

For all of the ambiguity, I still felt closer to the truth. "Thank you, Mr. Cannucci."

"Don't thank me. We're not through yet. You're not asking the right question."

That stopped me. "And the right question is?"

Now he was sitting upright. "*Why* did Victor change his mind and agree to become party to what you call 'the fix'?"

"Go on."

"Let's lay the real cards on the table. There were two parties that were pressing for assurances about the certainty of the outcome of that race. I'm still speaking hypothetically. Do you hear me? There was the usual group in the North End, shall we say, of Sicilian heritage. That's not unusual. But this time they were joined by a second group who shares your Victor's lineage. Are we clear?"

"Yes."

"Understand, it would make no difference to me. In fact, it might have doubled the fee to bring about the desired result in the race. Again, I speak from rumor. But on reflection, these are not your usual bedfellows. They're more likely to slit each other's throats over a block of drug turf. It suggests that the whole game was about more than the usual return on fixed bets, does it not?"

"Possibly."

"Yes. And you, my clever young friend, based on all you seem to know, are closer to the answer to that question than I am."

I gave a noncommittal shrug of my shoulders. "And therefore you're suggesting what?"

"Just this. If these people happened to have come to me with a suggestion of a repeat performance for a race at Suffolk Downs, hypothetically, and my assistance were sought by these same parties, my price could be affected by the knowledge of what's really behind it. A bit of leverage. You understand."

"And how does this involve me?"

"I want that information. And secondly, I want it known by the right people that I want in all the way. I want a piece of the real action. I want it for services no one else can provide with my reliability. Based on the people you seem to know on both sides, I suspect that you could deliver that message to the right parties as a go-between, you might say."

"I see."

"I want the message delivered to people at the right level that they're not dealing with some street corner bookie. The message might include the fact that a proper price, and I mean a proper price, will be paid by them . . . one way or another. I believe they'll understand my meaning."

I froze my own poker face and took a slow breath while the words rolled through my mind, "*How the hell did I become the messenger boy for this porculent, parasitic pile of corruption? And if I refuse, given the incriminating knowledge he assumes I have, what are the odds of my living long enough to catch that plane?*"

I stood on legs that were still deciding whether or not to hold me up. I smiled with the hope that my words did not sound as noncommittal as they were.

"I'll see what I can do."

He held out a hand to shake. I took it and felt myself being pulled to within a few inches of his face.

"I'd do more than that, if I were you. I'll be in touch."

The only thing that kept me upright on that walk to the door was knowledge of the e-ticket in my cell phone for a flight to Puerto Rico departing in exactly four hours.

EIGHTEEN

It was an eight-hour flight, with a two-hour stop off in San Juan, to the western Puerto Rican city of Mayagüez on the Mona Passage between the Caribbean and Atlantic. Mayagüez is home to the University of Puerto Rico, a world-class zoo, a sparkling seashore, a major harbor, my mother's sister (now deceased), an assortment of cousins I've never met, and if my prayers were to be answered, my client, Victor. The six-mile ride from the Eugenio De Hostos Airport north of the city to my hotel brought back flashes of my mother's descriptions of her former homeland. In some vague sense, I felt as if I were coming home.

It seemed the better part of discretion to stay at a hotel a bit removed from the center of the city in case my quest for Victor rattled any hornets' nests. The Mayagüez Resort was a comfortable two-and-a-half miles from center city. It was also a short hop from the seashore, always a comfort to a Bostonian away from Mother Atlantic.

I checked in and took to the road in a rented car. My first stop filled the need of both bodily and sentimental refueling. I'd heard my mother speak of the Restaurant El Siglo XX in her old neighborhood at 9 Peral as the closest thing to her home cooking.

It must be in the genes, because a certain comfort level engulfed me as I walked in the door. When I mentioned my mother's maiden name to the waitress and it was conveyed to Maria Sanchez, a woman of my mother's vintage, she came out of the kitchen with three of the staff. The tsunami of welcoming words and hugs revitalized every sleep-deprived cell in my body.

After the initial barrage of questions about my mother, the dishes began streaming from the kitchen like a column of ants bringing food to the colony. Thank God I hadn't eaten for at least eighteen hours. The shredded plantains with *huevos* alerted my salivating tonsils that they had hit the nirvana of Puerto Rican *cocina casera*. The *carne mechada* with red beans and rice alone could probably have made a meal for Fat Tony Cannucci, but it was surrounded by *tapas* from octopus to *carne de cerdo frito*.

After multiple courses, my taste buds were ready to collapse from exhaustion, when Maria brought out her personalized *flan*. Those same taste buds rallied to the occasion, and there was not an unappreciated spoonful.

The talk went on well into the afternoon. Word was sent to neighbors who came to join what was rapidly becoming a *fiesta*. I hadn't planned to spend that much time on what could hardly be described as a mere lunch, but it was an occasion I'll cherish forever. The stories and laughter flowed back and forth for hours. I vowed that I'd remember every disclosure of incidents from my mother's youth, embarrassing and otherwise, so that I could bring them up at our very next sitting in her kitchen.

When the grandfather clock chimed four, I was re-awakened to the reason I was there. When the conversation turned to Roberto and Victor, I mentioned as softly as possible the death of Roberto, but I skirted any reference to the cause of his death or why I was there.

At four thirty, before leaving, I had to repeat three times my promise to return before I left the island. My last words were to ask directions to a bar called Dos Hermanos on the Calle Del Rio, by a river called Rio Yagüez. It was the place given to me by Ramon Garcia to locate the only man he said I could trust—Nestor Ruiz.

That brought a chill like a fall frost on the festive spirit of every-one there. The others merely went into a deep silence. Maria came over to sit close to me. Her voice sounded so much like my mother's.

"Miguel, please, don't go there. On the life and soul of your mother, I'm praying this."

I was stumped for a response. I suspected that it had to be a gang hangout for the *Nyetas,* which would put it on Maria's for-bidden list. It was also my only source of contact with Nestor Ruiz. Without that contact, I'd be totally floundering. The hang-up was that I couldn't explain to Maria why it was necessary to go there without disclosing more about Victor than I thought appropriate.

I finally decided to nod and smile as if I were agreeing to follow her wishes. It was not so much a lie as a parting gift to those who had showered me with so much warm family feeling.

It was quarter to five when I was back behind the wheel of my rental. One lesson I'd learned that afternoon was to be careful about whom I asked for directions to the Dos Hermanos. I decided to follow the safest course. I stopped at a gas station and bought a city map. I figured I could find the address on my own without raising any hackles or sending any signals.

Within fifteen minutes, I was doing a slow drive-by. The clearest sign that Dos Hermanos was more than your friendly neighbor-hood pub was the door patrol in the form of two hefty, slouching *muchachos* with bulges in their waistbands and facial scars that don't come from shaving. The wired looks in their eyes said that their sense of restraint in dealing physically with this particular out-of-town drop-in might have been chemically altered.

Instead of attempting a walk-in without requesting passage, I parked and approached, open hands showing. I walked up to the one who seemed most nearly on this planet. He stiffened, with his right hand at belt level behind his back.

I decided to forego an ingratiating smile and just work on my calmly confident attitude. I opened my hands chest high. "I have a message for Nestor Ruiz."

That cut no ice.

"It's from Señor Ramon Garcia from the mainland." I almost said, "From the United States", but my conversation partner might have been touchy about an implication that Puerto Rico is not part of the United States. One thing I did not need was an unnecessary layer of *touchy*.

The one I addressed showed no response except to look at the other bookend by the door. He just shook his head to express, I assumed, nonrecognition. The first one turned back with a look that said that not only am I not going to get in, I may not be able to get out.

In desperation, I pulled out a name that at least could do me no harm among the *Nyetas*. "I'm a friend of Paco Morales. Pepe's bar. Jamaica Plain."

It had no effect on Goon One, but Goon Two nodded and pointed a thumb toward the door. I took it as an invitation and walked in. Goon Two was one step behind me. He put a fist on my shoulder and walked me to an old man sitting at the far end of the bar.

Goon Two mumbled something in muted Spanish. He had an accent with which I was unfamiliar. Nearly as I could tell, Goon Two had told the old man that I said I was from Paco. The old man swiveled in his seat to look me dead on. He smiled, but it reminded me of the look of a wolf smiling at a lamb.

"So, you know Paco. He's a good man. If he says you're okay, that's good enough. What's your name?"

"Michael Knight."

His eyebrows went up. He flashed a grin at the goon behind me. "Michael Knight, eh? Sounds like a gringo name. Why would Paco send a gringo here?"

"My mother's from this city. She married a man by the name of Knight. I'm half Puerto Rican."

He grinned again. "Really. Which half?"

"The half that's a lawyer representing a Puerto Rican jockey in a murder trial. Victor Mendosa. I came here to find him."

The grin softened into a smile. We were back to eye contact. He leaned back against the bar. "That's funny. I spoke to Paco on the phone yesterday. He didn't mention you'd be here."

"Then you must be a spiritualist, Señor. Paco was killed a week ago in Jamaica Plain by one of the *insectos*. I was with him when he died."

That caused a pause. I knew it was a test. I thanked God I could pass it. Temporarily.

"Then who sent you here?"

"I was sent by Ramon Garcia. They call him "Benito." He told me there's a man here who could help me find Victor. Nestor Ruiz."

I caught the first glint of recognition of Mr. Garcia's name, and it seemed to carry with it respect. The old man turned to the bartender and held up two fingers. The bartender filled two shots with a light amber liquid. The old man took one and handed the other to me.

"I hope you like good Puerto Rican rum. You won't find any finer. *Salud*."

We drank together with our eyes locked. He was right about the rum.

"And when you speak to Ramon Garcia, I hope you'll overlook any lack of hospitality by my men. These are dangerous times."

"I know."

"Yes. Now about Nestor Ruiz. He's entertaining some out-of-town players at the moment in the back room." He pointed with his chin.

I could see a grin spread across the face of Goon Two in the bar mirror. I looked back in the direction of a small side room with the door open. Four men were seated at a card table playing what looked like poker. I got off the barstool to walk to the room. The old man took my arm and kept me on the barstool.

"I wouldn't disturb him yet. Those three came in from San Juan looking for a game this morning. He'll want to concentrate. It won't be long."

I settled back. "How can you tell?"

"Trust me. Any minute now. The fuse is lit."

"What do you mean?"

"This is not a friendly game. It seems those three play poker as a team. It's 3 to 1 against Nestor. They've been winning."

"Seems like bad odds."

The old man shook his head. "No, 3 to 1 is about right. Have another drink, Señor half gringo. This may be your introduction to Nestor."

He motioned to the bartender. We shared another rum and watched. I whispered, "Which one is Nestor Ruiz?"

The old man leaned against the bar. "The man with his back to us."

I watched a hand of five-card draw poker being dealt by the man at the far side of the table. Three of the men picked up their cards. After a brief look, they all focused on the eyes of the man with his back to us, Nestor Ruiz. He sat there motionless, meeting the looks of each of them.

When the dealer called for the draw, each of the three discarded and drew one card. The man with his back to us simply patted the top of his hand without looking at his cards.

The player to his right bet a modest amount. Still without looking at his cards, Señor Ruiz pushed all of the cash in front of him into the center of the table. "It's late in the day, gentlemen. Shall we bet it all on this hand?"

The other three looked surprised, but not displeased. With a glance at each other, each of the three pushed all of the cash in front of them into the pot.

Señor Ruiz simply said, "Showtime."

Each of the others turned over their cards. With his cards still facedown and without looking at them, Señor Ruiz reached over and collected the entire pot. "I win by default."

Tempers ignited. The man to his right yelled, "The hell you did."

He reached over and turned over Señor Ruiz' hand showing three kings. "My four jacks beat your three kings."

Señor Ruiz spoke calmly. "They would. But two of those jacks in your hand were not in the deck when the cards were dealt."

The deepening red in the faces of the three out-of-towners framed the fire in their eyes. "You calling us cheaters?"

Señor Ruiz reached across the table for the deck of cards. He fanned them out face up and picked two more jacks out of the deck.

"Six jacks. Two too many, no?"

I could feel the explosion coming from the other three. Their hands moved under the table to reach for something in their belts.

I've never seen anything like it. In a fraction of a second, Señor Ruiz' right foot jumped to the wooden frame under the table. In one thrust, he drove the table into the sternum and chest of the man opposite. I could hear snaps, crackles, and pops of ribs like a bowl of rice crispies.

At the same instant, Señor Ruiz' left hand riffled the cards in the face of the man to his left, while his left foot drove the man's chair over backwards, pounding his head on the floor. In that same moment, Señor Ruiz' right fist flew straight out. It flattened the nose of the man to his right, sending him groveling onto the floor with his hands catching an outpouring of red fluid.

Two of them stayed twisting and moaning on the floor. The third began to get up. Señor Ruiz simply looked at him and pointed between his eyes. "Are you sure it's worth it?"

The man just dropped back onto the floor, rubbing the back of his head where he'd fallen.

Señor Ruiz rose to his feet. "Thank you, gentlemen. The cash in this pot will repay the amount you cheated. It might even provide a nice remuneration for the afternoon's entertainment."

As he turned, he said over his shoulder, "You might spread the word in San Juan. We frown on cheating."

Señor Ruiz walked out of the room. He nodded at two men at the end of the bar. They walked into the card room and removed the disabled visitors to the sidewalk outside of the bar.

The old man beside me called over, "Nestor, a gentleman to see you."

Señor Ruiz pocketed the money and walked toward us as calmly as if he were just returning from the men's room. He raised one finger to the bartender who immediately produced a large shot of rum that he seemed to have already poured.

Señor Ruiz poured a few drops over the cracked skin of the knuckles of his right hand without flinching. The bartender handed him a towel to dry his hand.

"This is Michael Knight. He's from the mainland. He says he was sent to see you by Señor Ramon Garcia."

Señor Ruiz drank the rest of the shot of rum in one swallow. I waited. He leaned both hands on the bar without looking at me. "Did Señor Garcia say anything else?"

I knew it was another test. I was groping for an answer. I finally said the only thing I could remember. "He said I could trust you. And that you were the only one I could trust."

I saw the trace of a smile. "He said the same to me about you." He looked over and started to hold out his right hand. When he saw that it was still oozing blood, he took it back. "Perhaps later."

I sensed that small talk was not Señor Ruiz' style. I cut to the chase in a low tone. "Señor Garcia said you could help me find Victor Mendosa."

"And why would I do that?"

I had the sinking feeling that my connection with this enigma was a fragile thread at best. The wrong word could break it, and I had no idea of the right word. "If it's my Anglo name that bothers you, I'm—"

"I'm half Puerto Rican, too. My father was Mexican. He was a *torero*. A bullfighter in your language."

"Then what are you—"

"Your bloodlines are of no concern to me, Mr. Knight."

"So what is?"

"Your heart." He tapped his chest. "If I commit to this quest of yours, it could be the last thing either of us will do on this earth. I want to know how committed you are. Like a *torero*, are your feet firmly planted, or do they shake and run when the horns of the bull come close?"

I sat back on the barstool, but I was looking into his eyes. "Words are cheap, Mr. Ruiz. I could tell you I'll never run under fire. But how would I know? I won't lie to you. I could tell you I haven't cut and run under fire yet, but why would you believe that either?"

The best I could say is that I had his attention. It was enough to go on. "I'll say this. Victor's my cousin. He's also my client. To some that doesn't mean much. To me it's everything. His life is at stake. I'll give everything I have to save it. That's all I can tell you. On that, you're in or you're out. If this is going to be what I think it is, I need your commitment just as much as you need mine."

I could see the hard crust of his look soften, almost to a smile. "That's what our mutual friend, Mr. Garcia, said you'd say."

He wrapped the bar cloth around his still oozing knuckles and held out his right hand. I took it. It was the beginning of a commitment that I felt sure neither of us would break. And four words consumed my mind: "God help us both."

NINETEEN

NESTOR REACHED OVER the bar and took the half-full bottle of rum out of the hand of the bartender. He took two fresh glasses and motioned with the bottle to a table in the rear of the bar.

I noticed that he took the seat that had his back to the wall. It being a small table, I sat with my back open to the rest of the bar. At that point, I had the feeling that I could have no one better watching my back.

We sat in silence while he filled the two glasses. He handed one to me and raised the other. "God help us in whatever lies ahead."

I wasn't sure whether it was a prayer or a toast. I drank to both. I also prayed that this might be the last toast of the afternoon while I could still hold a rational thought.

Nestor looked me eye-to-eye. He was not one to waste words on preliminaries.

"Why you?"

By way of groping for an answer, I stalled. "Why not?"

He took the cryptic return of his serve, so to speak, with a half-grin. He leaned his chair back against the wall. "Well, let's see. You say you're half Puerto Rican, but you look like a gringo to me. And probably to everyone else on this island. No offense. You asked. Your Spanish is good, considering. Even a touch of the Mayagüez accent, probably from your mother. But you still sound like you're working a second language. In a tight spot, you'd pass for an *hermano* like I'd pass for the Duke of York."

"I suppose—"

He held up his hand. "I'm just warming up. You know about Victor's race fixing at your little track up north, but I'd bet the pot that you're totally clueless about what this game is really about. How am I doing?"

"You make a good case."

"I'm still not through. You walk in here with nothing but a couple of names that may or may not be known down here—more likely not. You talk about all this concern for a Victor Mendosa, this jockey, who, by the way, nobody in this place gives a flying crap about. What I'm saying, it's a wonder you're still breathing."

That set me back about ten yards. "You mean . . ."

He leaned in close to the table and close to my ear. "I mean if that old man at the bar hadn't been here . . ." He grinned and shook his head. "Damn, you are clueless. If that old man hadn't recognized Paco's name, you'd probably be food for the barracudas. Are you beginning to get the lay of the land?"

On that one, I slugged down the last inch of rum in the glass.

"I repeat. Are you beginning to get wise?"

"I think so."

"I don't think so. This is not hometown U.S.A. This is a war zone. Except the soldiers don't wear uniforms. We have enemies sprinkled around this city that would give an arm and both legs to get through that door to bomb this place to hell. You hear me?"

"I hear you."

"Good. Then maybe my question makes more sense. The information I have is that your jockey, Victor Mendosa, is in the hands of those enemies I mentioned. The job your Boston friend, Ramon Garcia, passed on to me is to get Mendosa out of there, preferably alive. And so, who does he send for my right-hand man to ride into enemy territory?"

He held up his glass gesturing to me, before finishing the last few drops. "That said, you'll forgive my directness in asking—why you?"

I shook my head and couldn't suppress a wry grin.

He matched my grin. "You're offended."

I shook my head again. "Not in the least. I think I've asked myself that same question about two hundred times."

"And have you found an answer?"

It was my turn to look him in the eye. There was no grin now. "Yes."

"Good. Would you share it?"

"You said it yourself. I care about Victor Mendosa, apparently more than all the rest of you people put together. I told you. He's my client and he's my blood cousin. You might say I'm really the only one on this island who has a horse in this race. I'll do whatever it takes to get him home."

He just nodded.

"And one more thing, Señor Ruiz. I'm not quite the village idiot you describe. I learn fast. Especially when my life's on the line. Check around. I walked in here with a name and a prayer because this was my only lead. I knew the risk, but I had no choice. So that's the whole package. If you buy it, we're in it together. If not, with all due respect, to hell with you. I'll go it alone."

I caught the beginning of a smile. He rubbed the stubble of his beard and poured another round. "You left out one thing, gringo. You've got a set of rocks on you that may make up for all the rest. What the hell. No one lives forever."

He held out his hand. I was replaying in my mind the oration I'd just given. The thought occurred that I might have overstated my case. Especially the part about going it alone. Too late to take it back. In a "what the hell" moment of my own, I took the hand he offered and sealed the partnership.

"Now what, Señor Ruiz?"

"Now we drop the 'Señor'. If we're riding into hell together, it might as well be on first names."

"Done. I repeat, now what, Nestor?"

"It's school time. You need to understand what you may be giving your life for. Yes?"

"Could not agree more."

He took in a breath and let it out slowly. I think his problem was where to begin.

"You know about that fixed race at the track in Boston. That's what got you into this. What you don't know is why that race was fixed. This wasn't just to make a few bucks on bets. It was for that, of course, but a hell of a lot more. The group behind it needed a large and quick windfall of cash to buy into a major operation. It would multiply their winnings a few hundred times."

He was speaking softly, so I leaned in closer.

"Where the hell to start. If you know Ramon Garcia like he says you do, can I assume you're familiar with the group called the *Nyetas*?"

He looked over for an answer. My nod told him that I had a working familiarity with the gang. I didn't tell him how much history I had with a gang called the Coyotes associated with the *Nyetas* from my teen days in Jamaica Plain before Paco bought my release at a personal price. But the nod said enough. He looked straight into my eyes.

"Good. Because you're now sitting in the middle of one of our *Nyeta* headquarters. If you know us, maybe you've heard of the blood enemy I talked about. It's another Puerto Rican gang. We call them *insectos*. You understand that word?"

"It's about the same in English."

"Then listen. For the first time ever, the *insectos* partnered up with the Italian mafia in Boston for one big operation. The Italian mob did their part first. They did what they do. They fixed that race. Then they bet with bookies all across the mainland and in Canada. They won enough cash on that one race to finance an operation put together down here by the *insectos*."

He paused again in thought.

"Take your time."

"All right. Now you know the cast of characters." He checked the barroom behind me and leaned in even closer. "Let me ask you something. What do you think is the second largest illegal business in the United States? I mean right behind the billions of dollars made on illegal drugs every year. It's also the third largest international crime after the world trade in illegal drugs and arms."

No nod this time. I had no idea.

"It's the illegal poaching, smuggling, and sale of exotic and endangered wild animals."

He must have caught my reflexive look of disbelief.

"Just listen and learn. The trade is mostly in exotic wild birds, but it's also heavily into monkeys, tigers, bears, lions, fish, reptiles of all kinds. Anything that's exotic, and that means all of the endangered species. In fact, the closer to extinction, the higher the demand and the higher the price."

"No offense. I have trouble believing that."

"No surprise. Most people do, because they never hear of it. And most of those who hear of it, don't much care. That's what makes it easy money."

"It's just not what I expected to hear. Where do they get the animals?"

"Mostly the rainforest of the Amazon in Brazil. It's the richest source of wild animal species in the world. It's a chain operation. Traders in Brazil get the dirt-poor natives in villages in the jungles around the Amazon River to capture birds and animals. The more rare, the closer to extinction, the better. For the natives, it's a means of surviving. They trap and sell these animals to the traders by the hundreds of thousands every year for less per animal than the cash you've got in your pocket right now. Then the traders bring them by riverboats to the Brazilian coastal ports like Belém and Macapá."

"Then what?"

"That's the hell of it. These animals and birds get stuffed like sardines into tubes and boxes in every compartment of a ship to get them up here to Mayagüez. This is the major shipping port. From here they're carried by ship to get smuggled into the United States."

"Why Mayagüez?"

"Because the route's already been established years ago by the drug trade. The drugs, mostly heroin and cocaine, still come up from the cartels in Colombia and Venezuela to Mayagüez. They ship by the Mona Passage direct to Florida, usually around Miami. That traffic's been flooding the United States with drugs for decades. So when they needed a route to ship the animals, this was a natural."

It sounded like science fiction, but Nestor had a convincing way of telling it. He had my attention. "What do they do with them from there?"

"Once they're smuggled into the United States, there's a bigger market than you could imagine. There are about a dozen live auctions around the United States, but the biggest pipeline to the buyers is the Internet and specialized magazines. You can buy any exotic animal you want, even a species on the verge of extinction. It's almost as easy as buying a pair of shoes if you're willing to pay the price. You want a baby tiger, that's $1000. Just put it on your credit card. It'll be illegally poached and delivered to your back door. Hell, you can get a baby giraffe for $22,000. There's a price on everything. A little golden lion tamarin monkey can easily get $20,000. If they're nearly extinct like a Lear's Macaw, we're talking real money, at least $90,000."

"I've never heard of any of this."

"Most people haven't. But the organized crime gangs all over the world have. Russians, Chinese, Italians. Most of them are up to their ears in it. This is now a twenty-billion-dollar-a-year illegal industry. Some say it's already bigger than drugs and arms dealing. Even the major terrorist organizations are getting into it. And the hell of it is that the closer these animals are to extinction, the easier to sell and the higher the price. More species have gone totally extinct by this route than you can count. This, amigo, is the truth."

It was coming almost faster than I could absorb. "Where is this big market for animals? Who buys them?"

"Ah. That's the other side of this crap-eating picture." He stopped long enough to pour and swallow three more fingers of rum. "A lot of them are bought by thousands of people with more money than brains. They get their jollies out of owning a cute little exotic baby ocelot or tiger or monkey. Even bear cubs or lion cubs. The problem is these idiots have no idea how to care for them. Then, if they live at all, when they outgrow being cute and cuddly and become inconvenient, they get abandoned or bounced around like foster kids. They usually wind up being mistreated till they die in some sleazy roadside menagerie or, just as likely, at the wrong end of a gun or dumped in some vacant quarry. But I'll tell you this for sure, those clowns who buy them for pets are not the worst."

Another swig of rum. "There are the ones who buy them to stock hunting ranches for the sacks of crap who get an expensive ego-boost out of killing exotic animals, especially endangered species. The more endangered, the higher the price."

"How could I not have heard of any of this?"

"That just makes you typical. Then there are the wealthy, self-indulgent slimeballs who'll pay any price to make a damn meal on an endangered species."

"I still can't believe—"

"You better start believing. There are also the so-called scientists who pay the price to use thousands of poached monkeys to do illegal research. There are experimenters who pay over $30,000 for one illegally trapped endangered coral snake. And that's documented. Am I beginning to open your eyes?"

"If it's that big, why isn't it known?"

"Because, damn it, I mean it. Nobody gives a crap about these animals. No one cares enough to listen. And the worst part is that the rough way these animals are caught and shipped, ninety percent of them die a death you don't want to think about in the shipping. That's also a fact. But the profits are so high on the ones that survive it that the smugglers don't care about the ones they kill. Every year, the profits are rising higher than even illegal drug sales."

"Is that even possible?"

"Open your ears, Michael. It's true. Over thirty-eight million of these pathetic animals are taken out of Brazil every year. And trust me, what makes it possible is that no one gives a damn."

"Wait a minute, Nestor. I don't buy that. People care about animals. I know they do."

"Oh, is that a fact? Then how is it that the governments of every country involved know it's going on, and still, there are practically no laws against it, or the law's a joke. Only ten of your mainland states regulate the sale of exotic animals at all. Most of them just require a license so the state gets a cut. And if the traders are caught, which they almost never are, the fines don't amount to cigar money."

"But if it's a black market industry . . ."

"Here's the key. There's still no stigma attached to trading in animals. The few laws that exist are not enforced. The agencies are too understaffed and underfunded to make any difference. Last year, the percentage of smuggled animals recovered by the authorities was one half of one percent. And most of those animals were too far gone to save."

It was beginning to sink in. "I didn't know any of this."

"Well, you know it now. These slimeballs can operate as publicly as the corner meat market. The exotic animal auctions, the Internet, they're wide open. No need to hide. No one in authority is interested in even slowing it down. More entire species of animals and birds than you can imagine are joining the dodos and dinosaurs. So you tell me, where are all these people who care so much about the suffering and death and extinction of animals?"

I was groping for an answer, but there was none.

"And that, my friend, is why the *insectos* partnered up for the first time with the Boston Italian mafia to get in on the big profits. It's a hell of a lot less risky than smuggling drugs, where there is a stigma and heavy penalties when they're caught."

I was relieved when he sat back and took a break. This time I reached for the bottle and poured a shot glass full. Given the picture I was visualizing, the alcohol was no longer having an effect. When I could get my mind around what I'd heard enough to ask a question, I nudged his arm.

"How do you know all this?"

He came out of the thought he was locked in and looked over at me.

"I'm not the village idiot, either. Those *insectos* we're up against are no choirboys. They're as vicious as they come. If they tap into a source of funds to buy guns, bombs, whatever, they'll come at us with all they've got. I figured I'd better learn everything I could about what they're into and what we're going to be facing. Notice I'm including you."

"And again, how does all of this tie in to me and Victor Mendosa?"

"We got some information from an insider about what the *insectos* are up to. You don't have to know how. It's probably better you don't. The flood of money that came from that fixed race, and another one they're planning pretty soon, is being used to buy a major shipment of those birds and animals. There's a ship on the way here from Brazil right now. When the deal goes down, the animals will be smuggled into the United States."

"And the profits will go to the Boston mafia and the *insectos*."

"In the multimillions. With which they can buy a flood of weapons and soldiers. And God help us all. You catch on quick."

"When is the ship due here?"

"Soon. We need to find out exactly when."

There was still a gap.

"Victor's a jockey. He's been around Boston since his mid-teens. What's his connection?"

"Your jockey is from Mayagüez. He has an older cousin here. Chico Mendosa. They've stayed in contact all these years. Puerto Ricans take family seriously."

"I know." I thought of my mother who still sends more packages to Puerto Rican relatives than the USO.

"Chico's one of the heads of a gang here in Puerto Rico. They've been up to their ears in this animal trade from here for fifteen years. They have all the contacts with shippers from Brazil to here and from here to the Florida coast. They also have the bribes in place to smuggle the animals into the mainland. My guess is that the *insectos* need those contacts. Victor can put them together with his cousin—who's probably in it for a price."

"Why would Victor help the *insectos*? Especially after what happened to his brother."

"I don't know. I don't have all the pieces. Could be threats to his family. Could be something else."

"Like what?"

"Who knows? No use guessing."

I thought about that with another sip of the rum. Nestor leaned over closer. His voice was low, but his tone was strong. "And just in case you think that Victor Mendosa is the only horse you have in this race, think about this. The *insectos* have a major gang in your city of Boston. That's in addition to the Italian mafia. Those profits will fuel a flood of drugs, killings, and every other crime to take over territory like you've never seen before. Keep that thought in mind."

I had a flashback to the lunch with Billy Coyne at the Marliave. I could recall the depth of anxiety in his voice when he said that something a hell of a lot bigger than a fixed race was in the wind.

Nestor stood up and picked up the bottle. I caught his attention before he could walk away.

"I might as well ask this now. I may not get another chance. There's something here I wouldn't have figured. I mean beyond all the other stuff."

He stopped. He was listening, but he didn't look at me.

"This is personal. You don't have to answer."

He just stood, looking at the door.

"You really care about this. I mean the animals."

"Is that a question?"

"I guess it is."

He looked down at me. "I think someone should, don't you?"

"Yeah, but why you? If I could say it, you don't seem . . . "

His focus was back at the door. "I'm no choirboy either. I've seen a lot of suffering in this world. I've caused my share of it."

I didn't interrupt the pause.

"Those suffering animals never asked to be tortured and killed by that scum. I figure if I can do something about it—who knows, maybe it balances out some of the things I've done."

I started to speak, but he held up his hand. "That's your last question."

"I was just going to ask, where do we go from here?"

He looked back at me. "You go to your hotel. Now. Wait for my call. And don't wander into any more bars. You're no good to me sliced into fifteen pieces."

"Agreed. How about you?"

"I'll do what needs to be done."

TWENTY

I FOLLOWED NESTOR'S instructions to sit tight and wait. I have to admit, when I got back to my hotel, the Mayagüez Resort, it was no hardship to jump into a bathing suit, take a James Lee Burke novel, and just vegetate at the resort pool. I could feel the warming blanket of Puerto Rican sun baking knots out of nerves that had been strung like violin strings ever since that fourth race at Suffolk Downs. It would have been one of the most recuperative interludes of my life but for two things. I was wired to any cell phone sound that would bring Nestor and all that came with him back to the fore. The other thing was that try as I might, those haunting visions of animals, suffering just to feed the greed and ego of some level of humanity, kept penetrating the mental wall I was trying to erect.

By seven that evening, the dipping sun signaled time to change for dinner. I had actually dozed through the final two hours. When a slight chill in the air brought me back, I realized that the struggle between my white Irish pigment and darker Puerto Rican pigment had been won hands down by the former. Even the late afternoon sun had toasted my skin to a medium rare. When I managed to get vertical, my muscles were rebelling, my skin felt like a layer of fried bacon, my mind was fighting its reentry into the real world, and I think I felt better than I had at any time within any recent memory.

I dressed in pants and a shirt that would lay softly on skin cells that were exuding heat and pleading for gentleness. The hotel dining room was like an extension of the afternoon's vacation. The Puerto Rican menu specialties could have been improved upon only by importing Chef Ben Capone from his nook in Roslindale.

By nine o'clock, I was surrendering my taste buds to the local version of dulce de leche cheesecake. By then, my only thread of connection to reality was the thought that the Mayagüez Resort might be in the running for a honeymoon site for Terry and me.

Then at seven minutes past nine, the grating rasp of my cell phone dispelled every healing balm of the afternoon. In six words, Nestor's commanding tone brought me hurtling back.

"Where the hell are you, Michael?"

"In paradise, waiting for your infuriating summons back to hell."

Actually, I showed restraint. What I really said was, "My hotel. What's up?"

"Listen. Get this the first time. I have no time to repeat it."

"Go."

"Drive to the Plaza Colón, center of the city. Park on a side street. Statue of Christopher Columbus is in the middle of the plaza. There's a church, Catedral Nuestra Señora de la Candelaria. It's across the street behind the statue. Sit in the last pew on the right. Ten-thirty. Have you got that?"

"Yes. Plaza—"

Click. He was gone.

I got the impression that, like Mr. Devlin, he meant neither 10:29 nor 10:31. With that assumption, I was parked and sitting by the fountains under the statue by ten fifteen. The inscription by the statue said that Christopher Columbus, Cristóbal Colón in Spanish, had actually disembarked in Mayagüez—hence the statue and name of the square, *Plaza Colón*.

At 10:27, I started moving toward the cathedral. The Plaza was still alive with a passing combination of students from the University of Mayagüez and mixed ages of English-speaking tourists from the mainland. That was a bit of comfort.

The cathedral was massive, dark, and ancient. The heavy door in front was still open for an evening of late confessions. On the steps, I had to pass between two well-muscled and well-tattooed figures standing beside the door. I got the impression they were not there for confession. I noticed with some relief that they favored me with no more attention than they paid to any other passing gringo. Still, it felt like a wake-up call.

Inside the church, I tried to mute my footsteps. To my edgy mind, they still seemed to resound off of the stone walls. I stood against the back wall behind the last pew on the right to let my eyes adjust to the darkness. A middle-aged priest in black cassock was just coming out of one of the confessionals on the right side toward the altar. He turned away and walked toward the front of the church, passing the last two people kneeling in the front pew.

My eyes were slowly managing to read outlines more clearly. The only significant light was coming from a bank of votive candles at the altar. From the back of the church, I could just make out the form of an elderly figure, bent forward and wrapped in a shawl. The person was sitting in my destination—the last pew. It seemed like an unforeseen interruption to the plan.

I gave whoever it was until ten seconds before ten thirty to leave. That didn't happen. Since there was no plan B, I slid into the same pew a few feet away and sat in silence.

The voice with that familiar commanding tone came in a forced whisper. "Slide over."

I realized that it came from the huddled old figure. That in itself gave me the creeping shivers. If the warrior, Nestor, felt the need of a disguise, why in hell was I there with my face and all vulnerable parts exposed?

I slid over. I sat with my head down. My voice was so low I could hardly hear it myself. "What are we doing here?"

"You're going to confession. Closest confessional over there on the right."

It sounded like he was preparing me for my last moments on earth. I wanted to ask for clarification, but I wasn't sure I wanted to hear what he'd say. Instead, I just started to get up to follow orders. Another rasping command came out of the shawl. "Sit down. Not yet."

"How'll I know when?"

"You'll know."

"And in the meantime, what?"

"In the meantime, look around. Look where you are. You could do worse than to pray."

That thought had been on my mind too, but I didn't expect to hear it from my constantly surprising comrade in arms. I followed his advice.

After five minutes, I couldn't hold the question any longer. I whispered more loudly than I intended, "Hey Nes—"

"No names! What do you want?"

"Why do you get the disguise and I'm sitting here in plain view?"

"They know me. They don't know you. For the sake of us both, keep your mouth shut. No more questions."

Within another five minutes, a middle-aged priest came out of the clerical side of the nearest confessional, the one Nestor had mentioned. He followed the first priest to the front altar. Minutes later, a much older priest made his labored limping way from the front of the church and entered the priest's side of the same confessional.

There was one elderly person now sitting in the pew beside the confessional. She went in next. Within three minutes, she came out and headed toward the altar. There was no sound, but I felt a sharp kick on the side of my shin. I stood and walked down to the lay entrance to the confessional. The Latino aura of the church brought me back to my regular Saturday afternoon confessions in Spanish during my boyhood in Jamaica Plain. The two were distinguished only by the numbing sense of dread I was feeling at the moment.

The curtain fell closed behind me as I entered the small confessional. Whatever light was coming from the candles by the altar was a memory. I knelt down with my face next to the mesh screen. I heard the unmistakable sound of the wooden panel being drawn back by the priest on the other side of the partition. I reflexively whispered the familiar phrase, *Bendíceme, padre, porque he pecado*—"Bless me, Father, for I have sinned."

I was cut off at that point by a voice that hit me like a stun gun.

"I'm not your *padre,* Mike. But I bless you for coming."

I reacted with a jump that smacked my head off the side wall. The pain was just enough to clear my thoughts. Still, a logjam of questions froze my tongue. I could hardly get out the name.

"Damn it! Victor?"

"Unusual words for a confessional, but yes, it's me."

"I don't know where to start. How the hell are you? I mean ..."

"Don't worry, Mike. God's heard it before. I'm surviving. How about you?"

"Would you believe stunned out of my mind? I don't know what to ask first."

"Then just listen. We've only got about five minutes. First, thank you for coming. Somehow I knew you would."

I just nodded, forgetting that it was pitch dark. I was flashing back through the hell I'd gone through to get one answer from everyone else—was Victor guilty? I was truly shaken to be suddenly mouth-to-ear with the only one who actually had the answer.

"I'll make it the short version, Mike. Two days before that race, two of Fat Tony's goons ... You know Fat Tony Cannucci?"

"I've had the pleasure. Go on."

"They paid me and Roberto a visit. They offered a deal. We both pull our horses in that race. The main reward was that they don't do things to us and our families that . . ."

"I know. Go ahead."

"There was money involved, too, but the real payoff was that we get to keep our legs. We'd been through this before. We had promised each other that the next time, we'd tell them to shove it. No matter what."

"With what protection?"

"I told Roberto, if necessary, I'd go back to the *Nyetas*. A man I know."

"Benito? Ramon Garcia?"

"How do you know . . ."

"Another time. Keep going."

"When they came to make the deal, Roberto did tell them to shove it. And he stuck to it."

"And you, Victor. Think about this. Did you ever clearly tell Fat Tony or his men that you'd go along with the fix?"

For the first time in a week, I was thinking like a defense lawyer preparing a case. For that moment, it felt so good.

Victor hesitated long enough to make me feel uncomfortable.

"Actually . . . yes."

I'm sure he could feel my reaction. He had just cut off our most promising defense to a charge of felony murder. He jumped in before I could say anything, but I could tell he was still hesitant.

"I'm . . . not supposed to tell this to anyone, Mike . . . I think now I have no choice. Listen to this. This goes no further. Is that understood?"

"I'm your lawyer, Victor. It stays here. Lawyer-client privilege. Go ahead."

He took one long deep breath before he could say it. "When Fat Tony's thugs first offered me the bribe, with a threat, I said nothing one way or the other. I guess they figured I didn't have the guts to cross them. They let it go at that. Then the day before the race, I got a note to meet someone I didn't know after sundown at the bench across the street from Kelly's Roast Beef stand on Ocean Boulevard in Revere. I figured it was one of Fat Tony's people with the payoff."

"Had they done it that way before?"

"Something like that. Anyway, when I got there, there were two guys in suits. They said they were FBI. They said they wanted me to do something for them in that race. They could protect me and my family. I asked if they wanted me to ride to win. They said, 'Hell, no. we want you to go through with the fix. Tell Fat Tony you'll do it. We want you to work with us. Undercover.'"

"Did they show you identification?"

"They had badges. They wore suits. They looked like the FBI on television. That's all I knew."

"And you said?"

"I said, 'what the hell'. I was getting squeezed from both sides. I figured I might as well work for the good guys. Maybe they'll all cancel each other out. I could get back to riding."

"What did you tell Fat Tony?"

"I didn't have to tell him anything. He sent his goon with the envelope of money to my home that night. I took it. He just said, 'You're gonna be a good boy, right?' I just said, 'Sure.'"

"What happened then?"

"I went to see Fat Tony. I was wearing a wire. I'd taken the money, but I knew that he'd heard that Roberto wasn't in it. The deal I made was I'd go along with the fix as long as nothing happened to my brother. Fat Tony agreed. He said he could handle it without hurting Roberto."

That means Fat Tony was counting on the pebbles in the starting gate and the plan to force Victor's horse into Roberto's path to keep Roberto's horse out of the money.

"So what happened?

"You saw the race. I thought it was strange when they took the blinkers off my horse. He'd always spooked at anything beside him. When I saw Bobby Cataldo on Cat's Tale on my right flashing his whip at my horse's eyes, I knew what was up. I couldn't stop my horse from veering left into Roberto's path. I heard the hooves click. I knew there was a chance that Roberto's horse could go down behind me. It was risky as hell, but I didn't know it'd be that bad."

"I know. Then what?"

"I just broke. I even screamed out loud, 'To hell with those bastards.' I took my horse to the front and never looked back. Even if they disqualified my horse on a foul, I had to win. I wasn't thinking. I didn't know till after the race that Roberto had been hurt. That's when you and I went to the hospital."

I thought back to that race. "They must have wanted insurance in case you decided not to be a good boy. It was clever. Having your horse cross into Roberto's path would eliminate both of you in the same move. What happened after I left you at the hospital that night?"

"I was burning up inside. I couldn't tell you about any of this. All I could think of was, you know, Roberto may not make it, and I caused it. After you left the hospital, I got a call from Fat Tony. He was all condolences about Roberto, which was bullshit. He told me he wanted to see me at a place in the North End that morning. Something important."

"Did he tell you what?"

"No. Not then. When the doctor told me Roberto died, I went loco. I was going to meet Fat Tony, but not like he thought. I was going to take a gun and kill that bastard. I couldn't think of anything else."

"So what happened?"

"When I came out of the hospital, the two FBI guys were there. They took me into their car. We started driving around till I could cool off enough to listen. They told me this thing was a hundred times bigger than that fixed race. If I wanted to get Fat Tony, there was a better way."

"Which was?"

"It sounded crazy. They said that for the first time, two old enemies, the Italian mafia and the Puerto Rican *insectos*, were working together on a big deal. The Italians would raise the cash to finance it by betting on that fixed race with bookies all around the country. That way they'd get the best odds and no taxes. The *insectos* would then use the money here in Puerto Rico, in Mayagüez, to buy a big shipment of smuggled illegal wild animals coming in from Brazil. They could make millions in profit by getting the wild animals past customs in Florida and selling them around the U.S. The mafia and the *insectos* would split a big profit."

"Did they say how they'd get them past customs?"

"I don't know. Bribes, I suppose. They didn't say."

"What did all of that have to do with you, Victor? I mean, besides the fixed race. You're not into either gang."

His voice dropped another notch. "This is the first time the *insectos* have gotten into this business with wild animals. There's a gang here in Mayagüez that's been trafficking in illegal animals on a big scale for years. They have all the contacts to buy the animals here and smuggle them into the mainland. It's not that easy without the contacts."

"So?"

"So Roberto and I came from here. You know, Mike. About eight years ago. We have a cousin who's one of the big shots in the animal trafficking gang. Chico Mendosa. We were a close family when I was growing up. I've kept in touch with him ever since I left here. The FBI guys told me they had an informant inside the *insectos*. He told them about their plan. The informant heard the head of the *insectos* saying they needed to get me to talk to my cousin about letting them buy into the next big shipment of animals that was coming in from Brazil. They'd use the profits from the race to pay for the shipment. The *insectos* would take the risks in smuggling the animals into Florida. They'd pay a big profit to my cousin's gang just for putting them in touch with the contacts. The gang would get a cut of the profits off the top with no risks, financial or otherwise. But they needed me to arrange it with my cousin, Chico."

"What did the FBI want you to do?"

"They wanted me to play along. Set the deal up for the *insectos* with my cousin. I could let the FBI know when and where the animals were being smuggled into Florida. The FBI would move in and knock over the whole operation in one big roundup, mafia and *insectos*. Otherwise those big profits to the *insectos* would pay for a flood of guns and men to start a shooting war with the other gangs, the Russians, the Irish, the Vietnamese, even the *Nyetas*, all of them. Maybe even the Italians if the *insectos* pulled a double cross. They could take over territories from Boston to Miami. Drugs, weapons, human trafficking, pornography, everything big-time and wide open."

My mind was finally taking in the full dimensions of what Billy Coyne had sensed from the beginning was a hell of a lot bigger than a fixed race.

"So what happened?"

"I cooled off. I went to see Fat Tony at D'Angelo's Restaurant in the North End like he wanted. He was still all apologies, and what a great kid my brother was, and all this crap. I pretended to swallow it. Then he made me the deal. If I set it up with my cousin in Mayagüez, neither me nor my family would have to worry about anything ever again. There'd be a big payoff."

"How much?"

"For me, a hundred thousand if it worked this time. Maybe more if we did it again later."

"What did you say?"

"I bit my tongue and said that would be good for Roberto's family. I said I'd call my cousin, Chico. They said, 'The hell you will. You'll be on the next plane to Mayagüez this morning. You gotta be there to set this up in person.' That's why I had no time to contact you, Michael."

"So you came to Mayagüez and hooked up with the *insectos*."

"Right. But I also contacted Nestor Ruiz. He and I had known each other here from when I was with the *Nyetas*."

He paused, I think to check his watch. "And my time's up. I told the *insectos* I just wanted time to come to church. They let me, but they're waiting for me outside."

"Just one more question, Victor. When does all this happen?"

"When that ship full of animals gets here from northern Brazil. I'll know a short time before it happens. I'll get word to Nestor. He also needs me to find out which of the *insectos* is in charge of running this operation. Nestor's my only contact with the *Nyetas*. He's also my only real hope of getting out of here. When this deal is finished and that ship gets to Florida, they don't need me alive anymore."

"Nestor's outside. He's in the back of the church. Come with us now, Victor. He can hide you till we get a plane home."

"No. Not yet. I'm going to see this thing through for Roberto. I need you to contact the FBI agents and the U.S. attorney in Boston.

I'll give the name of the top *insecto* involved to Nestor and you when I get it. Tell the FBI guys this thing is much bigger than we thought. If I live through it, I'll testify against all of them."

"What else can I do?"

"Just wait. I'll get word to Nestor when I hear the ship from Brazil is coming in. He'll know what to do."

"Should we contact someone in the government here?"

"Hell, no. The *insectos* could never pull off anything this big unless the government people here are on the payroll. The problem is, we don't know who or how far up the line."

"All right. I'll stay at the hotel for whatever I can do."

"I know, Mike. Thanks. No better place than this cathedral to say God bless you for doing it."

"I say it back."

"Go on now, Mike. Get out of here. They don't know you, but they know Nestor. They may have men waiting for him. Adios."

* * *

I thought of the two tattooed goons at the front door of the church. I left the confessional and walked to the rear pew where I had left Nestor. He was nowhere in sight. When I looked back I saw the crippled old priest come out of the confessional I'd left and walk toward the altar. He ducked into a vesting room. In a minute, a short young man that looked like Victor came out and left by a side door.

They were just closing the large doors of the church when I left and walked down toward the square. The crowd had thinned, but I noticed that those who were left were clustered around the pool by the Columbus statue. They were buzzing about something.

I passed close enough to the pool to catch a glimpse of what was drawing the crowd. Two bodies with their necks and heads at an acute angle were floating face down. I didn't need to see their faces. I recognized the tattoos of the two who were standing outside the church.

As Billy Coyne would most certainly have noted, the body count was still increasing wherever I go. Lest my own be added to the count, I took an oblique path to my rental car on a side street. By midnight, I was in the bar of my hotel, nursing three fingers of Famous Grouse Scotch before calling it a day—one hell of a day at that. And in Boston, it occurred to me, the members of the bar were still living by the words, "The lawyer always goes home."

TWENTY-ONE

THE FOLLOWING MORNING
The Mayagüez Resort Hotel

THE FAMOUS GROUSE had helped me to put the vision of those two distorted bodies in the pool somewhere in the bottom drawer of my mind and get a night's sleep. An excellent breakfast on the sunny patio of the hotel dining room gave me a false expectation of a glorious day ahead.

Around ten o'clock, a call came in the clipped phraseology I'd come to recognize as that of Nestor.

"We need three things—a date, a time, and a name."

"Good morning, Nestor. It is a nice morning. Did you sleep well?"

"When this business ends, we'll have a nice long chat over a bottle of rum. Right now, we're about to do something you and I may or may not live through. For the survival of both of us, you need to know exactly what you're doing. Do you still give a crap about my night's sleep?"

"When you put it that way."

"Good. Then get this the first time. We need the date and time the shipment of the animals from Brazil is due in port. We also need the name of the man in charge of the *insectos'* operation. They haven't given Victor the details we need yet, and time's getting close.

They only keep him alive because they're afraid if they kill him, his cousin Chico will kill the deal."

"So who has the information?"

"Victor says we can get it from the informant we planted with the *insectos.*"

I wanted to ask if it could be the same informant who Victor said was working with the FBI. It could well have been the same man, working for the *Nyetas* for loyalty and for the FBI for payment.

"So why not ask him?"

"Because they found him out. He's . . . inaccessible."

"You mean dead."

"Not yet. They need time to confirm who he's really working for. He's tough. It'll take them a while."

"Then what does 'inaccessible' mean?"

"That's for me to worry about. The less you know about that for now the better."

"So what do you want me to do?"

"Do you know how to play dominoes?"

"You want to play dominoes?"

"Answer the question."

"Yes. Of course. I grew up in a Puerto Rican—"

"Just listen. At nine o'clock, I want you to go to a pub. El Garabato. It's on the Calle Post, 102. It's in a strip of bars beside the university campus. There'll be a mob of students in there. But they'll be gone by then until about midnight. The only ones there at nine will be the die-hard domino players. It won't be hard to get into a game. Bring some cash. They play for money."

"Can I ask why?"

"Because by nine thirty, you'll look like part of the scenery. They still don't know you. I need you to be there but invisible."

"Then what?"

"Listen to this. You'll have one chance to get this right. At exactly nine thirty, I want you to go out the door of the pub to the sidewalk. The Garabato's on a corner. I want you under the Medalla sign at that corner at exactly nine thirty. Smoke a cigar or something so you look casual. There'll be other gringo tourists there. Blend in."

"I'm technically not a gringo."

"You look like one. That's enough. I'm meeting someone across the street from that corner. Do not recognize me. One wave and you'll probably never see the sun come up. Are you listening?"

"I sure as hell heard that. Who're you meeting?"

"I got a message to the head of the *insectos*. I made him an offer. He's meeting me on the opposite corner at nine thirty to talk about it."

"What offer?"

"Doesn't matter."

"Will he accept it?"

"Not a chance in hell."

"Then why bother?"

"Sometimes the only way in is by the back door."

"Oh. Well, that clarifies everything. What am I doing there?"

"You're bringing a video camera. Use your cell phone if it has one. Like any other tourist, you're just filming a quaint section of town. You got that?"

"What am I actually filming?"

"Everything that happens with me on the opposite corner."

"That won't look suspicious?"

"If this goes the way I see it, all eyes will be on me. You just get the pictures. No matter what happens, you stay out of it. Go back to your hotel and wait for my call. If I don't get back to you within two days . . ."

"Yeah? What then?"

"Fly back to Boston."

"And do what there?"

"I don't give a damn. It'll mean I'm dead, and there's nothing you can do down here without me."

* * *

At about two minutes before nine thirty, I took a time-out from the hot domino game I'd struck up with a local. He used the break to get a beer from the bar. I walked out the front door and took a position with a good view of the corner across the street.

I set my cell phone to camera-video and waited. At exactly 9:30, as anticipated, I saw Nestor walk out of a bar and stand still on the opposite corner. I looked for someone who could be the head of the *insectos* to approach him. A few tourists passed him, but no one stopped.

At 9:32, every nerve in my body spiked to full alarm. Four city police officers were walking straight toward Nestor from four separate sides. It was their unified focus on Nestor that put me on alert. They were moving with a deliberate pace. If it caught my attention, I was stunned that the warrior, Nestor, wasn't bracing for action.

I played the tourist and started the cell phone video. The four police reached him at the same moment. The actions of all of them together seemed almost choreographed. I nearly dropped the cell phone when the cop coming from behind him swung a nightstick that caught Nestor in the small of the back. It doubled him over to the side. The one in front of him rammed his night stick into the middle of his stomach. That brought Nestor to his knees. I was stunned. Nestor still took no action to protect himself.

By now, the passing tourists were scurrying like rats away from the violence. It gave me a clear view to film the punches and kicks thrown by all four cops. Nestor was on the ground. He seemed unable or unwilling to defend himself. This man whom I'd seen dispatch three brawny card players in one motion just buckled without resistance under the blows.

I couldn't take it another second. I ran straight across the street. I was no physical match for any of the four cops, but I grabbed the one hitting him from behind around the neck. It took the cop by surprise. Big as he was, I was able to throw him off balance to the ground. I knew it was a useless gesture. One of the other cops spun around and planted a kick just below my ribs. Unlike Nestor, I went down with just one blow.

I couldn't get my breath back to fully stand up, so I just started yelling my head off at the cops. That brought blood in my mouth from an open-handed smack across my right cheek from another cop. It sent me tumbling back down on the pavement.

The next few minutes were a blur. I finally came back to seeing things in color with my hands in cuffs, riding in the back of a patrol wagon. I looked over to see Nestor. He was also in cuffs, propped up on the wagon's bench. He was still leaking red liquid from various openings. His voice had a raspy bass sound to it.

"Damn it, Michael. Why the hell can't you follow directions? You look like crap."

"Thank you. You're a thing of beauty yourself."

"So now they've got both of us."

"I couldn't just let them kill you."

I could swear I saw him start a grin, until it reopened the cracks in his lips. He just shook his head.

"Gringo, you're a piece of work. They could have killed you like stepping on a bug."

"I'm not a gringo. Besides, we're still alive. So that went pretty well."

Another head-shaking, this time with no grin. "Maybe I should have told you more. You might have royally screwed up any chance of this thing working out. I needed that video you were supposed to get."

"Why?"

He wiped some of the red streaming from both sides of his mouth. "I'll tell you what I should have told you before. The spy we planted with the *insectos*, they found him out. I'm sure they tortured him to find out how much we know."

"Did they get him to talk?"

He thought for a few seconds. "I don't know. I don't think so. I know him like a brother. I don't think he'd talk no matter what. But we all have limits."

"What does that have to do with—"

"Victor told me that our informant has the information we need about the ship."

"You said he was inaccessible. What does that mean?"

"It means the cops are the *insectos'* muscles. They have our informant in jail. I need to talk to him."

"So you need to get inside the jail. That's what this is about."

"I set up a meeting with the head of the *insectos*. He knew where I'd be at nine thirty. He wouldn't be there himself, but I figured he'd have his crooked cops there to take me out. The gamble was that they wouldn't kill me in public. I was hoping they'd take me in. Once I was in their jail, they could do what they wanted with me."

"And maybe you could contact the informant."

"That was the plan. The other half was that I needed your pictures of them beating me without any cause. I figured I could threaten to take it to the federal prosecutor. It could give me some leverage in jail to stay alive. Unfortunately for both of us, you chose to fight instead of film."

"It's not as bad as you think. I got most of it on video before I jumped into the brawl."

He looked over at me. "It is as bad as I think. The first thing they'll do is strip you and take away the camera."

"Maybe, but they won't get the camera. I figured you didn't just want the video for your scrapbook. I ditched it in a crack in the sidewalk before I attempted suicide to save your ungrateful ass."

That brought back the half grin. "Damn. Maybe you're not a useless gringo after all."

"Like I've been saying."

He closed his eyes and took a few breaths. I did, too. I opened them when I heard the unexpected words. "Thank you, Michael. It was a dumb move. But I'm damned if I know anyone else who would have done it for me."

I started to say something like, "You're welcome." He cut me off before I could get it out. "But next time obey orders."

*　*　*

They hauled us out of the wagon at the back entrance to what looked like a district court with a jail attached. I was still groggy from what must have been blows to the head. The cops half-dragged both of us inside to a room that looked like a decrepit courtroom.

They put us in a cage with what appeared to be a collection of the homeless of Mayagüez. I looked up to see a man in a black robe seated behind the bench. The sight of a judge roused the lawyer instincts in me. On the other hand, by this time I knew enough to keep my mouth shut until I got the lay of the land.

People sitting on the benches in the back of the courtroom looked like either the bottom rung of defense lawyers or relatives of the hapless souls in the cage with us. There was one older man on the back bench who stood out. He was clad in a well-fitting suit that looked even at that distance like silk. He held my attention. I caught it when he gave a nod to the judge that seemed to indicate us.

The judge returned the nod. He called two of the cops who had brought us in. He pointed to Nestor and me. The two cops opened the cage and took each of us by the arm. They took us both over to stand in front of the bench.

The judge looked over his half glasses. "What charge?"

One of the cops stepped forward. "Resisting arrest. Assault on police officers. Attempting to flee."

In the shortest criminal hearing of my experience, the so-called judge brought down the gavel. "Six months. Get 'em out of here."

I caught another nod, this time with a smile from the judge to the silk suit in the back. Again the nod was returned.

Two of the cops who brought us in grabbed Nestor by the arms. In one lightning move that reminded me of his action with the card players, Nestor brought a flying fist into the bulbous midsection of each of the cops. They were on the ground whining in one lightning second. Four other cops were on Nestor almost as fast. Two grabbed his arms while a third brought a nightstick down between his shoulder blades. Nestor went down and stayed down.

I took that as a cue. I threw what by Nestor's standards was a puny but well-aimed punch at the jaw of the cop to my right. That brought me a smack from behind that laid me flat on the floor beside my comrade.

The judge rose up to look over the bench. He yelled at the cops surrounding us. "Put 'em both in the pit."

* * *

I have no idea how much later it was that I woke up on the filthy, urine-smelling floor of a jail cell without windows. I had aches in body parts I didn't know I owned. My most overwhelming desire was to slip back into black oblivion. On the other hand, the squeaks and sounds of nonhuman toenails scurrying across the floor were an incentive to get on my feet.

When I managed to get upright, the single anemic bulb somewhere down the corridor gave just enough light to make out Nestor's form seated on a plank laid over a couple of buckets. Recognition of his voice, tainted though it was with a touch of irony, was the best thing I could say for the surroundings.

"Good morning, Michael. And tell me, did you sleep well?"

"Remind me never to ask you that question again. Where the hell are we?"

"Right where we should be. You may not believe it, but in your own prophetic words, that went well."

I flopped down on the plank beside him.

"You do have one ass-backwards sense of humor, Nestor."

"No joke. We just have to wait."

He hardly finished saying it when I heard two approaching sets of footsteps. One sounded human. The other sounded like the Sasquatch.

They left no doubt that they were heading for us. When they got in front of the bulb in the hall, I could see the outlines of two men. One was a guard of normal proportions. The other could pass for some mutant species with raging growth hormones. He was the largest human I had ever seen. Unlike most giants with gentle dispositions, this one gave no indication of gentleness.

When the guard inserted the key to open the cell, Nestor grabbed me by the shoulder. "This time listen. I've been hoping for this. Here's what I want you to do."

He gave me a couple of quick whispered instructions that ended with, "Then come back and glue your ass to this plank and keep it there. No matter what! Have you got that?"

Out of a fear that exceeded anything I can ever remember, I nodded affirmatively.

Nestor stood. I knew he had taken beatings that night that would keep any of the Boston Bruins on the disabled list for the season. But when he stood up, there was a smooth confidence in his motion that belied the pain. He simply stood there as if he knew what was coming.

The guard swung open the cell door. I could see him slink along the wall to crouch in one of the corners. The giant thumped on feet larger than I'd ever seen directly across the cell toward Nestor.

The giant was ignoring me. That gave me the chance to slip along the wall to the cell door. As instructed, I pulled it shut. The spring latch clicked into place and the four of us were locked in. I retreated to the nearest corner and plastered myself against the wall. I figured Nestor's instructions just meant stay the hell out of the way.

When the giant came within reach of Nestor, he raised both arms like two sides of beef to grab Nestor by the throat. With a flash of strength I thought by now would be spent, Nestor chopped his open fists like blades upward into the back of the elbows of the giant. The shriek of pain filled the entire block of cells and sent small furry beasts scurrying into holes in the walls.

Nestor ducked under the open arms. In a moment, he was behind the giant pulling him backwards off-balance by the shaggy shoulder-length hair. One kick to the back of the right knee and then the left crumpled his ponderous weight sprawling on the floor in a thud that shook the plank off the buckets. Nestor was on him with the straight spike of his fingers dug deeply into the outside of the giant's jugular vein.

Nestor said directly into his ear with a quiet gentleness that was unnerving, "Stay there. It's over. I can sever the vein before you even think of moving. You'll be dead before you can get to your feet. And for what? Do you hear me?"

At first the giant just froze in position. I was afraid of a sudden burst of motion that could break Nestor in half. As the seconds ticked on, I realized that being big as he was, and in severe pain from what Nestor had done to his arms, there was no sudden motion left in him.

In the next instant, both Nestor and I caught sight out of the corner of our eyes of the guard slipping along the wall toward the cell door. Nestor yelled to me. "Get him, Michael. Keep the door locked."

The guard was about my height and weight, but disadvantaged by a paralyzing fear that was broadcast by every facet of his face. I just positioned myself between him and the cell door. He backed off and slumped to the floor.

Nestor turned back to the giant. "Listen to me. I don't want to hurt you anymore."

The giant's eyes moved around to look in the eyes of the man who was holding him. The soft voice continued.

"I've heard of you. Your name's Jorge Conchas, isn't it?"

There was no response, but the giant was listening.

"None of this is your fault, Jorge. The people who sent you here, the ones who sent you to kill me, they don't deserve your loyalty. They'd kill you in an instant if they couldn't use you. That's all they're doing is using you. Do you hear me?"

The giant's breathing became slower and more regular. I could sense the slackening of muscles.

"I could have killed you just then. Do you understand that?"

The giant grunted something low that sounded like an affirmative.

"But I didn't. I promise you I won't hurt you. I'm not your enemy. If you give me your word that you'll stop fighting, I'm going to let you up. I'm going to trust you. Do you want that?"

A pause, then another affirmative grunt. Nestor took his hands away and stood back. The giant shifted his weight and sat up. He found that the pain in his hyperextended elbows still made his arms weak, but he managed to shift his weight until he was standing.

The giant and Nestor stood staring at each other for ten seconds before Nestor raised his arm to the giant's shoulder. The giant flinched back at first, but then he seemed to relax. Nestor's voice stayed calm, even friendly.

"Jorge, you've been misused by that gang of thugs. Those *insectos* treat you like a slab of beef. You deserve better. If you come with me, I'll take you to people who'll treat you like a man. With respect. Would you like that?"

Jorge seemed confused and hesitant. He finally nodded. "Why will you do that? I was going to kill you."

"Do you still want to kill me?"

"No. They said I had to."

"If you come with me, I'll take you to people who'll never make you do anything that's not right."

Jorge just dropped his head and nodded. I could feel a tidal change in that nod.

Nestor walked over to the guard, who was beginning to develop a distinct shiver. His voice was a whimper. "What are you going to do to me?"

"That depends on you. To begin, you're going to give me some information. You have a prisoner. His name is Santos. Mickey Santos. Where is he?"

The shivers magnified. "I can't. They'll kill me."

Nestor moved closer and dropped his voice. "Yes, they will, if you're lucky. Think about this. You're the man with the key to the cell. When they hear that you let us out, and they will, if all they do is kill you, it will be a mercy killing. You'll be pleading for it. Do you agree?"

The fear on his face was turning to panic. He stood speechless.

"I want an answer. Do you agree?"

He just nodded.

"Then it seems you have no choice. I'll have an answer to the question. Where is Mickey Santos?"

"What are you going to do to me?"

"If you do what I tell you, the four of us are going to walk out of this jail. Then if you have half a brain, you're going to catch the first boat to the mainland and keep heading west. Do you understand that?"

He nodded.

"Then answer my question."

"He's down that way. He's in solitary."

"Good. Then let's move. You're going to lead. If you change your mind about which side you're on, I'm close enough to break your neck with one swipe. Are we in agreement?"

He whispered, "Yes."

Nestor turned to me. "Michael, stay close to me. Jorge, walk behind us. They'll think you're still with them. Like you're guarding us. Are we ready?"

Nods all around. Lastly, but without equivocation, the nod came from the guard.

"Then let's move, gentlemen. We have promises to keep."

The poet, Robert Frost's words never held so much terror. I thought, "And miles to go before we sleep."

TWENTY-TWO

OUR LITTLE BAND of four moved out of the cell and down a scarcely lit underground corridor to the left. Silence was the rule until we reached a steel door on the right. The guard stopped. Nestor nudged him in the back.

"Is this it?"

"Yes."

"Open it."

The guard turned the key in the lock and pulled it opened. The four of us were looking into a pitch-black cell.

Nestor whispered a word to the guard. "Light."

The guard took a flashlight from his belt and shone it through the door.

The faint beam of light reached to the corner of the dank cell. A man's body was huddled there on the floor. He could have been on either side of the line of life.

"Inside."

The four of us followed the order while Nestor went over to bend down over the body of the lone prisoner. "Keep the light on him."

Nestor leaned close and spoke in his ear. There was no reaction. For the next minute, the question of alive or dead was a dice roll. Nestor lifted the man's chest and leaned him sitting up against the wall.

Nestor kept pouring words of encouragement into his ear to no avail until we finally heard a weak cough that slightly moved the man's chest. When his eyes slowly opened I tried to read what was behind them. The first message I got was cold terror. Then they froze shut again.

Nestor gently shook the man's shoulders. He spoke in an unwhispered voice. The eyes opened more quickly. The message this time was somewhere between disbelief and the faintest hope. I've never heard words spoken with more depth. "Nestor. My God! My God! Nestor?"

"It's me, Mickey. Tell me about you. Can I lift you?"

"Nestor. How did you find me?"

"Later, Mickey. We're going to get you out of here. Can I lift you without hurting you?"

"Yes. No matter. Whatever happens. Please."

"I'll do it as gently as I can. Put your arms around my neck."

Mickey raised his arms, but he used them to grab Nestor's shirt. He pulled Nestor's ear close to his mouth. He was barely forcing a whisper, but I could hear it.

"I didn't talk, Nestor. I told them nothing. Believe me."

Nestor hugged the weak body he was holding close to his own like a brother for several seconds.

"I know, hermano. I always believe you. Let me lift you now. We're getting you out of here."

Before he let go of Nestor's shirt, he pulled Nestor's ear close to his lips again. "In case . . . I don't make it all the way, listen to me. The ship is due into the harbor . . . in one day. Tomorrow . . . Supposed to be in the evening . . . They won't unload till the next day. . . . Ship's called the *La Nuestra Señora de Guadalupe*. Did you hear?"

"I did. Now—"

"One more thing—The *insecto* who's running the show." He coughed, and I could see the strain of speaking in his features. He took a short breath and said it loudly. "Jose Ramos—He's number one. You know?"

Nestor cast a look back at me. I took it to mean that Ramos was the *insecto* he had arranged to meet earlier on the corner on the Calle Post.

"I know him. That's enough now, Mickey. No more. Try to relax your muscles. If it hurts too much, let me know."

Nestor leaned in. He put Mickey's arms around his shoulders. Feeble as the remaining strength was in those arms, I could see Mickey straining to hang on. Nestor got his feet under him and lifted. I could see by the contortion of Mickey's face that the pain ran through his whole body. But no sound came out.

Nestor struggled to get him halfway to standing before he stopped. When he tried to lift Mickey onto his shoulders, it was obvious that the weight was too much for Nestor in his condition. They began to slant sideways. Nestor fought it, but they were slowly falling.

Before I could move to step in, I felt the giant form of Jorge move past me. In an instant he was beside the two men. He took Mickey's arms from around Nestor's neck. He put them around his own neck. The gentleness and ease with which he lifted Mickey's body into his aching arms and rose to his feet must have been a godsend to every cell of Mickey's body.

Nestor got to his feet. He assembled the group as before, the guard in front, Nestor and I in the middle, and Jorge close behind with Mickey in his arms.

Before we took the first step out of the cell, Nestor took the guard by the shoulders and turned him around. "Remember who your friends are, guard. One small lapse in your memory will be the end of your life. Understood?"

The guard had been noncommittal before, but when he said

"Understood" this time, he said it like someone who fully compre-
hended the thread by which his life was hanging.

"Good. Take that walkie-talkie off your belt."

He did.

"Call the sergeant at the desk upstairs. Tell him you need a patrol
wagon at the front door. Immediately. He'll ask why. Tell him the
prisoner is ready to give information. Say you called Jose Ramos
on his cell phone. He wants the prisoner brought directly to him
before he says a word. No one else is to hear it. You got all that?"

The guard followed orders precisely. A tennis ball lump came up
in my throat when I heard the sergeant at the desk tell the guard
to keep the prisoner in the cell until he called Ramos to verify the
orders.

The guard had apparently been truly converted. Without checking with Nestor, he came back to the sergeant without skipping a
beat.

"That's your choice, Sergeant. Just be sure he knows the call is
coming from you."

The voice came back. "Why?"

"Because this prisoner is on the verge of death. Señor Ramos told
me to bring him there personally. If this prisoner dies before I get
him to Señor Ramos, someone's going to be feeding the fishes. I'm
going to be sure it's not me."

There was a moment of hesitation. "I still think I should check."

"Go ahead. Call his personal cell phone number. He gave it to me.
Here it is. But you better know this. He's not at his headquarters."

"Where is he?"

"He's at that house by the ocean. He's with . . . do I have to tell
you who he's with? And when he's with her, and you interrupt him
to check on an order he's already given . . . Just be sure he knows it's
you calling and not me."

Another hesitation.

"Maybe you don't value your life like I do, Sergeant. But if I were sitting where you are, I'd get that wagon to the front door without messing around. We're bringing him right up. Be sure to tell Señor Ramos the delay is not my fault. Neither is the phone call. If you don't, I will."

There was no reply. On pure faith, the five of us marched down the corridor, up the steps, and directly past the sergeant's dais toward the door. We never slowed for conversation. When the sergeant yelled a confused, "Hey, where the hell are you taking those other two?"—which would be Nestor and me—the guard continued to play the role. "He wants to see them too. Jorge and I can handle it. Where's the wagon?"

On cue, a paneled police wagon pulled up to the front door. All of us but the guard got in the back section. The guard pulled open the driver's door. He yelled one word at the driver with an authority I think he was beginning to enjoy. "Out!"

The driver scurried down onto the sidewalk. The guard jumped into the driver's seat, threw it in gear, and the tires left four coatings of rubber on the hot pavement.

The wagon's siren cleared a convoluted path through side streets at a clip that would embarrass a Boston taxi driver. After ten minutes of evasive driving, the guard brought the speed back down to merely dangerous. He yelled back to Nestor for directions. Nestor gave him the address of a small clinic that was well out in a suburb that was, as I learned later, controlled by the *Nyetas*. Nestor used the guard's phone to call ahead to have medical assistance on alert for our arrival.

Within ten minutes, Jorge was lending his gentle muscle to the transference of the now unconscious Mickey Santos to a medical gurney outside of the clinic. From that point, we split up. Nestor and Jorge stayed with Mickey. I flagged a cab to go back to my hotel with instructions to wait for Nestor's call.

Before going on his way, the guard looked to Nestor for any last order. Nestor looked at him for a few seconds. I think he was calculating the odds that the guard would revert to his former loyalties. He must have decided in the guard's favor.

"You did well. I meant what I said. Your life won't be worth a peso when they put all this together. You've got a small window. There are ships leaving from the docks all the time. I'd ditch the patrol wagon and hop a cab if I were you."

"Thank you, Señor Ruiz. I will. I'm going to go to—"

"Don't tell me. It's safer if you're the only one who knows."

*   *   *

In spite of the idyllic trappings of the resort hotel, it was a night of wrestling with waking premonitions of the next "fine mess" we'd be wading into, interspersed with sleeping nightmares along the same lines.

I was into a third cup of coffee at breakfast when I got the next cryptic call from Nestor.

"Tonight. Midnight. Be at the front entrance of the hotel."

"Damn it! Could you just once soften it with 'Good Morning,' 'Nice Day,' 'How the hell are you?,' anything before the invitation to another walk into the bowels of hell?"

My cooler Irish side prevailed. What I actually said was, "I'll be there. What's up?"

"Mickey said the ship from Brazil docks sometime this evening. They won't unload the animals till tomorrow morning. I'm sure most of the crew will be off the ship tonight, probably in some bar. I want to check out the cargo hold while there's a minimum of security. You should be there to see it, too."

"Minimum security or not, how do we get through it?"

"Victor'll be with us. He told the *insectos* he'd have to go alone with his cousin to check out the shipment of animals. They apparently believed him since his cousin is their only contact with the syndicate that arranged the shipment. Victor says he can try using his cousin's name to get you and me on the ship. It might work."

"The key word in all that being 'might'."

"If you wanted a safe, predictable life, you should have been an accountant."

"Thank you for the career counseling. You're late by about ten years. I'll be at the front entrance at midnight. Meanwhile, have yourself a very happy day."

"Damn, you do love the small talk."

"Yes, I do. It reminds me that somewhere there's a civilized world of people who don't spend every waking hour trying to kill some living being. Like me. Right?"

There was a pause that took me by surprise. "I suppose. I haven't seen that civilized world in a long, long time."

I had a strong feeling that that last was not by his choice. I felt a small pang of regret at my tone and choice of words.

"I understand. At least I'm beginning to. Thank you for taking me along. I couldn't do what I have to do without you. I'll see you tonight."

* * *

That gave me the morning free. I took the time to retrieve my phone from the crack in the pavement. I also used the time to remind myself that there was a small circle of people in Boston who actually cared that I return intact. I walked to the beach where the peaceful, rhythmic lapping of waves on the shore would make an appropriate background for the most calming account I could give of my present status.

At the top of that short list was Terry—Terry, who was about to invest every hope for a future of love, children, stability, and happiness in someone who could not make a reasonably safe bet on seeing the next sunrise.

That was a quandary. She deserved the truth. She also deserved not to spend the next several days under a cloud of fear for the one at the center of those hopes. That was a tightrope walk. The best I could do was to dial her number in faith that the words would come.

And they did. Her excitement and joy in our being connected, even by the thin thread of a call, poured through the phone. And the words came to both of us.

For the first ten or so minutes, we simply poured out that joy in every possible form of expression. Eventually, however, the time came to answer the inevitable question. "When will you be home?"

I explained the uncertain timing in terms of meetings with our client, Victor, as well as conferences with an interesting new acquaintance by the name of Nestor, and several other Puerto Ricans who might be able to shed light on our defense strategy for the client. At the earliest possible moment after that, I'd be knocking on her seaside door in Winthrop, Massachusetts.

That pretty much summarized the true facts. It also syphoned off the terror that lay behind them. When that call ended, I renewed the silent vow to myself that if this case should be closed with all bodily functions intact, title searching and will drafting would consume my entire law practice. I might die of boredom, but it would be a considerably more drawn-out demise.

The second call on that short list was to my senior partner, Lex

Devlin. Presumptuous as this may sound, I knew that Mr. D. was suffering an anxiety level pretty much as high as Terry's for my safe return. I had left Boston with no more explanation to him than I was flying to Puerto Rico to follow a lead.

I knew this call would take at least the half hour that our usual morning chats over coffee consumed in his office. I decided to make the call through the one who I knew always had my back at the home front, my assistant, Julie.

"Michael! Are you all right? Where are you? Are you back home? Are you all right?"

"Julie, I'm fine. Never better. In fact, better for hearing your voice. How are you?"

"I'm always fine. I don't do dangerous things. But you . . . Are you staying out of danger for once?"

"Listen to this." I held the phone out to catch the gentle breaking of the waves. "Right at this moment I'm on an idyllic shore in the Caribbean, soaking up sun, good Puerto Rican cooking, an occasional game of dominoes. What could be more peaceful?"

"You have to say that to Mr. Devlin. He's been pacing around here like a caged lion. Have you been getting his calls and emails?"

"Tell you the truth, Julie, I've been too busy with meetings to catch up on either. I'll give him a full report."

"Good. I'll transfer you right away. Don't get too much sun on that Irish complexion. Do you have plenty of sunblock?"

"I do. The only problem is I'm a little short of bullet-block and nightstick-block." I left that last part out. "I'll see you within the week, Julie."

The next voice on the line came at a volume that almost eliminated the need for electronics. If Mr. D. had just opened his office window, I'd probably have heard him.

"Michael, where in the blazing bastions of hell have you been?"

I took him through the last three days, incident by incident, in a great more detail than I reported to Terry. He listened without interruption. We both knew that personal concerns aside, we had a professional obligation to the client, and we both knew going in that this would be no cakewalk.

I finished by recounting the prospect of a glimpse of the wild animal cargo on the ship that night, perhaps overemphasizing the optimistic aspects I'd gotten from Nestor. As we talked, I could visualize Mr. D. pacing in the space between his desk and the window facing Boston harbor, and far beyond, the island of Puerto Rico.

We finished the call by bringing deputy D.A., Billy Coyne, into a three-way connection on his private line. I took the lead in striking a deal. For our part, I gave him every bit of information I had. It substantiated what he had suspected from the beginning—that an enormous part of the iceberg lay below the surface—the fixed race at Suffolk Downs. I could tell from his tone that even that old court warrior was shaken by the prospect of the influx of drugs, guns, and violent turf wars that could flood his city as a result of heavy financing through the trade in wild animals.

I was also careful not to underplay the fact that my presence in Puerto Rico at the prospective scene of the crime was the best, if not only, chance of preventing that outcome, though God only knew how.

His part of the deal was to put a leash on the flaming ambition of his boss, District Attorney Angela Lamb. What little I knew of the details of the joint venture between the North End Italian mafiosi and the Puerto Rican *insectos* included one more fixed race at Suffolk Downs to complete the financing of the deal for the animals. I needed to be sure that Victor could return to the mainland to ride in that race without being snatched up prematurely on an arrest warrant for the felony murder of his brother.

Billy assured me that so far he had held her at bay. Through his stalling, the indictment of Victor was still pending finality with the grand jury. No arrest warrant had been issued yet. Since Mr. Coyne personally handled all major presentations to the Suffolk County grand jury, he'd see that his schedule remained clogged with other matters.

Billy signed off with a mutual exchange of promises to keep each other current. I was alone with Mr. D. on the line. I braced for an onslaught of commands and limitations, all calculated to keep me alive and in glowing health—and all impossible to obey, given the future prospects.

To my amazement, his voice lowered and he said just four words. "Come home safe, Michael."

I found myself swallowing a lump that clogged my throat. I knew that his words were as sincerely felt as any that have ever been spoken.

As were mine. "I will, Mr. Devlin."

PART FOUR

TWENTY-THREE

In the hold of the cargo ship, Nuestra Señora de Guadalupe

DAY OR NIGHT made no difference to Ancarit and his grandfather, Ansuro. The days of the voyage passed like one continuous night in the hold of the cargo ship, *Nuestra Señora de Guadalupe*. The only faint rays of light came from one weak bulb suspended in the center of the large chamber below deck.

Except for spells when they would collapse from near exhaustion, their time was consumed with bringing buckets of water to the crying mouths of the caged and bound animals.

For the first three days, the only sound to remind them that there was a world outside of their stifling enclosure was the labored chugging of the ship's tired engines. The longer it went on, the greater the hope that they could keep on with their routine without interruption until the journey ended. They knew that at that point, both their fate and that of the animals was out of their hands.

During the first day, rest periods had been spent in conversation to distract their minds from the constant dread of discovery. By the second day, even fear had no power over the demand of their bodies for sleep.

It was the beginning of the third twenty-four-hour period when Ancarit laid down the water pail he was carrying. Once again he had to take his grandfather by the arm and insist that he give his body rest. Without food for nearly three days, rest was the only restoration that kept their bodies capable of lifting the heavy pails of water.

Ancarit saw to it that his grandfather was lying beside him on the burlap mats on the floor before he let himself slip into the brief twilight that preceded sleep. Routine had become the narcotic that let his mind idle.

It was in that twilight that Ancarit flinched at the sudden grip of his grandfather's steeled fingers on his arm. At that same instant, blinding rays of sunlight burst through the hatch that had been pulled open at the top of the stairs above them. Their eyes recoiled in pain at the sudden brilliance. None of their senses gave them a clue as to who stood in the doorway.

Their only emotion was hopelessness. They were completely exposed to whoever stood at the top of the stairs. Hiding was not an option, and flight was impossible.

It was nearly a minute before their eyes could adjust to their first bath of sunlight in over two days. When they took the first painful glimpse above, they could make out the outline of one man. They watched for motion, but there was no movement. He simply stood above them—watching.

Ancarit was the first to stand. He helped his grandfather to his feet beside him to face together whatever was coming. With the passing seconds, it began to appear that the intruder was in no hurry to descend to attack them or to retreat to summon help.

Ancarit saw his grandfather raise his arms and hold them out to the side with his hands open. Ancarit took it as either a sign of peace or a plea for mercy. He did the same.

The figure on the stairs seemed to understand. He took one unhurried step at a time down the stairs that brought him close enough to be seen clearly. Ansuro's expectation was jolted when he recognized the features of a black African instead of a Brazilian like the rest of the crew.

"What you doin' here?"

Ansuro heard the English words in an accent that he recalled from his time in the west African country of Sierra Leone. To his grandson, the man's color, features, and way of speaking were beyond any he'd experienced. His grandfather had taught him some English, but not in this accent.

The size and build of the man told him that his grandfather and he would have no defense against anything the man wanted to do to them. At the same time, his way of moving radiated more caution than a threat of violence.

"Speak. You tell me now. What you doin' down here?"

The old man lowered his arms. He took one slow step toward the man and stopped. "We mean no harm. To you or the animals."

The man looked around at the cages that surrounded him. He was seeing something that obviously puzzled him. "What you do to these animals?"

"Nothing. I assure you. We haven't hurt them."

The man looked at the water pails, still moist from the last rounds. "You do somethin'. You tell me now."

"We haven't . . . Why are you asking about the animals? You see them. They're just as they were when you people loaded them."

The African straightened up. He looked into the eyes of both with an expression neither could read. The hearts of both men felt a constriction when the African turned without a word and climbed the stairs. They heard metal clang on metal as the heavy hatch locked into place.

Once more they were isolated in a darkness that seemed even more smothering than it had been before. Their presence and their awareness that a crime was being committed would be known in minutes to those above deck. The only certainty was that they would not be allowed to live.

Ansuro reached down and picked up the pail he had been using. Ancarit could hear his steady voice. "We can't help ourselves. But we can do what we're here for. God only knows when these poor creatures will have water again. Shall we do what we can?"

Ancarit picked up his own pail. He tried to smile at his grandfather for what he thought would be the last time. Together they filled the buckets and began carrying water to all of the animals they could reach before time ran out.

They had watered nearly a third of the animals when the sound came again. This time without looking, they knew the heavy hatch was being pulled open. They froze where they were until they could see how many came down the steps to take their lives.

When their eyes could focus above, they saw the silhouette of the African. He was still alone. When he came down the steps, they could see two bundles under his arms.

He moved more quickly this time as if he sensed a reason for haste. When he came to within ten feet, he dropped the bundles on the floor in front of him. He spoke in a quiet voice.

"I know what you doin' down here. Why you do it?"

Ansuro spoke first. "We're doing no harm. Please let us finish before—"

"I see you helpin' them poor beasts. Why you do it?"

Ansuro had no idea of what to say but the truth. "Because they're suffering."

The man looked from one to the other before speaking. He pointed to the two bundles he had dropped. "This one for you. That one for them."

He turned and walked back toward the stairs. Ansuro called after him. "Wait. Are you going to tell them about us?"

The African looked back. He nodded to the bundles on the floor. "Use it now. We reach port tonight. The evenin'. They won't unload till just before dawn."

"Thank you. Will you—"

"Be quiet. Listen to me. When the men come to take the animals, you get behind them cases all the way over there. Stay there. You hear me?"

"Can you help us?"

"Just do like I said. And keep quiet."

"You're going to help us, aren't you? What's your name?"

"It don't matter."

"Why are you helping us?"

"That don't matter either."

"Yes it does. Why?"

The African looked over the rows of caged, frightened faces. His voice was lower. "Because they sufferin'."

He turned and climbed the steps. Again they heard the heavy clang of the hatch being closed and secured.

Together Ancarit and Ansuro bent down over the sacks the African had dropped. They each pulled one open. Even in the dimmest of light they could see that one sack held loaves of bread. The other held fresh fruits they had not seen since leaving their rain forest village.

They each ate enough of the food to bring back their energy. The renewed strength propelled them to move as fast as they could. They tore off pieces of the bread and fruit to put into open mouths that begged through the bars of every cage. They rationed it until it went as far as it could go. When it was gone, they went back to bringing water until, once again, they fell exhausted onto the mats.

This time, the exhaustion was mingled with a sensation they thought they would never feel again. Hope.

* * *

Ancarit and Ansuro were in the midst of another round of water delivery when they felt the ship slowing. They could sense turns in the ship's motion until a sudden jarring threw them off balance.

Ansuro whispered. "We've docked. Now we wait."

They crouched behind the cases of animals at the rear of the chamber as the African had told them. It was an hour later that the hatch above clanged open. They recognized the soft footsteps of the African. They could tell from the sound that he came alone.

They came out of hiding to meet him. He brought them more food in a sack. This time he was close enough to hand it to them.

Ansuro spoke for both of them. "Where are we? And tell us, how do we call you?"

"My name don't matter. We in port. Someplace in Puerto Rico. I been here before on this ship."

"What will they do with the animals?"

"Listen to me. Not much time. They gonna unload the animals here. Sometime they gonna ship 'em to the coast of the United States mainland."

"Will they put them on a different ship?"

"Yeah. But not yet. I heard them talk. This time they gonna put 'em on trucks. They take 'em somewhere first. Somewhere inland."

"Why do they do that?"

"I don't know. I never been there. Listen to this. Pretty soon most of the crew be off this ship. They go in town to the bars. They gonna leave one, maybe two men to watch the hatch upstairs."

"Will they come down here?"

"No. They don't like the smell down here."

"What can we do?"

"You wait. The men from the trucks gonna come get the animals.

They come in the dark sometime before dawn. When the men from the trucks come down here, they won't know you. They maybe think you with the ship's crew. You can sneak out then."

"If we do, what's going to happen to these animals?"

The African looked from one to the other. "Whatever happen to them gonna happen anyway. You can't stop it. You did something good here. Now you gotta get out. No good for you to die, too."

Ansuro and Ancarit felt the same conflicted emotions. There was new hope that they might yet live another day. Still, their looks to each other carried a feeling of futility if what they'd done would have no effect on the fate of the animals they'd kept alive.

Ansuro looked back at the African. He pointed to the food. "I don't know how to thank you."

"Then don't. I know what you been doin' here."

"How did you know? You never saw what we did."

The African nodded to the cages. "Them. I done this trip three times before. I never seen this many of them still alive."

Ansuro had no answer. Before he could speak, the African turned to go. "Remember. When the men come from the trucks, you just walk off like you one of the crew."

They were alone again with fear for all of the pleading faces in the cages that surrounded them. They used the time for one last merciful delivery of water to the open mouths of the animals.

Then they lay down to wait.

TWENTY-FOUR

IF THERE WAS anything I had failed to absorb about the discipline of being on time during my three years with Mr. Devlin, Nestor had filled the gap. At ten minutes before midnight, I was in front of my hotel. I had shopped for the typical attire of a Mayagüez longshoreman at a store by the docks. My choice of clothing drew curious glances from those who could afford to stay at the resort hotel; but then, this was not the crowd with which I needed to blend.

When the black sedan pulled up to the curb, I jumped into the front seat while it was still on a slow roll. By now I knew enough to finesse any "How was your day?" patter.

"Where to, Nestor?"

I detected a brief smile of appreciation for the brevity. "The docks. The ship's in."

"Did Victor tell you when they'd unload?"

Nestor gave a slight backward nod of his head. "Ask him yourself."

"Hello, Mike."

I nearly got whiplash spinning my head toward the voice in the back seat. "Victor! Where the hell did you—"

"Long story. I'll give you a quick update."

I sat in silence as more of the missing pieces that had been gnawing at my sense of direction in this case poured out of Victor's mouth.

"When I got to Mayagüez, I got in touch with my cousin, Chico Mendosa. He told me to meet him in the back of a bar on the north side of the city, about fifteen minutes from here. I went with Jose Ramos, the big shot in the *insectos*. I introduced him to my cousin like I'd known Ramos for years. It seemed to go all right at the time. My cousin listened. He didn't say anything up or down. He said he'd have to check with his people and get back to us."

"It was that easy?"

"No."

"Why not?"

"When we started to leave, Chico asked me to stick around to talk about the family. We all shook hands. Jose went out the door. When I turned back to Chico, he grabbed a fistful of my hair with one hand and stuck the point of a knife to my throat with the other. I was scared crapless."

"So what happened?"

"Nothing. He just held me there for about ten seconds. I could feel my neck getting wet where he'd broken the skin. When I could get the words out, I said, 'What the hell, Chico?'"

"And?"

"He pushed the knife in a little deeper. I thought he was going to bleed me out right there. He pulled my head up next to his mouth so I could hear him whisper."

"What'd he say?"

"Damn! I can tell you his exact words. I'll never forget. He said, 'Blood is thick, Victor. But money is thicker. If I take you to my people and you're not on the level, this is exactly where they'll have us both. Only they won't stop with a little bloodletting. Do you understand me?' I said, 'Yes.' He said, 'Are you on the level with me?' I said, 'Yes.' He said, 'Do you swear it on your brother's soul?'"

Victor went silent for a few seconds. We gave him time.

"I love my brother. I said what I thought he'd want me to say. I said, 'Yes. I swear it.'"

"Did he buy it?"

"I think so."

"So what happened?"

"The next day he called me. He told me to come back around midnight to that same bar. He said we could do business. I asked if he wanted Jose Ramos, the *insecto*, to come with me. He told me he just wanted me. The fewer the better. He told me to bring $900,000 in cash for the first payment. When I told Jose, he said he could get it for me from the winnings on that fixed race. That night, Jose gave me a satchel to bring with me to the meeting."

"How did that go?"

"Quickly. When I got to the bar, the bartender brought me to the back room. Chico was there alone. He took the satchel and just set it down beside him. I asked him if he was going to count it. I hadn't even looked inside."

"Did he count it?"

"No. I think that was part of the show. The message was that no one would dare shortchange these people. But I'll tell you this. When I handed it to him and he set it down, he grabbed me with both arms and just held me there. I just about crapped my pants. Then when I looked at him, he was smiling. I realized he was just hugging me like a cousin. Somewhere I got the strength to hug him back."

"How'd he leave it?"

"He told me the ship with the animals we were buying had left Macapá. It's a port in Brazil. It was about a four- or five-day trip to get here. He'd let me know when it would get in. I was supposed to get word to Jose Ramos and the *insectos*."

"To do the unloading of the animals?"

"No. He said his men would do that. They had to take them somewhere first. Then they'd be brought back and put on another ship for somewhere on the coast of Florida. That's where they'd be smuggled into the mainland for sale. His people would set up the contacts. We could use their warehouse in Florida to keep the animals while they were being sold."

"Sold to whom?"

"Chico said he'd set up the deal with the wholesaler his people used. But he made it clear that once that ship left Mayagüez with the animals, it was up to the *insectos* to take charge of the operation. That way, the *insectos* took the full risk of smuggling them into the mainland. That was the deal."

"You said the $900,000 was the first payment. How much more?"

"Chico said we had to pay another $900,000 within a week."

"Where will the *insectos* get the money?"

"That's the worst part. They're flying me back to Boston tomorrow. Fat Tony is going to fix another race in a couple of days. They want me in the race as an insider to see that the other jockeys make it come out their way. If I think any of the jockeys are not going along, I'm supposed to tell Fat Tony. His boys will take it from there."

"So they trust the *insectos* to come up with the next $900,000."

"Trust, hell. Even the *insectos* are scared out of their minds to cross Chico's gang."

Nestor had been listening in silence. I looked over and noticed a look that said trouble. "Why are they taking the animals someplace else before they ship them?"

"I don't know. Chico didn't say. I wasn't about to ask. Maybe they have to check them out."

We all went silent for a few seconds. Nestor and I were ingesting a deeper glimpse of the bigger picture than we'd had since day one. The discontented look on Nestor's face intensified.

"What, Nestor? What's your problem?"

He looked at me for a few seconds. "There's a piece missing. We still don't have all of it."

I could almost read his thoughts, but I wanted to hear it. "Like what?"

He shook his head. "I hear what you're saying, Victor. It still doesn't sound right to me. Chico's gang can make a big profit on that shipload of animals and keep it all themselves. They've been doing it for years. Why would they be willing to share the profits with the *insectos*?"

"How about the $900,000 I delivered to them, with another $900,000 in a week? That pays for the animals and gives them the profit before they even have to make delivery."

"Have they ever had trouble financing these deals themselves in the past? I don't think so."

"Maybe they liked the idea of shifting the risk of getting caught in the smuggling to the *insectos*."

Nestor looked at Victor in the rearview mirror. "Why now? Word is they've been greasing the customs agents somewhere on the coast of Florida for years. No one raises a big fuss over smuggled animals. Even if they're caught, the fines are a minor business cost."

Nestor looked at me. He just tilted his head to ask if I had the same feeling. I nodded. "It's got me, too. We're missing something."

Victor raised his hands. "I guess we go with what we have. What else can we do? It's too late to pull out."

This time Nestor turned around to look Victor in the eye. "We can be damn careful. Especially you, Victor. You're the closest to them. What we're not seeing could come down on you."

"I know. Which brings us to tonight. Now that the ship's in, the *insectos* want me to check out the animals for them. They figure I can get on board by using my cousin's name. That's why I contacted you, Nestor. I thought you two might want to go along."

Nestor gave me a "what the hell" look. "Then let's do it."

TWENTY-FIVE

NESTOR LEFT THE headlights off. He cruised to within a hundred feet of the gangplank up to the sea-worn ship with the name *Nuestra Señora de Guadalupe* on its stern. The three of us walked to it in silence through a shroud of fog.

A few faint lights fore and aft were the only indication that anything human might be on board. There was a rhythmic slogging of waves against the hull that caused the old bucket to groan and give out enough death rattles to scare off a battle-scarred wharf rat.

We climbed the gangplank single file with a wary eye to anything or anyone who might challenge our coming aboard. Nothing stirred. If the condition of the ship was an indication of the caliber of the crew, Nestor was probably right that they were all well into their rum in the nearest bar. Still, even on that sultry night, I could feel the fight-or-flight chills tickling the base of my spine.

Nestor took the lead. The storage of anything large had to be below deck. Instinct more than sight took him toward a large hatch in the center of an open section of the deck. We closed ranks to keep a close unit as we approached.

Nestor took hold of the massive handle on the hatch. He looked back at us before hoisting it. His facial expression did nothing to settle the chills.

Victor and I both gave him a go-ahead nod. Nestor put his back into the lifting of the hatch. It gave off a creaking groan. The shrieking command, "Drop it!" that came from behind made us bolt straight up.

The three of us spun in the direction of the pitch-black darkness that covered the source of the voice. I went into a tight crouch and took the path of silence. Nestor's breathing was the only thing that gave away his state of shock—that, and the slight glint of light on the barrel of the gun in his right hand. The best he could do was aim it at the voice in the dark. He was the first to be able to speak. "Who the hell are you?"

The voice came back. "The question, mate, is who the hell are you?"

The blinding beam of a flashlight caught the three of us dead center. Whoever held it responded to the gun first. "Put it away, mate. You have one second before I blow the three of you to hell."

Nestor didn't drop it, but he was realist enough to lower it to his side. By this time, Victor was regaining control of his voice. "You do and you'll answer to Chico Mendosa. He sent us. He told us to check out the animals."

Apparently the name of Victor's cousin was the effective password. The voice came down half an octave and softened. "Why the hell didn't you say so? I could have blown your heads off."

I heard him hit a switch on the metal wall behind him. Another weak bulb came alive above our heads. It gave enough light to see a scruffy, bearded sailor in the act of lowering a double-barrel shotgun.

"They're down there. You doin' the unloading?"

"No. Not yet. They'll do that later."

"It can't be too soon."

"Yeah? Why?"

"Open that hatch. You'll see. Close it when you go down. I have to breathe up here."

With that ominous preface, the three of us looked at each other for solidarity. None of us wanted to take that next step.

Nestor took another grip on the hatch and put his weight into pulling it open. A cloud of stench like nothing I'd ever experienced engulfed us as if it were literally dying to escape from whatever was below.

We gave it a few seconds to let the acid smell that stung our nostrils dissipate, if it would, and to get control of the clenching muscles in our stomachs. Nestor looked back at the sailor. "Let me use your flashlight. This won't take long."

Apparently Chico Mendosa's name was still working its magic. He handed it over.

We looked at each other for a decision on the marching order. Nestor bowed to our hesitation and took the lead. He took the first five steps down into the chamber below. I could see the beam of the flashlight in his hand coursing around whatever was down there. I'd have followed next, but Nestor stopped cold. I heard him utter words to no one in particular in a tone I never expected from him. "My God. So this is hell."

I had to force my legs to take the steps behind him. My eyes followed the beam of light as it played across a scene that no words could describe. I saw the faces of animals, birds, creatures I'd never seen before, crammed body to body on top of each other in cages too small for any one of their kind. I could say that the stench was what made my knees nearly buckle, but that wasn't really it. If ever fear and desperation could be distilled into one sea of faces, so overpowering that no mind could encompass it, this was what gripped our eyes, our minds, and our souls. Somehow I found the voice to answer the words Nestor hadn't really addressed to me. "This must be hell."

At the bottom of the stairs, the three of us made our way together following the light in Nestor's hand. We passed through a narrow passageway between the stacks of cages. I was stunned to notice that practically no sound came from the animals. Their confinement had apparently been so torturous and so prolonged that it stifled even the hope and strength necessary to cry for help.

By the time we had passed halfway to the back of the room, we had seen enough. There was no point in going further. Nestor signaled us to turn around. He pointed the light beam behind us. We started back toward the stairs with Victor in the lead, me next, and Nestor behind.

We had taken about three steps, when a sharp pained grunt from Nestor followed the sound of something heavy coming down on flesh and bone. I spun around, but the flashlight he had held was rolling across the floor. In the darkness, I could only hear a scuffle between Nestor and what sounded like two men.

I ran to where I heard the flashlight rolling against a cage. I grabbed it and spun around to cast light on the scuffle. Nestor was trying to throw what looked like an old man off his shoulders. Another younger man held him in a grip around his throat.

I could see the strength that came from desperation in the faces of the two attackers, but even together they were no match for Nestor. In two moves, he had the two forced up against the stack of cages. He had one in each hand in a tightening grip on their throats. Their arms and legs were flailing at him, but Nestor clearly had their lives in his hands.

I was certain that within moments there would be two more lifeless bodies in that room. And there would have been, but for a voice that boomed and echoed from the steps. "Stop it! Leave them two alone! Now!"

The three of us turned to see a massive black African man descending the stairs. The club he held in his giant fist seemed more threatening than a gun. Nestor froze in place.

"Let them men go. You hear me. They not your enemies. They not hurtin' your animals. They keepin' 'em alive."

Nestor relaxed his grip on the throats of the two men. He turned to face the approaching African.

"You leave them two alone. You hear me? You hurt them two, you answer to me."

The African was just a few feet from us and still approaching with the club raised. Nestor spoke from behind us. His voice was calmer and lower than I expected. "We're not your enemy, either. They're not our animals. Listen to me. We came to help them. I think we're on the same side."

There were a few seconds of indecision. The six of us were frozen in position. Nestor and the African were each trying to read the face of the other. Nestor moved first. He pulled the gun out of his belt from behind his back. I was afraid he'd use it just to be sure. Instead he just showed it to the African and laid it down on the floor. He held his arms and hands out straight. Victor and I did the same. The African looked into each of our faces for a few seconds before he raised his hands in the same gesture.

The African brushed past me and Victor and bent down to help the two men Nestor had been holding. They had dropped to the floor when he released them. The African took the hand of each of them to help them up. "You all right? He didn't hurt you too much?"

The older man shook his head. "We're all right. I think we have to trust him. And these two men. We have to trust someone or we'll all be dead. Then no one will help these animals."

The African nodded. He turned to Nestor and Victor and me. "Who are you? Why you want to help?"

Nestor took the lead. He explained quickly what had brought the three of us down those steps. He made it clear that each of us had reasons of our own for wanting to help the caged animals. Different as those reasons were, they put us all on the same side.

"And who are you?"

The older man spoke first. "My name is Ansuro. I'm from a village on the Amazon in Brazil. That's where many of these animals were captured. This is my grandson, Ancarit."

Ansuro gave a brief account of what had brought him and his grandson to the hold of that ship, and more importantly, what they had been doing during the voyage. They pointed to the African, who had previously told the two of them that his name was Martin. "This man, Martin, he's from Sierra Leone in Africa. He is an angel of God. Without him . . ."

Ansuro's voice caught, but even without specifics, we knew what he was expressing. While time permitted, there was more to say on each side. Every part of it cemented the six of us more tightly in a single purpose—to save the animals that were still alive. The fundamental question for all of us was how it could be done. Amazingly, in that new brotherhood, none of us was asking, "And how do we escape with our own lives?"

Each of us was aware that the hour of dawn was approaching. According to Victor's information, the men from his cousin's gang would be coming before daylight to remove the animals. We assumed from what Victor said that they would be taken by truck to land. We had no idea where or how to follow them.

Eventually a rough plan took shape. It was far from foolproof, but each of us signed on without reservation. Victor, Nestor, and I climbed the steps back to the deck. The sun had yet to make an appearance to give us away to any unfriendly eyes.

We passed the lone sailor who kept watch when we had come aboard. We had intended to mumble something inconsequential on the way by, like "*Adios,* mate," but it was unnecessary. Their watchful guard was deep in the arms of Morpheus.

On the dock, Nestor, Victor, and I took up a position out of sight beside one of the storage buildings. We settled in to watch. Within a half hour, three large army-type trucks with canvas covered beds pulled up alongside the gangplank. A crew of three dressed in what looked like longshoreman garb got out of each of the trucks. No words were spoken as they mounted the gangplank single file. They went straight to the hold in the center of the deck.

Within minutes, we saw the men reappear from the hold below, each laboring under the weight of a cage crammed full of animals. They hoisted the cages into the canvas-covered backs of the three trucks.

The rough, callous handling of the cages of defenseless animals by these thugs spurred a heartfelt, but ill-advised, impulse to send a few rounds of ammunition in their direction. Cooler thoughts prevailed. We all knew there was much more at stake than what was happening before our eyes.

A slight hint of sunlight was beginning to light the sky by the time they finished. The light was enough for the three of us to spot Ansuro and Ancarit bending their backs to join in the carrying of cages along with the trucks' crews. As we had hoped, the thugs apparently thought they were part of the ship's crew lending a hand. They were not about to refuse help with a job no human could possibly enjoy.

We watched closely toward the end of the loading. In the sparse, dusky light, the truck crew, sweating and weary from their labors, never noticed that Ansuro and Ancarit stowed away among the cages in the third truck.

As the trucks turned and pulled slowly away from the pier, I felt that sense of helplessness welling up again. It was probably shared by Victor and Nestor. I could not imagine what emotions the two

Brazilian natives must have been feeling. They were now part of the contraband shipment heading God only knew where, but most certainly into the hands of a gang that valued profits well above human or any other form of life.

There was nothing to do now but wait. When we forged the rough plan together in the hold, I had given the cell phone I had received from Nestor to the old man, Ansuro. Assuming that he and Ancarit survived the unloading undetected and could describe their location, the plan was that they would use the phone to inform Nestor. That could be hours or even days away.

* * *

The sun was well up by the time Nestor dropped me at my hotel. I knew Victor would be phoning his report on the animals to the head of the *insectos,* Jose Ramos, before flying back to Boston. He had one more fixed race to pull off for Fat Tony Cannucci to raise the second installment of payment for the animals.

It must have crossed Victor's mind, as it did mine, that once that fixed race was run, and the animals were smuggled into the mainland and sold for an enormous profit, Victor's usefulness to the two gangs involved would have run its course. He'd be a liability as a witness to people who seldom left such liabilities breathing.

Nestor and I agreed that I could be of more use on the Boston end. He could keep me informed of anything he learned from the two Brazilians.

I had three calls to make from my hotel room. The first was to book a seat on the next plane that morning to Boston. The second was to Mr. Devlin to let him know that he still had a living, breathing partner, who would soon be making the most joyful entrance of his life into the Boston offices of Devlin & Knight.

The third call was the most important. I knew it would take longer, and I didn't want it to be rushed. On the drive back to the hotel, I had done one of the most serious life evaluations of my twenty-seven years. I let a decision percolate long enough to be sure it wasn't the result of stress or exhaustion. When I reached my hotel room, I waited to pick up the phone until I was as certain as I could be of what I was about to say.

Then I dialed Terry's number.

TWENTY-SIX

My phone call reached Terry at home in Winthrop before she left for work. When the excitement of reconnecting had been fully felt and expressed between us, I settled down to explain to Terry the conclusion that I found inescapable from a consideration of the previous three days. I had thought and rethought of the number of times in that short period that every dream of our life together could have been snuffed out in one fatal instant. The immediate days ahead held prospects of the same kind of uncertainty. That forced the making of a decision for each of us. We go forward with the dream, or we say it would be kinder and wiser to end it now.

For me, the decision was easy and irrevocable. We cling to the dream and live it for as long as God keeps it alive. But the decision had to be hers, too. I left it equally in her hands.

I asked the question, and my breathing stopped. It began again in three seconds. That was the time it took her to express her decision. I was apparently engaged to a lady who was as impractically in love as I was.

That was important, but it was just the first part of the decision. I had also concluded for my part that our dreams were far too precious to leave indefinitely in the grip of an unpredictable future. I couldn't guess what the next twenty-four hours held, let alone the next eight months.

That being so, I suggested to Terry the possibility of our meeting with our wedding planner, Janet Reading—who would undoubtedly consider the two of us mentally deranged for even considering it—and moving the date of our wedding from sometime in the spring to the following Saturday.

Terry's only response was, "I'll call Janet. Let's put it together tomorrow at lunch."

My heart took a small trip upwards into my throat. I could hardly get out the word, "Where?"

It was a foolish question. The Parker House, of course.

* * *

Some sights and sounds imbed themselves so deeply in our memories that instant recall is available forever. High on that list is the joyous, squealing sound of the rubber tires of that 747 grabbing the asphalt on Runway 27 at Logan Airport sometime after midnight. The sight that went with it was equally joyous—the view across Boston Harbor of that sleepy peninsula called Point Shirley in Winthrop.

I was in mid-debate with myself about dragging my sleepless bones and unshaven face directly to the Andrew Street address on that peninsula and waking Terry out of a sound sleep, or waiting until morning. Logic had no place in the debate. When I walked off the plane into the nearly abandoned terminal, the decision had already been made to offer a hefty tip to any cabbie who knew the shortcuts to Winthrop.

It turned out that I was not the only one with a total disregard for the hour. When I came through the ramp into terminal C3, I could hardly believe what I was seeing. I can still recall every nuance of joy radiating from Terry's smile. Her arms were open, and I was in them, and every trace of the paralyzing fears and frustrations of the previous week dissolved.

That night I slept the sleep of one who could finally let go of every fear and dread of the day ahead—at least for one night. The next morning, the sweet aroma of my own blend of coffee in my own apartment on Beacon Street said "You're home." I won't say that the elevator ride to the Devlin & Knight suite of offices on the seventh floor of 77 Franklin Street was exactly the "Stairway to Paradise," but it was so damned close, it could have fooled me.

I made no stops between the elevator door and the corner office of Mr. Devlin. He was behind his desk when he saw me. The emotion that framed that crusty old trial warrior's face will also remain with me forever. He walked around his desk as if he had difficulty believing what he saw.

We just looked at each other for a second. He was the first to get his voice back. "Michael—Don't you ever—I don't give a damn who the client is—"

His words ended there, but for the first time in the three years we'd known each other, he held out his arms. I moved to respond, and we actually hugged each other like the father and son we'd grown to be.

There was so much to say. In my usual verbal reports to Mr. D., I frequently underplay the danger of situations I stumble into in defending our clients. I do it both to save him the anxiety, and, frankly, to save myself the barrier I know he'd raise to my doing what I know has to be done. In this case, I laid out every bit of it, no punches pulled.

We agreed that a meeting with Deputy District Attorney Billy Coyne was in order. I also knew that nothing could take precedence over my lunch with Terry at the Parker House. Mr. D. and I agreed to meet at our usual Marliave Restaurant for dinner at seven. He knew that Mr. Coyne would cancel anything to be there, salivating for any details I could give him, as well as a dinner at the hands of John Ricciutti.

I next checked in with my assistant, Julie. It turned out that she was so emotional about our reunion with my life intact that she ignored, let alone forgave, my abandoning her to the depredations of incensed clients and opposing counsel. There was another hug there, and for a brief humbling second, I gave thanks for the blessing of those three people who cared deeply that I was still alive.

The lunch meeting with Terry and Janet at the Parker House was a complete hoot. Janet was to meet us there a half hour after we arrived. That gave Terry and me time to reaffirm our decision not to waste an unnecessary hour of our lives apart. It meant moving the date of our wedding up to that Saturday. We knew we needed a united front on the date before breaking the news to Janet.

True to form, Janet blew into the main dining room her accustomed ten minutes late. The radiant smile on her face said she had no inkling of what we were going to lay on her. We stuck to small talk long enough to let her polish off most of her Beefeater's martini.

Terry and I had decided that I should break it to her on the chance that she'd be less likely to come sailing across the table for my throat. On that supposition, I simply said, "Janet, brace yourself."

The smile froze. "For what, Michael?"

"The wedding that you're so meticulously planning for a date eight months from now—"

"Which," she broke in, "is already stressing me out. You know I need at least twelve months—"

"Janet, grab the table with both hands and hold on tight. The wedding is going to be next Saturday."

She just smiled. "Michael, your damned Irish sense of humor is going to have me planning my own wake instead of your wedding."

She signaled the waiter to bring another Beefeater's, telling him to skip the vermouth. "Now Michael, Terry, can we have a civilized conversation?"

"We can, Janet. Here are the details. It will be next Saturday. It's going to be here at the Parker House. If they give you any grief, which they won't, use Mr. Devlin's name. That will break any log-jam. Terry and I will contact the members of the wedding party. You have the guest list. Same list as before. If anyone can't make it on short notice, we'll connect with them for a dinner later."

At first, her eyes just glazed over. Then, as it sank in, I could see the fire intensifying in each pupil. Just before the explosion that I knew would accompany the words, "Absolutely impossible", I laid any argument to rest—for better or worse. "Janet, listen to me. That date is fixed in stone. Everything else we leave in your capable hands."

She froze. The recalculations that were spinning her mental wheels had her locked in stunned silence. I stood up and gave her a kiss on the cheek. She never moved. I thought her eyes were going to start spinning like a casino slot machine.

Her first movement was to reach across the aisle to snatch the second martini from the tray of the waiter. While she ingested it in gulps rather than sips, I looked at Terry.

I kissed her and whispered, "That should calm her. Can you take it from here?"

"I'll get her a third martini. She'll be fine."

"Call me if you need fortification. I have a dinner tonight with Mr. Devlin. Let's meet later at Big Daddy's. Around eleven?"

"I'll see you there."

* * *

There were five hours open before meeting Mr. D. and Billy Coyne at the Marliave. It was time to step out of the calm I was so enjoying and wade back into the vortex of the storm. One of the major loose ends that I had left dangling when I jumped from the frying pan in Boston into the fire in Mayagüez was still hanging, much as I'd have loved to ignore it.

The night after my meeting with Paco, my now-apparent savior from the wrath of the Coyotes years ago when I chose to leave the gang, there was an incident that I could ignore only at considerable risk. By the time I found Paco at Jamaica Pond he had been fatally wounded. His killer came within a count of three of putting a bullet through one of my own vital organs. Had it not been for a shot from somewhere around the dark edge of the pond to the heart of my intended assassin, this recounting would have been cut decidedly short.

That left three pressing questions: Who, with an incentive to kill Paco, knew about the time and place of our meeting? Why, at that point, would that person want me equally dead? And who was the marksman whose bullet kept me alive? These were more than curiosity. I had no reason to hope that putting an end to my existence had lost its appeal to someone. In fact, if there was a connection between that night and the bombing of my sweet Corvette, which was likely, I realized I'd do well to make the answers to those questions a high priority.

In about twenty minutes, I was parking my replacement Corvette in Hyde Square, Jamaica Plain, in about the same spot I had parked that morning about a hundred years ago—or so it seemed. I figured that the twelve-year-old kid who showed up to watch my car that morning had claimed that stretch of sidewalk as his private turf for car-watching. Sure enough, he was there sitting on the sidewalk, waiting for me to pay tribute so that his implied suggestion of the possible desecration of my car might be magically averted.

I doubled the fee, which lit up his larcenous little eyes.

"What's your name, son?"

"Armando. Why?"

That told me just one thing. Of all the Latino names in the register, his was not Armando. But at least I had something to call him. I needed five minutes alone with him away from spying eyes that could be in any window of any building.

"How would you like a ride in a Corvette, Armando?"

To any twelve-year-old in almost any other neighborhood, that would sound like fun—and, being a car ride with a stranger, just the thing their mothers had warned them against. I could see enough of myself at twelve in little Armando, or whatever his name was, to see his mind calculating a profit.

"Why not. Can I drive?"

"Just get in the car, Armando."

We drove in silence the ten minutes to the lonely Jamaica Pond area. I pulled over to the curb by the shore. I looked over. Armando sat there with the slight grin of one who is about to get an offer that could only result in ready cash.

"I need some information, Armando."

"Don't we all, boss?"

"About a week ago, you watched my car."

"Who could forget? It wasn't this one, though."

That surprised even me. I thought they were identical. That was good news. This little bundle of precocious greed had an eye for detail.

"Two funny things happened that day."

"That a fact, boss?"

"The old man, they call him 'Paco.' He came out of Pepe's bar. He gave you a note and told you to slip it into my pocket when I picked up the car."

"You don't say."

"I do say. And you did just that."

"Amazing I don't remember that, boss."

"Don't worry about it. We haven't gotten to the cash part yet. You read the note before you put it in my pocket."

"Hey, man, you think I don't respect people's privacy?"

I pitched my tone to the twenty-year-old attitude of a street-educated kid that had been my attitude too at his age.

"Let's get real, Armando. I have no intention of doing you any harm whatsoever. In fact, I feel rather protective for reasons I'm not about to explain. I want you to start ringing that cash register in your head. All I want to hear at the end of this is the total charge in cash for one bit of information. Can we cut the preliminaries?"

I could see what looked like a bit of surprise in his frozen grin.

"Hey, man, you supposed to be some big-shot lawyer. How come you talk like that?"

"Not so much 'big shot', Armando. But someday the fact that I'm a lawyer might do you a lot of good. That's for another day. Today, we're doing business like two *muchachos*. You read the note because you figured there may be a buck to be made with the information. I'd have done the same thing at your age right there on that same street. Let's move on."

He just looked at me. The brick wall between us seemed a bit softer.

"And you did make a buck on it. Someone asked you what the note said. Now you're going to make another buck on it. I need that name."

I reached in my shirt pocket and pulled out the two twenties, neatly folded, that I had put there when I first saw Armando on the sidewalk. I held them out. I knew he saw them. He just kept looking out the front window.

I knew the language. I took the other two twenties I had folded out of the same pocket. Now he was looking at the ceiling. I took out one more twenty. He turned away to look out of the side window. Again I read him. I slipped all of the bills into his shirt pocket.

I put the car in gear and drove back to where I had picked him up without either of us exchanging a look or a word. He got out of the car and took up his position on the sidewalk. I drove off without attracting any more attention than necessary.

I was on the outskirts of Jamaica Plain when I pulled over. It was no surprise that I had felt nothing. And yet, when I reached into the same pocket where I had found the previous note, there was another. It had just three words written in juvenile handwriting.

"Pepe's bartender, Manuel."

TWENTY-SEVEN

IF I'D NOT been too distracted to give it a few seconds thought over the past week, I could have narrowed it down to Manuel. The only ones who might have known about that meeting at Jamaica Pond were Paco, me, the boy . . . and Manuel. It was disturbing to think that I'd missed that. In this game, that kind of lapse could easily prove terminal. Lesson learned.

* * *

Pepe's Bar was dark and devoid of any of the Coyote or *Nyeta* members who tended to hang out there. The Puerto Rican salsa that was playing in the background kept Manuel from hearing me approach the bar from the side. I slipped under the break in the bar and came up behind him.

One tap on his shoulder triggered two reflexes. The first was a spinning jump backwards away from this intruder. The second, when he saw my face, was a stab of the left hand into the shelf area under the bar. His eyes were riveted on mine, while his hand ran like a windshield wiper over the shelf.

I gave him a few seconds to search.

"Is this what you want, Manuel?"

I held up the snub-nose pistol that I'd lifted from the shelf before

I got his attention. His eyes went from the pistol back to me. The fire that burned in those eyes could have started a barn fire.

I moved around to a point where I had him facing me and pinned against the bar. For the first time in recent memory, I had the advantage of a good five inches of height, fifty pounds, thirty years in age, and possession of the only gun in the house. It inspired the sense of control I needed.

"What the hell you doin' here? You get outta here. You made your choice a long time ago."

"I don't think so, Manuel. You and I are going to talk to each other. We should have done it that first day. It could have saved a good man's life."

"I don't know what you talkin' about. But you go ahead and hang around. You stay till our boys get here. Won't be long. Then you get what you shoulda got a lot of years ago."

He was locked onto the bar with both fists. Beads of perspiration started appearing on his balding head. I could sense his every nerve and muscle on high alert. It was not what I wanted. I needed to deactivate the bomb ticking inside of him.

I dropped my voice an octave lower, just above a whisper, and filled it with a soothing balm. "Go easy, Manuel. I'm not going to hurt you. We're just going to talk like two rational people on the same side."

"The hell we're on the same side. When my boys walk through that—"

His eyes fell on my hand holding up the key that he recognized as being from the front door. They flashed back to the window with its blind drawn and the sign I'd turned outward to read "Closed."

"I'm giving you the afternoon off, Manuel. We'll have a talk. Then I'll leave. You can reopen. Nothing more than that. Yes?"

It took a few seconds, but the intense heat seemed to subside. I emphasized my calming goodwill by backing off and walking around the bar to a table. I laid the gun in the middle of the table and sat down. He watched the whole performance before he followed me to the table.

"Sit down, Manuel. We've got things to talk about."

"Yeah." He said it quietly, but I caught an instant's glint of the old passion rekindling in his eyes. He leaned over the table as he pulled out the chair. I looked away for a second. I heard the chair tumble backward. I looked back to see him move faster than I thought he could. He snatched the gun off the table and backed off a step.

I froze in position. His right arm was straight out. The gun was shaking, but never leaving the target of my face.

"This is for Paco!"

There were expletives with it that poured out of him like fifteen years of pent-up rage that was about to be fulfilled in one final act of revenge. I forced myself to keep calm.

"Don't do it, Manuel. We need each other."

"Like hell!"

The hand and gun were shaking violently now.

"You can do more for Paco if you let me live. You don't understand. You kill me and you'll be helping the ones who killed Paco. There's nothing the *insectos* want more."

That seemed to buy me a few more seconds. He was caught between two hatreds, undecided which trumped the other.

"It was an *insecto* who got to Jamaica Pond ahead of me. He cut Paco's veins till every drop of his blood was drained. Listen to me, Manuel. Paco loved us both. You know that. Would he want this? You answer that. And be honest."

I just looked into his eyes in silence. The battle raging inside of them seemed to give way slowly by inches to more rational thought.

Whatever I said that tipped the balance seemed to help settle the waters. I could see the gun fall away by inches. When it was by his side, I picked up the chair from behind him and held it open to him.

"Just sit, Manuel. Talk to me."

"Talk is cheap. You walked away from the gang. Paco stood in your place. He took the beating that should have put you in the grave. You did that to him."

He pointed the gun back in my direction, but his finger was off the trigger.

"Yes, Manuel. Now I know it. I didn't then, but that was my fault. I have to live with that." I leaned across the table, closer to the gun, but also closer to his face.

I put all the intensity I could into the words. "But you did worse. You found out about my meeting with Paco. You told someone about it. And that—listen to me. Listen to the truth. That caused Paco's death. I may have hurt him, but you killed him. Which is worse?"

The gun hand fell to his side. The moisture was not sweat now but tears. His head hung down. He seemed lost in the guilt he had been able to suppress under his hatred for me.

"Sit down, Manuel. Guilt is no good for either of us. It just eats us up. Let's do something together for Paco. Let's see that he didn't die for nothing."

He dropped into the chair. He was staring straight ahead, but I sensed that he was listening.

"Manuel, that day that I came here, Paco left a note for me with the boy. You paid the boy to tell you what was in the note. You heard that Paco and I were meeting that night at midnight at Jamaica Pond."

He looked over at me. There was no denial in his expression.

"You told someone. It might have gotten Paco killed. I know it's not what you intended. I'm not blaming you. But for Paco's sake now, whom did you tell?"

I leaned closer to hear what I expected to be the name of one of the heads of the *insectos*. It was my turn to be stunned when he barely whispered the name. "Ramon Garcia."

It took me a second. "Why Ramon Garcia? He loved Paco."

"That was why. I didn't trust you. I figured you asked for the meeting. I thought you might be setting a trap for Paco. I told Mr. Garcia about the meeting so he could protect Paco. I don't know what happened after that. The next day, I heard Paco was dead."

It took me a few seconds just to sort out the possibilities. Like every other time I got an answer in this quagmire, it just led to more questions.

I stood up and put my hand on Manuel's shoulder. "If I get this thing sorted out, Manuel, I'll come back and tell you what happened. Just don't shoot me the next time I come through that door."

I started to leave, but he caught my arm. "You trusted me." He held up the gun. "You left the gun where I could grab it. Why? I was ready to kill you."

"I had to get you to trust me. Otherwise you wouldn't have told me what I had to know. Would you?"

He shook his head. "No. I wouldn't."

I looked in his eyes that no longer seemed to burn with hatred. I figured one last shot of honesty couldn't hurt. I took his hand. I turned it over, and dropped into it the bullets from the gun that I had removed before I put it on the table.

I saw the faintest trace of a smile. He just shook his head. "Never trust a lawyer."

"Except this one, Manuel. You can trust this one."

* * *

It was about three in the afternoon when I parked a block away and walked to the Puerto Rican Restaurant, El Rey de Lechón, off Roslindale Square. I'd parked there before on Ramon Garcia's instructions. This time it was out of pure self-preservation. I figured the less known about my whereabouts, the more likely my continuing to breathe.

I walked through the alleyway to the kitchen entrance. The door was open to exhaust the heat. The aromas of whatever magic Ben Capone, the chef, had performed for the lunch menu flowed out as well. I caught the unmistakable scent of *huaraches de Nopalitos.*

Ben was alone in the kitchen. I caught his attention as he was drying the last frying pan. It was good to see someone who flashed an instant smile when he saw me.

"Couldn't stay away, could you?"

We shook hands, and I held his hand as I asked, "*Huaraches,* right?"

"You have a good nose."

"Damn. And I missed it. If you ever tell my mother, I'll deny I said it. She's the best, but you could take her to school. You sure you're not full-blood Puerto Rican?"

"Not unless a few *muchachos* landed on the east shore of Sicily. Come on in, Michael. He's inside."

I walked into the otherwise empty dining room. Mr. Garcia was at a far table, back to the wall. He was on the phone, but I caught the blossoming of a smile when he saw me. These welcomes were good for the soul. I had to do this more often.

I accepted the hand-wave invitation to sit opposite him. He signaled something to Ben as I sat down. Whether for privacy or courtesy, he cut the call short. We had a few minutes of warm casual conversation before I heard Ben's footsteps behind me.

Before I could look around, Ben set in front of me a plate of hot *huaraches* that took my breath away. Mr. Garcia could only grin when he saw the expression on my face. He gave a nod of approval to Ben, who retired with a grin of his own to his kitchen chores.

Mr. Garcia held his hands out in invitation. "We'll talk while you eat, Michael. You'll never find better."

And I never will. I tried to follow the casual conversation, but my mind was clearly savoring every nuance of flavor Ben had woven into the magic he had set before me. Since I'd been too pressed for time to order anything at the Parker House, every corner of my empty, growling stomach was pleading for the next bite. I finished with regret the last morsel on the plate and just sighed. Mr. Garcia caught my meaning.

"Now, Michael, we have more serious matters. I've heard from Nestor Ruiz. He called me from Mayagüez. I'd say you and he had an adventure or two."

"There were some interesting moments."

"So he said. Enough to convince me that if there were any doubt of your . . . commitment, shall we say loyalty, there could be none now. I hope you feel the same. We need to share information so all the pieces will fit. Do you agree?"

"More than I could say. Let me begin, Mr. Garcia. Without any more vague hints, I believe I can assume that you are the head of the *Nyetas* in Boston, perhaps Massachusetts, perhaps New England."

I paused while he leaned closer in silence. When he spoke, it was in a voice that seemed to say that he was crossing a difficult threshold. "I wouldn't say this to another living soul, Michael. Even the men I command. I hope you appreciate the level of trust."

My eyes never left his. "I do."

"And I hope you realize that if one word of this reached the ears of any number of people, my death would be assured."

He said it calmly, but the weight of it suddenly descended on my shoulders. I held his eyes and spoke with the same deliberate calm. "I do understand, Mr. Garcia. As I heard recently from the bartender, Manuel, words are cheap. These words are not. You'll never feel the pain of betrayal from me."

"So I'm told by our friend Nestor. Then to your assumption, I'll say a simple 'Yes.' Now, you first. What can you tell me?"

"You probably heard at least part of this from Nestor. The informant you had with the *insectos* in Mayagüez was discovered. I was there when Nestor rescued him from a jail cell. He was close to death. God willing, he's recovering."

"And so he is. Nestor says he's growing stronger every day."

"Good. He was tortured by the *insectos* to the extreme. Nestor might have told you, but I can confirm it. He said he told the *insectos* nothing. For what it's worth, I believe him."

"It's worth a lot, Michael. I trust Nestor with my life. But two opinions are better than one. What else?"

"I talked to Victor. The *insectos* keep him involved because they need his influence with his cousin in Mayagüez. His cousin's gang has the contacts for shipment and smuggling of the animals into Florida."

"Who will they sell them to in Florida?"

"I don't know. Victor's cousin says he has contacts there, too. I only know there's a great deal of money involved."

In the disconnect of Mr. Garcia's gaze, I could see that he was calculating the threat of open warfare with the *insectos* that infusion of that kind of money would make inevitable.

"There's more, Mr. Garcia. Victor says the *insectos* don't have enough money to pay the full price of the animals yet. They made a lot on that fixed race, but not enough. They need to fix another race to get the rest. They sent Victor back to Boston to help pull it off."

"Will Victor do it?"

"Not alone. He'll ride in the race and keep tabs on the other jock-eys. But it's the Italians, the mafia in the North End. They're in this too. There's a man called Fat Tony Cannucci. He's the mafia expert in fixing races. The *insectos* need that expertise. It's not as easy as it sounds. I'm sure the profits from the animals will be split between the *insectos* and the mafia. From what I hear, there's plenty to go around."

"So if we get Victor to refuse to go along with the fix . . ."

"I don't think so."

I could see an instant reaction in his eyes. "Why not?"

"Because we haven't seen the bottom of this well yet. The animals came into the Mayagüez port on a ship. They could have sailed on to the Florida coast once they're paid for. Or they could have been loaded onto another ship for transport. They weren't. They were loaded onto trucks and taken somewhere inland."

"Where?"

"I don't know."

"Why?"

"That's the question. I don't know that either. Yet."

That last word raised his eyebrows in the obvious question. I leaned closer. "I may know soon. Before we talk about that, could we discuss something else?"

He raise his hands in a "why not?" gesture.

"That night Paco was killed at Jamaica Pond. Manuel told me that he got word to you that I was meeting Paco there at midnight. What happened?"

I could see the pain in his eyes when he thought of it. "When I came here that evening, I got the message Manuel left. He was concerned that you were meeting Paco secretly to do him harm. Clearly, he didn't trust you. You and I had never met. I had only his word."

"What did you do?"

"I sent a man to Jamaica Pond to be there at midnight to protect Paco." There was a pause. "He got there too late. Before midnight, Paco had arrived. When my man got there, Paco was tied to a bench, bleeding. He was too far gone to save. You found Paco a couple of minutes later."

"And that same man who killed Paco, that *insecto,* he was about to kill me. It was your man who fired first."

"Yes."

"And saved my life."

"I say 'Thank God' now. My man could see that you were trying to help Paco."

"I'll never forget the debt I owe you, Mr. Garcia."

He just smiled and patted my folded hands on the table. I reached over and took his arm in my hand. I stood and urged him to his feet. In the blink of an eye, a major domino had tumbled in my mind.

"Before I leave, my car's just down the street. It's sort of a classic. A Corvette. I've heard you have a great interest in special cars. You might find it interesting. Would you like to walk with me?"

"Of course, Michael."

I hesitated. "One last thing. You asked about Victor. Let me explain. I think we should tell Victor to go through with the fixing of the race."

"And give them the money they need to do this thing with the animals?"

"Yes. Even so."

"Why?"

"I know these people, Mr. Garcia. I know of this Fat Tony Cannucci. If Victor does anything to block their plans, he'll die. His family will all die. I needn't tell you how. I think you know that Victor is not just my client. He's my cousin. He's my blood. I can't let that happen to him. Don't lose hope. I may have another way to upset their plans."

I could see that something was not sitting right with him. He thought for a moment before getting it out. "But Victor defied them before. They tried to force him to pull his horse in that first race. And yet he rode to win. His horse was disqualified, but he rode to win. Why didn't they kill him then?"

"I'm sure they would have, but they needed him to make the deal for the animals with his cousin Chico's gang in Puerto Rico. That saved his life."

"I understand. But what about now? How can they trust him to play their game in the next race?"

"This time they use both a carrot and a stick. The stick is still the threat of death for him and his family."

"I could protect him."

I held his arm and looked in his eyes. "Mr. Garcia, you know better than I do that if people like that want a man dead, there is no protection."

He met my look for several seconds before nodding.

"And the carrot?"

"They've promised him a small cut of the profits. To Victor, it's a lot of money. Especially for his family. There's not much financial security in a jockey's life. They're counting on that."

I could see he was still having trouble with supporting any plan of the *insectos*. But for reasons I could not reveal at that moment, I needed him on board with my idea.

"I'm meeting with my cousin, Victor, tonight. We're meeting at that same place by Jamaica Pond at ten o'clock. I plan to tell him to do whatever Fat Tony Cannucci tells him. Do I have your agreement?"

There was no smile now. I could see hesitation in his eyes. He finally nodded again. "You have to follow your conscience, Michael. I know you feel no disloyalty to my interests. We'll talk again."

"I'm sure."

Mr. Garcia and I stepped outside the door of the restaurant. We both tipped up our coat collars against the chill wind. At my lead, we began walking east on Cummins Highway. We got three steps before I heard the querying voice beside me.

"Michael?"

"Yes, Mr. Garcia."

"Would you be offended if I told you—and this is no reflection on my feelings for you—I don't give a damn if your car has six wheels and flies. My interest in your car is nonexistent. Why would you think otherwise?"

"I don't."

"Then why are we out here in the cold when we could be inside opening a bottle of fine Puerto Rican wine?"

"That wind from the east is good, bracing, ocean air. It clears the mind."

"My mind was clear where it was warm. You have something to tell me. What is it?"

I said it low but distinctly. "I should know in a day or two why they're taking the animals inland in Mayagüez."

He stopped me with his hand. "Tell me."

"Nestor must have told you about the two native Brazilians who were stowing away on the ship that brought the animals to Mayagüez. They were keeping most of them alive with water, no thanks to the crew of the ship."

"He mentioned them. Go on."

"They hid out on the trucks that are taking the animals inland. When they see where they're taking them, and why, they'll use a phone we left with them to call Nestor. That's assuming they're still

alive. Nestor will call me. It may be that we can put together a plan
at that point. We may have some help. I'm afraid I can't be more
explicit right now. I just want you to know that much."

"Will you keep me informed?"

I needed a deep breath to think. The air came out as vapor. "I
don't know, Mr. Garcia. If I can, believe me, I will."

"Why wouldn't—"

"I'm thinking three steps ahead. It may be that whatever I learn
will be in a confidentiality I can't break."

I was thinking of the meeting ahead with Deputy D.A. Billy
Coyne. I could sense his mind making the connections. "I see."

"This much I can promise you, Mr. Garcia. I'll never betray any
confidence between you and me. No matter what."

He was looking straight into my eyes. Whatever he saw must have
satisfied him. He nodded. He started to turn back to the restaurant.
I held his arm.

"One last thing. If anyone beyond you and me hears about the
Brazilians, those two men will be dead on the spot."

My eyes were searching for assurance. He gave it in a nod.

TWENTY-EIGHT

AT LAST, I was getting the feeling that if I were not on solid ground, at least I was not treading in quicksand. I had one clear straw to grasp at.

On my walk back to the Corvette, I speed-dialed Tom Burns' private line.

"Tom. This one is major. I'm literally putting my life in your hands. Do I have your attention?"

"Completely. What're you getting into this time?"

I told him my plan for the evening.

"You do have a proclivity for the insane. Why this?"

"I need to nail down an answer. It's critical, and I can't come up with a plan B. It's back-to-the-wall time. I need the best man I can think of behind me."

"That, of course, would be me. That aside, listen to me. This could put you beyond even my considerable ability to keep you alive. Do you know who you're playing with?"

"Probably better than you do. I have no choice."

"Then at least carry a gun like I've been telling you."

"No good, Tom. I'm still not a shooter."

"That's too bad, because you have a hell of a habit of being a target. I don't like this. You'll be like a staked goat."

"That's why I need your man's eyes on my back. Are you in?"

There was a pause that I read as concern. "Always."

"Then there's one last detail. Without this, it's all for nothing. Here's what I need. "

I gave him his final marching order.

"Damn, Mike. Why don't you just commit suicide and be done with it?"

"Because I have confidence in you and your man. Come on, Tom. Tell me it's a piece of cake. Tell me he's the best there is. I need all the false courage I can get here. By the way, who'll I look for?"

"I want to think about it. Whoever it is, call him 'Marty.' He may have to do something that he doesn't want linked to his real name."

"Roger that. Thanks, Tom. I feel better about it."

"Just don't feel so good that you ever think of doing it again."

*   *   *

It was past three in the afternoon when I was driving along Commonwealth Avenue on the way back to the office. I thought I might field a few of the more pressing calls that had been plaguing my faithful assistant, Julie. It would fill the time until dinner with Mr. D. and Billy Coyne at six. More to the point, it would take my mind off my ten o'clock rendezvous that evening.

I was between Clarendon and Dartmouth Streets when my cell phone came to life. I checked the caller ID and pulled over to the curb. I needed full concentration for this one. It was from Nestor in Mayagüez.

"Nestor, what's up?" I remembered to honor his disdain for polite niceties.

"I have the answer we were looking for. It's not a good one, but it finally makes sense."

"You heard from the two Brazilians. Are they all right?"

"So far. I just got the call. The three trucks with the animals went inland from the docks about an hour northeast of the city. They said it felt like a dirt road. They stopped in a clearing in the trees in front of a large warehouse-type of building."

"Do you know where it is?"

"They described the country around it. I know the area. I'm sure I can find it."

"Go on."

"The men in the trucks unloaded the animal cages. They carried them into the warehouse. Ansuro and Ancarit stayed hidden under a tarp in the truck. After dark, they sneaked around the building. There was a back door."

"Unlocked?"

"They don't need security. There's nothing out there but trees. When they got in, they were able to conceal themselves behind the cages that were stacked inside."

"And?"

"You remember what I said when we went down into that hold on the ship?"

"Hard to forget. You said that it was hell."

"Yeah. If that wasn't, this is."

My mind braced to visualize the picture I could see coming. "Tell me."

"When they brought the cages into the warehouse, there was a crew of six other men waiting there. They pulled the birds and monkeys, all of the animals, out of the cages. They were still taped up. They threw all the dead ones into a big pit for burning."

"Were many dead?"

"Yeah, but the workmen kept saying not nearly as many as usual. The two Brazilians were praying they wouldn't figure out it was because they'd been feeding and watering them. That would have led to a search."

"But it didn't?"

"Not yet."

"What about the animals still alive?"

"That's the real hell. They had other cages in the warehouse. Just as tight. Maybe tighter. They stuffed the animals back into the new cages. Our two men said it took them most of the night."

"Why change cages? Certainly not for the benefit of the animals."

"Not a chance. But it does make sense. Finally."

"Tell me."

"Let me say this first, in case we lose contact. The Brazilians heard them say they have to keep the animals there for a few more days before they ship them."

"Why?"

"The *insectos* need time to raise the rest of the money to pay for them. Victor's cousin Chico's gang isn't about to release them before they get the cash."

"That means they'll have Fat Tony and Victor fix a race at Suffolk Downs in the next day or so. Then what?"

"Ansuro said he heard one of them say they'll take the animals back to the ship in Mayagüez. Then they get shipped to the coast of the mainland."

"Where will they smuggle them into the mainland?"

"Ansuro said he heard they have two places they use on the coast of Florida. They've greased the customs people so it's a smooth run at either place. He'll keep listening to get a fix on which place they'll use and where it is. He and his grandson are still hiding out in the building."

"Did he say—"

"Listen to this. We may lose contact. There's one bright spot for the animals. Before they stuffed them into the new cages, they gave them some food and water."

"That's out of character."

"Not so much. It's not for the animals. Since they have to keep them at least a few days longer, they want to keep their investment alive. No one buys a dead monkey."

I had to pull myself back from a distracting vision of the animals in that warehouse. I needed full objective concentration for what was coming.

"So end the suspense. What's the piece of the puzzle we've been missing?"

"It's about the only thing that could make this thing worse than we thought."

I got a mental grip to take it in. It did no good. When he laid it out, I was blindsided and numbed anyway. What Nestor described raised the stakes higher than I could comprehend.

"My God, Nestor. This thing has no limits."

"Yeah."

"Give me a second."

"That's about all I have."

I rested the phone on my lap. My eyes were on the Boston drivers pushing the speed limit on Commonwealth Avenue without really seeing them. I was forcing every brain cell to get the tumblers to fall into place for a plan.

It was a new game, with a completely new deck of cards. It took about thirty seconds, but out of the floating jumble of possibilities, a barely rational idea began to take shape.

"Your second's up, Mike. I've got to move."

The voice brought me back to the phone. "Move in what direction?"

"The only one possible. We don't have the firepower to take on the *insectos* and Chico Mendosa's gang at the same time. I don't like it, but there's only one choice."

"Hell no, Nestor. If you're thinking of taking it to anyone in the government down there, don't do it. There's no one you know you can trust. You've got the scars to prove it."

"And you have a better idea?"

"Yes. Stay close to the phone. Just sit tight, and keep quiet."

"Now there's a hell of a plan. Why didn't I think of that?"

"That's not the plan. I have a dinner meeting with the deputy district attorney tonight here in Boston. Let me try to put something together on this end."

Silence.

"Listen to me, Nestor. What you just told me could be the best news we could get. When you hear from the two Brazilians, see if they've heard where the two points of entry are in Florida. I need specifics. And which one they plan to use. If you hear anything, get back to me as soon as possible. You listening?"

There was a pause. It could have been the total vagueness of my so-called plan, or the fact that he'd be taking orders from this junior associate. Or both. Eventually he came back with a disgruntled but vaguely positive, "Yeah."

I decided to go with that and hung up.

It had been so long since I'd felt the vaguest twinge of optimism, I hardly recognized it. When I rethought the scant hope it was based on, it ducked its little head back undercover.

Instead of driving to the office, I parked in the underground lot under Boston Common. I walked to a bench beside the swan boat pond in Boston Garden. Some of my best plan formulation over the years has been done in the almost mystical peace of that setting. And I was in need of some magic. I was pulling strands of ideas from some far-flung reaches to amass something I could sell as a plan to Billy Coyne.

The sun was well set, and I was chilled to the bone without realizing it when I checked my watch. It was time to walk to the Marliave for dinner with Mr. Devlin and Mr. Coyne. I rehearsed one last time what I was about to propose.

* * *

Our little trio was escorted again to the private room at the top of the stairs. Chef John presented the bare outlines of a suggested menu to Mr. Devlin. When he began describing his recommended choice of wine, I moved my hand close enough to give a light touch to Mr. D.'s elbow. He read me instantly and told Chef John that we'd be foregoing the wine. Billy Coyne caught the signal and glanced at me. My expression must have conveyed the fact that what was to follow was not casual conversation.

As soon as we heard the click of the lock behind Chef John, Mr. Coyne leaned closer.

"What is it, kid? What've you got?"

Mr. Devlin stepped in with one sharp word. "Billy."

It brought Mr. Coyne's eyes up in surprise. "What?"

"He's not a kid. He's my partner. What he's about to tell us came at serious risk of his life. His name is 'Michael.' Nothing less."

I may not have moved, but I felt as if I were sitting three inches taller. For the first time since I've known him, Mr. Coyne looked at me as if he actually saw me. "What have you got for us, Mr. Knight?"

I had to suppress a grin to think that he actually knew my name— let alone used it. He looked at Mr. D. for mock approval.

"Don't overdo it, Billy. You're still old enough to be his grandfather. 'Michael' will do."

With the name game concluded, all eyes were back on me, and the tone could not have been more serious. I knew that Chef John was ensuring our complete privacy, but I still brought it down nearly to a whisper.

"I have the answer you've been looking for, Mr. Coyne. It makes complete sense, but you're not going to like it."

"Let me have it."

I knew that what I was about to say needed a boost for credibility. I went through most of the details of my excursion to Mayagüez. Before leaving, I had retrieved the phone from the crack in the sidewalk where I'd stashed it. I showed him the video I'd made on my phone—the Mayagüez police in uniform coming at Nestor and beating him. I explained to Mr. Coyne that the police were corrupt muscle for Chico's animal-smuggling gang.

I knew I could trust Mr. Coyne with the names of Nestor and the two Brazilians. Out of respect for a promise given, I kept the name of my new-old friend, Ramon Garcia, head of the *Nyetas* in Boston, off the table.

By the time I got to the message conveyed by Ansuro to Nestor, I had built enough suspense to have Mr. Coyne edging forward in his chair. I sensed that I'd also built the solid base of credibility I needed to get him on board with the only plan that made sense to me.

"This is the piece we were looking for, Mr. Coyne. None of us could understand why Chico Mendosa's gang, that's been smuggling and selling wild animals for years, was willing to sell the animals to the *insectos* and let them take the profits. I can give you the answer now in one word."

"What?"

"Drugs. Pure, uncut heroin. A hellish massive amount of it. Direct from South America. It's worth many times the value of the animals once it hits the streets in cities on the east coast—Boston included. It's enough to flood the current epidemic of heroin addiction."

Billy Coyne sat back and just breathed while his mind absorbed the unbounded specter of that poison pumped through the veins of his city's people, from high school on up. The deaths from overdoses alone would be staggering. I knew his mind was also flooded with images of gang massacres and deaths of innocents that would inevitably result from the influx of weapons bought with drug money. I paused until he looked back at me.

"This is how they're going to do it. They took the cages of animals off the boat from Brazil in Mayagüez, Puerto Rico. They trucked them inland to a warehouse out in the country. They re-stuffed the animals into new cages with false bottoms. Every cage holds enough pure heroin to cause more deaths than an open war."

Mr. Coyne jumped in. "You said it made sense. Why did they get the Italian mafia and the *insectos* involved?"

"Because the risk has gone up about a hundred times what it was in the animal business. You know yourself, no one takes the trade in wild animals seriously. The chance of being caught smuggling animals is minimal. The customs people at the entry points are open to bribes as long as they're just harming animals. And no one else cares. Most people don't even bother to learn about it. And even if they were caught smuggling animals, the penalties are minor fines. Barely a cost of doing business."

I could see he was thinking a step ahead of me, but I said it anyway. "But if they're caught smuggling a boatload of pure heroin, there'd be hell to pay. The FBI would be on them like flies. So would the other feds. The DEA. Even the customs people would come down on them. We'd be talking about prison sentences at the top of the spectrum. The feds could even reach their people in Puerto Rico since it's part of the USA."

"Yeah."

I couldn't tell if he said it to me, or if his mind was running with it alone. I finished the thought anyway.

"That's why they were willing to get the *insectos* and the Italian mafia involved. This way, Chico's gang first makes a profit of nearly two million selling them a shipload of animals. Then they let the *insectos* use their contacts with the bribed customs people and the animal wholesalers on the mainland. That way, the *insectos* and mafia take all the risks of smuggling the cages into the mainland without even knowing they contain drugs. If they're caught, the *insectos* and mafia people take the fall—and it would be heavy."

Mr. Coyne was listening, so I stayed on a roll.

"On the other hand, if the smuggling of the cages works like it always has, Chico's people take the drugs out of the cages, reap a fortune, and Boston and every other city on the East Coast will be torn apart with gang killings and swimming in heroin."

I stopped there and gave it a chance to sink in. I had filled Mr. D. in on it before. The two of us just watched Billy Coyne with his hands folded in front of him, staring at nothing, with a look on his face that said he felt as if he were carrying the welfare, if not survival, of his city, on his shoulders.

After a minute, I leaned forward and touched his hands. He just looked up at me without words.

"Mr. Coyne, they say, 'It's an ill wind that doesn't blow someone some good.' I think we just got an advantage."

His expression was somewhere between curiosity and disbelief. His eyes asked the question. It was time to make my pitch.

"Here it is. As long as it was just the animals, it was just me and Nestor and a few others who gave a damn. They had it all their own way. When they made it drugs instead of just animals, they stepped out of their safety zone. I think we can take them down. But I need your help in a big way."

He looked at Mr. Devlin for some assurance that the one he had always called "the kid" had any claim on believability. Mr. Devlin nodded. I had his attention again.

"I need two things from you, Mr. Coyne. They're big things, but I need to depend on you to pull it off. If you don't come through, my neck will be on the chopping block. And that's not a metaphor."

"What do you need, kid?" He caught Mr. D's look. "What do you need, Michael?"

"Two things. Contacts. I need you to set the trap on a tight spring. I'll explain what I mean in a minute. And it has to be absolutely leakproof. If one name gets out, the obituaries will start piling up. Beginning with mine."

"What's the second thing?"

"Money. A lot of it. I'm hoping you can tap into federal money. If this works the way I hope, I'll get most of it back for you."

"Why money?"

"I think all of these gangs have gotten themselves in a tight circular bind. The *insectos* and the mafia owe Chico's gang another $900,000 for the animals. But so what? Why is that holding up the deal? Why doesn't Chico's gang let the *insectos* have the animals right now? Let them smuggle the animals and the drugs into the mainland. Chico's gang could make a quick windfall with the drugs. The profit they'd make on those drugs would make the $900,000 due for the animals look like chump change."

"So what's the answer?"

"It took me a while. I finally realized that this is probably the first time Chico's gang has dealt in drugs. They could only buy that amount of drugs directly from one of the big cartels in Central or South America. My guess is that they owe the cartel the $900,000 to finish paying for the drugs. And they can't welch on that one. The boys in those South American cartels make Chico's gang look like Cub Scouts."

Mr. Coyne was nodding in agreement, so I finished it off. "My bet is that Chico's gang doesn't have the $900,000 to pay the cartel until they collect it from the *insectos* and mafia for the animals. And the *insectos* won't have the money to pay Chico's gang until they collect their winnings from the race that they want Victor and Fat Tony Cannucci to fix at Suffolk Downs in the next couple of days."

I could see by the burning look in his eyes that Mr. Coyne was following every step of what I was talking about. My only fear was that he'd start peppering me with questions about specifically what I was going to do with the money I was asking for. That could lead us into a part of the plan that neither he nor the state or federal government would be anxious to take on as an investment. I knew what was coming as soon as he said the words, "And what are you going to do with the—"

I cut him off in mid-question. "Mr. Coyne, consider this. I'm asking you—actually I'm asking the government—to put up less than a million dollars to save every city on the East Coast from a disaster like none of us have ever seen. I'm putting up my life. Literally. You can confirm that with Mr. Devlin. At this point, I've told you everything I can without breaching confidences that I won't break under any circumstances. That's the deal."

We were eye to eye, but he said nothing. It was time to go all in.

"Mr. Coyne, you've got one chance to make one hell of an important decision. If you make the wrong choice . . . I may not be alive long enough to give you a second chance. And that's not Irish dramatics. I need an answer now."

Mr. Devlin and I both sat counting the seconds. I think the only reason Mr. D. was not vetoing the plan immediately—in spades—was that I hadn't told him what I had in mind for the evening.

The seconds continued to tick. At some point, Mr. Coyne looked up at Mr. Devlin. "Lex, where the hell did you find this piece of work you call a partner?"

"Actually, he found me. And you can start thanking God right now that he did. The question is, what are you made of, Billy? I've always thought it was the same Irish courage that made the Republic. Shall we see? The chips are down. It's your play."

I'm sure in my soul that it was Mr. D.'s timely playing of the Irish Republic card that tipped the balance. Whatever it was, Billy nodded, and we were game on.

TWENTY-NINE

BEFORE WE ADJOURNED the dinner, I asked Mr. Coyne where he would be at ten p.m. that evening.

"Where would you like me to be?"

"Your office would be good. Alone, except for a couple of Boston's finest. Detective level. And two you'd trust with your life—and mine."

"That can be arranged. Why?"

"I may want to make a personal delivery."

He nodded, and didn't press for more on that subject. I was getting the impression that he almost welcomed help in something that was over all of our heads. "Anything else?"

"Just one thing. I need to have my jockey client, Victor Mendosa, able to ride in a couple of days. It's critical. Can you keep him out of jail?"

He knew I was referring to pressure from his boss, Suffolk County District Attorney Angela Lamb. Given the scent of a headline from a case involving the juicy topic of race fixing, I knew she'd want Victor nabbed, tried, convicted, and put beyond reach faster than even she could say "governor's office."

"I've kept the indictment on the back burner. She had me present the evidence to the grand jury, but I've been dragging my anchor in putting it to a vote on the actual indictment. I keep slipping cases in ahead of it, but I can't do it forever."

"You won't have to. Within the next week, I'll give her cases that'll draw headlines that will blow her mind. She'll be shopping for a governor's inauguration gown. You can dangle that in front of her. Just don't be too specific."

"That will appeal."

"In the meantime, she has a couple of cops on Victor's trail. They were at the track the morning after Roberto's accident. She proba-bly wants him picked up for questioning. Malloy and his partner. You probably know him."

Mr. Coyne winced. "Not exactly the pride of the force."

"Can you put a leash on them? Victor has to ride in a day or two. There's a lot more than a race at stake."

"I'll see if I can get them on another assignment."

He stood and walked to the door. Before he left, he turned and looked in my direction. "Stay out of harm's way . . . Michael."

I could almost believe he meant it.

* * *

I went back to my Beacon Street apartment to change into clothes that suited the evening's agenda. The temperature was in the low fifties, but the thought of what I was about to do brought on chills. I dressed for the chills.

At nine forty-five, I was parked close to Jamaica Pond, on a quiet street that ran behind the once-home of the last politician to build a voting base on personal handshakes and family favors. As I walked past that house on the Jamaicaway and crossed the street to the dark path around the pond, I tried to calm my nerves by focusing on that perennial survivor, James Michael Curley, who actually won an election while serving a sentence in prison for taking an exam for a friend.

I could feel the darkness swallow me up as I walked from dim light to dimmer light along the pond's edge. I had intentionally mentioned in my last conversation with Ramon Garcia at the El Rey de Lechón restaurant that I'd be meeting with my client, Victor, at a bench in a particular deserted area halfway around the pond. It was a test. After something he'd said, I figured it was the next best thing to sending an engraved invitation to anyone who might want a clean, unobserved shot at ending my existence.

In the almost total darkness, I was approaching a bench that was about thirty feet from the bench I had designated. The termites in my stomach were breeding more rapidly the closer I got to the meeting spot without seeing any sign of the protector promised by Tom Burns. He had never let me down, but the unwelcome thought occurred that, contrary to his proclamations, even Tom is subject to human failure.

Just when my legs were on the verge of convincing the rest of me that the better part of discretion was to let them carry me in the opposite direction, I spotted my salvation. When I got close enough, I saw a form sprawled out prone on that first bench. Even in that dim light, I could distinguish the oversized, torn overcoat and ragged hat that covered the body of an apparently homeless man.

And I thanked God. I knew that Tom had come through. His man was a master of disguise. As I passed, I whispered without looking down, "Marty, I'll be right there on that next bench."

I saw a hand come out of the folds of the overcoat to let me know he was fully conscious and tuned in.

With renewed courage, I took a few more steps toward the appointed bench. My eyes were scanning the small area of pathway fifty feet ahead that fell under a weak cone of light from a lamppost on the side.

My feet stopped cold when a dark form passed slowly into the dim light ahead, moving in my direction. I could just make out the outline of a slender figure about six feet tall. Even without more details, my pulse accelerated into triple digits. It nearly doubled again when I saw, or perhaps imagined, a tiny glint of light off what I believed in my heart to be the barrel of a handgun.

I backed up a few steps to get within whispering distance of my guardian on the bench. I forced the words through gritted teeth.

"Marty! This could be showtime! Could we get a little action here?"

I nearly jumped out of my shoes when the hand that had come out of the overcoat tapped me on the knee. I looked down. My knees almost crumbled. The hand was turned palm up. It went with a raspy voice from under the overcoat. "Hey, buddy. I need a drink. Can you spare a couple of bucks?"

The words just about leaped out of me. "Holy crap in spades! This guy really is a bum. Where the hell is Tom's man?"

I looked back down the path. Even by that dismal light, I could see the hand with a gun pointing in my direction. I started a prayer, and got as far as "My God—"

A voice cut me off. "Knight! Down!"

I dropped like a sack of grain. Two shots split the air. I thought I could hear the instant whoosh of air followed by two thuds. When I looked back at the shooter, I saw two figures walking toward me in lock step. One was behind the other and seemed to be holding tight to something around the neck of the one in front.

They were about fifteen feet away. I could make out a gurgling sound from the one in front. Over the gurgling, I heard the same commanding voice. "Get up, Knight."

I was about to obey, when something like a dead weight tumbled over and pinned me to the ground. I struggled my way clear. The man giving commands flashed a light on the fallen bulk. By the time I'd scrambled to my feet, I recognized the panhandler from the bench.

In pushing my way clear, I had touched his chest. My hand came away drenched in a sticky fluid. He had apparently sat up and taken the bullets that were intended for me.

I looked back at the man who had a cord of some kind around the neck of the man in front. He had loosened his grip. He still held him secure, but the gurgling had stopped.

"Marty?"

"Correct. Sorry for the close timing. I could have taken him out sooner, but your specific instructions were to keep him alive."

I was still panting as if I'd run a hundred yard dash. "Right . . . Well done."

"What's your pleasure?"

"Tie his arms, Marty. Do you have a car?"

"I do. Just over there." He pointed with his chin.

"Good. We need to make a delivery. Let's go."

I noticed that instead of using the cord on his arms, Marty produced a pair of handcuffs. It made me wonder about Marty's background before he became a member of Tom Burns' finest. I decided not to ask.

Before leaving, I leaned down to the man in the overcoat on the ground by the bench. I felt for a pulse and found that he'd had his last drink on this earth.

The three of us made our way to Marty's BMW. I took his keys and sat in the driver's seat. Marty pushed his prisoner into the back seat and sat beside him with a gun planted in his upper ribs.

It was a silent trip to the back of the building that housed Billy Coyne's office. A call on the cell phone reached Mr. Coyne in his office as promised.

"Mr. Coyne, I have that delivery for you. Can you meet us at the back door, preferably with the help I mentioned? The fewer eyes that see any of us the better."

We waited in the car until the door opened. Mr. Coyne appeared with two plainclothes police officers. Marty kept his gun in the ribs of the prisoner while he took back his handcuffs. At Mr. Coyne's order, the officers took custody of the prisoner and escorted him into the building and up the stairs.

"What have we here, Michael? I'm assuming to keep it legal you made a citizen's arrest."

I nodded. "The charge is attempted murder. Mine. Can you get him to an interrogation room? Alone."

"That's where he's headed."

Before I followed them into the building, I turned around to thank Marty. I barely caught sight of the BMW rounding the corner out of sight.

Mr. Coyne and I stopped first at his office. "You want to fill me in, Michael?"

I had apparently fully graduated to the "Michael" status. Somehow it made the move I had in mind easier. I gave him the background.

"What I need, Mr. Coyne, is five minutes in the interrogation room with the prisoner. You're welcome to watch. In fact, it might go better if you're there. But I may need to say things that wouldn't go well coming from you."

He looked at me as if I'd just dropped back to the "kid" stage.

"Just words, Mr. Coyne. No rough stuff. You can call it off any time you think I overstep."

It took him a few seconds. "On that condition."

"Agreed. Only before you step in, please remember what's at stake."

I got a look that was intended to remind me who was the deputy district attorney, and who was not. I dutifully nodded, and we walked to the interrogation room.

There was a tall, stringy man in his thirties, sitting at the table, hands folded in front of him. I'd never seen him before, but my first impression was that he looked like a soldier with either the *Nyetas* or the *insectos*.

I took the chair across the table. I could feel Mr. Coyne's presence behind me, standing in silence, giving me first crack at the suspect.

My first choice would have been to do it in Spanish, but that would have cut Mr. Coyne out of the loop, and I needed his approval of where I intended to go.

"What's your name, amigo?"

Silence.

Just in case it was a language barrier, I tried *"Cómo te llamas?"*

Still silence. Back to English.

"You don't like that question? Try this one. Because this is the only other question I'm going to ask you. Who sent you to kill me?"

He pushed the chair back with his long legs. I could see a grin start to creep across his face. The attitude was setting in fast. I knew there was nothing we could do to him within the law that would shake loose his pride in soldiering up in silence.

"Okay, amigo. That's it. That's everything. You're free to go."

I don't know if that caught him or Mr. Coyne more off balance. The grin froze, and I could feel Mr. Coyne stiffening up behind me. Thank God, he let me roll on.

I stood up. "What's the matter, amigo? You don't hear too well? I said you're free to go. There's the door."

The grin turned to a glare. He mumbled it in Spanish, *"De qué hablas?"*

To keep Mr. Coyne on frequency, I translated. "What am I talking about? I'm talking about you walking out that door. No one's going to stop you. Only before you go, you want to make a little bet? I'll put my money on, I don't know, maybe an hour. Perhaps less."

"An hour for what?"

I leaned over the table toward him. "An hour before your brother *insectos* pick you up. I see the tattoo under your shirt collar. On second thought, probably less than an hour."

"What the hell you talkin' about?" Now it was in English.

"What I'm talking about is this. Someone in that gang of yours sent you to put a bullet through me at the pond. You took a shot, but you missed. That's attempted murder. You killed that homeless man back there. That's murder. You were taken to the district attorney's office. Right here. Ten minutes later, you're turned loose. The police are on their way now to arrest the man who sent you. Yeah, I can guess who it was."

As I talked I strolled to a spot behind him. I leaned down and whispered a name in his ear. The grin was gone.

"By the time you hit the street, I'll see that the word is out about how grateful the police are for your cooperation. You were obviously released because you gave up the name of the man who gave you the order. Then my guess is that the target will be on your back instead of mine. Only it won't be a couple of quick shots to the head, will it? I've heard stories when I was a kid about what they do to snitches. I figure your brother *insectos* will have you where you don't want to be. My guess is less than an hour."

I could hear Billy shuffling his feet behind me. I knew I was probably over the line, but in the context of what was happening, I prayed that he had redrawn the line to give me two more minutes. I needed time to play on the look of near panic that was freezing the face in front of me.

"You look like you've been around, amigo." I used my finger to trace the line of scar on his face that ran from his forehead to his jaw. He never moved.

"You know what your brothers do to an *insecto* who spills it to the cops. I've heard the stories, but I bet you've seen it."

The silence continued. He was a hard shell to crack.

"Is there anywhere you can run that they won't be able to get you? I don't think so. But maybe you want to risk it."

The quiver in his hands and feet said it was time to go for broke. I figured I was also at the end of my leash with Mr. Coyne.

"On the other hand, amigo, maybe there's a way out. Maybe you get to live another day."

He looked me in the eye for the first time.

"Here's the deal. You do two things. You plead guilty to the murder and attempted murder. Then you give us the details. You name the man who sent you and anyone else involved. You make a full statement and sign it."

He shook his head with a sarcastic laugh. "I go to prison, I wouldn't be alive for ten minutes."

"I know. That's why you get protective custody. You'll be kept out of the prison population. You'll be pleading to a federal charge of racketeering. That way you can be transferred to a prison somewhere in the country beyond the reach of the *insectos*. A new name. No one in that gang will know where you are. You'll get a reduced sentence because you cooperated. When you get out, you maybe start a new life."

He stared at the table in front of him. For the first time I looked back at Mr. Coyne. I'd been running solo without approval of any of it. He held his hands out in a way I read as "We'll see." I knew he couldn't commit for the Feds, but at least he was not squelching the offer.

"That's the offer, amigo. It has a short life. Decision time."

I walked over and held the door open. "You're in or you're out. Right now."

He sat there in limbo. I called in one of the detectives who was waiting outside the door. With absolutely no authority, I gave the order. "Take him out, Detective. He's free to go. No charges. He's been very helpful. You can spread the word."

That did it. The detective took him by the arm. He pulled away and grabbed the table with both hands. "All right. All right."

"All right what?"

"I'll talk. I want the deal."

I gave the detective a nod to let go and exhaled the breath I didn't realize I was holding. On my way out of the room, I whispered to Mr. Coyne, "Can I get a written copy of his statement?"

"I'll send it to your office."

I started to walk out.

"Michael."

"Yes, Mr. Coyne."

"None of this gets out of this room. This never happened."

I nodded. I started to leave again.

"Michael."

I turned around. He just gave me a slow nod of the head and the faintest crack of a smile. Coming from him, it was like a blast from the Harvard cheerleading team with the marching band playing the victory march.

THIRTY

BEFORE I LEFT his office, I told Billy about the dead homeless man on the bench beside Jamaica Pond. I knew he'd send someone to pick up the body and take it to the morgue. I had one last request.

"Mr. Coyne, could you put the word out to the press that a body was found last night by Jamaica Pond with two bullet holes? And could you withhold identification or any other details?"

"It's possible. Why?"

"The one who ordered it will probably assume the dead body is mine. It could give me some slack without another attempt for a few days."

"And to even the exchange or favors, you might want to share the name of the one behind it."

"I do want to. And will. As soon as one more piece fits into the puzzle. I don't want to mislead either one of us. I'll be in touch."

* * *

It was around ten thirty when I aimed the nose of my Corvette toward a spot on Beacon Hill that for six years had been my personal Monday night refuge from all of the pressures and anxieties of my peculiar practice of law. I parked on Beacon Hill and walked down the small circular staircase that led to Big Daddy's Jazz Club.

Big Daddy Hightower was a particular idol of mine. His driving bass had accented the New York club and recording dates of the jazz giants of the '50s and '60s from Charlie Parker to Miles Davis and even Oscar Peterson, when Ray Brown was out of town. He and Charlie Mingus carried the bass line of so many iconic jazz groups that their names became synonymous with the stand-up bass.

Then the day came when he got "an offer he couldn't refuse" for an exclusive recording contract from one of the New York mafia bosses. He refused the offer, and what they did to his hands took him off the bandstands of the first string New York jazz clubs permanently. After years of rehabilitation and wood-shedding with his bass, a number of the musicians he'd made sound even better in the old days staked him to a small jazz club near the top of Boston's Beacon Hill. He was the nightly headliner, together with every noted jazz instrumentalist who passed through Boston.

By the time I settled onto my usual third barstool from the back and took that first transporting sip of the three fingers of Famous Grouse Scotch that Sonny, the bartender, automatically set in front of me, I could feel knotted muscles start to unwind. By the second and third sip, I was in a more peaceful world.

Across that small room that Big Daddy kept in nearly total darkness to focus attention on the music, I could take in the gentle rhythms he was laying down under a dreamy version of Errol Garner's "Misty." I did not have to look up to recognize the languid sax of Jim Redeker, a West Coast disciple of the breathy tone of an Ellington alumnus, Johnny Hodges. The guitarist was up to their level, but unfamiliar.

That first unwinding in as many days as I could remember continued all the way to the Land of Nod. I never heard the end of the set. My first conscious thought was that an arm the size of a small side of beef was resting on my shoulder.

"My music never put you to sleep before, Mickey. I must be losing it."

"Daddy, the day you lose it is the day we close the book on music. That was beyond beautiful. I was just resting my eyes."

"And your feet, and everything in between. You been gettin' yourself into all kinds of mischief again?"

"Not a bit of it. You know me, Daddy. Safety first. Words to live by. I see Jim's in town. Nice he came by."

"Yeah, it's nice. I never known him not to when he comes east. Keeps Old Daddy young, jammin' with these babies. How come you're here? This is not Monday night."

I thought back. "I had a couple of things going on Monday. This is my make-up night. Terry's meeting me here. Have you seen her?"

"Not yet. Why don't I give you a table for the two of you down front there? Can't have that pretty lady sittin' at the bar."

"Thanks, Daddy. That'd be nice."

He picked up my Famous Grouse in one hand and took my left arm in the other. He led me weaving through the barely visible tables to one beside the musician's stand. He laid the Famous Grouse on the table. When I started to sit in one of the two chairs, the arm kept me moving past the table, up the step, directly to the piano bench. Under slight pressure of the big hand, I sat.

"Here we go, Mickey. Let's make up for Monday night. See if you pick up on this one."

I could feel the vibrations of Daddy's driving bass deep in the base of my stomach. It somehow spurred enough adrenaline to bring my fingers instinctively in touch with the keyboard. Within four bars, I picked up on the chord changes and followed his lead into a medium-tempo run of "'Round Midnight."

We had improvised about six choruses in comfortable sync with each other's thoughts, when I heard the lush, throaty sax of Jim

Redeker take the lead. I could just fall back into backup and happily coast. For the next four choruses, my entire conscious world lay between Big Daddy's bass line and Jim's transporting improvisation.

When Daddy gave the signal, we came back down to earth for a final chorus as Thelonious Monk had written it. When we finished, there was applause that reminded me that there were other people in the room. I was back in the world I'd left, but, as always, with a peace that made the sharp edges softer.

I shook hands with Jim, and exchanged smiles with Big Daddy. I saw him cast a big wave in the direction of the table by the stand, and my entire world brightened. Even in that dark room, I caught the glowing warmth of Terry's smile, and I was there beside her in a second.

Big Daddy said to the other people in the club, "This here's a personal message between two people who found what this whole life gig is all about." He whispered a word to Jim, and together they just enfolded Terry and me in the warmth of "There Will Never Be Another You."

When it ended, I waved them a "thank you," and Terry blew Big Daddy a kiss before taking my handkerchief out of my suit coat pocket.

I knew that I had to make the most of the limited time I had with Terry. While Big Daddy took a break, we caught up on any loose ends that needed tying before our wedding that was now a fast-flying four days ahead.

Apparently our wedding planner, Janet, had reached an emotional plateau by the third martini that afternoon. It enabled her to approach the whole production with a fatalistic "What the hell, it's their wedding" calm.

She had been astounded at how the mention of Lex Devlin's name to Terry Griffin, the function manager of the Parker House, had freed up the very ballroom we had in mind. I hadn't mentioned to Janet that it was Mr. Devlin's magic in years past that had dissolved a certain tax tangle that could have given our friend Terry state-funded living quarters for three to five years. Justice had been done, and I've never known Terry to refuse any request Mr. Devlin had made since.

With that issue secured, the details of caterer, band, flowers, limo, and even expedited RSVPs from guests had apparently been, could I say, a piece of cake. The real *sine qua nons*—the church, the priest to perform the ceremony, the substitute for Terry's deceased father to give her away, the maid of honor and best man—those had been preordained from the moment we became engaged, and we knew that every one of them would cancel their own funeral to be there.

Terry and I stayed for one more set. It seemed that every note was directed at us. We could blissfully have stayed until Daddy laid down the bass at closing, which was usually one side or the other of three a.m., but the early day ahead promised its share of challenges.

* * *

Before coming to Daddy's, I had contacted my client, Victor, by cell phone. Since his return from Mayagüez, he had been staying out of public view with a cousin off Hyde Square. At my suggestion, he had gotten in touch with Fat Tony Cannucci to let him know he was available to do his dirty work on command. Fat Tony knew that Victor had been the key link between the *insectos* and his cousin, Chico, to set up the contacts necessary to smuggle the animals into the mainland. It had been easy to sell Fat Tony on the notion that Victor was now in for a cut of the profits on the deal to market the wild animals. Given that, it was an easy next step to convince Tony that he could rely on Victor to go through with the fix.

Since Victor had not been available to ride recently, he agreed to let Fat Tony know when he could arrange for a mount in a race in which he could oversee the fix of the other jockeys.

I got home from Daddy's around two in the morning. When the alarm went off at five, I had to persuade each muscle individually that it was worth the effort to leave the bed. I doubled my usual Starbucks intake, and drove to the backstretch of Suffolk Downs.

I saw Victor standing with Rick McDonough by the corner of Rick's row of stables. Rick saw me and waved me over to the coffee shack. The three of us joined up and walked with yet another cup of coffee to an unpopulated section of the outer rail of the track before any of us said a word.

I had set up the meeting the night before. I figured it would take a good bit of backfilling and persuasion to get Rick on board. I knew it would cut against the very core of his nature. Still, there was no one else I could trust enough to lay bare the plan.

First, I laid out more of that vicious web that had engulfed both Victor and me than I ever thought I'd share with anyone. By the time I had him up to speed on the inhuman animal trade, the unholy alliance between the mafia and the *insectos,* and the crucial part the detested race-fixing manipulations of Fat Tony Cannucci played in it, I had his full attention. I also had him emotionally on board, since the death of his favorite jockey, Victor's brother Roberto, had been a direct result of it all.

I saw him taking a long look down the track where the earliest workouts and breezes were just beginning. His eyes were on the horses, but I knew he was digesting the enormity of the evil he was hearing. I gave him time with it, because I knew what I had to ask.

When he looked back at me, I could read in the lines in that old cowboy's weathered face a determination to be on board. Now I had to harness that determination in a direction he would hate.

"You've got something to ask me, Mike. What?"

"I want you to give Victor a mount in tomorrow's eighth race. You've got a horse entered. Brown Beauty. He's in post position three. My guess is the morning line will have him a favorite."

He looked at the ground. This was hurdle one. "You know I've already got Alan Garcia on that mount. I made the deal with his agent."

"I know. And you know you can still change riders. Alan won't fight it. Neither will his agent. He wants more mounts from your stable. You can tell him Victor knows the horse from the morning workouts. That's the easy part."

This time he looked me dead in the eye. "And what's the hard part?"

I'd known Rick since he trained horses for my adopted father when I was spending mornings before school shoveling out stables. Subtlety and soft selling would never cut it. If he caught a whiff of deception or dilution of the hard truth, I'd be seeing the back of his boots.

"Victor's going to promise Fat Tony Cannucci to pull your horse. It's a fixed race."

I could see his nostrils flare. He looked at Victor for denial. The set of Victor's face told him there was no give there. He looked back at me with an anger that burned white hot for even suggesting it to him.

"That's the thing we need, Rick. I can't dress it up nice and pretty. It's ugly. I know you hate it to the bottom of your soul. So do I. And you can imagine how Victor feels. His brother was killed that last time they pulled this."

Our eyes were locked. I hadn't lost him yet. But this was the moment a bullfighter would plunge the blade over the horns into the heart of the bull. This was the *"momento de verdad"*—the moment of truth. I had one shot. Rick would not stand still for a second.

"I also know this, Rick. Unless we can break the back of this partnership from hell, thousands of defenseless animals will die a wretched death. And they'll be giving their lives to put an arsenal of guns on our streets and on every city street on the East Coast. And worse, heroin in the veins of more kids than I can even count. And the race fixing you and I detest will still go on until every jockey at this track has sold his soul to Fat Tony Cannucci and his bloodsuckers. Every bit of that's the truth."

Rick looked down at his feet, but I wasn't finished. "Listen to me, Rick. I hate what I'm asking even more than you do. I've been living with it a lot longer. But I'll be damned if I can figure another way to break this thing. It's part of a plan."

I'd run out of words. Rick was looking me dead in the eye to find one flicker of deception or lack of commitment. I gave him none. He turned and leaned both elbows on the track rail. It took thirty seconds while we waited in a tense silence.

"And if I do this, is whatever you've got planned going to work?"

I'd have given anything, up to and including my Corvette, to have said, "Yes. It'll work." But I couldn't.

"I have no guarantee to give you, Rick. I have none myself. For what it's worth, I'm putting my own self-respect—and my life—into the pot on this hand."

That last part caused him to look back at me. Then his eyes were back on the horse that was flying past in a wide-open breeze. I could hardly hear the words, but I seized on them.

"Okay, Mike. I'm in. This once."

THIRTY-ONE

THE DOMINOES WERE starting to tumble in line. Victor put the colt Brown Beauty through a light gallop before leaving the track. He wanted to feel the rhythm of his next mount. It also put truth behind Rick's excuse for changing jockeys from Alan Garcia.

Victor used his cell phone to reach Fat Tony while I was still there to listen. Fat Tony jumped at it. The fix would be in for the eighth race the next day. His goons would pay calls on each of the other jockeys riding the race. Victor agreed to be on the alert for any jockey who showed signs of rebelling.

Before hanging up, Victor asked Fat Tony which horse he wanted to win the race. I heard Fat Tony's voice on the speakerphone get tense. "None of your damn business. Just see that it's not your horse."

Victor swallowed what he wanted to say and left it at, "I hear you, Mr. Cannucci."

I left Victor and Rick with the clear three-way agreement that this once, and never again, Rick's horse would be an intentional "also-ran."

On the way to my car, I whispered to Victor the words, "Just in case, keep an eye out for any message I might send."

* * *

I reached the office a bit past ten. I took time to drop in and bring Mr. Devlin up to speed on what was happening at the racetrack. He had been in touch with Mr. Coyne. I held my breath while Mr. D. ran through the federal and state connections that Mr. Coyne had tapped into. With each click of another positive domino reported on, my pulse came back down another ten beats. We had apparently harnessed a wolverine in setting Mr. Coyne to the task of lining up the authorities on our team.

Our entire counterattack was, however, still in limbo when I asked about the ultimate hot button—the $900,000 in federal funds. Mr. Coyne left word that that approval had to come from the top echelon. He was still waiting for that shoe to drop.

At least the answer was not "No," or as I rather anticipated, "Hell no!" That duck was still alive, and the rest of them on Billy Coyne's side were now in a row.

It was time to put my last piece in place. For that, I needed the privacy of my own office. I promised Julie on my way past that I'd spend the afternoon on the phone being a traditional lawyer. The sigh of relief came from her toes. She was ready to grant any favor in return. I had just one. No interruptions from any source for the next half hour. She was so grateful, she would have stationed a Swiss Guard at my door, if she had one.

I figured it was around eight a.m. on the West Coast at the Berkeley campus of the University of California. What I knew of the habits of my closest friend from our Winthrop House roommate days at Harvard College told me that Harry Wong would be into his second cup of Oolong tea over the *New York Times* crossword puzzle.

Harry and I had solidified a symbiotic friendship in college as the only racial misfits on the house wrestling team. My Latino determination and his Asiatic martial arts mastery had won us a measure of acceptance from teammates with more homogenized ancestral roots. A supercilious attitude is hard to sustain when one is being pinned to the mat.

Wherever in the world Harry's academic pursuits might have carried him during the intervening years since graduation, our annual Thanksgiving dinner at my mother's home always blew away the cobwebs of a year's absence in one reuniting hug. More to the point for my present needs, Harry had always answered my calls over the years to play a willing role in helping to resolve some of my more bizarre cases.

"Michael, good to hear your voice."

"And yours, Harry."

"I know it's not Thanksgiving and it's too early for your wedding. Do I dare hope you're not about to ask me to put my life in mortal danger again for some ungrateful client?"

"Absolutely, Harry. You can always hope."

"And will my hope come true?

"No."

Silence.

"I have a small favor to ask, Harry."

"Damn. And would it be presumptuous to ask when my plane leaves?"

"Three this afternoon, your time. I'll send you the e-ticket. I just booked it. I'll meet you at Logan Airport at seven tonight."

"Why the hell do you always assume I'll say 'yes'?"

"Because we're like two musketeers. One for both, and both for one, you might say. In other words, we'll each do anything the other one asks."

"Then why is it you do all the asking, Michael?"

"Because you're in a profession of sane people. I can only wish I were. Besides, admit it. You enjoy a little excitement, a little danger, as a relief from all those predictably boring algorithms."

"I admit nothing. Let me have it. Who do you want me to be this time?"

"I think you'll have a more enjoyable flight if I tell you when you get here. Seriously, I appreciate this more than—"

"Don't tell me how much you appreciate it. It'll only make me more nervous. Anything special I need to pack for?"

"Not a concern."

"How long am I staying?"

"You'll see when you get here. Let me just tell you this. You'll love your accommodations."

"That is not a comforting sign."

"Good-bye, Harry. Safe travels."

*   *   *

I picked Harry up at the airport that evening. Our first stop was an elegant dinner at the Four Seasons on Boylston Street. I kept the conversation as light and irrelevant as possible. After dinner, we dropped into the sumptuous Avery Bar in the Ritz-Carlton for drinks and more casual chitchat.

When he was sufficiently mellowed, I fielded his question, "Where actually am I staying tonight? Or am I?"

"You are, Harry. Upstairs. Here. Ritz-Carlton."

He nearly choked on his Black Russian. "Michael, dinner and drinks in these high-end places, that was to soften me up. But if I stay here they'll want the gold in my teeth."

"As they used to say, 'don't bother your head about it.' Come on. Follow me."

I escorted him up to the top floor, to what Mr. Ritz and Mr.

Carlton call their "Luxury Suite." Harry hesitated to cross the threshold.

"Shall I carry you across, Harry?"

"No, save that for Terry. Michael, a straight answer. What the hell are we doing here?"

I took his arm and led him through each opulent room of the suite and showed him the magnificent view clear to Boston Harbor.

Then I sat him down on the bed. Beginning with the race in which Roberto Mendosa lost his life, I took him through every hair-raising incident up to the then present moment with no omissions. By then, the dinner drinks and Black Russians had spent most of their effect, but he was still settled enough to listen in a state of calm while I explained exactly what I was about to ask of him, and why I wanted him to get comfortable in opulent surroundings.

While he was still contemplating the level of risk, I walked him to the spacious bedroom closet. I pointed out a small but complete wardrobe of clothes that bore the signatures of world-class designers who show no shame in affixing a price tag.

"This is why you only need a toothbrush, Harry."

"What's wrong with my clothes?"

"Your taste in clothes is, what can I say, professorial. My assistant, Julie, has high-end taste. She did the shopping. I assumed that that absurd diet of yours kept the sizes the same."

He took it all in, and true to the heart of a musketeer, when he walked back to sit on the bed, he had just one question.

"When do we start?"

* * *

The next afternoon, I was nervous as a cat on the drive to the track. I couldn't keep my mind from counting the ways in which this whole anticipated train of events could be derailed.

I came in just before the third race and began counting the hours and then the minutes to the start of the eighth race. When the seventh ended, I stationed myself by the saddling paddock in a spot where I could catch the attention of Victor's valet, Lanny, as he was bringing the saddle and saddlecloth with the number 3 to the third stall.

He caught my nod and came by where I was standing.

"What's up, Mike?"

"I need to get a message to my client, Victor Mendosa."

Without looking at me, he took the small envelope I handed him. He almost palmed it as if it were the formula for Coca-Cola. Track security since the fixed race that had ended Roberto's life had gone from tight to near paranoid.

"Be careful with that note, Lanny. It's a plan to bomb the statehouse and kidnap the governor. This makes you an accessory."

Actually, I didn't say quite that. I wasn't sure of Lanny's sense of humor. Even mine was running on fumes at that point. I just mumbled, "Thanks, Lanny. Have a neat day."

His nod concluded the conversation.

* * *

Within ten minutes, the bell at the jockeys' room rang and the colorful succession of silks came out the door. Victor never looked my way on his walk to stall three for last-minute instructions from Rick. Given the plan, the instructions were minimal.

The call for "Jockeys up!" rang out. I saw Victor take a leg up from Rick and swing aboard Brown Beauty as if he'd been riding daily. As Victor's horse was led by the stable-hand close to my position at the rail, Victor pulled a small corner of a slip of paper out of the waistband of his pants. He gave a momentary glance at me with a question mark written all over his face.

I looked as deeply eye to eye as I could for emphasis and gave a minimal but unwavering nod, "Yes!" The envelope that Lanny delivered contained a two-dollar betting ticket on Brown Beauty. It was a ticket to win. It had just four words written in my best hand on the back: "Ride like the wind."

Victor's first reaction to my nod was one of stunned doubt, but as the message sank in, a smile began to crack the solemn set of his mouth. It was a full-blown grin by the time he passed through the gate onto the track. Brown Beauty began a high prancing trot in the post parade as if he were reading the body language coursing through every inch of his jockey.

The race was six furlongs, a three-quarter mile sprint. The horses were loaded in the starting gate without incident. I could see the race starter on his platform take the starting button in hand.

There was just time for one last prayer as I turned back to spot Fat Tony and his overstuffed entourage sitting in a front box in the clubhouse. The satisfied look on his face said that he and his mafia associates had managed to place high wagers with every bookmaking syndicate across the country. Victor had heard that Fat Tony had muscled his way into the animal deal for a cut of the profits. Within about one minute and eleven seconds, his fixed long-shot winner would bring in the $900,000 needed to pay Chico's gang the second installment for the animals.

* * *

"They're off!"

That call always sent my blood pressure into a steep climb. This time, it gave me an instant case of the chills. My eyes were glued to the springing gates of the number three chute. Brown Beauty exploded out of that gate as if he knew what was riding on his race.

It took him four giant strides to propel him a full neck ahead of the pack. Victor gave him the whip once and then crouched on his neck with the reins in both fists, pumping forward with every stride.

When they reached the turn at the end of the backstretch, Victor had driven him into a two-length lead, clear of the other racers in case Fat Tony had some backup plan for scuttling Brown Beauty.

When they were halfway around the turn, the lead was three lengths, and my worry center lit up. Was the pace too fast? Would Brown Beauty have enough left in the tank for the long homestretch?

Victor apparently did not share my worries. He drove Brown Beauty off the turn and onto the homestretch. Over the crowd tumult, I was vaguely aware of the track announcer screaming, "Here comes Brown Beauty, and Beauty is flying!"

I looked at Victor's face as he passed the eighth pole. His left cheek was nearly touching the blowing mane of the horse, and I was sure he was yelling something at the top of his lungs.

I knew at that moment that with every foot of track Brown Beauty was consuming with his stretching stride, the greatest race I had seen in my entire life was all but in the books.

I stole one glorious look back at the twisted face of Fat Tony, contorted as it was with pure rage, and a shiver of joy ran through my entire body.

By the time Victor and Brown Beauty crossed the finish line, I was running full out for the winner's circle. I nearly ran down an old track tout ripping up betting tickets when I glanced away from my path to see Victor rise, standing straight up in the irons with both fists in the air, still yelling something to the skies—perhaps to his brother, Roberto.

I stood by the rail just outside the enclosure where the jockeys have to weigh in before the race can be declared official. I knew there was a second race that had to be run. I could see Fat Tony screaming orders at the two goons in his box.

They began running to the clubhouse exit as fast as their fat bowed legs could carry them. I knew they were heading for the path Victor would take back to the jockeys' room with guns drawn. There was no one anywhere near that path, and the crowd noise would cover up any shots fired.

I jumped the rail and grabbed Victor's arm as soon as he came close. He was still grinning. I made time for one long overdue hug of victory, and then pulled him into a dead run. We jumped the rail on the other side of the path and ran full out to the side of the parking lot where I'd parked a nondescript rental car.

I thanked God for the map I had in my mind of every backstreet from Revere to Route 1 north of Boston. I gave Victor a ride that must have rivaled the one he had just had on Brown Beauty.

He changed into the street clothes I'd brought for him, while I apologized for keeping the change of plan from losing to winning from him until the last minute. I wanted him to be able to promise a fixed race to Fat Tony with no trace of doubt in his voice. I explained that the rest of the plan called for him to simply stay out of sight. Fat Tony's mobsters would be scouring every corner of the city and beyond for him.

My sincere hope was that the *insectos* still thought the body of the homeless man found shot at Jamaica Pond was mine. That gave me room to operate as long as I stayed out of Puerto Rican haunts.

I veered off of Route 1 into the parking lot of a hotel on Newbury

Street in Danvers. The choice was easy. How could I resist the Knight's Inn?

I registered Victor under a name from a bygone era. I was sure none of the young crowd there would remember Darrel Madden, the leading jockey who rode my first winning horse at Suffolk Downs.

THIRTY-TWO

IT MAY NOT have been the greatest win in racing history, since all of the horses except Victor's and the longest shot on the board for whom the race was fixed were being pulled by their jockeys. But it sure felt like it. I saw more emotion on Rick McDonough's flushed face in the winner's circle than I thought he could muster. He caught sight of me by the weigh-in scales. I read an instant look of consternation in his expression because I had not trusted him with the real plan, but the elation of the unexpected win clearly drowned it out.

Now events would start to move at warp speed. I set up a quick meeting that evening with Mr. Devlin and Billy Coyne. I chose a spot that would be least likely to be frequented by Fat Tony or the local band of *insectos*. It was also one that would give us the absolute maximum security I needed—St. Anthony's Mission Church at 100 Arch Street, a short walk from the office of each of them. Brother Bruce Lenich, with whom I've gone one on one on a basketball court with personally humiliating and expensive results more often than I care to admit, let us use his office.

At this point, there was no choice but to lay all the cards on the table—face up. I explained the presence and purpose of Harry Wong, now stashed in a luxury suite of the Ritz-Carlton, in the most optimistic terms I could manage. My explanation drew the "Are-you-serious?" look I expected from Billy Coyne. Mr. D.'s expression sent me a generous, if tentative, "benefit of the doubt" message. I took a breath and launched into one of the hardest sells of my life.

"Mr. Coyne, I think you're probably wondering why in the world you agreed to line up the federal forces behind this little plan." He nodded. "And you're also wondering how in hell you can squeeze $900,000 out of the federal executive budget to carry it off." The next nod was more vigorous.

"It had to be done this way. I need Harry Wong at the center of the action to pull it off."

I explained why. Mr. Coyne's forehead was still deeply furrowed. It was time for my last fastball right over the plate.

"I'm counting on the fact that at this moment, Fat Tony and the *insectos* involved in this animal smuggling scheme are scared totally crapless. They owe some $900,000 to Chico Mendosa's gang in Mayagüez for the animals that are waiting to be delivered. They counted on the winnings from that race this afternoon to pay it. As we planned, Victor blew their dreams to pieces by winning the race. They not only lost all the winnings they expected to use, they lost all the money they bet on the race with bookies all over this country and Canada, plus the cost of fixing the race. They are in one hell of a hole. And they know better than anyone what Chico Mendosa's mob will do to them when they don't come up with the cash. Chico's boys will send a message in pure pain and blood. Right now, Fat Tony and the *insectos* would sell the souls of their grandmothers for a bailout."

At least the grimace was gone from Mr. Coyne's face. On to point two.

"There's a second level. Chico's boys will double the squeeze on Fat Tony and the *insectos* because Chico's gang owes at least that much to the South American drug cartel to pay for the heroin they're packing in with the animals. They need to be paid by Fat Tony and the *insectos* in order to pay off the cartel. And if Chico's gang can be inhumanly vicious in collecting their debts, you can at least double that for the cartel. Chico's people will be grasping at any straw that floats by."

The furrows were gone from his forehead. Mr. Coyne was just murmuring, "Mmmm."

"This plan could work, Mr. Coyne. Harry and I are putting our lives on the line for it."

"I suppose."

"You better suppose. Like the pig said when the hen invited him for a ham-and-egg breakfast. 'For you it's just a pain in the ass. For me it's a matter of life or death.'"

I thought it, but not to deflect his focus with similes, I just said, "That's the plan. I have to know now. The clock's running. Are we in or out?"

It took ten more weighty seconds before he mumbled, "I'll get the cash for you. Are you sure you need all of the $900,000?"

"No. I recalculated. I need an even million. Can you have it in cash, in a large unmarked briefcase? I'll pick it up from Mr. Devlin in his office at nine tomorrow morning."

I didn't wait for an answer. Some things you leave to faith.

My next contact was indirect. I couldn't risk a face-to-face meeting with Fat Tony Cannucci in his then state of mind. But I needed a chance to defuse him with a possible escape hatch.

I first called Paulie Caruso at his quasi-office at D'Angelo's Restaurant in the North End. The first thirty seconds of the call I spent calming his tantrum over the non-fixed race. I did it by calling my client, Victor, every synonym for a traitorous, backstabbing, lowlife, scumbag I could think of. That confused Paulie.

"I'm on your side, Mr. Caruso. I know about the animal deal. I'm actually in it for a cut of the profits. That damned jockey betrayed me, too."

That brought his temperature below the boiling point.

"But I've got a solution. We can still save the deal."

I'm sure he heard that as "We can still haul your condemned ass out of the fire pit."

"Yeah? What?"

I laid out a plan for a meeting the next morning at ten. I commissioned Paulie to convey the invitation to bring Fat Tony with him. That was half of the cast. I also needed Jose Ramos, the head of the *insectos* in Mayagüez on board since they were partnered in the animal deal with Paulie's Boston mafia family. I asked Paulie to bring Ramos into the loop by conference call.

Before Paulie reached Ramos, I figured a little preparation of that ground would be in order. I called the restaurant, El Rey de Lechón in Roslindale. Ben the Chef answered.

"Hi, Mike. You missed my best specialty tonight."

"Be kind to me, Ben. Don't tell me what it was. You don't want to hear me cry. Is the big man there?"

"We're just closing. He's having a brandy in the dining room."

"Is he alone?"

"Sure. I just hung the 'Closed' sign. Hang on."

The conversation switched to Spanish. I was not sure what to make of Mr. Garcia's greeting.

"Michael! What the hell is this? I heard you were killed last night. At Jamaica Pond."

"You know what Mr. Twain said. 'Rumors of my death have been greatly exaggerated.'"

There was a pause. "What a relief, Michael. Thank God you're all right."

"Thank you. I have just a minute. Can we talk privately?"

"Certainly. Go ahead."

"The fixing of that race backfired. Victor rode to win. I thought that would kill the *insectos* deal for the animals. That would be the best thing for your *Nyetas*."

"Yes. I know."

"But now there's a new wrinkle. Someone else showed up. I hear he wants to put money into the animal deal. He's a big shot with the Chinese tong. They run organized crime in every city that has a Chinatown. He has almost unlimited funds."

"Who is he? Where's he from?"

"That's all I heard. Nobody outside of the tong itself knows much about any of them. They're a complete island. I only know it looks bad for the *Nyetas*. This guy is the real deal."

There were a few seconds of silence. "That's bad news, Michael. Where'd you get the information?"

"One of those confidential sources I mentioned. An old friend in Chinatown. We've exchanged favors over the years. I just wanted to give you a heads-up. I know you'd do the same for me."

With that seed planted, I let a splash or two of the Famous Grouse untangle tightly wound nerves to get a solid night's sleep before a day that promised to be memorable.

* * *

By quarter of ten the next morning, I was giving Harry Wong the kind of last-minute prep I'd have given to a critical trial witness. He sat sipping coffee out of a Spode cup in a $2000 suit with the silk shirt and Bally shoes that I had previously stocked in his closet. He exuded the air of one to the manner born.

His increasing comfort in the role of a member of the luxuriously wealthy class was reassuring. At the same time, it was scaring the hell out of me. Harry has been known to play it over the top.

"You're sure you've got it, Harry? I want you relaxed and on top of it. At the same time, not too relaxed. Remember that one slip and we're hamburger."

He gave me a look.

"Is that how you comfort your witnesses?"

"Just trying to tune you up."

The phone rang. One of us jumped three inches, and it wasn't Harry. I got it.

"Sir, there are two . . . gentlemen asking for Mr. Chin An-Lo."

I sensed that the concierge was stretching his understanding of the word "gentlemen" to the rupture point. I asked him to show them to the elevator up to Harry's room.

A soft, sonorous bell sounded by the door leading to Harry's private elevator. I answered the door and escorted Fat Tony and Paulie Caruso into a royally appointed sitting room that had their necks on a constant swivel. I invited them to sit on Chippendale chairs, while I made the call with the number I got from Paulie that brought the top *insecto* in Mayagüez, Jose Ramos, into the conversation on speakerphone.

Harry let them sit and absorb their surroundings for thirty seconds, and then fidget for another thirty seconds, before making his entrance. I was about to summon him by the scruff of the neck for overdoing it, when suddenly our Harry appeared.

I was stunned myself. He coasted across the floor looking like a million dollars from head to toe—literally. The two thugs on the Chippendales were on their feet instantly. They each held out a hand as he approached. I nearly lost my breakfast when Harry ignored both hands in passing and simply glided in for a landing on a sofa that could be sold for the price of my Corvette. He was solidly in the role. The silent words, "So far, so good," slowed my heart rate a trifle.

He finally acknowledged them with a glance. I started to

introduce them, but Harry cut me off in mid-introduction. "Mr. Knight, there is nothing you can add. I know more about these people than their own mothers. And you there on the telephone, you as well. That said, let's not quibble about facts. You have a business transaction regarding live cargo. It interests me."

Paulie Caruso found his voice first. "You have an interest in the animals, Mr. . . ."

"Not in the slightest. I have an interest in money, Mr. Caruso. Your cargo represents money. What you don't have is the capital to bring it off. I do."

There was a soft knock at the door. I leaped up to open it. It was a finely liveried employee of the hotel. He spoke from the doorway directly to Harry, "Mr. Chin, may I bring you and your guests beverages and refreshments?"

Harry's answer was decisive. "No. These people will not be staying long enough to bring coffee. You're dismissed."

I closed and locked the door behind the rapidly retreating hotel employee. Harry continued the monologue. "I am prepared to invest the $900,000 you need to consummate the purchase of the cargo."

Paulie and Fat Tony looked at each other. If they had been in any other surrounding, they'd have bounced their fat butts off the Chippendales and high-fived. I could almost hear a sigh of relief over the speakerphone.

Harry read it in their faces. Before they could speak, he continued. "Before you agree, it comes at a price. Exactly what profit do you expect from the sale of this cargo?"

This time Fat Tony found his voice. "We understand . . . three million . . ."

Harry smiled. He looked at Fat Tony with a glare that could cow a rhinoceros. "The figure is four million five hundred thousand. I would expect you to lie, Mr. Cannucci, because you're a thief and a blackguard. However, that said, if you ever try to deceive or defraud me again in the slightest matter, you will most assuredly lose more than my investment. Do you understand that completely?"

As if to lend punctuation to Harry's words, two amazingly muscled young Chinese men, dressed head to toe in black, entered the room from the door of Harry's entrance. Harry had apparently felt the need to add a supporting cast. They caught the attention of Fat Tony and stifled in mid-throat any intended reply. He simply nodded.

"Good. Life is simpler when there is no room for misunderstanding. Now to the price. I have two conditions. My portion of the profits shall be 35 percent."

"*Oh crap, Harry. Control yourself. The plan was 25 percent. That's what I mean by over the top.*" The words resounded between my ears, but never left my mouth.

"If there is the slightest disagreement with that figure, my associates will escort you to the elevator. This is not a negotiation."

I could see Paulie and Fat Tony weighing the loss of 35 percent of the profits against the impending loss of bodily parts to Chico's thugs. The nods came within five seconds. I heard a mumbled, "No objection," over the speakerphone.

"Good. We won't speak of this again. Secondly, your supplier of this cargo is Señor Chico Mendosa's organization in Mayagüez. I need to reach an arrangement with Señor Mendosa before the $900,000 is at your disposal. Señor Ramos, you'll arrange a meeting with Mr. Mendosa."

The voice of Jose Ramos, the head of the *insectos,* came over the speakerphone. "When and where?"

"This afternoon. Two o'clock sharp."

There was a pause. "Excuse me, Señor. He could not possibly get to Boston by then."

"Of course not. But I can be in Mayagüez. My plane is being readied now. Two p.m. Sharp. Mr. Knight will arrange the place. He will be accompanying me."

Harry looked at the silent faces and stood. "Excellent. If my meeting with Señor Mendosa produces results that satisfy me, you'll have the money you need this evening. Now one last item."

Harry looked at one of the palace guard standing by the door. I could read him. I all but whispered, *"Don't snap your fingers, Harry. This is not a 1940s movie."*

He snapped his fingers. The guard disappeared through the door. He returned in seconds with the largest and finest leather briefcase I have ever seen. Harry nodded at the table in front of the guests. The guard placed the briefcase in front of them.

"Gentlemen. Lest you're ever temped to take my words less than seriously . . ."

Harry took a key from his pocket, unlocked the case, and flipped it open with a feigned nonchalance that I almost wanted to applaud. The eyes of the guests nearly left their heads. They had never seen the color green in such profusion as in the $900,000 lying in front of them.

Harry gave it ten seconds to sink in. He flipped the case closed, picked it up, and strode through the door he had entered without one syllable of salutation.

It was a remarkable performance.

THIRTY-THREE

THE PRIVATE JET I chartered for Harry was in the air ten minutes after we arrived at Logan Airport. During the flight, I reached Nestor by cell phone in Mayagüez. His skepticism when I outlined the plan was overcome only by his lack of any Plan B.

There was a car to meet us at a secluded edge of the runway at the Eugenio Maria De Hostos Airport in Mayagüez. Harry and I jumped aboard, and the car took off. The driver wore a black shirt and pants with a cap pulled low over his forehead. We turned onto Highway 2 heading north at a good clip before the driver pushed back the cap and cast me a wary smile.

"Nestor! Good to see you. I thought you'd send a driver."

"You know you're dealing with the devil here, Michael. I thought I better watch your back."

"Thanks, but this time I think we're safer if you stay out of sight. The fewer competing gang entanglements, the safer. Besides, if they wanted to just shoot the three of us, what could you do?"

"So how do you two plan to stay alive? Chico Mendosa's bunch is the worst of the worst."

I could feel a shiver run through Harry on the seat beside me.

"We have something they want. $900,000. They don't get it until we get back to Boston alive."

"Suppose they decide to just kidnap you two. A couple of days of torture and you'd be sending home for the ransom. Your buddy here looks like money walking. No offense."

"None taken." Harry smiled as he said it. He held a hand over the seat to shake hands. Nestor looked at him as if he were a potential sack of ransom cash in unmarked bills. He ignored the hand and just kept driving. "I repeat the question, Michael."

"They're no dummies. I figure they've been moving contraband animals for years. Now they're on the verge of a drug score that makes the rest of it look like small change. Are they going to jeopardize it by killing two American citizens?"

He looked at me through the rearview mirror. "I don't know, are they? Maybe you give them too much credit for smarts."

Nestor turned off on a small, one-lane side road. He headed northeast.

I decided the subject needed changing. "How did you set it up, Nestor?"

He just shook his head, apparently resigned to the fact that the die was cast. "I got a message through to Chico Mendosa about the meeting you wanted with their head man. I did it through one of their men I knew from the old days. We have no open fight with Chico's gang at the moment."

I knew the "we" meant the *Nyetas*.

"So where do we meet?"

"'Where' is not the problem. They chose the place. 'Who' is the problem. He'll have an army with him."

"That's okay. He needs me. Actually, he needs Harry."

The one-lane road turned into a dirt road that led to the shore of a river, the Rio Grande de Añasco. Two men with what looked like AK-47s blocked the road. I realized that this was my show from here on.

"Slow down, but keep driving till we get to them."

The two guards split, one on each side of the car. I patted Harry's arm. I whispered, "Buck up, Harry. Just like we're valet parking for the Boston Symphony Orchestra."

He whispered back, "Damn, Michael. What's the Spanish word for 'No'?"

"It's '*No*'."

"Remind me of that next time you call and it's not Thanksgiving."

We each stepped out of the car on our own side. Two other goons appeared and frisked us for weapons. They led us up a path through the trees to the front steps of what in Montana would be called a hunting lodge. Inside, we climbed a second set of steps to a door at the top of the landing.

Goon One knocked. Goon Two responded to the voice from inside and opened the door. For all we knew, we were prisoners of the man who sat at the head of the large oval table in the center of the rustically decorated room. He sat in the high-back chair at head of the table. I was sure that the regal chair and the cigar he smoked while seeming to ignore us were props to convey to us who was in charge.

Prisoners or not, Harry strode, rather than walked, to the only other high-back chair at the table, directly facing our host. I sat in the low-back chair beside Harry.

Harry pulled his chair up to the edge of the table with what seemed to be a maximum of thumping sounds. I knew it was intended as an annoying counter to our host's air of authority. He clearly took it that way. His glare moved from Harry to me.

He indicated Harry with his chin. "Can that one do it in Spanish?"

Before I could answer, Harry addressed the man sitting to the right of our host, whom I assumed to be Chico Mendosa. "Can that one do it in Chinese?"

A taut silence settled in for about five seconds. Finally, our host addressed Harry directly in English. "Let's get this on the table. You're here at my allowance. I could have the both of you shot right now with one word. Understand that."

Harry faced him with a stare I'd never seen before. He pounded his fist on the table. I was halfway into a solemn prayer, when Harry fired the words. "Then do it!"

Another silence, more frozen than the last. "Do it! Do it now! I have no time for this juvenile posturing."

Our host had the firepower on his side, but still seemed to be the one grasping for control. "Do you know who the hell—"

"Do I know who you are? Of course I do. Why do you suppose I came here?"

Before our host could reload to fire another verbal volley, Harry settled back in his chair with a sense of calm that went beyond impressive. "Let's start making sense here. You have two choices. You could go on playing the big shot for your peons here. You could even get your jollies ordering the killing of two men you know are unarmed. Or . . . you can stop playing a pissant gangster and act like a businessman. I came here to make a deal that will bring you more money than you could imagine in your wildest dreams."

That last part seemed to gain an edge on the rest. Our host was chewing at the end of his cigar with narrowed eyes. "I hear you already made a deal with the *insectos* and the Italians back in the States."

"You heard right. Those people couldn't even pull off a fixed race. I had to put money into it to get those animal crates moving. Without me, you'd have a warehouse full of dead animals and no way to move what this thing is really about. Now, if you're through wasting my time, let's talk about what's going to make the real money. For both of us."

"What're you talking about?"

"I'm talking about what's in those cages besides animals. I'll say it if you won't. Heroin. Pure. White as the driven snow. Probably more than ever came across the mainland border in one load."

The cigar-chewing became more intense. "Where did you hear that? Who told you that? I don't even know who the hell you are."

Harry matched the penetration of his eyes. "And you never will. Unlike you, I belong to an organization that has the discipline to keep its identity to itself. I'll give you a name. The Chinese tong. Say it to most people, they'll say it hasn't existed for decades."

Another pause before he spoke. "Then why would I want to do business with this tong that maybe doesn't even exist?"

"I'll give you the only reason that matters. You have buyers for the heroin after it's smuggled in. A few mafia families. The Russians. The Irish. Whatever. How much are they offering for it?"

"Why should I tell you?"

"You don't have to. I know what they can afford. Get your head out of a hole in the ground and listen. Take what they're offering for the drugs . . . and triple it."

I could see our host's eyes bulge involuntarily. "The hell."

"No. Not 'the hell.' The fact. There's a reason I can pay this and still make more money myself than you ever dreamed of. I can cut it, package it, and distribute it through every Chinatown in every city in the United States and Canada. The demand is something you can't even comprehend."

Our host sat in silence running mental calculations. Harry gave him the space by slowly checking his watch and looking at his cell phone. When he looked back at our host, he leaned forward as if he were ready to stand.

"I'll add one element. This is just the first time. If I find your organization reliable . . . This could be the beginning of a beautiful friendship."

My respect for the depth of Harry's cool just doubled with his tossing off that last line from the movie *Casablanca*.

Our host was beginning to swim in dreams reaching fantasies. "How does this work?"

"The simpler, the better. As planned. The gang you call the *insectos* will do the smuggling into the mainland wherever you have the connections already greased. I assume somewhere on the coast of Florida. The bribes will still work because everyone will still think they're just smuggling animals. My people will have no part of that. When it's in and unloaded, you tell us where it is by phone. I'll be waiting. I'll check it out. If it's what it's supposed to be, I'll wire the first payment to be sure it goes through. You acknowledge receipt. Then I wire the rest of the payment in full."

Harry took a pen and piece of paper out of his pocket. He wrote a dollar amount per kilo on the paper, folded it, and slid it across the table. Our host grabbed it and opened it.

Harry stood. "I want to hear just one word, and I leave."

Our host had the cigar chewed down to the wrapper. "I need to talk with my people."

"No, you don't. You knew what this meeting was about. You're the man in authority or you wouldn't be here. Either you have the rocks to make a decision right now that will make you the wealthiest man in Puerto Rico . . . or you're just the pissant gangster who sat there preening himself when we came in. One word. Yes or no."

I was very nearly in need of a bathroom for the next five seconds. If the word was "no," there was no reason not to order both of our heads blown off forthwith.

Our host tossed his masticated cigar into a wastebasket. He stuffed the paper in his pocket and nodded in the affirmative.

My feet were nearly on the way to the door when Harry gave my blood pressure one last bounce.

"I'd like to hear the word. Out loud."

Our host seemed to regain some sense of control from the decision-making process. I could see him chafing at being given an order in front of his men. He spoke calmly, but the underlying threat was clear. "Be careful. The day may come when you will cross the line. In spite of the money."

Harry returned the calm. "I'm sure you'll let me know if that day comes."

"Oh, you'll know. You'll know. In the meantime . . . may we both prosper."

Harry nodded, and the deal was sealed. Our host began to stand. Harry cut short any thought of an uncomfortable parting word on either side. He preceded me directly through the door, down the stairs, and into the waiting car. The instant we were aboard, Nestor put the car in motion for the drive back to the airport.

"I don't have to ask how it went. You're both still alive."

When we cleared the post of the two armed guards, I looked over at Harry to shake his hand. He had held it together as long as necessary. In the ten seconds since we had gotten into the car, his breathing rate had doubled, and the hand I took was trembling enough to mix paint. I looked at his face, now bathed in rivulets of perspiration.

"You were magnificent, Harry."

He managed a weak smile. "Piece of cake, Mike."

THIRTY-FOUR

EVENTS WERE NOW up to sprinting speed. All the dominoes were set to tumble. The trick was to keep up with them, stay alive, and not miss any important turns.

As our flight back neared Logan Airport, I called Fat Tony to set up a meeting with him and Paulie Caruso at seven that evening to complete the deal for the animals—$900,000 in cash. Fat Tony was with Paulie waiting for our call.

They suggested we meet at Paulie's restaurant, D'Angelo's, in the North End of Boston. Harry was listening on the speakerphone. He grabbed my hand with the phone, put on his Chin An-Lo voice, and yelled into the phone. "What have I ever said that would suggest to you that I'm that dimwitted? Mr. Knight and I will be in a private room upstairs in the China Pearl Restaurant on Tyler Street in Chinatown at precisely 7:00 p.m. If you're both there, on time, alone, without so much as a nail file in your pockets, we'll do business."

Before I could speak to soften it, Harry reached over and tapped the "end call" button on my phone. He had apparently more than recovered from our last hairy episode. I was afraid he was beginning to enjoy this altogether too much.

"Harry, could we remember that we're still dealing with people who would kill both of us—emphasize *both*—with sadistic joy."

"I've got it, Mike. I'm in total control."

"Hmmm."

With Harry's connections at the China Pearl Restaurant, we had the privacy of a top-floor room, well adorned in Chinese décor with a profusion of rich red accents that clearly implied that it was Harry's bailiwick.

At 7:00 p.m. precisely, Paulie and Fat Tony were shown through the door by the owner. Harry had the two Chinese muscle men who had been with us at the Ritz-Carlton in attendance by the door.

Harry and I were seated at the table when they arrived. Harry pointed to two empty seats as an invitation. Fat Tony walked to the chair with a strut that looked more self-assured than natural. Paulie looked around for someone to give him the expected frisk. Harry nodded to a chair.

"Sit, Mr. Caruso. I trust your discretion. If you were foolish enough to bring a weapon . . . well, I needn't describe the consequences in these pleasant surroundings. Sit."

A few words in Chinese from Harry to the proprietor ensured the same privacy we would have had at the Marliave, minus the dinner. The proprietor withdrew, followed by the two muscle men—whom I later learned were actors Harry had engaged from a Chinese theatre group.

Harry took the lead. "Gentlemen, to the point. To review, I am financing a shipment of live cargo, to be passed through customs at your risk. It will be delivered onshore in the mainland to wholesale buyers with whom you have an arrangement. I understand that they will pay on delivery, and, lest we forget, I shall receive forthwith 35 percent of the agreed price. Are we still in agreement?"

Paulie looked at Fat Tony without speaking. Fat Tony began shifting in his chair. "I don't know. Thirty-five percent. It seems we take all the risks and you—"

Harry's fist came down on the table with a resounding smack that could be heard in the North End. I should have been getting used to Harry's outbursts, but I still came three inches off the chair and grabbed the table. One glance told me that the other two were frozen in place.

"Before you say another word, all bets are down. You play the game as agreed, or I recover my expenses in cash—or pain—before you leave. I do no business with weasels. Speak now!"

Paulie began nodding immediately. Without his army of thugs around him, he was no superhero. Fat Tony was a tougher nut to crack. I could see his mind running numbers. Perhaps it was the promise of reaping the somewhat diminished profit on many future occasions that swung the balance.

"All right. Done."

Harry was a human roller coaster. He could go from a volcano of erupting emotion to a sedate businessman in a flash, once his feathers were smoothed.

"Done indeed."

Harry stood and clapped his hands once loudly. Poor Paulie flinched again. Fat Tony just looked curious until the door opened and one of the muscled actors entered the room. He placed the fine leather briefcase in front of Harry.

Harry produced a key, unlocked the case, flipped it open, and spun it around to face our guests. Their eyes were riveted on the fresh, green, bound stacks of presidential portraits.

Harry gave the briefcase a shove. It glided to a halt under their noses below two sets of staring eyes.

"Nine hundred thousand dollars, as agreed. Count it if you like."

Fat Tony pulled it toward himself. He dug through the top packets to see that the cash ran straight through to the bottom layer. He looked up at Harry with a slick smile and closed the case. "I think we can agree that the unpleasant results of any deception here would flow both ways."

Harry smiled. "It's a pleasure to do business with gentlemen who understand the parameters."

Fat Tony snapped the clasps on the briefcase and placed it at his side.

"Now, gentlemen," Harry said, refocusing their attention. "To conclude this pleasant meeting, when will the ship with the live cargo sail?"

Fat Tony locked eyes with Harry while he hit one button on his cell phone. He said three words into the phone. "I have it."

He listened for several seconds and ended the call. He turned back to Harry. "The ship sails this evening. It will dock in two days. Early morning."

"Good. Where will it come ashore?"

Fat Tony looked at Harry with a wary eye. "I don't know. What difference is that to you?"

"Just a curiosity. However, my 35 percent is not a curiosity. I'll expect your call in two days. I'll give you instructions then to wire the money to my account."

* * *

I noticed that the two stayed close to each other as they descended the steps of the China Pearl Restaurant. I watched through an open window upstairs. When they hit Tyler Street, they were engulfed in the dinner hour sea of Chinatown denizens. There was a large sprinkling of tourists in the crowd, but after my planting thoughts of the Chinese tong in their minds, every Asiatic face that crowded them on the sidewalk drew them closer together. Fat Tony was carrying enough cash in that fine briefcase to make anyone paranoid under the circumstances.

Fat Tony hailed the first on-duty taxicab he could find parked by the sidewalk. They hustled their fat butts through the cab door, slammed it, and gave orders to the driver to get them the hell out of there.

I have to admit, it tickled me to the point of the first actual out-loud laugh I could remember. Harry gave me a quizzical look.

"You seem jolly after just giving away $900,000 of taxpayers' money to two of the lowest parasites on earth."

"I don't know, Harry. Maybe it's being in your fine company. Maybe it's having those parasites out of our sight. Or maybe it's the fact that the driver of that cab they got into is one of the few Chinese members of the Boston Police Force. They don't know it, but their next stop is the Eighth Precinct station house for book-ing on race fixing and smuggling charges. That fine briefcase of tax-payers' money is actually on its way back to the office of Deputy District Attorney Billy Coyne."

Harry was grinning now. "The hell you say."

"I do say, Harry. And, as far as the mafia in the North End is con-cerned, neither you nor I had anything to do with the arrest. We can still go to dinner at Lucca's anytime we like."

I couldn't help thinking of the joy and relief the arrest of those two would bring to my client, Victor. With the heads cut off of the race-fixing organization, he could not only come out of hiding—he and every other jockey at Suffolk Downs from that day on could ride every race to win.

* * *

Our next move was to get Harry back to his sumptuous digs at the Ritz-Carlton. On the drive, I got a call from Nestor. He had heard from the two Brazilians. Ansuro had told him that the whole crew at the warehouse was suddenly busy loading the new crates, repacked with the animals, on the three trucks. They'd be pulling out for the trip to the docks in Mayagüez sometime after midnight.

"Has Ansuro heard where they'll come ashore on the mainland?"

"He heard them talking about two sites. One is just north of Boca Raton on the east coast of Florida. The other is on the east side of Key Largo. There's an inlet off Garden Cove inside of Rattlesnake Key. He couldn't hear which one they'll use."

"Don't worry about it. If it's down to two, I can find out which one. It's time, Nestor. We need you in position to lead the people we talked about to the warehouse area."

"I'm ready."

I hung up and dialed Billy Coyne. He was waiting for my call at the federal building office of the U.S. attorney.

I gave him all the information, including Nestor's number. "It's on, Mr. Coyne. Are you ready to put it in gear?"

"Soon as I get the word."

"You've got it. Right now. Go."

I dropped Harry and drove directly to the El Rey de Lechón Restaurant in Roslindale. It was close to closing. This time I came in through the front door. Ben, the chef, was just carrying out the last dish from in front of the lone diner, Mr. Garcia, at his usual table. He and I had the room to ourselves.

Mr. Garcia seemed surprised to see me. He waved a gracious hand toward a chair at his table. He called to Ben to bring more wine and another glass. He did, and returned to the kitchen cleanup for the night.

I sat and accepted both the wine and the toast to my health from Mr. Garcia. I told him that my time was short, but I had some news. I told him that the animals were about to be shipped from Mayagüez. It was too late for anyone to stop it.

He asked if I knew where they'd come ashore. I took a deep draft of the wine and looked at him directly. At this point, we switched to Spanish. "Yes, It's a point just north of Boca Raton. They'll smuggle the animals ashore there. The customs people know about it, but they've been bribed before."

"Is there anything you can do to prevent it?"

I leaned across the table. "This is a life-or-death confidence, Mr. Garcia. But I know I can trust you."

"Of course. It goes both ways. Tell me."

"I got the Suffolk County District Attorney's office involved. The deputy D.A. is coordinating everything with the federal authorities. This is gang-related criminal conduct across state lines. It's also international smuggling and a RICO violation on a large scale. That means he was able to get the FBI and the Coast Guard directly involved. When the ship pulls into the dock north of Boca, they'll have a surprise welcoming committee."

He leaned back with a smile and lifted his glass. "*Felicidades, Miguel. Buen trabajo.*"—"Good work, Michael. Well done."

I touched glasses with him. "*Quizá. La semilla es plantada. Esperemos que se necesita.*"—"Perhaps. The seed is planted. Let's hope it takes."

Actually, that was a silent prayer. All I said out loud was, "*Gracias, Señor Garcia.*"

* * *

The next day, I felt like a juggler who has a couple more balls and clubs in the air than he can keep flying. I had to get my feet on solid ground with at least one of them.

I took Terry to lunch at the No-Name Restaurant on the Boston docks for a revitalizing, overflowing plate of the best fried whole clams this side of Ipswich.

Terry gave me an account of the mind-boggling details she had been nailing down for the wedding, which was on for four p.m. the following day. An amazing number of guests, some going back to our grammar and high school days, had altered schedules and travel plans to be with us on "our day."

I realized then that the shortening of our wedding date meant that Terry was engaged in a juggling act that rivaled mine. The only noticeable difference was that if she made a miscue, none of our guests were threatening to blow our brains out.

* * *

The following day was D-Day. It was crunch time in so many different directions. I was grateful for the superstition about not seeing the bride on the day of the wedding until she came down the aisle. It left me the freedom to accomplish what seemed impossible before four o'clock.

The previous night, Harry and I had flown the private plane Billy Coyne's funds were still providing to a small airport on the southern end of Key Largo. We rented a car and drove to the docks by the inlet on Garden Cove across from Rattlesnake Key toward North Creek Sound. We each took turns sleeping while the other scanned the coast for the lights of a ship.

Just as the sun was beginning to cast thin rays of light over the horizon, the ship pulled into the deserted dock. Harry called Chico in Mayagüez to have him notify the ship's captain that we were to be permitted aboard to examine the merchandise before unloading.

The word must have been passed. No one stopped us when we boarded the ship and went right to the hold. We descended the steps with flashlights. The odor was less pungent this time. Each of the cages was covered with a tarpaulin.

Without lifting the tarp, Harry picked a cage at random and used a knife to dig a small hole in the side of what looked like a solid base. When the knife penetrated, a tiny trickle of white powder flowed out. Harry touched a damp finger to it and tasted it.

He made a face that could mean anything.

I whispered, "What, Harry?"

"These bozos have tapped into the mother lode. This stuff is the purest of the pure."

"And you'd know?"

"Take it on faith."

I did. I dialed the cell phone of Chico. The boss of the gang was with him waiting for the call. I let Harry talk.

"The shipment looks good. I'll take it. Give me the number to wire the money."

Harry wrote down the number and hung up. He dialed another number and set up the immediate transfer of funds—specifically, $50,000.

We waited. My phone jumped in three minutes flat. Harry answered it. It was Chico. "What the hell is this? I could get $50,000 for a tenth of one case on any street corner. We had a deal."

"We still have a deal. The rest is coming. The $50,000 was just to be sure of the transfer numbers. Just send back a formal acceptance of the money and I'll send the rest. Do it now."

Harry nodded to me as he hung up. "He accepted the first payment."

I grabbed the phone and hit the number for Billy Coyne. He caught it on the first ring. "It's done. He took payment for the drugs. The crime's complete. Let it rip."

Billy Coyne was on it. "I hit the button, kid. It's a go on both fronts."

I ignored the "kid" and hustled Harry up to the deck and down the gangplank for a front row seat in the shadows.

Billy was on top of his game. Men and women with the big letters

"FBI," on both sides of their jackets came out of nowhere with guns drawn. They poured onto the dock and up the gangplank.

The quiet of dawn was pierced with shouts of "Drop it!," "Hands up!," "Down on your knees," all over the ship. We heard the FBI leader tell the captain that the ship was confiscated for smuggling drugs.

A line of the crewmen with hands cuffed behind them started moving down the gangplank and into the waiting federal vehicles. I could hear pieces of Miranda warnings echoing all over the ship.

Harry grabbed my arm. "Let's get the hell out of here. Time is running."

I was about to run with him, when I saw something that had to be done. I ran back up the gangplank past the line of arrested crewmen to get to the FBI leader. I made my strongest lawyerly pitch in rapid-fire whispers. He held firm until I told him what the black African crewman, Martin, who was then halfway down the gangplank in cuffs, had done to save the animals and the two Brazilian stowaways, Ansuro and Ancarit.

He finally relented and shouted an order. One of the agents uncuffed the African, who looked back in surprise. He saw me and understood. He bowed to me, and I returned it, before he ran down the gangplank to his personal freedom.

Before Harry and I left, most of the cages had been stacked on the dock to be guarded and picked up by government trucks later. I got a nudge from Harry. "Hey, Mike, what about the animals?"

"Go take a look."

Harry ran down the row, lifting tarp after tarp to stare into empty cages.

"Where the hell are the animals?"

"Come on, Harry. I'll explain on the way."

THIRTY-FIVE

OUR CHARTERED JET was headed top throttle back to Boston when I got the call from Billy Coyne. God willing, the second of many shoes was about to drop. My hopes rose when I detected a grin in his voice.

"Smooth as silk, kid—Michael. I had the FBI office in Puerto Rico on alert. It didn't take much when I told them whom they were about to bring down. When you gave me the word that Chico Mendosa and the top brass of that gang of scum had accepted the payment for the drugs, the FBI troops stormed their headquarters like Patton's army. They've been trying to break that animal smuggling operation for years."

Now I was grinning. "Way to go, Mr. Coyne."

There was a pause. He said it quietly. "No, Michael. I have to admit it. This was yours. You set them up like tenpins for us. That partner of yours is going to be busting his buttons when I tell him about this."

That was the part that put the smile deep in my heart. Two down, one to go.

When we landed, I drove Harry back to Ritz-Carlton—he'd made no offer to move out of the lap of luxury he now no doubt felt he deserved. I had one more door to close before I could give every ounce of my attention to Terry and our wedding.

I drove directly to the El Rey de Lechón Restaurant in Roslindale.

The lunch crowd of old-timers was just breaking up. I joined Mr. Garcia at his table just as the last of his companions went out the door. Chef Ben was in the kitchen.

"What would you like, Michael? Ben's kitchen is still open for you."

This was the most bittersweet moment I could remember, and the bitter part was weighing heavily on my heart.

I said this completely in Spanish. "Mr. Garcia, I'm so sorry. I'm going to break your heart."

I could see lines of pain form on his forehead. I kept on in Spanish. "I'm speaking now to your chef, Ben Capone."

"I don't understand. Ben's in the kitchen. Shall I call him here?"

"There's no need, Mr. Garcia. Ben is listening to everything we say. He has been every time we've spoken in confidence. Look under the table. I'm sure you'll find a listening device. And he understands Spanish perfectly."

I could see disbelief as well as shock on Mr. Garcia's face. I put my hand on his arm. I went on in Spanish.

"I'm speaking to you now, Ben. I know you hear and understand every word. You're a traitor to Mr. Garcia and to the *Nyetas*. I know you passed everything you heard us say on to the *insectos*. That first day when Manuel, the bartender at Pepe's, sent a message to Mr. Garcia that I was meeting Paco at Jamaica Pond, you delivered the message to Mr. Garcia. Then you notified the *insectos* so they could have a man there to kill Paco and me. You and Mr. Garcia were the only ones who knew about the meeting, and Mr. Garcia would never deal with the *insectos*."

Mr. Garcia stopped me. "*Esto no puede ser verdad*, Miguel."— "This can't be true, Michael."

"I had to be sure, Mr. Garcia. I had to test it. A few days ago, I came here to tell you I was meeting my client, Victor, at the same place at Jamaica Pond. It wasn't true. I was going there alone. I said it privately to you, but Ben must have overheard it in the kitchen. That night, an *insecto* was there again to try to kill me. He's in police custody now. He named Ben Capone by name."

I could read pain in every line of Mr. Garcia's face. "But know this, Mr. Garcia. Ben's treachery served a purpose. It was the key to breaking their entire scheme. The last time you and I talked here, I knew he was listening. I specifically told you that they were planning to smuggle the animals ashore at the place north of Boca Raton. I said the federal troops would be waiting there. That wasn't true. I didn't know which of two places they'd choose. I figured Ben would relay the information to the *insectos* and the mafia so they'd use the other point, Key Largo, as the smuggling point. That's just what happened. The FBI's troops were waiting there to round up their whole crew."

Mr. Garcia looked toward the kitchen door. The look on his face was burning anger. He started to rise. "And what about Ben?"

We heard the sound of running footsteps and the slamming of the kitchen door. I knew that Ben had heard every word. He apparently decided that it was time to cut and run for his own life. And that was all right. I knew he'd be running right into the arms of the FBI team Billy Coyne had arranged to have there to block his escape.

* * *

I beat the clock by five minutes. The drive from Roslindale to my apartment to dress, and from there to Monsignor Ryan's Sacred Heart Church in Charlestown would take a non-Bostonian a good hour and a half. It would take a Bostonian an hour. It took this Bostonian forty-five minutes.

Father Ryan was a close boyhood friend of Mr. Devlin. We had even shared a few adventures with him in the past. He was there in full priestly garb to meet me at the side entrance at five minutes of four. He gave me a three-minute briefing to take the place of the usual rehearsal that in my case had been out of the question.

I had no time to explain why I was shaving the time so closely. Just before we went out to the altar he stopped me. "Are you sure you're ready to enter into this, Michael?"

I thought of the past three weeks. The only bright spots that bubbled up out of the morass of evil and pain were the moments I had spent with Terry. "Like gangbusters, Father."

He laughed. "Then let's do it right now."

We took our position at the altar. From somewhere, Harry Wong appeared at my side with a hug. I looked at that long, lean, smiling figure, who had proven yet again that he would ride into hell for his closest friend. The emotion got the best of me. I could only return the hug silently from the bottom of my heart.

Terry's maids of honor, Pat Plese and Helen Lee Potter, joined us at the altar. Big Daddy Hightower joined us to stand beside Harry. The stage was set.

At four, the ancient bells in the church steeple tolled the magic hour across all of Charlestown. My mother was in the front pew with Victor and my other cousins. I knew we would all be together soon for a memorial Mass for Roberto. I looked out at pew after pew on the right of faces that had influenced and brightened every era of my life from grammar school through law practice. There were more smiles and nods than I could return in those precious minutes.

And then they all disappeared. My heart jumped until I thought my body couldn't hold it in. I think there was organ music, but I can't even remember that. I can only remember seeing my entire life from that moment on in the smiling face that radiated whatever is beyond beauty coming down the aisle toward me.

She held the arm of Mr. Devlin, who was standing in for Terry's father since her parents were deceased. He was bringing me the greatest gift since his friendship. He kissed her gently before putting her hand in mine.

The ceremony began. I can recall that Father Ryan seemed to take immense personal joy in fusing the three of us—Terry and me and God—into one being.

*   *   *

The reception in the grand ballroom of the Parker House under the personal supervision of Terry Griffin was beyond flawless. Janet Reading looked like she had just brought off a second invasion of Normandy with four days' planning. She had one request. "Don't ever do this to me again."

I looked at Mrs. Terry O'Brien Knight sitting beside me at the head table. "Janet, I doubt that it will ever be an issue."

Weddings come in all different types. This one could only be called "joyous." I was so proud to introduce Terry to the friends of every phase of my life, and she did likewise to her friends. The wine flowed, and stories from our friends about things either Terry or I had done since childhood—some of them true—brought barrages of laughter.

The laughter was suspended when my best man, Harry Wong, stood to make the toast. I could never recapture the words here, or even the depth of spirit in which he said them. I only know that when he raised the glass, if there was a dry eye in the house, I didn't see it. Of course, I was looking through moist eyes myself.

It was time for our first dance as a married couple. We walked to the floor and stood waiting for the band to begin. I saw the musicians putting down their instruments, as the bandleader said that the music would be supplied by a very special friend.

We heard the sound begin to come from an organ in one corner of the room. We looked at each other and knew that John Kiley had kept his promise to play for our first dance. We both blew him a kiss, as I took Terry in my arms to dance to John's gift of "It Had to Be You."

I wondered if Terry was also thinking of that night at the Molly Waldo Restaurant when, as we danced to John's music, he said, "Michael, if you don't propose to this beautiful lady this evening, I'll personally have you committed." And I did.

* * *

It was around eleven o'clock when Terry and I left by limo for the airport. I was uncertain about answering the call on my cell phone, but I've always been glad that I did. I heard the voices of Nestor and the Brazilians, Ancuro and his grandson, Ancarit. They were beyond jubilant. They kept cutting in on each other to tell what had happened at the warehouse where the animals had been kept.

As I pieced what they said together, it seems that once I gave the word to Billy Coyne about payment being made for the animals, he had a force from the Puerto Rican office of the FBI ready to join Nestor. Nestor led them to a point in the road a few hundred yards out of sight of the warehouse. As soon as Chico accepted my payment, his gang loaded the cages of animals that now held the heroin as well, onto the three trucks. When the trucks moved out of sight of the warehouse toward the docks, the FBI force intercepted them with a full show of armament. They arrested the men, seized the trucks, and held them there.

What I didn't anticipate was that the agents of the FBI then

brought Ansuro and Ancarit back to the warehouse in the darkness. They gave the Brazilians four packages to sneak into the back
of the warehouse by a small door they had been using to spy. Under
orders, the two planted the packages inside and ran back into the
woods.

When the moment was right, one of the FBI agents pressed a remote switch button. The four packages inside went off in successive
explosions that shook the tin of the warehouse roof. The men inside
who had loaded the animal cages ran full tilt out through the front
door as if their feet were on fire. They ran smack into a line of FBI
troops with assault rifles that brought them to a dead stop. Within
fifteen minutes, they were handcuffed and ready to be transported
to FBI headquarters.

That much I got mostly from Nestor. When he finished, Ansuro
and his grandson broke in, one on top of the other, to tell the rest.
They were as excited as children home from their first day at school,
wanting to tell everything that happened. After a minute of both
talking at once, Ancarit let his grandfather tell it.

"The animals. I never dreamed of it. I thought when they drove
off, they'd mostly die on the journey. It was heart-breaking. Then,
after they arrested the men at the warehouse, we saw it coming from
the road. The trucks were bringing the animals back to the warehouse. We ran to help the FBI men unload them. Now we've turned
the whole warehouse into a clinic for the animals."

When Ansuro's emotions tightened his throat, Ancarit picked it
up. "They helped us build pens so we could let all of the animals out
of the cages and be as free as possible. Some of them we could help
right away. But a lot of them needed help we couldn't give."

Ansuro was back. "They're bringing veterinarians in from all over
Puerto Rico. Some will even come from Brazil where the animals
came from. They'll bring them food and bandages . . ."

Ancarit chimed in at a voice level that more than filled our limo. "We have a plan, Mr. Knight. The best part. They said we could use the ship that had been taken from the smugglers by the FBI. When we have the animals that survived back in good health, we'll use the ship to take them back to their homes on the river in Brazil. Thank God, Mr. Knight."

I could hear Ansuro now in the background. "And thank you, Michael. You should see this. You'd cry for joy."

When I looked over at Terry, I could see teardrops running streams of mascara down her cheeks. We rode in silence for a few minutes. I needed the time to absorb what Ansuro and Ancarit had said. It was the bright light at the end of what had been a seemingly endless tunnel.

Terry broke the silence. "Michael, I think it's time you finally give away the secret. I know you wanted to plan it as a surprise. But now, where are we going on our honeymoon?"

I held my breath when I broke the surprise I'd been planning for a week. "Are you ready?"

"Anywhere you say. Just together."

"Would you mind if we start our life at the Mayagüez Resort in Puerto Rico? I first planned it just because I think you'll love it. But now . . ."

I could see her face light with an excitement I could not have anticipated. "But now, Michael, we can see . . . maybe even help with the animals."

AUTHOR'S NOTE

WHAT YOU HAVE just read is fiction. Unfortunately, the unlawful trade in wild animals, birds, fish, and reptiles that form the background for the novel is not fiction.

The illegal wild animal trade is, in fact, second only to drug dealing in terms of profitability in the United States, and third behind drugs and arms dealing in the international criminal trade. Profits worldwide are expected to exceed 20 billion dollars annually.

With an estimated 38 million animals taken out of the Brazilian rainforest, including parrots, monkeys, crocodiles, reptiles, and tropical fish each year—at least 90 percent of which die in the capture and smuggling process—the number of species that have been driven into endangerment or complete extinction is staggering. And it is growing. The illegal trade in ivory has reduced the African elephant population from 1.2 million in the mid-seventies to well below 500,000.

The market in the United States alone is vast. It includes specimens for animal exhibits and collectors, subjects for illegal research and experimentation, personally owned exotic pets, animal parts for mythical medicinal use, and ornamentation for everything from shoes to watchbands.

Over 1,925,000 reptiles and lizards were brought into the United States in one recent year to be sold as pets to owners without the vaguest notion of their physical and behavioral needs—resulting in radically shortened lifespans in captivity. The same fate awaits the thousands of monkeys, lions, tigers, parrots, iguanas, and other exotic species bought and sold as pets.

The rarest animal species, closest to extinction, bring the highest profits on the illegal market. Certain breeds of blue macaws bring a few dollars to the rainforest natives who trap them, but once smuggled into the United States, they sell for $70,000. A golden lion tamarin, an endangered tiny monkey, brings over $20,000.

The lack of interest of the public, and therefore the government, in making or enforcing laws to curb this inhumane industry is evident from the fact that animals on the endangered species list can be purchased openly at dozens of auctions across the country. A number of magazines provide advertisements from dealers. On hundreds of Internet sites that are growing steadily, for a simple credit card charge, home delivery within a few days can be had for a baby Bengal tiger ($1000), a baby baboon ($5000), or even a baby giraffe ($22,000).

Typically, when the baby tiger, lion, bear, ocelot, or python quickly outgrows the baby stage and is big enough to tear the house apart and attack family members, it is generally "gotten rid of"— sometimes to some roadside menagerie, sometimes by abandonment in the wild with little or no chance of survival, or frequently at the business end of a gun.

Proof of the expanding profitability of this illegal trade is the fact that nearly all of the major national and international organized crime syndicates have entered the field in major proportions. The reason is simple. The profits are commensurate with or exceed those from illegal drug and arms dealings without the dangers of prosecution. Since there is as yet no stigma attached to the animal trade, such as that which drives enforcement of laws against drugs or arms dealing, the chances of being caught are minimal. And if caught, the penalties—if imposed at all—are absurdly low, making it a minor cost of doing business.

In fact, for that reason, drug dealers are increasingly using the smuggled animals themselves as vehicles for the smuggling of drugs as well. In fact, the enormous and increasing profits from the illegal animal trade are more and more symbiotically funding the other activities of both organized crime and terrorists.

The downsides of this burgeoning illegal activity include, in addition to the incomprehensible suffering of the animals:

1. Extinction and threatened extinction of countless species that perform integral and important functions in the complex machinery we call our planet's ecology;

2. The unregulated spread of "zoonotic" diseases—diseases that are passed from animals to humans—including SARS (Severe Acute Respiratory Syndrome), Heartwater Disease, Avian Flu, Plague, Ebola, Yellow Fever, Hepatitis, Malaria, Tuberculosis, Rabies, and Salmonella. One government report states that "The most dangerous emerging infectious diseases, in terms of total fatalities and fatality rates, have come from wildlife."

3. The introduction of "Invasive Species" when former "pets" are released into the wild, resulting in the endangerment or extinction of native animals by competition for prey or spreading of disease, and disastrous destruction of local ecosystems—for example, the immensely destructive overrunning of southern Florida by rapidly breeding Burmese pythons.

* * *

If the current apathy of the public, and therefore the government, toward addressing both enactment of laws and enforcement of those laws to quell this currently invisible disaster stems from lack of knowledge of the facts, then perhaps the first step toward a solution is to cast a blazing light on those facts. That hope is what compelled me to write this novel.

9 781608 093724